To Jeremy

Lots of love
^ Best Wishes

Elaine Pomm

(elainepomm@yahoo.co.uk)
(omit www) zoologyll.tripod.com

Edinburgh Knights

by
Elaine Pomm

(The Clown of Hearts)

authorHOUSE™

1663 LIBERTY DRIVE, SUITE 200
BLOOMINGTON, INDIANA 47403
(800) 839-8640
WWW.AUTHORHOUSE.COM

First published by AuthorHouse 6/27/2006

ISBN: 1-4259-0455-6 (sc)

Printed in the United States of America
Bloomington, Indiana

This book is printed on acid-free paper.

Chapter One

'Reader, attend - whether thy soul,
Soars fancy's flights beyond the pole,
Or darkling grubs this earthly hole,
In low pursuit;
Know, prudent, cautious self-control
Is wisdom's root.' - Burns

'She looks a bit of alright.' Lawrence heard Joe comment as he tried to doze. It had been a long coach journey from Waterloo to Edinburgh the previous day and now the compulsory city tour was proving too much, even for a 26 year old. Lawrence slightly opened one eye to humour his best friend of eight years and glanced at the subject of interest. She was a pretty young thing, bunched blonde hair, micro skirt and legs right up to her armpits. Just as he was about to open his other eye, he noticed a man close behind patting her bottom.

Now Joe also closed his eyes, enjoying the August sunshine which brazenly penetrated through the claustrophobic tour bus window and soothed him back to sleep. Lawrence was Jewish, Joe Catholic. They had met at Oxford University when they were both eighteen. Lawrence had been reading psychology and history, Joe had read philosophy and art and liked the course. Art was more practical than academic; an easy way to impress the yuppie girls was to offer to paint their portraits.

He began to wish Lawrence had studied something other than history. Throughout the long journey his companion had given him frequent lectures about Edinburgh's history, including the books he'd read about the Holy Grail and the Stone of Scone. Lawrence had insisted that Joe also read the books because it was about his Catholic heritage, or so he'd claimed. He'd given him a boxed set for Christmas, wrapped in a gold ribbon. Sadly for him, the only Scone Joe was interested in was of the sultana variety. Even so, their similarities vastly outweighed their differences. Both had attended private prep, then public schools; well indoctrinated, educated and tailored into suits of success. This included a large chunk of parental wallet, stocks and shares, and of course the Received Pronunciation had been thrown in by their nannies for good measure. Although nurtured on middle class values and traditions, least of all its code of conduct, Joe was the first to admit that by nature and inclination he was just a pleb. He preferred the company of Essex girls, less expensive to bed than the sisters of his friends and less complicated. Some of the Etonians in his year had jokingly nicknamed him '*Jack the Ripper*' due to the East End dives where he'd occasionally hung out. But he hadn't been with many whores, no need when he could easily get it for free.

Suddenly, the engine of the tour bus revved. Lawrence gave Joe a nudge, 'wake up, you'll miss everything!' Joe grumbled and opened his blue eyes. More passengers were boarding, his attention now focussed on a girl dressed as a jester carrying a guitar, obviously a busker entertaining at the Fringe. Behind her stood a tall, fair haired creature, at least 6 ft. Male or female, he wasn't sure, the clothes gave nothing away.

'Ladies and Gentleman,' the tour guide standing at the front of the tour bus suddenly commanded their attention in a clipped Scots accent.

'Welcome aboard the LRT Edinburgh Classic Tour. I hope you will enjoy seeing and hearing about the many places of interest we will pass on this short drive around the central part of Edinburgh. The ticket you have purchased is valid all day on this tour, so you can leave the bus at any point along the route to visit a place of interest, and then board another LRT Classic Tour bus to continue the drive. Well, off we go!'

'Joe, look, over there...a piper!' Lawrence pointed excitedly towards the pavement below as the bus pulled away, where a kilted soldier played the bagpipes.

Joe wasn't as much into this as Lawrence. He'd only agreed to come for the Edinburgh Fringe, and of course for the sake of wine, women and clubbing. Joe was a good looking young man. He had blue eyes, dark hair and was of Irish descent on his mother's side, the Kennedy's' of Dublin. His maternal uncle was Paddy Kennedy the king of Dublin bookmakers, now a wealthy stud farmer. His father Randolf Hill was a self made man, but as to what business he did, Joe was never sure. The only certainty about the said business was, as Lawrence put it, 'it's definitely not kosher.' But of one thing Joe was sure, and that was his father's win at the recent election as Tory M.P for Knightsbridge.

'As we leave Waverley Bridge, we have on our left two monuments to famous Scotsmen. One is a statue of David Livingstone the African explorer and missionary, who died searching for the source of the Nile,' the guide expounded. But Joe was too tired to care about those living, let alone those dead. Of what interest was history in any event? Living in the past, studying ghosts and tragedies. Better to dance with the demons of today than wrestle ghosts of the past.

Beggars were sitting on the pavements, hands outstretched.

'*Send them to work camps*' he'd often say to Lawrence, '*begging should be illegal*'.

'...And under the archways of the 200 ft gothic spire is a seated figure of Sir Walter Scott, perhaps Scotland's greatest literary figure. If you have the energy you can climb 287 steps to the top platform and obtain magnificent views all over the city in all directions,' the voice continued, as Joe closed his eyes.

'We are now on Princes Street, Edinburgh's main street, once known as the Lang Gate or the long walk. The two pillared buildings on the left in classical Greek style architecture are art galleries.' Joe suddenly sat up. The word art reminded him of university, a time of fun and falsehood playing hopscotch between the lines of adolescence and maturity.

'In front we have the Royal Scottish Academy, built in 1836, this houses exhibitions of the work of contemporary Scottish artists, while the National Gallery at the rear completed in 1854, contains Scotland's National art collection.'

'The contemporary rubbish of blobs on canvas you have to pay to see,' Lawrence whispered across to Joe. 'Yet the paintings by the geniuses in the other Gallery is free...barmy world don't you think?'

'Both buildings were designed by the same architect, William Henry Playfair whose use of the Greek style on many buildings he designed in the city has given Edinburgh its title of the *Athens of the North*,' the guide expounded.

'Athens, here? Ha ha. Well, Joe, it's all Greek to me,' Lawrence laughed, trying to shield himself from the flash of the camera coming from the seat in front.

'Who's he then, Zorba?' Joe withdrew a cigarette from his jacket pocket, referring to the tour guide. He was regretting not having gone on the murder weekend which he'd been invited to by his dealer friend from Sloane Square.

'On our left we have a fine view of the old town of Edinburgh standing on the ridge that runs down from the Castle rock to Holyrood Palace,' the guide continued, ignoring the coughs and sweet papers being unwrapped.

'We can see the jumble of buildings overlooking the valley in front of us where the Waverley Station now stands. In years past this site was covered by the Nor Loch, a stretch of marshland and water.'

A murder weekend would have been fun, lots of pretty girls screaming for him to offer comfort, booze, spliffs, perfect. Why on earth was he here then? Joe groaned to himself.

'Should have gone on a murder mystery weekend like I said.'

'I'd have thought that you'd had enough of murders what with your mother's housekeeper. And don't forget there were also those murders not so far from your parents' home. Mind you, they'll have probably caught the meshugener by the time we get back.'

'For someone who's studied psychology you have overwhelming empathy for your subjects.'

'I do have empathy, Joe, you know I do. I thought I made myself clear during our debate last night exactly my views on contract killers.' Lawrence tried to atone for his lack of compassion. 'Remember that I said they are either mentally ill or sadistic. You know, innate, genetic, can't help the way their brain works.'

Joe just gave a shrug of indifference, but once Lawrence had started there was no stopping him. He always did that when he felt guilty, unlike Joe.

'In fact, I'd take a bet that committing murder by proxy happens more often than we realise. Yar, I suppose that even the contract killer must be a type of psychopath, you know, without conscience. I've always said that everyone is capable of murder, even me...even you, Joe.' Lawrence gave a sigh, wishing he'd never broached the subject.

'So you think one has to be what you call a meshugener, mad, to commit murder? How do you know he's mad? In fact, he might even be a *she*.'

'So why would a woman kill your mother's housekeeper?' Lawrence demanded, taking a sly look at his Cartier watch with dragon motif.

'She wasn't a housekeeper. In fact she was a rather voluptuous au pair. No more than twenty I'd say. Great tits.'

'Joe, please!' Lawrence sighed, 'show her some respect, she's dead.'

'Princes Street, lined with shops on one side, and gardens overlooking the railway line that had once been Nor Loch on the other,' the familiar voice intruded on their dispute. 'Its backdrop, the skyline of the old town of Edinburgh.'

'Looks medieval, gothic, weird really. As if a pied piper might pop out,' Lawrence mumbled, his eyes transfixed to the skyline of flagpoles and spires. The magnificent buildings rose high above Princes Street gardens, resembling an illustration from a children's book of fairytales. Perhaps Lawrence was right, Joe pondered, having recently re-read the poem himself. Maybe Browning's piper had piped in Edinburgh, piped just once too often, and the city's children were still festering within the hollows and chasms.

'The many buildings that are huddled together on the top of this ridge also run down the sides, so that while a house may have four or five storeys on the High Street, at the rear that you can see now there may be as many as thirteen storeys,' the Scots voice explained, as his passengers all listened intently. 'This is where the people of Edinburgh lived, crowded within the city walls until the new town was built in the late 18th and 19th centuries. And, on our left we have a basalt rock, some 400 feet high, all that remains of an ancient volcano. And on that rock overlooking the city is Edinburgh Castle.' The guide pointed up to a steep, rugged, grass covered hill topped with a castle. A child started to cry.

'Trust the brat to spoil the serenity of an almost perfect moment,' Joe snarled, wishing someone would strangle the kid.

'The origins of the Castle are shrouded in the mists of time, but we do know that there was a fortress of the Northumbria kings on the rock in the 8th century,' the guide raised his voice above the shrieks of the child. 'The oldest building in the Castle today is St. Margaret's Chapel, dating from the end of the 12th century and built for Queen Margaret, later St. Margaret, the wife of King Malcolm Campbell.'

'The Castle shrouded in the mists of time' the words played in Joe's head, his crystal blue eyes staring up towards the fairytale citadel. How Katie would have loved to see it. She was always such a romantic, Joe reflected, slyly inhaling the tobacco, hoping other passengers wouldn't complain.

Strums of a guitar emerged from the pavement; tourists were crowded around the music like rats.

'Sounds like your song, Joe,' Lawrence grinned, causing Joe to strain his ears. But, it was impossible to hear the busker who was dressed as a clown. Lawrence had of course been referring to his namesake *'Joe Hill'* as being his song. Joe loathed it. His mother forever sang it. *'I dreamed I saw Joe Hill last night, alive as you and me. Says I, but Joe, you're ten years dead. I never died says he'.*

'Don't know why you always grunt when you hear it, Joe, many believed it to be a great song, great man Joe Hill. A song writer like you... a militant trade unionist. Apparently, they say, he made the industrial workers of the world into a singing organisation.' Lawrence's eyes still focused on the busker.

'Lucky you can sing, Joe, great gift singing. When your father is sent to prison at least you'll have something to fall back on.'

'Yar I know, Lawrie, my old man's a crook, but tell me, what politician isn't? As for Joe Hill, his reward by the government for his selfless efforts was execution. Yar, yar I've heard it all before.' Who cared? Joe Hill was just another clown like the one on the street, and no one cared about clowns. From his own philosophical studies he'd decided that every action, whether selfish or selfless, was down to what the philosophers termed '*psychological hedonism*'. At the end of the day even martyrs sacrificed to make themselves feel good. Joe's own song writing was not going too well of late, not since Christmas really. 'You'd think it was the end of the world,' Joe's mother had mumbled when Joe had opened the package containing his returned demo discs. No, he knew it wasn't the end of the world, Lawrence had already told him Nostradamus had predicted that for the 4th July, 1999.

'Did you know Edinburgh is built on a volcano?' Lawrence interrupted Joe's reminiscences. 'Think the guide book said there was a leper hospital on Carlton Hill at the end of the 16th century, and possibly a Carmelite monastery. But then, perhaps I've got it wrong.'

'Give it a break, Lawrie, we've paid for him in the hat to tell us about this ultra exciting city, you don't have to as well!' Joe barked, referring to the guide standing at the front of the tour bus holding his microphone.

'I was only trying to be nice,' the dark haired Lawrence sulked. He hadn't changed since they'd met during their fresher year, not intrinsically. Obviously from a physical level, the once proverbial slug was now a red admiral that still didn't have a clue how to sail his own ship. Well, not how Joe would have sailed it. At eighteen he'd been positively ugly, gawky, bespectacled and so boring. How thin he'd been, sprouting a ridiculous haircut and a face full of boils and blackheads. In those days it was Joe who got all the girlies. If it hadn't been for the fact that Lawrence had been his room mate on campus, plus the fact he frequently offered to help Joe with his essays when they had both attended lectures on the philosophy of mind, they would never have become friends.

7

How times had changed. Joe glanced at his handsome young friend with the muscular build and roguish stubble on his face. He was the one who seemed to get most of the girls nowadays. Yet, underneath, he was still the sensitive, insecure, too considerate Lawrence Mossman.

'Don't get uptight, Lawrie, it's just that you're always going on about history, and I need a break. I mean, who takes history seriously these days? Most of what we read is fabricated, it's just not relevant. You just take everything too seriously, that's your trouble.' Joe turned to his friend with a smile, 'clubbing tonight? Bet I can pull more than you.'

'No spliffs,' Lawrence returned a smile.

'Alright oh sensible one, no spliffs,' Joe laughed, and turned his attention back to the window as the bus drove into an adjoining road lined with shops. Joe knew it was the dream that was bugging him. The same dream he kept having every month, it was worse than PMT. In the dream a baby died. It was more like a nightmare, for Joe would wake sweating and shaking. It seemed to happen around the time of a full moon. Katie had accused him of being evil, perhaps she was right, a man without a conscience she'd said. Even Joe had to admit it was intriguing how water around the brain and the tides were affected by the moon; perhaps he should have studied astronomy instead of philosophy.

'We are now entering the new town of Edinburgh begun by the city fathers in the mid 18th century, when living conditions within the confines of the walled old town became so intolerable that urgent action had to be taken,' the voice continued. 'A competition was set for a design for a new town of Edinburgh to be built on moor land across the loch north of Edinburgh Castle. This was won by a young local architect called James Craig, and building on his plan, which was in the form of a grid iron began in 1767.'

'What are you thinking about?'

'I was thinking of what you told me about Nostradamus predicting the end of the world,' Joe mumbled.

'He was Jewish!' Lawrence volunteered with sudden enthusiasm, but then stopped smiling. 'He believed in the occult, you know astrology. He was actually asked by Catherine de Medici to write

8

horoscopes for her seven children, she was Mary Queen of Scots' mother in law. Nostradamus died in 1566, the same year as David Rizzio was murdered.'

Joe's eyes were closed, he wasn't listening. He hadn't a clue who David Rizzio was and didn't care; these people were of no interest to him. Joe didn't even bother to open his eyes to glance at the objects which the guide referred to. How he could bear to do his job Joe could not imagine. This was why Joe was currently unemployed, apart from the brief assignment in France. No point in working if it was boring, life was too short for that.

As he snoozed he could hear the voice continue.

'…Statue of William Pitt, the youngest person to be Prime Minister of Great Britain and the man we have to thank for introducing income tax…James Craig…statue at each end…St. Andrew patron saint of Scotland…Freemasons Hall…Dr. Chalmers…Robert Adam…'

The sunshine was lulling Joe to sleep, penetrating through the glass furnace of the bus window. A road sweeper pushed his broom along the gutter, pausing momentarily to let a young girl pass. She was obviously part of the Fringe, dressed in period costume, balancing a large basket on her head brimming over with plastic fruit.

'Many notable people lived in these houses around the square over the years, such as Alexander Graham Bell, the inventor of the telephone.' The guide's words now flowed in and out of Joe's consciousness; he was catching only snippets here and there.

'Earl Douglas Haig, commander of the British forces in the 1914-18 war… Lord Cockburn…Lister…antiseptics…Philip…tuberculosis…Prince Albert…'

Joe was now fully asleep, dreaming of the girl on the bus with the blonde bunches who stripped naked as he was being knighted by Queen Victoria. He walked across the Forth Road Bridge re-named Melville Street. It was there he met a Mr. Walker. The dream was quite pleasant until the said Mr. Walker punched him in the side because the blonde girl was his wife. Joe then awoke to discover the digs were from Lawrence.

'See, Joe, the statue of the dog! Amazing! I've seen the film years ago, and Scotland isn't so far from London yet we've never been before. Aren't you glad now I persuaded you to come?'

'Ecstatic,' Joe grunted, now fully awake.

'On the corner of the roadway to the left is a drinking fountain, and on top a statue of a little dog. This is Greyfriars Bobby...' The guide expounded, as the bus slowly made its way along George IV Bridge, past the beggars wrapped in blankets who sat in doorways, then turned up a hill towards the Castle.

Joe wasn't listening, catching only random words.

'Crown jewels...oldest in Europe...Stone of Scone or the Stone of Destiny.'

The bus stopped to let off some tourists at the Castle's esplanade.

Of course when the tour guide had mentioned the Stone of Scone, Lawrence nearly jumped out of his seat. Joe sniggered, his friend hadn't changed that much, he used to wet himself at school on occasions from over excitement. As for Joe, well he wasn't interested in any stone, other than making his own destiny being stoned for the rest of this dire tour.

'Do you fancy getting off here? Joe!' Joe was unresponsive, Lawrence didn't pursue the issue.

Other coaches were pulling up beside them. Tourists who looked to be from the orient filled the one nearest to them, cameras filming, voices jabbering. Lawrence wanted to get out and follow them into the Castle, see the jewels and hear of the centuries of intrigue and murder. He wanted to understand the minds of those past. But, he didn't want to upset Joe too much so he let the sleeping dog lie.

'Have you ever heard of the magazine Brith, Joe?' he asked with feigned enthusiasm, just to stimulate conversation. 'It's published by a society who believes that Britain is the new Israel. They believe that the Stone of Scone is God's throne and given to the Royal House of David.'

The bus now turned around in the Castle's esplanade, and headed back down into the olde worlde cobbled street. The route was packed with tourists and stalls. Entertainers were strumming guitars and performing free reviews to advertise their shows, obstructing the path of the bus until the police moved them on.

'Odd there are no statues of females.'

Joe didn't respond.

'We are now entering Lawnmarket, and it's where we join the Royal Mile. So called because it's a mile from the gates of the Castle to the entrance to Holyrood Palace, and where the most powerful people in Scotland once lived.' The voice continued to drone, as Lawrence also began to nod off.

'On the left the house of Thomas Gledstaines, a wealthy Edinburgh merchant of the early 1600's. On the right is Brodie's Close. William Brodie, councillor for the city by day, but at night he became a burglar. And with true moral irony, he was hung in 1788 on the city's new gallows which he himself had designed. His story inspired Robert Louis Stevenson's book Dr Jekyll and Mr. Hyde.'

Throughout that long, tiresome journey to Scotland Joe had tried to sleep whilst Lawrence had rambled on, mostly about Scottish history, monarchy and Edinburgh. Typical Lawrence, he even managed to suggest the present royal family had some Jewish connection due to the Queen Mother's maiden name being Bowes-Lyon. Joe was snoring now; Lawrence gave a start, uncertain which of them was making the noise. He wanted to rebuke Joe for being so disinterested, but he knew that he'd only get grief for insisting they travelled by coach when Joe had wanted to fly. Joe was tired, having just returned from Paris a few days earlier. The coach tickets had been a prize, won by Lawrence's mother at one of her Rotary club raffles. Naturally, his father had harassed her to join the Order of the Eastern Star, some Masonic group for women. But she'd remained with Rotary. Once again the bus was forced to stop due to the street entertainment. This time a fire eater had attracted a huge crowd of spectators who were cheering and participating in his act. Even the police seemed absorbed in the performance until the bus driver gave a toot, and they assisted him through.

'On your right is St. Giles Cathedral, the high Kirk of Edinburgh. There has been a church building on the site since the 9th century. One of the most famous ministers to preach in the church was John

Knox, the great reformer who had many a heated argument with Mary, Queen of Scots, over her allegiance to the Roman Catholic religion. It was also in St. Giles that the incident took place in 1637 when Jenny Geddes threw her stool at the head of the minister who was preaching the English form of service.'

Lawrence began to doze off again; the journey from London was taking its toll.

'On the right is the Mercat Cross around which the markets were held in old Edinburgh and where proclamations were made. Three days later than in London as it took the messenger that time to get here. On the left are the Edinburgh City Chambers...'

Joe was waking and sleeping intermittently, the words of the guide infiltrating his dreams. 'The building dates from 1790... underneath is the hidden city of Edinburgh, Mary King's Close... plague...ghosts...'

The tour bus suddenly stopped beside a period house, its timber fronted gallery prominently jutted out over the shop below.

'The house of John Knox!' the guide spouted with pride, causing Joe to give a yawn so loud that the guide would hear, but the man continued his rhetoric unperturbed.

'Just before I mention the house of the famous Kirk minister John Knox, there is another famous building right next door. Moubray House,' the guide boasted, wiping the sweat from his brow. 'It's the oldest building on Edinburgh's Royal Mile. Although the frontage dates from 1630, the house was originally built around 1477, by Robert Moubray. Andrew Moubray built a new house at the rear in 1529.' All eyes glanced across futilely, knowing full well before they looked that they wouldn't be able to see the rear of the building from where they sat in the coach.

'It was here that Daniel Defoe edited the Edinburgh Courant, and it was restored by the Cockburn Society in 1910.'

'Daniel Defoe, didn't he write Robinson Crusoe?' Lawrence whispered. 'I've always fancied myself on a desert island, one would learn so much about oneself.'

'He wrote Moll Flanders,' Joe grunted back.

'Outside in the street is one of the wells which used to provide the water supply for the old town,' the guide pointed to the stone well standing on the pavement.

'Next to Moubray House is the famous house of John Knox, minister of St. Giles. The Mossmans owned this house now known as John Knox House. They were goldsmiths, loyal to Mary Queen of Scots.'

'Same name as me, Joe! Wow, what do you think, Jewish? No, couldn't be. I mean there were no Jews here during the 16th century. Must have some different root, like the man from the moss or something.'

Joe made no comment, singing the words from a song, '*moss doesn't grow on a rolling stone*...Mick Jagger looks a bit moss ridden, I suppose.'

'What did you say, Joe?'

'No, you're right, Lawrie; moth ridden would be more apt.'

'Look, Joe, as you seem so averse to history, perhaps we can debate psychology...unless you have any objections?'

Joe wasn't listening, his eyes spying out the public houses along the roadside.

'So what do you think?'

'What, do I think what?' Joe snapped, irritated by his friend interrupting his concentration, focusing on an oriental little dish who flashed her camera in his direction.

'So what do you think about the subconscious, Joe? Answer me!' Lawrence demanded, once the bus revved up.

'What about the subconscious?'

'About hypnotism. Joe, are you listening? I told you how many times that one of my main papers I'm submitting for my PhD is about hypnotism.'

'Yar, I heard, well, what do you want me to say?' Joe replied with an air of nonchalance.

'At least as my best friend say you wish me well. Or even that as a fellow intellectual, one of the top 3% of the country that you find it even vaguely interesting. Or even go as far as to say that if you could help me in any way you'd be delighted,' Lawrence replied, the hurt showing in his eyes.

13

Joe laughed, still the same sensitive boy inside his masculine adult façade.

'Lawrence, you know I wish you well, even if you are a Yid and killed my God, and...' he began to cough, and now it was Lawrence's turn to laugh. How often they had sat in the tiny room they had shared in their Oxford Halls of Residence during the three years they were undergrads, debating all the topics in the universe, including religion and its appendage angel, prejudice. Those were the days, long before Katie and the baby. No point in seeing Chloe. Too upsetting. Although when Lawrence had asked, Joe had lied and said he'd seen her regularly. The truth was that he'd only seen them once since Christmas, on Chloe's second birthday earlier that month, just before he'd flown out to Paris. They'd held the tea party in the back yard of Katie's tenement block, staying out there long after Chloe had fallen asleep in her buggy and the sun had gone down. Number 49 Magdalene Towers. Even a rough old tenement block looked almost attractive beneath the light of the moon. Katie had remarked that it was a full moon and forecast no sleep for Joe, but thought it might be a good omen for herself. Her horoscope had foretold a drastic change in circumstances. Joe didn't believe in astrology, in fact he had very little in common with the mother of his first born, even to the point of choosing the baby's name. When Joe first learned that he had a daughter he'd settled on the name 'Lettuce' after his favourite great aunt Letty. Katie had adamantly refused, saying that they'd call her 'Leaf' or 'Salad' at school. Lawrence had suggested the name 'Tamar'. This time Joe objected, claiming the kids at school would nickname her 'Bridge' if they ever moved to Devon.

Of course, none of his family knew of the child's existence. Well, Katie was from a council estate. As if his mother would accept a grandchild with those genes.

'I suppose if you have a kid you'll call him Moses.'

'Some say Moses wasn't even Jewish,' Lawrence responded. 'Well, not fully. Personally I accept what the Torah says...but the arguments for him being the son of a pharaoh are interesting.'

'What a lot of bollocks!' Joe jeered, as he pulled another cigarette from the packet.

'No, seriously, Joe, I mean the argument from a non religious standpoint is valid. Why would the daughter of a Pharaoh take in the enemy's kid and bring him up as her own? Did you know that even Freud believed that Moses wasn't a Jew, but an Egyptian?'

'Oh well, enough said. I mean if Freud said it, then it must be true. I mean according to you, Freud is God!' he coughed.

'No, seriously though, Joe, I mean odd isn't it, that all our great leaders had dealings with the Egyptians? Your own namesake Jacob's son, for example. Even your Jesus' ancestor Abraham, well his wife was really his sister.' Lawrence turned his body around to face Joe as if excited by the possibility of a prolonged debate.

'So you're saying that Abraham, your great father Abraham, the patriarch of your chosen race, shagged his own fucking sister?' Joe took a long, slow drag at his cigarette.

'No. I mean...well, I'm not saying it...it's what the Torah says. Anyhow the Pharaohs all slept with their sisters.'

'But Abraham wasn't a fucking pharaoh!'

'Well. No, and yes. He was a king wasn't he?' Lawrence began to stutter.

'And here we are at the Netherbow Port.' The voice of the guide momentarily distracted them, all eyes now focussed on the attractive renaissance architecture.

'When was it that your lot were thrown out of Britain?' Joe turned away from the object of his gaze and took another long drag on his cigarette.

'Why? Since when have you been interested? We were thrown out in 1290. It was Cromwell who brought us back in 1665.'

'No, you've got it wrong, Lawrie, Marlow wrote, *The Jew of Malta*.'

'Marlow was born in 1564, died in 90 something. Just like Shakespeare who wrote about Shylock, neither man had ever met a Jew. There were no Jews either in Canterbury where Marlow was from, or in Stratford upon Avon. Got it, Joe? No Jews by law. We have often been likened to rats!'

'I suppose you'll tell me next that Browning's poem 'The Pied Piper' was about your lot, and God had the ultimate revenge on their abusers by taking the gentile children.'

The girl in the jester outfit stood up to retrieve something from her rucksack, some juggling balls accidentally tumbled from her pocket.

'Wish she'd play with my balls,' Joe mumbled under his breath.

'Although having said that...there were the Marranos. I think they were in Britain. I suppose Shakespeare may have met them,' Lawrence conceded. 'But there again, they wouldn't have been obvious, you know like the Fagin type, caricatured. Interesting that gentiles never portray Jesus looking or speaking like Fagin do they? You do know who the Marranos were don't you, Joe?'

But Joe's eyes were fixed on the pretty jester and her patterned leggings, so tight that they exposed the line of her knickers.

'Joe, after all these years of friendship, you still don't care what happened to my people. I've always suspected that deep down you were racist, not your fault of course. It's been indoctrinated into you.'

'Ha ha, yar, you're right, Lawrie, definitely think it's a great idea, get rid of Jews, blacks, gays,' he teased.

'May I remind you, Joseph, that the Celts arrived here only about 150 B.C and the blacks were brought here as slaves in 1555. They didn't first arrive here in the 1960's. The same goes for the Asians, they were forced here as servants in 1630.'

'Whatever.'

The bus had stopped at traffic lights, a group of men dressed in highland plaids, carrying swords and shields crossed the road. He heard one shout, 'for Scotland and freedom!' the tourists laughed, some snapping them with their cameras.

For a moment both men were quiet, absorbing the sights. Joe noticed that the car in front had the sign of a fish on the back window. Christians, he groaned to himself, but why the sign of the fish Joe had no idea. It was when the guide mentioned the word *'clan'* once too often that Lawrence started off again.

'The 12 tribes of Israel were clans you know. Do you remember I told you about some books I've read about the Ku Klux Klan? Apparently they have a big membership up here in Scotland. They had a big recruitment here in the late 1980's. In fact, Joe, I've heard through certain sources that Special Branch has recently investigated the KKK here. In fact only last year...'

'Yar, yar,' Joe yawned rudely.

'Well, if you're not interested...in fact if your only interest is women, then we may as well have stayed at home, I mean...'

'Only joking you sensitive Jesus' gene carrier. So what happened in 1996? No really, Lawrie, I'm interested,' Joe laughed, his good looks matched his confidence, nothing fazed him. When he smiled, dimples appeared in his cheeks, extra bait for the girlies he'd often boasted.

'Who else would spend most evenings listening to you rant on about the morons in the Bible and the Holy fucking Grail?'

'I wish you wouldn't swear, Joe. Well, if you really are interested. But I expect you already know what I know, seeing as you've contacts in Special Branch.' Lawrence raised his brows knowingly.

'You recall David Duke, Republican candidate for Louisiana. Big name with the KKK? Well, he went on about his Scottish roots, his family's supposed to have come from Edinburgh.'

'Better hurry up and lose your virginity then...before they come in their white hoods and flaming crucifix to get you. Word will be out in Edinburgh by now you know, *Jew boy hits city*!"

'Odd when one thinks of it, Queen Elizabeth the virgin Queen.'

'Virgin...I bet she shagged more men than...Well, bet she had a good old seeing to.' Sniggering, Joe scratched his balls.

'Elizabeth I ordered the Lord Mayor of London, this was 1601 you understand? She ordered him to expel London's black population. And yet, Joseph, only 29 years later, the Asians were brought here as servants, so her logic makes little sense.'

'Whatever,' Joe grunted, sniffing his fingers.

'But, I think it wasn't until the 1700's that immigration, well, forced immigration increased to a large degree. But perhaps you are of a different opinion, Joe.'

Joe yawned.

'Always on about Jews, Lawrie, as if only your race has been chosen. If you are the chosen race, then what does it say about the rest of us? Does it mean that the mythical creature known as 'God' doesn't care about the rest of us goyim?' he coughed.

'No. Well…well no, I didn't say that.'

'You don't need to, that's what you think. Just like the Asians, keep the blood line pure. But if the Jews are the only race to wear God's designer label, then where does it leave the rest of us?'

'Well…I suppose theoretically perhaps those who are chosen will all have some Jewish genetics somewhere in their DNA, even the Scots. I mean the crusaders put it around a bit, didn't they? It doesn't mean you are totally worthless just because you don't have my genetic coding.'

'Fuck you! You're such a fucking racist, Lawrie, such a fucking wanker! That is if you can wank with half a dick!'

Joe glanced about in search of the jester with the tight pants.

'Royal House of fucking David,' he seethed under his breath. Lawrence didn't respond.

'Kosher cunt…Oh no, I forgot, that's Rachel!'

'The borough of Canongate was a separate borough,' the tour guide expounded as soon as the lights changed. Joe noticed in one of the shop windows a display of birthday cards and teddy bears wearing tartan hats, perhaps he would send a bear to Chloe. He tried not to think too much about his own past. Although he had gone to confession just that once, after his grandmother had died and mentioned Chloe. Obviously he'd not bothered about the full penance, one Hail Mary was quite enough, particularly with a hangover.

'And there before us we have the Palace of Holyrood.' The guide wiped his brow as the passengers made various comments to one another as they gathered their belongings. Most of them were intending to vacate the tour bus in order to take a closer look inside the Palace.

'So what shall I do about the research for my PhD?' Lawrence asked, as the bus travelled down the road towards the impressive black gates of the Palace.

'About what?'

But just as Lawrence was going to blast, Joe, being sharp of mind said, 'oh, you mean about hypnotism…well, I don't believe in it myself. It's for the weak minded, and I thought Jews weren't supposed to dabble with *iffy* things.'

18

'What are you talking about *iffy*? Even King David had a seer called Gad. Anyway, anyone can be hypnotised.'

'Course they can't, it's self induced!' Joe retorted, his eyes resting on the huge, impressive Palace.

'There's no way you could hypnotise me in any event...hey look at *that!*' Joe directed his friend's attention to a girl waiting outside the Palace gates dressed in micro skirt and high boots.

'Bet you a fiver I can.'

'Bet what, you can bed her first?' eyes still glued to the micro skirt.

'No! Oh, Joe, why can't you think of anything else other than women! It's not as if you are happy with them...look at Katie.'

Immediately Joe left the object of his gaze, his eyes fell towards the bus floor.

'Well, are you up for it?' Lawrence said more light hearted, trying to cheer his now depressed companion.

'Yar, okay, but make it a tenner and you're on!' Joe suddenly bounced back in typical Joe style and jumped to his feet, ready to follow the other tourists from the bus. Some were taking their camcorders strapped about their person, others carried children. There was even an oriental woman and her son carrying a large trunk of jewellery.

'Japanese?' Joe asked his companion who stood at the door, but Lawrence was busy delving into his small backpack searching through papers.

'Utter waste of time, Lawrie, it won't work on me,' Joe scorned, and hurried down the steps behind the blonde in bunches.

'Now, wait a minute,' Lawrence instructed, looking around as he placed his index finger against his right temple as if in thought.

'Well, at least let's go in!' Joe said, spotting two teenage girls tottering on high heels, arm in arm through the black iron gates protecting the Palace courtyard.

'For goodness sake, Joe, they're kids...and probably dykes the way they're walking.' Lawrence reprimanded, dragging his friend by his shirt sleeve towards the ticket inspector clad in the Ancient Hunting Stewart tartan of green and blue. His black Glengarry perched rook-

19

like on his head as he inspected their tickets, and then allowed them into the courtyard.

'That must be Arthur's Seat.' Lawrence's brown eyes scanned the high, grassy hills, splashed with an overwhelming brilliance of orange gorse.

'Like a mountain of gold isn't it, Joe?'

'Hurry up!'

'Let's go over there...the gardens I suspect,' Lawrence suggested.

The young men sat on the bench near the shell of what looked to have once been an abbey. Joe was silently inspecting the large, perfectly laid gardens, interspersed with flowers and shrubs, as Lawrence carefully removed various items from his backpack. The girlies would be long gone by the time he got away. Joe now wished he'd come by himself, or at least that he hadn't been so stupid to have called Lawrence's bluff about this hypnotism. Never mind, there were still the clubs that night to look forward to. A couple of pints and a few whiskeys and Lawrence would be excellent fun. The girls he pulled even made Joe jealous. How he'd changed from that lanky, ugly fresher to a sexy hunk was a shock to all who'd ever known him. It was a punishment to all the other male freshers who'd ignored him, when in his third year the frog had gone through metamorphosis and lured their women away.

What a laugh they'd had with the twins Amy and Sian. Then there were the two from Jamaica, they'd had a great week with them on the yacht in Cowes, except Lawrence wouldn't try some coke. Joe smiled as he thought about the mother and daughter Rita and Michelle they'd met two years ago at 'Stringfellows'. Joe had the mother and Lawrence the daughter, and then they'd swapped. Such a whiz...until Katie had found out, all due to the big mouthed Louise who Joe had dumped for Rita whilst Katie was pregnant. Well, he supposed it was for the best.

Lawrence was going in for one of those planned marriages. A Jewish girl called Rachel to whom he'd recently become engaged, daughter of a high court judge and that was just her mother. Joe still felt slight pangs of guilt whenever he thought about Katie. Her mother had died when she was only 14. Her father had raised her and her two siblings single handed, that was when he wasn't in the pub.

'Look, Lawrie, you're wasting your time I can't be hypno...'

'Just give it a chance, Joseph, you are so impatient. You were the same at Oxford, and you've been the same ever since!' Joe knew that it took a lot for Lawrence to snap, but when he did it was usually when there was an issue of utmost importance, and then Joe knew that it was time to show some reticence.

'Well, how can you make a conclusion from this hypothesis, to prove that it has worked?' Joe asked, suddenly taking an interest in his friend's project. He had seen stage hypnotists numerous times at university balls, but nothing ever convinced him that the subjects weren't merely weak minded individuals. His attention momentarily focussed on a family of French tourists entering the gardens.

'You went to France earlier this week, Paris wasn't it? I bet it was more work for MI6. Oh, don't think I don't know about your work for them, Joseph, I saw you constantly talking into that secret earpiece of yours last night. We're not best friends for nothing.' He laughed, and then winked his eye.

'So, where did you stay? What did you do? You haven't said a word about it?'

'Just had a liaison that was all. Stayed in Marne La Vallee in Paris...so, anymore questions?'

'What was she like? Hope she was worth the journey,' Lawrence winked again.

'Yar, Lawrie, she was well worth it.'

Paris was an interesting city, Joe reflected. His stay had been too brief to have done the city significant justice, although he'd managed to cram in The Moulin Rouge. The cancan was much the same as it always was, feathered girls covered in sequins. His dinner guest had eaten the same as Joe, Foie Gras de Canard en gelee a l'armagnac, followed by Scottish salmon and then Filet Mignon with Morilles crèmees washed down with champagne. For dessert his guest had chosen nougat glacé, but Joe was full and just had the cognac and cigar. He didn't pull that night, perhaps he ought to have taken his paints and offered to paint the dancers. In hindsight it may have helped if he'd begged on his knees; apparently they were partial to dwarves, Joe sniggered to himself.

'French women like little men don't they, dwarves?'

Lawrence looked back at Joe blankly.

'Do dwarves have little dicks, or normal sized ones? Odd don't you think? What would have happened if say...your Moses had been born a dwarf?'

'He couldn't have been.'

'Why? I mean you'd argue that God doesn't dish out the crap, you know, like deformity. So if it's not His will for someone to be a dwarf, then why couldn't Moses have been one if it's purely an accident of birth? It begs the question, would anyone have followed him across a puddle least of all an ocean had he been?'

'Would anyone still worship your Blessed Virgin if she had been?'

Joe hesitated before giving an answer then laughed. 'There's no such animal as a virgin, blessed or otherwise. All women just want a good fuck.'

'Was she the Virgin Queen? Oh, no of course not, that was Elizabeth. The Virgin Mary was the Queen of Heaven or something wasn't she?' Lawrence screwed his face, uncertain of Catholic doctrine.

'I need a fuck, Lawrie. It's your fault keeping on about virgins.'

'Although I think Elizabeth played an instrument known as *'the virginals'*,' Lawrence continued, as if he hadn't heard his friend's comments.

'I wouldn't mind playing them...virginals, do the notes come easily?'

'Joe, your double entendres do you no credit, and you'd have done better to have visited the galleries in Paris than spend your time on lesser pursuits. Mary Queen of Scots spent her childhood in France you know?' Lawrence suddenly digressed.

'I read a book about her not so long ago. It was written in the 1800's yet the author referred to Mary as the *'Queen of Hearts'* just like Princess Diana...or Diana Princess, whatever is politically correct these days.'

'It's Diana Princess of Wales,' Joe mumbled, his mind still at the Moulin Rouge watching the cancan.

Behind them the French tourists were taking snapshots of the ruined abbey; Joe moved to be out of their range.

'Strange, do you think she would have been like Diana? I've heard that she's abroad with that Dodi guy, you know, Al Fayed's son.'

To Joe's mind Diana was grossly overrated, just an ordinary yuppie who was a nursery nurse with big connections. She was slightly unbalanced and vaguely attractive, she would have been more so had she not constantly thrust her head to one side making her look somewhat demented. An actress of course, she enjoyed the limelight far too much. Naturally her main occupation was discrediting her husband, as all women loved to do.

'Mary was tall, slim, supposedly beautiful and married to that awful Henry Lord Darnley and then the Earl of Bothwell. That was of course after her first husband Francis, the King of France, died. She was so young to have suffered so much.'

'Who cares? Women shouldn't rule anyway, even your Bible tells you that.'

'Diana has a link to the Stewarts you know. Possibly a Jewish connection, Irish too. Brian Boru. Both she and Charles have a common ancestor. Bit like Mary Queen of Scots and her husband Lord Darnley.' Lawrence continued his historical lecture, ignoring Joe's disinterest. 'I read that Queen Elizabeth, you know our present Queen has the same coat of arms as James 1. You see he was a Stuart...or perhaps it's the Queen mother and her late husband who had the common ancestor, but whatever...'

'Whatever. Who cares, Lawrie? Who fucking cares?'

'Well I've read books about the Stuart bloodline, yar. The authors claim they are related to the Jews through that line. I told you all this earlier, but I don't think you were listening, Joe. Were you, Joseph?' he demanded like a rebuking father.

'No, Lawrence, I was asleep, so humbly sorry and all that. Look, we could go and find a bar what do you...'

'I've even read claims that they might be a lost tribe of Israel,' Lawrence ignored his friend's apathy.

'Princess Tamar went to Ireland with Jeremiah. You can read it in the Bible, she was supposed to be a Jewish princess, the daughter of King Zedekiah. There's another female, Scotia, or Scota something like that. Well, the term *Scot...*'

'Oh shut up, Lawrie, this is so fucking boring,' Joe snarled, following with a loud belch hoping to embarrass his friend into silence.

'Anyhow, as I was saying, it has been suggested that Scotia might have been a daughter of an Egyptian Pharaoh.'

'Perhaps Dodi Al Fayed is related to this pharaoh of yours. Don't look at me like that, Lawrie, I mean he's Egyptian isn't he? Maybe he's descended from him, and Diana from Scrotum or Tamar, what do you reckon?'

'I don't know if there was a link between Scotia and Tamar, who was said to have married a King in Ireland, Eochaidh or something like that.'

'Ha, don't tell me...your latest theory is that both the Royal House of Ireland and that of Scotland are both rooted in Judaism! So tell me, where did your family come from, Lawrie, the line of O'Cohen or McLevy?' Joe mocked.

'I hope Diana does find happiness with this Dodi guy, she deserves it.'

'Why? Some say that if she stays with him she will be pro Palestinian, how would you feel then?' Joe said, trying to provoke his friend.

'I have no problems with Palestinians. As you know, Joe, I had some very good Palestinian friends at Oxford. And genetically we are related, Jews and Arabs are cousins through the line of Abraham.'

'Well, what would happen to the royal family if Diana got herself pregnant to this Dodi?'

'Egypt is a great heritage to be proud of. It once had the greatest minds, culture and royalty the world had ever known,' Lawrence responded, refusing to take the bait.

Joe gave up; his eyes fixed to the Palace gates, wondering how they were still friends after all these years. His parents adored Lawrence, they wished Joe would be more like him or so they'd said all too often. Perhaps Joe was adopted. He'd hoped he was, but knew from just looking in the mirror that his eyes were genetically cloned from his mother.

'They say that when Tamar went to Ireland with the prophet Jeremiah they took the Stone of Scone with them, you know the Stone of Destiny, the one I told you about before. She was buried...well, so they say, on the hill of Tara and all the subsequent kings of Ulster were crowned on that stone. Did I tell you that some believe the stone to be Jacob's pillow?'

'Yar, I'm sure he rested his head on a stone, very comfortable. More probable that he spent the night humping a camel, or the hump of a camel,' Joe sniggered.

'I've read that the Irish Celts whom the Scots conquered were from the tribe of Dan. They say it was this King Eochaidh who united the Irish Celts and Scottish Gaels.' Lawrence continued his story undeterred by his companion's insults.

'In fact, Joe, they say that the Scots got their name from a king called Eber Scot, or some pronounce it Heber Scot, think it means *father of the Scots*. Well don't you think it a little odd yar, that in Hebrew father is almost the same word, *abba*? Not so different to *Eber*. Amazing isn't it?'

'Yar, fucking amazing.' Joe belched again. 'I thought you said the Scots got their name from some female.'

'Apparently some believe that Scota...or could be Scotia, what do you think?'

'Scrotum probably.'

'They say she was the great, great grandmother of Heber Scot the king.' For a moment there was silence, and then just as Joe began to close his eyes he was interrupted.

'I don't know why you said before that women shouldn't rule. Deborah from the Bible was a leader you know. Read the book of Judges, interesting book, very interesting.'

'Yar yar, get on with it, Lawrie. Anyhow, I bet you won't let Rachel rule you once you're married.'

'It's respect that matters, Joe, women can lead just as well as men. We Jews elevate heroines like, well, like Dahia Al-Kahinah. She led her tribes against the Muslims.'

'Is that it, one whole heroine?'

'No…No…er…there was Havivah Reik. She was a parachutist during the Second World War, taken prisoner and shot.'

'Yar, and I bet if I asked your mother she'd say that she'd never heard of her!' Joe sneered.

'Well, read the book of Judges in the Bible. You'll not merely read that Deborah was a great warrior and leader over the whole of Israel, but that there's more to heaven and earth than you could know,' Lawrence assured him. 'I'm surprised, Joe, with you being a philosopher, that you don't philosophise more. You should read Judges, the bit about Elijah. He went to heaven and didn't even die. And then, years later your Jesus apparently spoke to him on a mountain top.' Lawrence sat up straight, enthusiastic for what he hoped would be an in depth debate, just like the old days at university.

But Joe turned away disinterestedly in order to light a cigarette.

'I mean, your lot say that without Jesus' death and resurrection none of us can live after death. And that we are all pre programmed with evil which means we all die in sin.'

'So?'

'So Elijah didn't die. Which means that Jesus didn't die for him. He apparently didn't need the crucifixion to take place, and Moses was also on that mountain top, also resurrected prior to the crucifixion.'

'So?'

'So what?'

'So tell me why you make Rachel sit separately from you at your synagogue and why she's not allowed to touch the scrolls if you're so into women's rights?'

Lawrence didn't reply, merely digressed.

'As a graduate of psychology I must confess, Joe, I've often wondered whether your Jesus had suicidal tendencies from a young age. You often find that with children who don't have a stable upbringing.'

'What do you mean? Of course he had a stable upbringing, he was born in a fucking stable wasn't he?'

'Well, seeing as you were the one who claimed to be an atheist, and has now apparently transformed into a Catholic fundamentalist, perhaps you can enlighten me and reply to my former argument. How was it possible for Elijah to be resurrected prior to Jesus' crucifixion if, according to your Catholic doctrine one needed the crucifixion to happen in order to be resurrected? Now, if you take the blood line of the Royal House of Stuart...'

'It's not my fucking doctrine, I haven't been to church since my grandmother died!' Joe inhaled on the cigarette, as if relishing every atom of nicotine.

'I'm not the least bit interested in the Bible or the history of any royal fucker!'

'Well, I'm still impressed by Mary, Queen of Scots, and I find it fascinating to think that there might be a Jewish link there to Princess Tamar...and possibly Egypt,' Lawrence retorted despondently. 'Odd that there's that rumour about Diana Princess of Wales being a descendent of...'

'Oh don't say she was also born in a fucking stable!'

'No! I wasn't going to say that. But it's a little more than interesting that her boyfriend Dodi Al Fayed is an Egyptian. And I wish you'd stop swearing, Joseph. You accidentally swore when you last saw Rachel, and let me tell you she was not impressed.'

'What you need, Lawrie, is a good shag. Anyhow, if Jews were banned from Britain from the dates you've told me they were banned, what was it, from the 12th century and not allowed back for hundreds of years? Then there would have been no Jews in Scotland when Mary was on the throne. So she obviously didn't give a shit about your lot either!' Joe gave an ignorant yawn, glancing in the direction of a coach parking outside the gates, hoping to glimpse some pretty girls.

'I've got it, Lawrie!' Joe suddenly became animated in order to change the subject. 'You try to hypnotise me back in time, so then it will show without doubt any anomaly in your hypothesis.'

'What hypothesis?'

'Oh...any, all of them. You know, Mary Queen of Scots, even throw Princess Diana in for good measure if you want. Perhaps Diana's the reincarnation of Mary for all you know. Hypnotists, good ones, claim to get their subjects to go back in time you know? And it's kosher, you told me yourself that the Hassidic rabbis believe in reincarnation.'

Lawrence looked at his companion sceptically, whilst Joe glanced down at his shorts and wondered if they were appropriate for pulling.

'I thought you said it's Diana Princess of Wales, not Princess Diana anymore. And kosher merely means clean as you well know, Joseph Hill!'

'Oh you mean that blood business? The blood is mine sayeth the Lord, whatever that means. How can the blood be His? What blood? A lamb's blood? Look, Lawrie, if I'm willing to give this hypnosis crap a go, then you should be. And if I experience things I couldn't have known in this lifetime then I'll believe you really did hypnotise me. Fifty quids in then?' Joe pleaded, unable to take anymore history lessons. 'And I'll prove that women in every age were always inferior. Let's be honest, all the knights were men. It wouldn't even sound right would it? Queen Ethel-in-bed and Sir Val-a-Had. Mind you, I suppose they would have multiple orgasms if they lived in Camelot,' he sniggered. 'Yar, Lawrie, I'll prove to you that there were no female knights, not even in Edinburgh.'

'Alright, you're on!' Lawrence replied, now copying Joe and glancing down at his own shorts wondering what they were supposed to be looking for.

'But,' Joe interrupted, his blue eyes now staring directly at his friend. 'You have to leave me alone, for a few hours at least, or else the test won't work. Go and study the history of the Palace if you want, and leave me here by myself. Just direct me into any historical time zone you choose, and then come to find me at say...what's the time now, Lawrie?'

'12.13,' Lawrence replied, slightly anxious about the project he'd embroiled himself in.

'Well, say about 3 o'clock. Come and find me if I don't find you first, and then you can ask me what happened,' Joe said, surprising Lawrence by his sudden enthusiasm.

Joe often surprised him, feigning to be a shallow, selfish soul. Yet bubbling beneath the surface there was more than a hint of compassion and sensitivity. Lawrence had never forgotten the time

28

when he'd had the brief affair in Cowes with one of the Jamaican girls. Joe had arranged for and paid for the abortion without Lawrence ever knowing about it until after she'd returned to Jamaica. Joe knew only too well that Lawrence's family would never allow him to marry a *shiksa*, let alone a *shvartza*, and thank God Rachel never found out. Joe was a friend in a million, even though his testosterone frequently seeped into his brain.

'It wouldn't be safe, Joe,' Lawrence warned, though he was quite intrigued by the idea.

'Of course it will. I bet it doesn't even work. If you stay, you'd only be accused of influencing me into artificial experiences, but, if you aren't around then you will have proved your argument.'

Lawrence had no idea that Joe's sudden enthusiasm had nothing whatsoever to do with concern for his friend's academic interests. He would merely be at liberty to salvage the hours he had left to find some female to flirt with and pass the time. Joe felt slightly guilty at the deception, but, if no one was hurt then why worry? Lawrence would be happy with his research and Joe's overactive hormones would be placated.

'But it would be almost three hours, far too long...'

'You can't do it can you? Now at last you have got me willing to try this nonsense you're backing out,' Joe knew that this would be the addictive carrot for the kosher donkey.

'Lie down on the bench,' Lawrence instructed. Joe was uncharacteristically obedient, and immediately sprawled himself across the wooden bench.

'Close your eyes. Now, you can only hear the sound of my voice...relax, you're now on a beach...the sun...'

'Hey, Lawrie!' Joe's voice interrupted the moment.

'If you want, I'll see if I can find you any of your women warriors from the past, you know, some knights with frilly knickers. Well, at least we'd get one decent Edinburgh night!'

'Are you going to take this seriously or not, because if not then...'

'Yar, alright, calm down. Wouldn't find a female hero in any event, fucking contradiction in terms,' Joe sniggered, then threw his cigarette stub to the ground and closed his eyes.

'Female hero is a heroine, Joe.'

'Well, let's see if we can find you an Edinburgh heroine then, or a Queen. Yar, a Queen of Hearts or Queen of Heaven or whatever.'

'Now we must do this as professionally as possible, and I'll try and see if we can get you off those cigarettes. Now, today's date is August 30th 1997. Time, 12.20.' Lawrence rambled on trying to guide Joe's brain into some sort of hypnotic state.

'...And you are now counting backwards,' he heard Lawrence cajole, having failed to listen to any of his previous instructions which had gone on for ten minutes at least.

'Nineteen, eighteen, seventeen...'

The warm sunshine caressed Joe's face as Lawrence's voice wafted off into the Scottish air, and long legs and big breasts filled his mind.

Chapter Two

'To Ed'nburgh, sir, when e'er ye come,
I'll wait upon ye, there's my thumb,
Were't frae the Gill-bells to the Drum,
And take a bout,
And faither I hope we'll no sit dumb,
Nor yet cast out.'   (Allan Ramsay)

Now that Lawrence was out of sight, Joe had eagerly followed the two girls in micro skirts up the steep flight of turnpike stairs, and into what looked to be a museum dotted about with display cases containing artefacts of historical interest.

'Hi,' Joe smiled to the girls who giggled back. He was well aware of the effect his smile had on women, just one look at his dimples and the glint in his Irish eyes and they were his for the taking. Even two of his white teeth had a canine point on them. Sexy the girlies had said, although Katie had said they were the teeth of Dracula.

Joe fixed his stare on the girl with the biggest breasts, and motioned towards an open door that had a rope across forbidding entry. The girl followed him, leaving her friend to be the lookout. Inside the door there were steep spiral steps, Joe took the girl's hand and led her up until they were out of sight.

'What's your name?'

'Joanne. What's yours?'

'Joseph. Ha ha, both called Joe. There, we were fated to meet. Where are you from?'

'Befnal Green. You talk posh.'

'Does it bother you?'

'Na, still fancy yer, dun I?'

'Not as much as I fancy you.' His blue eyes stared into her green ones, hypnotic, seductive. He pressed his lips onto her own painted mouth, softly biting and kissing, his tongue slyly invading the moist hollow. Her own tongue responded, in and out, in and out, dancing tongues, wet and sticky.

Their bodies pushed against each other; strangers, intimate strangers. Just like animals, Joe considered, as he slowly took her hand and pressed it against the flies of his shorts. The girl didn't pull away, instead she began to move her fingers adeptly around the bulge that had grown. How many women he'd had, the sperm he'd wasted, all that potential life going to waste. Sperm that resembled tadpoles teasing their ejector with their potential of what they might have been had they been allowed to live. Perhaps some moralist could accuse him of murdering his own children.   For that's what they were, his children, fruit from his loins. Who was to decide which of his offspring should live and which should die?

Joe suddenly heard a cough from down the stairs, the girl's friend was signalling. Probably just a warden passing by, nothing to worry about, but obviously he wouldn't be able to shag her there. Joe took her hand and placed it inside his flies.

'Just a wank then yar? Please,' he said, pressing his head against her breasts.

'You've got great knockers, huge, bet the men in Bethnal Green can't keep away from you.'

Joanne giggled, her fingers now clutching hold of his penis, pushing the skin back up and down.

'Do yer fancy me then?' she blew into his ear.

'What do you think?'

'Going to buy me and me mate a drink later then?'

'Of course. Meet you in an hour. Meet you by that John Knox house okay?'

'You will turn up?' she blew again into his ear.

His mouth pressed into her fleshy breasts.

'You won't stand me up?'

'Of course not,' he panted, 'not if I can have another feel of these tits later.'

The girl giggled, lifting her head to allow him room to manoeuvre. His tongue was reaching for the nipple, sucking, licking.

Her own hand suddenly became more enthusiastic, working faster and faster. Up and down, up and down, harder, faster. His breath quickened, his penis hard, large and rigid. Up and down, up and down. Harder, bigger, faster, faster, faster.

'I've come,' he sighed. The fluid dribbling down into his fallen pants.

The girl looked at him, trying desperately to make eye contact, hoping that the pleasure she'd given would secure his own pleasure in her. But relief was over in every way, the relief of emission and departure.

They both descended back down the stairs and out into the room with the glass display cabinets. The girl still trying to make eye contact as they bid their farewells, Joe avoiding such contact as he raced down the stairs for a smoke and the sudden need to urinate.

Instead of finding himself at the front of the Palace, he now faced a grass covered piazza enclosed by aisles resembling cloisters.

The sun was shining in his eyes. For a moment or two he couldn't focus having emerged from the darkness of the Palace stairwell. Looking about for the gents, he noticed a sign for the toilets at the end of one of the aisles. Joe hoped upon hope that Lawrence hadn't felt the need to urinate at the same time. Of course he liked Lawrence, loved him like a brother, best friends and all that. At the clubs Lawrence would be the life and soul with a few drinks inside him. But, he was sometimes such a pain, too serious, too moral. Perhaps it was due to his recent engagement to Rachel. She was very pretty, not Joe's type of course. Her family were orthodox, her uncle Hassidic, not exactly wild people. They vaguely reminded Joe of the Amish cult in the States, stuck in a time warp.

After relieving himself Joe hurried back out into the sunshine. Yet, when he emerged into the daylight he was disorientated, he must have taken the wrong exit from the toilets.

Straining to see the entrance leading back into the Palace, Joe couldn't even place the door, let alone see a guide in sight. The grass piazza was still there, a quad within the centre of the four walls, reminding Joe of a medieval monastery.

His eagle eyes flew around the stone walls and walkways, trying to relocate the turnpike stairs.

He thought it peculiar the sun had suddenly gone in, it had been blazing only seconds before.

'What was that?' he shouted, startled by the sudden noise like the roar of a lion. Obviously he was mistaken, or perhaps the tourist guides were showing a film about lions. He'd noticed a red lion motto on various souvenirs in the shops when he'd first arrived in the city. Lawrence had teased him saying that Scots were yet another lost branch of Jewry, for the Jews also used an emblem of a lion, the lion of Judah.

The only person in sight was one of the passengers whom he'd seen on the coach, the tall beautiful being with fair hair, whose gender he'd been unable to ascertain. Yet, the person was now wearing some sort of fancy dress, a black cloak that reached to the ground with a cowl attached. Perhaps attempting to portray a monk or nun, or merely an authentic tour guide in period costume. Overhead the sky darkened, the clouds became grey, almost black, threatening a storm. Grey clouds of the unknowing, the words crashed through his mind with the sudden onset of a flash of lightning striking Arthur's Seat aflame. *'The cloud of the unknowing'*, a book he'd been forced to browse through at university, its author aptly also unknown. Was this the cloud? Joe wondered, his eyes transfixed to the great volcano overshadowing the Palace. A cloud, dark and impenetrable, unknowable.

'Some of these men the Devil will deceive their ears with quaint sounds, their eyes with quaint lights and shininess, their noses with wonderful smells – they are all false'. Words he never knew he'd read, let alone absorbed seeped into his head.

Yet, what did the author conclude? That God could not be reached by human intellect, only through love. A special, unique love that could pierce through the *'cloud of unknowing.'* Joe focused on the tall, cloaked being, who was beckoning him to follow. Not unduly worried, although he hadn't taken ecstasy for months. Not since a girl from the '*Viagra Cabana Club*', the best night club in his home town, whom he'd once bedded had died from it. She was only 16. Once again he found himself climbing turnpike stairs. Yet, these were different from the steps he'd previously climbed. They were less steep yet wider, with more windows and spy holes through which he could see soldiers on horseback appear through the mists of Holyrood Park.

'Was King Arthur here then?' Joe called up to the guide ahead of him, still struggling to work out the person's gender. The cloaked figure didn't reply, leading him into a large chamber adorned with elaborate black velvet drapes at the head of the staircase, reminding Joe of a drawing room in mourning. A long wooden table was surrounded by a variety of chairs neatly placed about the rush covered floor. All overshadowed by giant tapestries and drapes covering the walls. A large crucifix was fixed onto a pilaster in the corner overlooking a small statue of the Madonna and child.

'Cockburn, just call me Cockburn,' his guide suddenly volunteered in an educated Scots accent.

'Joe, Joe Hill.'

How beautiful she was. Joe knew now Cockburn was definitely female, well almost certain. Lawrence had told him angels were tall and genderless from his Jewish studies when he'd attended a Stamford Hill Torah Trail course. Joe presumed it was something akin to a Billy Graham mission week. Although he'd argued with Lawrence that just because his own uncle Brendan believed in Leprechauns, it didn't prove necessary existence. Anyhow, the biblical angels were merely astronauts; and Cockburn was more like an Adonis than a Venus.

A group of men were laughing beneath huge tapestries and wall hangings over on the far side of the room. They were all attired in 16th century dress and appeared not to notice the intruders as Cockburn led Joe away from their direction.

'Dinnae ken why they are happy whilst ma Queen is fighting for her country. They should be with her, nae eating her food and drinking her bevies.'

One of the men sitting down called out for more wine, but Cockburn ignored him.

'Who's your Queen, do you mean Queen Elizabeth?'

Cockburn's face suddenly reddened, and then she spat phlegm onto the ground.

'Dinnae ever say that here, dinnae ever mention the bastard and Queen in the same breath!'

'Sorry I'm sure. So what Queen then?' Joe rolled his eyes, uncertain if this Cockburn was quite all there. Perhaps she meant some gender bender queen.

'Ma Queen's Marie of course, who else could ye call Queen? But then ye cannae be worse than her half brother James Stewart, Earl of Moray. Killed her mother although nae one will speak of it.' Cockburn's eyes were now focussing onto the lump of gob she'd spat on the floor.

'Traitor that he is encouraging rebellion. But ma Queen got her ain back. D' ye ken that on the 14th day of this very month the crown seized the properties of the rebel lords?' Cockburn gave a snigger. 'And then she replaced their Protestant provost with her ain, Sir Simon Prestoun of Craigmillar.'

'Catholic?'

'Of course. It was only a few days back she donned her helmet and pistol wi' her husband, that lang streak of piss, and led her army oot of Edinburgh efter her brother Moray. And taeday, wha's the date taeday? I cannae remember wi' all this commotion, nae thing's the same when her Majesty's awa'.'

'30th August,' Joe grumbled, thinking Cockburn only asked to ensure that he was still listening to her waffle.

'Aye, nae thing's the same. She's now leading her army. Over 5,000 men frae Glasgow. Heard that rain ha' flooded Glasgow taeday.'

'Yar, I've been told it always rains in Glasgow. Well that's what Lawrence said.' Joe responded, as Cockburn led him into the bedchamber, the large four poster bed taking precedence, adorned in heavy, scarlet drapes.

'She left here, well, it wa' aboot four days ago, she rode tae Linlithgow Palace.'

'What's that smell?'

'Oh, it's only Angell Marie...she's the perfumer, just delivered the flowers and pomanders for her Majesty. Nae that she's expected tae return for some time. But ye ne'er can tell. I shall pray tae the Blessed Virgin. The Holy Father the Pope is also praying for her.'

'I always pray for a blessed virgin...but rarely get one.'

Perhaps someone had spiked his drink that morning when they'd stopped off at a wine bar on the way to the Waverley Bridge to catch the tour bus, Joe conjectured. Cockburn stood at the end of the bed with arms folded, foot tapping impatiently on the rush covered floor.

'Where are they?' she asked crossly.

'Who?'

'The Queen and her army, where is she? I just cannae rest until she's hame safe!'

'I thought you said she was in Glasgow,' Joe muttered sarcastically, but the tall guide failed to respond to his taunt.

Two women in period costume stood chatting in one of the small adjoining rooms. Perhaps it was a dressing room Joe considered, his eyes focusing upon the younger of the two busily folding a rug. Yet, even now he wasn't unduly concerned, presuming that the staff were expected to wear authentic garments. The pungent smells of wax and perfume filled the air making him slightly heady as he glanced about. The floors were highly polished oak covered with numerous carpets and rushes. Oak tables, elaborately carved with the royal crown and cipher, accommodated high backed chairs of gilded leather and cushions of brocade and damask. Some were covered in velvet bordered with gold thread.

'Well, I dinnae ken why ma Queen does listen tae Master Rizzio, if he deceived her once then he'll do it again.' The girl with blonde locks escaping from her white cap warned the older woman in broad Scot, who now followed her into a small side room richly decorated in crimson and green. Joe was now totally bemused as to how he understood her every word. He'd never been any good at languages at Eton, even failing first year exams in the philosophy of language and linguistics at Oxford.

'Wha' do ye mean, Betsy?' the older servant asked.

'Aye, it's true; it was Master Rizzio who arranged the Queen's marriage tae ma Lord Darnley, ken how she was sae full of the passions?' Betsy momentarily stopped what she was doing.

'We must'na call him *Lord Darnley*, he's tae be called King now. And they've only just been wed, why should she nae be full of the passions?'

Then, giving out a loud sigh, the older woman conceded.

'Aye, I suppose ye're right, Betsy lass, they say the Queen was tae ambitious and tae passionate...particularly aboot *him*.'

'Maybe they'll both be killed taeday,' the girl sniffed back her tears.

'Nae, lass, dinnae greet, I ken everything's in turmoil. All this blether aboot the devil starting a civil war inside the Flodden wall. But her Majesty, she'll nae let us doon.'

'Excuse me,' Joe interrupted, 'are you tour guides?'

Both women glanced at one another curiously, brushing down their skirts and caps.

'Nae, sir, just servants of her Majesty,' the middle aged woman curtsied.

Before Betsy was able to follow her lead they were untimely interrupted.

'What are you two standing around in her Majesty's supper room for? Oh, forgive me, my lord, I didn't see you there.' The intruder was a middle aged woman, but wearing grander attire than those whom she'd addressed.

'Mistress Margaret Carwood, I'm one of her Majesty's women of the bedchamber, my lord.' The woman spoke in French and gave a short curtsy, then immediately turned on her staff. 'Now get on with your work! Would you come with me, sir, into the banqueting hall?'

Obliging, Joe followed her into the outer chamber. He was too dazed to question where he was going, least of all where Cockburn had disappeared. The said Mistress Carwood guided him towards a chair, and then exited through the outer door towards the turnpike staircase like a bit part actress anticipating no curtain call.

Joe, unable to sit still, found himself wandering back towards the door that led into the bedchamber. He eavesdropped on the two women cleaning the rooms, slyly searching for the girls from Bethnal Green.

'Aye trust me, I ken for a fact that oor beloved Queen Marie's mother, Marie of Guise, had an affair wi' Cardinal Beaton.'

'But ma Jock wa' in the stables shoeing the horse belonging tae the Earl of Argyll, and he wa' bletherin' tae his companion that it wa' a different maid who Cardinal Beaton gave bairns tae ken? Had lots of different maids sae ma Jock said!' Betsy expounded as she threw some dead flowers into a box and replaced them with new ones. 'And forged the King's will he did that Cardinal Beaton!'

'Aye, sae they say, lass. I'm old enough tae remember when St. Andrew's Castle was seized by Beaton's murderers.'

'Tae think that Master Knox was captured and sent tae galleys as a galley slave.

If only they'd hung and quartered him, oor beloved Queen would'na hae tae fight for her crown sae hard.'

'Hush…Master John Knox has ears everywhere,' the older maid cautioned, then dropped to a whisper. 'Anyway, they blame Cardinal Beaton for the Protestant Wishart's death. Some might say that it's divine justice that the Protestants then killed him.'

'John Knox, but I thought he wa' alive. Still giving his Catholic hating sermons in St Giles.'

'Nae, lass, John Knox is very much alive. I mean Cardinal Beaton…oh, nae mind ken. Best finish these rooms afore Mistress Carwood returns or else we'll be as deid as Cardinal Beaton.' The women were now cleaning under the four poster bed so Joe was unable to hear their mutterings.

An animal growled, or at least it sounded like an animal, the noise coming from outside the window. But, as no one else appeared to have heard it Joe began to wonder if he'd gone totally mad.

Perhaps no one existed, not even him. The world just made up from random hallucinations in the mind of God. Whether God Himself existed was another matter. If He did, was He a rationalist or empiricist? None of Joe's Oxford tutors had ever said. Perhaps He was a utilitarian or a psychological hedonist.

Rationality was a virtue of God by necessity, Joe had suggested during a university tutorial, the deity's reasoning based on the

Principle of Sufficient Reason. As to whether God was the First Cause, or embodied the necessary and sufficient condition of life Joe had grave doubts. Joe's tutor had definitely not been impressed in his fresher year when he'd handed in a paper disproving God's existence. In the said paper Joe had stated that God was an atheist, and His only spirituality was His leanings towards Buddhism and Nirvana in order to self annihilate.

The women suddenly emerged from beneath the bed now dusting and polishing the furniture.

'Nearly twenty years have passed sae quick since his murder. Aye, time flies hen, ma Queen wa' just a wee bairn.'

'If ye want tae ken aboot oor Queen, ye only needed tae ask me.' The voice made him jump. It was Cockburn, she'd appeared seemingly from nowhere.

'Have you seen two girls, they're wearing really short skirts...and very high heels?'

'Ma poor young Queen inherited her crown in 1542, just six days old.'

'What?'

'Thirteen years in France, ye cannae ken how lang that is for a wee lassie. In her heart and mind she's French. This land is tae wild for her. A flower surrounded by deadly thorns.' Cockburn spat out something from her mouth.

'Of course Master Knox is the instigator of the gossip aboot ma mistress bedding ma lord Darnley afore they wed. Yet, Knox himsel' is bedding the wee lassie he's just married. And tae ken he wa' once a Catholic priest, his bride is nae mair than a bairn hersel'.'

Joe just gave a slight smile for the sake of politeness, perhaps this beautiful creature was part of the tour package.

'As ye just heard, they say that Marie de Guise the Queen's deid mother bedded Cardinal Beaton. But I dinnae believe she did, after all Beaton wa' her husband the King's ain envoy.'

Through the narrow window Joe could hear the thunder explode overhead, then the anticipated flash of lightning. The heavens opened.

'Dinnae fret, it's only the sons of thunder…Would ye care for one?' Cockburn held out a small bowl of nuts towards him with some fruit mixed in, Joe declined.

He went to search for his cigarettes in the pockets of his shorts, only to discover that his pockets weren't there. Looking down towards his legs Joe suddenly saw that his shorts had also gone, he was now wearing russet and green doublet and hose. Along with a cod piece, leather purse, small dagger and gloves.

'I…I don't understand…am I tripping?'

'Her mother's initials are up there.' Cockburn pointed up to the elaborate wooden ceiling before Joe had a chance to react to his transformation.

'And you can see the French fleur de lys,' Mistress Carwood interrupted, as she carried a large tapestry under her arm.

'Master Pierre Oudry is here with the new tapestries, Cockburn, tell Master Rizzio…oh, I see you are taking care of our guest.' Before Joe had a chance to reply, Mistress Carwood left the room followed by the said Pierre Oudry and his tapestries.

In the corner of the room musical instruments were piled high, Joe noticed a lute, but he had no inclination to play. As if sedated, he felt too tired to care overmuch about anything, least of all the disappearance of his clothes. Joe's main concern was his cigarettes. Of course it had happened to him before when he'd found himself in a strange venue without knowledge of how'd he'd arrived there. On one occasion he'd even found himself naked. He'd either taken some illegal substance of his own volition or else someone else had spiked his drink, but he'd never worried overmuch, all part of the club scene.

'She oversteps the mark speaking tae me as if I were a mere kitchen servant!' Cockburn spat angrily.

'You were telling me about Cardinal Beaton.'

'Aye, the great Catholic, succeeded his uncle as Archbishop,' she mumbled, her eyes still focussed on the door through which the housekeeper had exited.

'Genetic spirituality then,' Joe remarked sarcastically.

'Ne'er heard the Mass called that afore.'

'So is he here today?'

41

'Many would abhor your jokes, sir, as ye ken David Beaton was executed many years ago. And as for your mention of '*taeday*', it wa' nae a guid day tae arrive here, Joseph.' Cockburn shook her head pensively. 'Moray, the Queen's half brother advances on this city whilst oor Queen ha' gone tae fight the rebel lords. Mar, the governor of the Castle ha' asked if he must fire cannons against the invaders.'

'Well yar, that sounds like a sensible move.'

'Nae sae sensible if it means killing the innocent citizens if a cannon is fired! Ye must excuse me, I have tae make preparations for supper taenight. If ye need anything ask a servant.' Cockburn hurried out of the room before Joe had a chance to remonstrate.

The black rain clouds had passed as quickly as they'd appeared. The sunshine was now stabbing laser beams through the windows, randomly highlighting the numerous ornaments and tapestries.

The two maids were still inside the small room adjoining the bedchamber setting out food, jugs and knives.

'...And politicians, aye politicians, the religion of the damned, well, that's wha' ma Jock says.'

'Aye, hen, all tae much for those like us. Aye, all tae much,' she sighed. 'But there hae been great feasts. Remember her Majesty's wedding tae Lord Darnley? Allowed me tae help her dress she did. Took off her widows weeds efter the service, and put on the brightest, most fashionable dress in all Christendom. Aye, lass, but wha' are memories?' The older maid rubbed her heavily bagged eyes.

How often Lawrence had tried to discuss memory with him, but Joe hadn't been interested. Psychology was his friend's field, and nothing about it appealed to him; although Joe did recall having touched on the 19th century philosopher and psychologist William James during his studies at Oxford. James had argued something about memory proper being the knowledge of a former state of mind after the event had been dropped from consciousness. Joe's own argument had been that a dream could also be described as a former state of mind after waking. Therefore, he'd concluded, theoretically at least, that memory of real events could claim no greater authenticity than those that were imaginary.

42

Lawrence had once mentioned a reporter in Moscow who could reproduce reports verbatim without ever taking notes. The man was a mnemonist and had developed tricks to help him. Tricks such as visualising a street, then positioning the objects to be remembered at some point along the street. Joe had merely responded with a scoff, for he hadn't even been interested in his own research degree let alone Lawrence's academic studies.

'...And the food, remember the swans at her wedding feast, they were decorated like brides? And the dancing, how her Majesty and her husband danced that day! Aye, she wa' sae beautiful, wi' her red hair and golden eyes...and sae tall,' the young Betsy chattered with the enthusiasm of a child.

'And the gold coins that ma Queen threw tae the crowds,' the older servant dribbled through the numerous gaps in her teeth as she carried a bowl of jelly into the supper room.

'Ma niece collected five coins. Ha' tae punch oot the fishwives teeth tae get her share ha ha!'

An auburn haired young woman interrupted them as she carried a sack of logs towards the fire, she was soaked to the skin. A ginger haired toddler was strapped about her body.

'And why aren't you helping Nan with the logs?' a man's voice suddenly bellowed causing Joe to jump.

'Sorry, ma lord,' the women curtsied and hurried to the aid of the girl, relieving her of the logs.

'Nan, if you go to the servants' kitchen there will be some bread and honey for you, and something for Rabbie,' he smiled at her.

'Look at your hands, they're bleeding. You shouldn't be doing this work you know, there's no need. Least of all to live where you do.'

'I'm alright, sir, we manage.'

'Even so, I insist you take this for your trouble,' he pushed a bag of coins forcibly into her torn hand.

Once they were both out of sight the servants resumed their gossiping.

'Ye ken why he gave her the money?' the older woman said in a whisper.

'His mistress?'

'Nae, lass, as if Lord Seton would do such a thing tae one of her Majesty's ain…he worships Queen Marie.'

'Well then why?'

Joe was about to ask what she'd meant by *'her Majesty's ain'*, when suddenly loud explosions could be heard outside setting the younger maid into panic.

'Dinnae greet sae, lass, ye'll be safe enough here.' The older woman tried to console the younger who was now weeping uncontrollably. The thunderous roars of gunpowder grew louder and more frequent.

'Come on stop bletherin!' the voice belonged to Cockburn.

'I dinnae ken why ye're greetin' sae, the guns are only being fired by oor ain soldiers, practising, just in case. Sae wipe yer eyes…her Majesty will return frae battle and have nae bed tae sleep in!'

'So, who's the dude…is he shagging the girl with the kid then?' Joe asked Cockburn when the explosions outside had ceased. 'That's Lord Seton, half brother tae Marie Seton, one of her Majesty's ladies in waiting. He's the Master of the Hoosehold.'

'So what did they mean about the girl being your Queen's own?'

'Here ye are, Master Hill,' Cockburn thrust a miniature book into his hands.

'What's this?' Joe glanced at the tiny Bible she'd given him, as they sat on velvet covered chairs in the banqueting hall.

'Ye will need this, it's yer instruction manual if I'm nae around,' Cockburn smiled, a detached, yet impish smile.

'What are you talking about? Listen, I think I'll go and find Lawrie, I need a drink. Do you think I have salmonella poisoning, it's rampant at home?'

'Ye are far tae agitated, lad, relax, I'm just yer servant, Cockburn. Related tae the Cockburns of Ormiston. Although most of ma family are Protestants, I mysel' belong tae the true religion.' Cockburn offered him some wine from a jug. Joe never declined booze, and happily lifted a goblet from the tray whilst she poured.

44

'John Cockburn of Ormiston, ma uncle, is a great Protestant supporter of the Reformation and of the minister of the Kirk of St. Giles, Master John Knox.

Ye may hae heard of him?'

'My friend Lawrence would argue against Rome being the true religion,' Joe remarked, gulping down the red grape juice. 'You see, he'd say that Jesus wasn't a Roman.'

Cockburn made no reply as she poured herself a goblet of wine.

'So, are you trying to tell me that this is back in time...you know, like really the 16th century?'

'Of course it is, laddie, are ye blootered?'

'So what are you telling me, Cockburn, that this is what? The 30th August 1600 and something?'

'Joseph, please dinnae piss aroond, ye ken very well it's 1565... although ye are correct aboot it being August.'

'Ah, but you gave me a Bible...And, if King James isn't yet born, then how can there be a Bible? Gotcha!'

'I'll call the servants tae get mair wine.' Staggering slightly, Cockburn made her way towards the top of the turnpike stairs.

'Mair wine!'

'I feel strange, I mean where is Lawrie? Did someone give me an E?' Joe squinted his eyes at Cockburn who looked bemused.

'An E?'

'You know, ecstasy.'

'Ecstasy? Och aye!' she gave a wry smile, 'ye are a Catholic tae!'

Joe was puzzled, but now on his fourth cup was too drunk to care.

'Yar, I'm looking for a blessed virgin...will I find any in Scotland?'

'Aye, Knox married his 17 year old virgin only a few months ago. His second wife.'

'And the Queen's married I suppose, her first marriage presumably?'

'Nae, where hae ye been, lad? She wa' married tae Francis II, he deid of cancer of the ear. Ye ken wha' Master Knox said? *'that rotten ear that would'na hear the gospel.'*

'I'll tell you a riddle about Monsieur Knox,' a voice interrupted in French. It belonged to a girl wearing a jester's outfit and hat, designed as a dress rather than body suit. The girl began to speak in gibberish, her behaviour bizarre, hands moving about erratically.

'Go away, Nicola, we dinnae hae time tae be amused,' Cockburn rebuked.

'The Kirk minister Wolfart Bruce is hanging aroond in the courtyard, gae and annoy him!'

Again Joe heard what sounded like the roar of an animal, he presumed it came from some nearby forest.

'You have no joie de vivre, Cockburn, but it matters not. Our Queen Marie likes me the best of all, well, better than she likes you.' The girl headed towards a tray containing an assortment of fruit and began juggling half a dozen small pomegranates into the air. Noticing that she had no audience the girl stopped, replaced the pomegranates into the tray in exchange for a red apple.

'You see this pomme, monsieur?' She handed it to Joe. 'Open it up with this knife si vous plais.'

Joe obliged, taking the knife she offered, and cut into the moist flesh of the apple. To his surprise he found himself retrieving a tiny egg from behind the pips. The girl snatched the fruit he was examining away from his grip, and in an instant both apple and egg had vanished.

'I've seen it all before, ye get boring efter a while, Nicola, better ye'd gone tae Glasgow wi' the Queen than get on ma nerves.'

With that, the girl went away, eager to torment the group of men dressed in 16th century attire sitting on the far side of the room by the turnpike stairs.

'Who's she?'

'Nicola Ambruzzi…she's the Queen's fool, Joseph.'

'Yar, she does seem more than a little foolish. Funny, I'd always thought fools were supposed be astute. I suppose it's different for women, I suppose for women anything goes. Did she find her in a sort of workhouse? You know, a sort of lunatic asylum?'

'Please dinnae be fooled, she's nae stupid. She's mair sharp than yersel' and mysel'.'

From the far side of the banqueting hall Joe could hear the men laughing as the said Nicola Ambruzzi entertained them. How they roared. Life was indeed a comedy Lawrence used to say, a comedy of errors.

Joe's eyes were closing. The dark, red juice now dribbling down the sides of his mouth like a kiss of blood.

'Why, ye look half deid, Joseph, come we will eat.' Cockburn placed an arm through his as he staggered to his feet.

'Right, Joseph, ye must hae heard of the bell book and candle, used in excommunications in the Catholic Church?' Cockburn sighed. 'Efter pronooncing sentence the priest closes his book, quenches the candle by throwing it tae ground, and tolls the bell like ye would for someone who ha' deid.'

She was growing impatient.

'Look, the book symbolises the Book of Life. The candle...that's the soul, it's removed frae the sight of God, as the candle is frae the sight of man! Oh come on, what ye need is some fresh air!' Cockburn now dragged him towards the staircase where the servants were bustling to and fro carrying trays and steaming, covered dishes.

Outside the fresh air hit him full on. The drink impaired his balance as he tried to keep up with Cockburn who led him across a drawbridge flanked by soldiers and into the main courtyard.

Again he thought he heard an animal roar.

'What was that?' But his escort failed to answer.

Joe noticed a high wall enclosing the area to the left of the drawbridge, which stretched from the turreted corner of the Palace into the western gardens. The lower half of the wall was stone, the upper, high wooden fencing. Opposite, not far from the drawbridge, was a large fish pond surrounded by a magnificent rockery. Draped in flowers resembling narcissi, the pond nestled within a bed of lilies intermixed with green, purple and lemon shrubs. In the centre of the fish pond was a dragon spouting water from its mouth. Below, sculptured smaller dragons and lions heads also sprayed water. Joe was almost certain that this area had been the east side of the Palace. Now it appeared to be the north.

'There used tae be otters here ken, but tae much trouble. Follow me!' Cockburn instructed, heading in the opposite direction towards an abbey that appeared to be in the throes of repair.

Workmen balanced precariously on the top of the broken structure, their wet ropes and ladders stretching insecurely across the large gaps in the roof. Everything was soaked from the recent downpour.

'There's nae roof on the choir…ye'll see mair graves here than choirboys, lad, aye mair graves.'

As they made their way beyond the damaged abbey, bordered by a small herb garden, Joe wondered how his guide wasn't boiled in her long, black cloak. The smells of the lavender, violets and rosemary wafted through the warm air as they headed through an ivy and rose covered trellis into the eastern gardens. Ruins of what looked to have once been part of the abbey carpeted the ground, harbouring large puddles. Workmen meandered around the ruins wheeling cartloads of wood towards the nave, followed by a couple of donkeys laden with building materials.

There were numerous wells scattered randomly in the eastern gardens beyond the ruins, adorned with flowering arbours and sculptures. Beyond the wells in a nearby field were stone lodges, Joe was uncertain if they housed the more important staff, or were guest houses.

Cockburn led him through another rose covered trellis and they emerged into the southern gardens. The high braes above were partially covered in woodland. As if ablaze with burning purple and gold flames, heather and gorse carpeted the peaks. His eyes scanned the scene, settling on the ruins of what looked to have once been a chapel standing alone on the crag above overshadowed by pine trees, as twilight settled over Holyrood.

Butterflies and bees were in abundance, Joe's own head also buzzed from the alcohol as his eyes scanned the vast, elaborate gardens illuminated by the sunset and multitude of blazing lanterns.

Trees dripped with fruit; apricots, pears, apples and plums, even peaches carpeted the grass below. Baskets laden to the brim with fruit and berries were being carried away by children. Joe was surprised that fruit trees could thrive in Scotland with its bleak winters, as his focus now centred on the exotic flowers and plants, a carpet of multi coloured sunshine. All the vibrant hues of the rainbow cascaded over small artificial ponds and ornamental fountains and rock gardens. Classical figurines stood sentry-like intertwined between the sculpted bushes soaked from the recent storm.

The smaller shrubs danced off the raindrops beneath an oak tree, incited by the wind. Naughty children overseen by the school mistress, whose splintered, wooden arms waved with wild enthusiasm. The gardens on this side were sectioned into eight plots of equal measure. The plots were divided by numerous paths and trellises. Flowers were laid out in precise design, some in the pattern of fleur de lys, rosettes, wheels and the occasional sundial.

Joe followed Cockburn through the trellises, failing to comprehend why she had gone to such trouble to try and explain her bell, book and candle. Perhaps it was the title of a film, maybe they were actually participating in a film. He'd always secretly fancied himself as a star. Maybe there would be a steamy sex scene, if so, he was up for it. Cockburn was tall, good body, face beautifully surreal.

'Well, ha, do you…are you…want a quick roll in the hay?'

'Ye are nae here by chance, Joseph, ye were sent. Ye are here wi' us tae learn the meaning of life and death, ye are a philosopher aye?'

If there was one thing that was irresistible to Joe and almost as good as a shag was a challenge, a puzzle, especially those of the cryptic kind. Perhaps he was going to get his murder mystery weekend after all. He wondered if Lawrence had set it up as a surprise.

'Yer mission is tae find the bell, book and candle, and tae help ye along yer way ye will be given riddles tae solve, and every answer will reveal a letter from the alphabet. Tak' each letter ye find, and ye will have enough letters tae make the word ye need, ken.'

Joe gave a smile; this was going to be fun.

'I'm surprised to see that fruit grows so well here.'

'Aye, but nae always…most years we hae tae import fruit like peaches and figs frae England.'

Nearby he noticed archery butts and courts.

'Do you play tennis?'

'The Queen plays cachepull. Mainly plays in her private garden, it faces the Canongate, west side, faces the toon. Cachepull disnae require anything but a ball ken.'

'Volley ball, is that what you mean? Or is it something more dangerous like an extreme sport?'

'Wha'? Do ye mean the archery butts in ma Queen's private gardens? Here, tak' this.' The guide withdrew something from inside her cloak, it was a ring.

'If ye are feart of danger, lad, just show it tae anyone and ye'll hae the protection of the crown.'

Joe fiddled with the ring she'd given him. It was gold with a black stone engraved with a golden lion set within a square and compasses, the sign of the masons. Joe began to laugh; this wasn't so different from Knightsbridge after all.

'Of course ye must find the key, as the only way ye can escape frae here is wi' the key. But I dinnae hae time tae explain, must hurry.'

'I thought we were going to eat!'

'I'll be back for ye soon, laddie,' Cockburn gave a nod and started to walk away.

'Oh, Joseph!' she called behind her, 'watch ye codpiece ken, it's tae wee and ye bits are hanging oot...and ye are mingin' ken!'

It was after Cockburn had disappeared that Joe made his way towards the courts where cachepull was played. A large wooden ball still remained in the court, Joe bent down to inspect it. It seemed too big to hit with a bare hand, perhaps it belonged to a different game, cricket or croquet maybe.

'Catherine de Medici hates her!' Joe glanced up to see two men walking nearby, they spoke in Italian.

'You know, Mingo, that our Queen Marie calls her a *merchant's daughter*,' the shorter man laughed. 'Catherine should have more love for her former daughter in law don't you agree? Marie was not much more than a child herself when she was widowed to her son Francis, but Catherine de Medici is hard, cold...some say she's evil.'

'She gave the magician Nostradamus gold crowns to tell her future, what do you think of that, Davey Rizzio? You, who happens to be favourite valet, musician and secretary to our Queen!' Upon the mention of 'Nostradamus' Joe's ears pricked up. 'Apparently, he foretold Francis's death you know. He knew Marie would be widowed without children, and he prophesised that two islands would be thrown into war.'

'They say he's a converted Jew.'

'Lucky for her Nostradamus wasn't born in England then, there Jews are banned from Christian shores on pain of death. Catherine de Medici's the niece of the Pope, more than a little interesting don't you agree, Davey?' Mingo asked, stealing a peach from one of the remaining baskets.

'What do you mean?'

'Well, what with her consulting Jewish magicians rather than the Holy Father.'

'Not every land, Jews aren't banned from every land. Well, not from Scotland. Anyhow, our Queen Marie doesn't need Nostradamus, she needs the support of Rome. She needs Rome's armies!' The swarthy Rizzio took a swig from his flask. 'And with no adult succession of Stewarts since the fourteenth century, she has a long battle on her hands. And what with the English court jeering at my poor Marie behind her back, they even mock her name because it originated from the stewards of the kings of Scotland.'

'Well you do surprise me, Davey, speaking against the Pope, you of all people! Yet I, a mere valet de chambre wouldn't dare to speak likewise. But then of course, rumour has it that you're the one that they say is the Holy Father's secret spy here ha ha.'

'I've never spoken against the Holy Father, Mingo, just concerned as to why the support her Majesty should rightfully enjoy hasn't been dispatched from Rome.'

Joe returned his gaze to the wooden ball in his hands once the men were out of sight, focusing on the join circling its centre embossed with a red lion. The join moved slightly, obviously the ball was broken.

His sweaty fingers twisted against the join, twisting and turning. The ridge was stuck, slightly mouldy. Joe tugged and pulled, gripping hard at each side of the orb until at last the ball opened. Hollow inside, except for a book that had been bent in half to fit into the ball. Even so, it was tiny, the same size as his Bible, but this book was written in French. It was when he noticed the signature, '*Nostradamus*', that Joe's heart began to race. The book was bound in crimson and gold with the royal crest in each corner. The cover was illustrated with a picture of a tarot card, The High Priestess. There was a message written inside the cover, it read:

> **'Nostradamus prophesised, and the true lineage isn't David's seed. Tamar was Queen of the hive and Deborah was the bee.'**

Below the message was a Biblical reference.

> **'Exodus 28: 34 – so find Elijah don't be dense, but the clues might not be in sequence.'**

Joe grabbed the miniature Bible Cockburn had given him, and searched for the reference.

Immediately, he realised that his jibe to Cockburn about the King James Bible had been irrelevant, as every page was written in Latin.

Considering his previous knowledge of Latin was minimal, as with his command of Scots, French and Renaissance English he was suddenly able to read every word fluently. At the appropriate verse he noticed that a section had been underlined.

> *'A golden bell and then a pomegranate.'*

Joe was none the wiser, now scrutinizing the book of Kings for all references to the prophet Elijah, but there was nothing to connect with the clue.

He presumed the Palace had its own hives, but he'd already had his ego stung that day, there was no way that he was going to get his body stung too.

Eventually, Joe gave up and threw the Bible to one side.

What a disappointment, what a let down, Cockburn was just a run of the mill Bible basher.

'Huh, stupid female, all just weak parasites!' he spat at the ground.

Someone was humming a tune, who was singing his song? His head shot around, but there was no one there, yet he could hear the tune of '*Joe Hill*'.

A sudden chill was in the air. It reminded him of what his nanny was wont to say, '*as if someone has walked over my grave*'.

A voice, almost like a breath of wind blew into his face

'Queen Scathach female warrior of Skye. I taught the weak male how not to die.
And when the Reformers come to take the crown, they'll call lasses 'witches', and they will all drown'.

Joe blinked, what was it that he'd heard? A real voice, or was it his imagination?   Who was Queen Scathach? He'd never heard of her, he must have momentarily dozed off.

The moon was full that evening as the sky slowly disappeared into the thick mist of night, obscuring Arthur's Seat.   The day had passed so quickly but Joe didn't know where. Nearby, he noticed several soldiers racing around like headless chickens.   Men in saffron shirts and blue hats followed them, carrying weapons akin to pickaxes and sticks, only a few carried knives.

'Here, Joseph, this is for ye.' The voice belonged to Cockburn, now showing him the long, black cloak that she carried in her arms.

'What's going on, why the soldiers, has there been a murder or something?' he joked.

'Aye, sae ye've heard hae ye, laddie?'

'What? You're not serious. Why, you are serious.   Well, who's been murdered?' Joe was confused, his mind still beating out the words he'd heard in his dream of Queen Scathach.

'I think ye met the poor wee lass when ye were up in her Majesty's apartments.   She wa' preparing the Queen's rooms.'

'You don't mean that young girl with the blonde curls, the one with the cap on her head?'

'Betsy.'

'Yar, that was her name I think, yar, Betsy. Wow, so she's been murdered. Wow. So who did it, I mean have they caught him?' Joe shivered; he'd only seen her that afternoon.

'Here, Joseph, ye'll need this, tak' it,' she pressed the cloak into his trembling hands.

'Now follow me and I'll show ye where tae sleep taenight, but we'll eat first.'

Joe draped the cloak about his shoulders, ensuring his ring remained on his finger, and followed his guide through a small side door near the drawbridge leading into the Palace. A fire roared in the corner, over the flames hung a spit. Other servants sat around the fire. A group of young children were turning the spit whilst the revellers were eating and drinking, some dancing whilst a fiddler played. All were dressed in 16th century costume like Joe, who was now getting used to wearing hose, although he'd accidentally pissed down them twice.

No one seemed to care about the murder, not like at home. No press, no police, and no ambulance. Maybe it was because the region appeared to be in the midst of a mini war, but it seemed to Joe that poor Betsy's life was deemed to be worthless. Perhaps the murderer had done her a favour, he thought, liberating her from a life of drudgery. Whatever, it appeared to Joe that no one cared whether she lived or died.

Taking an empty stool, he sat down by a table. Before him on a platter lay the leftovers of a cooked swan, its long throat hanging down over the side of the table. Joe was hungry, never one for over sentimentality he accepted the food offered.

'Here tak' this,' Cockburn handed him a knife.

'The Queen uses forks, but I prefer just the knife like most folk.'

Nicola, the Queen's fool was doing her party piece. This seemed to consist of a handstand whilst juggling two fish with her bare feet, the fish miraculously turning into two pig's eyes. Ignoring the music and entertainment, Cockburn shouted above the noise.

'Catherine de Medici, she wa' the mother of the Queen's first husband. Well, she introduced forks tae France frae Italy. The English say forks are *'effeminate'*, tha's why I dinnae use them.'

Joe wanted to remind Cockburn that she was a female, but thought better of it.

'So this is the kitchen,' his eyes searching around for a girl to bed for the night.

'Nae, this is just the servants' kitchen. Next door, 'tween here and the abbey are her Majesty's kitchens. There are pantries, cellars where she keeps her wine, a bakery. We e'en brew oor ain ale. Aye, Joseph, her Majesty ha' over 200 servants ken.'

'All called Ken.'

'Wha'?'

Sitting over on the far side of the room he noticed the girl who'd brought the logs earlier that day, her child lay on her cloak asleep. If only he wasn't so drunk he'd go and ask her what the servant had meant by, *'as if Lord Seton would do such a thing tae one of her Majesty's ain'*. Perhaps the girl lived there, maybe they all lived in that one room, but Joe didn't really care. He was too drunk, too tired to care about anything, least of all where Lawrence was. If it wasn't for the kid with her he'd have made an effort to speak. She looked fit enough for a blow job, but there was little point if she came with excess baggage.

Other fools and jesters had joined them now, along with a multitude of dwarves. All were singing and dancing, swigging down the ale, wine and anything else on offer.

Although he would have preferred to be thought of as more aristocratic rather than find himself amongst servants, it didn't take him long to feel at home. Eagerly joining in with the drunken revelry, he ate and drank his fill as the fire lulled him into a false sense of security.

It was the early hours of the morning when Cockburn came to fetch him. Joe still wanted a shag, it would have ended the day nicely. But his guide seemed resolute on removing him from the room before he had a chance to charm out the talent. Perhaps Cockburn would be up for it he wondered, as she led him into another room on the ground floor of the Palace. The tiny cell housed a bed, a lantern and not much else except a portable toilet, it reminded him of the commode his grandmother used before she died. In the near distance he could still hear animal wails and growls but he'd almost become accustomed to them, wild animals prowling in the forest, nothing more.

The lantern burnt dimly, barely highlighting an old, worn tapestry that had failed to hide the huge crack in the stone wall. Joe was too drunk to notice much about his whereabouts as he took the nightgown and cap Cockburn handed to him.

'Are your pubes blonde too?' he asked drunkenly, struggling with the gown.

'I like blonde pubes…I like dark pubes, in fact, Cockburn, in fact I want a sha…'

Suddenly he stopped, Cockburn had gone.

Drifting off to sleep the moment his over indulged head hit the feather pillow, Joe began to dream of the Eiffel Tower. Lawrence was dancing on the top of the tower dressed in a kilt. In the dream Cockburn was pointing under the kilt shouting, *mark of the Jew ken*!' Then she dragged Joe off to a nightclub, where he was seduced by some big breasted female jesters who skilfully juggled his balls.

Chapter Three

'A Man's a Man for a' that:
For a' that, and a' that' - *Burns*

It was still dark when Joe awoke with a headache, he'd slept, no more than a couple of hours. In need of some Paracetamol he struggled from his bed, throwing his nightgown and cap to the floor before peeing into the commode.

The lantern had burnt out, and he'd no idea how to re-light it. Just the same as when he'd attended summer camp as a boy, a military kindergarten for those who would be officers and gentlemen.

Dawn was beginning to break as he cautiously opened the oak shutters attached to the small glass window, he peered out through the iron grill into the mist spitting with rain.

Horses were being led across the courtyard towards the distant stables, followed by some geese and dogs.

Heading out of his tiny room towards what looked like the main entrance, Joe found himself surrounded by swarms of servants, overseen by soldiers, bustling about. He was now able to distinguish the French servants from the natives by the colour of their clothes. Many of the Scots servants wore crimson and yellow livery, the French servants wore black.

'Er, excuse me...' he tentatively approached a boy carrying a brace of geese. But the boy ignored him. He needed a shave, perhaps he looked like a criminal.

'Do you know someone called Cockburn? I...' he called over to a couple of men walking with hounds, but they didn't appear to hear him. By now Joe had endured enough, he needed a fag and a cuppa.

It was just when he found himself before the raised portcullis that he heard a mighty roar. Glancing about nervously, he was unable to comprehend how wild animals would be allowed to come so close to the Palace. The noises seemed better suited to a zoo. Joe knew nothing about acoustics in Knightsbridge, least of all those below Arthur's Seat.

The drawbridge was defended by guards, standing between Joe and the world. Why they weren't with their Queen in Glasgow Joe had no idea and didn't much care. The soldiers ignored him, their gaze directed down at his hand as he headed across the drawbridge. Catching sight of the iron grill fixed to the window of the room where he'd spent the night, Joe tried to get his bearings. The room was squashed up alongside numerous store rooms beside the kitchen and servants quarters to the right of the drawbridge. To the left was the high walled enclosure opposite the ornate fish pond.

Joe hurried towards the high, ornate, iron gates on the opposite side of the overcrowded, misty courtyard; packed with horses, dogs, carriages and servants. In front of him as far as the eye could see were more gardens, trees, stables and fountains elaborately adorned with figurines. Some appeared to have been destroyed. There was one particular figurine that caught his eye in the middle of the courtyard. It was the centrepiece of a small fountain. The goddess Diana was positioned above the marble basin, into which jets of water flowed from the statue's breasts. Above the statue's head was a crown and a crescent moon, in her arms she held a bow and arrow. Beneath the basin were carvings of hunters, lions and thistles. Joe knew it was Diana from his art studies at university. He'd even done a few sketches of her for his portfolio, Diana the huntress.

Soldiers stood at the iron gates. The gates were embellished with lions, initials, emblems, coats of arms and an abundance of golden thistles which he'd noticed all over the Palace. The guards glanced down at his hand and allowed him to pass without comment. Joe gave a slight nod, and proceeded through the gates beyond a large gatehouse, stables and small stone houses, following the road that led up a steep hill.

Servants scurried about the cobbled street, some carrying buckets of water and brushes, others tools and boxes. Milkmaids yoked with urns hurried into the mansions. Coachmen were holding the reins of well groomed horses as they waited in front of the large, well tended lawns that harboured intricately designed flower beds. Some of the more lavishly ornate coaches were occupied, the well dressed passengers visible through the glass windows. On the other side of the street there was a group of older men wearing robes trimmed with fur even though it was August, protecting them from the nip in the early morning air as they hurried into a tavern.

The area was spotlessly clean, the only litter being rose stems that had fallen from the basket of one of the flower sellers. Yet, there lingered a vile smell.

Joe gave them a casual glance as he headed towards a high turreted wall and large stone gateway that blocked his entry into the city.

Like a demolished castle without sides or back, just a frontage, Joe gazed up at its turrets and flags that waved from the top of the gateway.

Guards were busy hassling some of the merchants for a toll fee. The men held the reins of their tired horses and oxen attached to covered wagons and open carts. Joe grew nervous having spied a troupe of soldiers galloping on horseback down towards the gateway with guns and swords in hand.

'Ye hae nae need tae pay, ma lord, unless ye are a merchant frae awa',' one of the guards shouted over. 'I've seen ye ring, that's guid enough.'

Bemused, he looked down and realised that the man referred to the gold ring embossed with the lion, square and compasses that Cockburn had given to him. He wondered if he needed to give the guard a strange handshake or something, but thought better of it and walked through the large archway. Beside him limped a man carrying a shovel full of dead rats, causing Joe to wonder if this was Hamelin after all, and he was the Pied Piper.

Nearby, merchants, jewellers and sword salesmen were setting up their wares from small booths situated around the turreted wall. The smell of cakes wafted past, momentarily stifling the other more noxious smells.

This appeared to be a wholly different world, a new scene in this surreal play. Beggars were sitting near piles of garbage, even those who weren't begging looked filthy, especially the children who were climbing ladders and carrying heavy loads on their backs.

Animals roamed everywhere, some with their owners on the way to market, others scavenging for food amongst the debris.

A drum beat loudly causing a hoard of people to hurry to and fro, obviously to work.

'What's the time?' Joe called out, but no one responded. A cannon exploded, followed by gun shots, Joe's heart jumped. The animals wailed in their beast-like vernacular, babies howled, horses bolted.

'Moray! Moray! He's come tae tak' the Castle!' a voice cried, as half a dozen soldiers carrying swords and guns ran down the road towards the Palace followed by others on horseback.

The commotion lasted but a few minutes, and then the populace resumed its place in the renaissance play. A few lice ridden heads poked out from various hideaways like rats in a sewer.

Had Browning and the rat catcher mistaken the location and Joe had been sent to pipe them away to where, *'honey bees had lost their stings and horses were born with eagles wings'*? He recalled the poem from his recent visit to see Katie; she'd informed him that she was reading it to Chloe. Joe thought it ridiculous, Chloe was far too young to understand.

'Just when you became assured that your lame foot would be speedily cured!' Joe called out to the man limping behind him with the shovel. 'The fucking music stopped. What a bummer!'

The surrounding houses appeared to be stone constructions with wooden frontages and projecting balconies over shopping booths. Not as grand as the houses he'd seen on the other side of the stone gateway, but attractive nonetheless. A few men were running around the area extinguishing lanterns.

'Hello, my lord!'

It was the girl he'd seen carrying the logs at the Palace. Looking cleaner, her head uncovered, golden red hair reflecting the dawn light. He could envisage how it would glow if the sun ever decided to shine that summer morning. The child wasn't with her, in its place a sack of washing.

'Hi, where's the kid?'

'You mean my son? Old Ma Ragg has him...only while I do Mistress Kemp's washing.'

'Where am I now, is this the main road?' Joe asked, disgruntled that he'd smoked his last cigarette.

'You've just left the Canongate, my Lord and the Netherbow Port, over there is Swift's Close, last close on the King's Hie Gait.' She pointed towards a narrow alley. 'Did you hear the cannons? They say that the Earl of Moray is here to take the Castle and Palace whilst the Queen is away,' she complained. 'And to think how she trusted her brother. Aye, he'd happily see her dead. Trusted him all her life, he even went to France with her when she was a wee bairn.' Joe thought her accent strange, spoken like a Scottish aristocrat, with occasional French overtones.

Beside them a man sat in the stocks whilst a group of young boys threw various lumps of garbage at him. One even threw a jug, cutting the man's head, but no one seemed to care.

'My name's Nan, sir,' she gave a curtsy.

'Joseph Hill. Do you have a second name?'

'Aye, Joseph Hill.' It was the first time he'd seen her laugh, she was pretty with good teeth, Katie had good teeth.

'So, what's your surname?' he demanded, trying to avoid the horse dung and other excreted delights which infiltrated the road. 'It stinks!'

'What, my name?'

'No, the smell, can't you smell it?' Joe snapped, irritated by her apparent stupidity.

The girl smiled, unable to appreciate his nasal problems, obviously used to far worse odours than the one now wafting along the street.

'Where's Princes Street?'

The girl looked puzzled, Joe pointed to his right.

'Oh, you mean the other side of the Nor Loch…most call it the Lang Dykes.'

'I wouldn't mind some long dykes.'

Nan didn't hear what he'd said. Too busy licking her fingers and running them through her hair, as if it might magically transform her from a pauper into a princess.

'If you're looking for sights to see then you'd best go up near St. Giles Kirk. Stop at the Mercat Cross, might be a beheading if you're lucky.'

Joe failed to respond.

'The Maiden's there now, better than the heiding sword.'

'I have no idea what you're talking about,' he sneered.

'The Maiden, it's a guillotine, it was built by the Earl of Morton… the only one in Scotland,' she boasted proudly. 'Perhaps my lord would prefer seeing naked lassies getting a whipping by the Bow near the West Port. But it's a wee bit early in the day for that.'

Joe was uncertain if she was being serious or sarcastic.

'Isn't that John Knox House?' He pointed to the large house beside him that had a timber gallery projecting out over the street, above an assortment of open fronted shops that traded from below.

'No, sir, it belongs to Master Mossman, the goldsmith and silversmith…jeweller to the Queen,' she boasted. 'The luckenbooths are used mainly by his own family, although he rents out some spaces to other traders. The upper floors are Master Mossman's private home. Sometimes he lets me and my son Rabbie warm ourselves by his fire or invites us to supper.'

Merchants were already opening the shutters of the luckenbooths ready to trade.

Pigs chained to small wooden cots in place of garden gnomes seemed to be a feature in the front of booths and houses alike. The swine content to lie down in anticipation of the sun's visitation some time during that August morning.

'Andrew Moubray rebuilt the house next door to Master Mossman,' she added. Joe felt sure that a drinking fountain had been outside Moubray House when he'd gone past on the coach with Lawrence, yet he noticed that the only well in sight was situated on the other side of the road.

The route leading from the Palace of Holyrood up to Edinburgh Castle was one long road.

'Down there is the Kow Gait.' Nan pointed to the side of the ridge edged with twisting lanes and labyrinths leading steeply down both sides into a valley of edifices and gardens.

'And this is the Royal Mile?' Joe tried to show off his little knowledge.

'No, this is the King's Hie Gait, but we call it Hog's Back Ridge. There's a wall around the town, some say we live on an island.'

'Why? There's no water.'

'Course there is...the Nor Loch silly!' she laughed, showing a pretty smile. He hadn't noticed she was so pretty that previous day. It didn't make sense why a girl of her obvious intelligence and looks would be working as a servant.

'The Black Friars used to live on the east, and the Grey Friars on the west. It's the most exclusive street in Edinburgh. Greyfriars has the big graveyard now, it was a Franciscan friary until a few years ago.'

Noticing Joe's sudden interest in a lane leading off Hog's Back Ridge where a market was being set up, she said, 'Marlin's Wynd'.

'It stinks here, what's that smell?'

'It's the Tron.'

But Joe was none the wiser.

'How interesting, it's got proper street pavement...how odd, yar?'

'Oh you mean the road, aye, it's the only paved street in the burgh.'

Horses, donkeys and oxen were being unloaded, whilst unloading their own dung onto the paving stones. Weigh beams and scales of various descriptions were being hoisted up as men piled heavy sacks against the sides of the weigh beams. His eyes suddenly focused on a man trapped in some stocks.

'Oh, don't worry about him. He's only having his ear lopped off for stealing a book. Have you seen the Queen's library?'

Joe shook his head.

'You must go sometime, she has the most wonderful books there...I can read.'

'Okay, Barbie, so you can read, I'm impressed.'

They headed up the hill beyond the guard house surrounded by horses and donkeys, towards a church. It seemed to be the busiest and noisiest part of the town. A steeple overshadowed the area, so much higher than the rest of the buildings. Joe had noticed it rising above the whole burgh from when he'd first stepped through the Netherbow Port.

'St. Giles Kirk...and that's the Mercat Cross,' Nan murmured, as they approached the 40 ft monument beside a black platform supporting a guillotine. A pillory and scaffold stood between the beheading apparatus and the Kirk. A large gathering of people were there, taking occasional refreshment from the nearby well. Joe's head throbbed from their high pitched shouting and banging of a drum.

'They make their official proclamations from here,' his companion explained.

Joe's eyes were concentrated on the Mercat Cross, the tall shaft rising from the centre of the octagonal monument. His focus drifted beyond the scaffold toward the guillotine.

'Don't be alarmed, sir, they rarely execute anyone with the Maiden. Well, no one who's poor. They just get their heids chopped with a sword or axe...or get a hanging.'

Joe failed to respond as the Edinburgh rains began to fall. A man was busy sweeping the street; he stopped to make way for a washerwoman who balanced a large basket on her head.

Joe glanced about, desperately trying to locate the City Chambers. If his memory served him correctly, on the bus tour he thought the Chambers were on the opposite side of the road to St. Giles Cathedral, as was Mary King's Close. As he scrutinised the area there was nothing except narrow alleys harbouring tumbledown tenements, and an influx of traders packed like tinned sardines. Servants, beggars and the upper classes all seemed to have congregated around the nearby market stalls.

'Come on hurry, sir, the rain is coming in heavy now, look at the mists.'

Nan's frail, young body wrapped in a black shawl looked almost ethereal as she led him down a narrow, cobbled lane not more than 8' wide. There was hardly any space between the doors of the tenements on either side. The path was steep and uneven. The further down they went the filthier the ground looked, and the stench grew stronger. Joe had little doubt that he walked in human excrement, but, as his companion seemed unperturbed he kept silent. Steep and smelly, the narrow alley was lined with wooden shutters displaying numerous spy holes.

Suddenly, the ground dropped steeply, causing him to trip. Managing to catch his balance he noticed water ahead.

'Nor Loch, sir.'

The stench rose in his nostrils, he could feel the vomit in his throat. From where he stood the loch looked like a huge sewer. Yet the inhabitants appeared unperturbed. The women mended their fishing nets whilst their children played as if it were a beach. Even sheep roamed the edge of the marshy loch. Over on the far side of the Nor Loch and marshes he could see moor land. A few cottages, animals and numerous fields led the way to the distant sea. How close it looked, he'd never thought of Edinburgh as a seaside town before.

Nan began to dance a jig, as if refreshed by the rain; her eyes were sparkling, teeth so white. Joe suddenly thought her quite beautiful.

'Nice teeth,' he mumbled, but Nan couldn't hear him through the pelting rain as she grabbed his arm and ran towards a doorway pushing him inside.

It was too dark to see clearly, the ceiling was low, the few lamps stinking from fish fat.

Nan opened one of the shutters slightly, just enough to let in the light but keep out the rain.

'What did you say to me out there?' she called, banging against one of the shutters.

'Oh, just that you have nice teeth.'

'The mother in law of the priest John Knox was going to take a few of them to keep for herself. But I said I'd report her to Lord Erskine if she did...and I never heard from her again after that.'

'Why on earth would a lord help you?' Joe demanded insensitively. But the girl didn't appear to take offence as she began to wring out Joe's hair for him.

'Now remember, sir, this street is called *'Towris Close'* if you need to find it again, but you have to be careful as there are other wynds that look identical to this.'

'Why would I need to find this again?' Joe gave her a sarcastic look, as he wrung out the sleeves of his jerkin.

'Hello, Nan, is that Mistress Kemp's washing?' a young girl interrupted.

Joe couldn't see the person clearly, due to the dim lighting of the doorway.

'Aye, Lizzie, I have it here.' Nan handed over the sack to the girl, who then made her way back out into the rain. The stench inside seemed almost as bad as that outside, like rotting meat.

'What's that smell?'

'What smell? Oh, you mean the flesher's smell. Master Gilchrist's shop's through there if you want to go and see. The blacksmith's forge is just along from the flesher.'

'Oh, don't be ridiculous! It's not even big enough in here to swing a cat let alone shoe a horse!'

Suddenly, there was banging on the wooden shutter causing Joe to catch his breath.

'Oh, it's only my friend, she watches out for me.'

'Bonjour, Nan. Just come to check you aren't being frightened by the pistol shots. The Queen's brother is still here.'

'Who's her brother Henry VIII?' Joe interrupted sarcastically.

'Earl Moray, monsieur, Lord James Stewart of course, you must have heard he's taken the city. And the Queen of Hearts is not due back today to defend it!' the girl shouted back through the open shutter. It was then Joe realised that the voice belonged to Nicola the fool, who stood outside in the pouring rain.

'Who's the Queen of Hearts, do you mean Princess Diana?' Joe called back to Nicola. Not that he was particularly interested, just irritated by the fool's intrusion, thinking her far too well connected to be *'a friend'* of anyone who lived in Towris Close. But Nicola failed to reply. Instead, she comically shook out her wet hair and went on her way.

'The Queen of Hearts?'

'He means our blessed Queen Marie. Surely you must know that's the term her loyal subjects use. She is Queen of their hearts.'

'Come on, lass I'll give ye some broth! And ye'll want yer bairn of course!' an old woman shouted out from the adjoining room.

Joe followed Nan through an unlit narrow passageway into the next room. In the centre of the room was a tiny fire, on which balanced a black, badly broken cauldron. Shadows danced on the stone walls between the unlit broken lanterns. The room reeked so badly that Joe felt nauseous.

An old woman sat by the dying embers, rocking a toddler in her arms. A large pig lay by her feet snoring.

Her breast heaved over the child's face, suffocating it like a pink, ballooned jelly. The infant was scrawny, its humanity seeping away with the sewerage that ran along the sides of the stone walls, wet with urination and damp humidity. Before Joe could ask why they were sitting inside this dismal pit by a fire when it was August, the old woman croaked, 'sit ye doon, laddie. The wee one's been nae trouble hae ye ma bonny wee man?'

'Ma Ragg, I've got some money to pay you,' Nan held out the money that she had just been given for the washing.

'Ye keep that for ye and Rabbie.'

'No, really, it's alright, I was given extra at the Palace, you take this and buy yourself a new shawl.'

'Ha, wha' would I need a new shawl for, lass? Nae as if I were going somewhere, nae like ye mixing wi' royalty ha ha! And who are ye, lad?' the toothless woman turned to Joe.

'Joe, Joe Hill,' he replied with a slight nod. 'Er...um, I wonder if you can help me?'

The old woman beckoned him nearer. Cautiously, he edged closer and knelt on one knee by the fire. He could smell her foul breath and body odour; he could see the urine stains on her legs beneath her skirt.

'You see, someone set me a riddle, but I don't know where to start.'

'Start efter ye've ta'en some broth, lad.' She looked at the dish of steaming soup which Nan handed him.

A young boy ran into the room and gave the old woman a small loaf of bread; Joe noticed the child only had one hand.

'Sir, I ken ye've seen his hand,' Ma Ragg muttered, as she rocked the toddler in her arms. 'It wa' a fiere of that Lord Maitland, he stole some cakes frae the baker's stall when he passed by.' Joe was now even more puzzled.

'They all ken it wa' a noble, but when he blamed the wee one they ha' tae punish him.' The woman dabbed her heavily bagged eyes with her apron.

'I'm sorry, but you've lost me. Have you got a cigarette by any chance?'

'Ye ken, lad, this lord wa' tae high a man tae be prosecuted, and of course nae man would dare, sae they had tae use this wee one.' She pointed to the child.

'You mean a sort of whipping boy?'

'They tak' wee laddie here tae the Mercat Cross and tied him up and chopped off his wee hand. The Kirk said it wasna sae bad, as it wa' his left hand.'

Joe glanced at the child's hand. Well, it was tough, sure, but he wasn't going to lose any sleep over it. In any case, this wasn't real, just a hypnotic hallucination, an ecstasy overload.

'Joe Hill,' Ma Ragg called to him across the fire, holding up a piece of paper. 'Here, Elijah sent this for ye.' Joe froze. Elijah had been the name haunting him since the previous day.

'Well tak' it, lad!' the old woman scolded, noticing the child slipping from her lap.

The fire was almost dead; the only light came from the open shutters in the other room where Joe now headed. Warily, he opened the scrunched up paper. There was nothing inside except for a small object encrusted with diamonds and shaped into the letter '*R*'.

Joe tentatively examined the wrapping paper, written inside were the words:

'The Exodus and the pomegranate don't go to hell, so find the bell.'

Joe returned to the room, having just experienced excreting into a half filled bucket of sewage. He was still deliberating as to whether the old girl had meant that the Biblical Elijah had sent the riddle and diamond studded letter 'R' direct from planet Pluto, or whether the local postman was called Elijah. Suddenly, there were loud explosions outside, followed by the sound of gun fire. Rabbie began to cry, along with other children in adjoining rooms. All around the burgh dogs were barking, horses neighing, pigs screeching and humans running about like beheaded cockerels. Desperate for a cigarette, Joe spent the next hour asleep on a straw bed, sodden from the rain which dripped down through a hole in the window shutter.

'Come on, sir, wake up, they've stopped firing now, we must go.' The voice belonged to Nan who was heading for the door with her son in her arms.

They didn't speak all the way back down the main street, Joe unclear whether its proper title was the King's Hie Gait or Hog's Back Ridge. The rain had stopped, the sky looked brighter, but the ground was soaked. Puddles slyly waiting to surprise him as they hurried, almost running down the hill.

Joe hadn't noticed the clothes of the populace before, not properly. Yet even he could tell the rich women from the poor who wore tartan shawls, and were mostly barefoot. The men with them wore a virtual uniform, blue cap, saffron shirt and looked unkempt.

Numerous beggars were crippled or blind, many with limbs absent, making do with an old stick as a prosthetic or the empathetic shoulder of a companion. Joe could smell them when he walked by, their body odour reeking, causing him to wonder if that was the time in the burgh's history when the appellation, *'Auld Reekie'* was initiated.

It was just as they reached Marlins Wynd when he caught sight of a man with long ginger hair and dressed in black from head to toe beating a gypsy girl with a birch rod.

'What's he doing?'

'That's Wolfart Bruce,' Nan replied, her cheeks had visibly paled. 'Some distant relation to the Queen through the sister of James II, who married a Count Wolfart.   Wolfart Bruce is one of the burgh's hangmen.'

'Suppose he's the one who chopped off the kid's hand.'

'He's a priest of the new reformed church, sometimes assists with the administration of our justice system.'

'What collecting fines and whipping women?' Joe snarled sarcastically. 'Looks more like Rasputin to me, how is it his hair's so long?'

'He's a good friend of Master Knox. I would not upset him if I were you,' the girl warned.

Ignoring the advice Joe headed across the road.   Just as he was about to speak, the sound of gunfire boomed out from the Castle and everyone ran for cover; including Wolfart Bruce, allowing his victim to escape.

Only beggars remained perched by the wet roadside, hands stretched out in hope, as the wealthy thundered past in horse and carriage. Clothes of the aristocracy were noticeably different from the local peasantry, adorned with ruffs about the neck and wrist. Men wore hats of varying shapes and sizes, many festooned with feathers; they all wore gloves, some carried a watch.

'Why is it so filthy, you'd think they'd clean it?' Joe grumbled, searching with his eyes in the debris for a dog end.

'You should see it on Saturdays, sir, it's piled high then, even the pigsties smell better than our streets.'

'They used a drum to call people to work this morning, is that every morning?'

'Aye…but not in Aberdeen, they use a whistle there.'

Joe noticed two nuns scurrying down a nearby lane, one hurried so fast that she tripped over her habit and fell to the floor. He was surprised that no one ran to her aid even though she appeared to bleed.

'Isn't anyone helping her?'

'St. Catherine's Convent was destroyed by the English in 1544, and they say that those Sisters who still live in the area are soon to be evicted. Partaking in Mass can mean death. The few nuns and priests who remain all live in peril, sir, many have already died.'

'So, where did she run to?'

'Kow Gait, my lord. It's down at the bottom of those closes. It's where our men of rank live, cattle are herded there all the way from the Grassmarket. There's even a fish market in the Kow Gait, my lord, and there are many clean wells.'

It was just as they reached Mossman's building, the house with the timber gallery overhanging the sales booths which the tour guide had referred to as, *'John Knox's house'*, when Nan stopped.

The area was almost empty, apart from the few merchants that were closing the wooden shutters of their booths, and the soldiers fully armed, who were attempting to secure the vicinity. All were adorned in their renaissance period costume, like a fancy dress party with strict 16th century dress code.

The building above the booths appeared to be about three storeys high with an attic perched on the top. A maid waved down from one of the glass windows on the first floor. In front of him workmen were loading and unloading the carts and donkeys, throwing numerous sacks and barrels down into a cellar below the booths. Women and children were amongst the workforce, heavy loads strapped to their backs. Their arms overloaded whilst balancing baskets on their shawl covered heads.

'Master Mossman was recently knighted by our Queen. He's a great man, I expect you know him.' Nan glanced at Joe, but he made no reply. 'Anyway, my lord, this is where I have to work today. I have to clean the top rooms, you are welcome to come in and wait, or look around the luckenbooths.'

'Why do you have to clean? I mean that well to do person yesterday knew you; and that fool woman, you know, the clown. I mean, if you have such good connections…'

'I accept no charity, sir, also I'm the only one who is trusted in Sir James Mossman's private rooms.'

'I'll see you in, but I can't stay. Cockburn will be expecting me… and I hardly know you,' Joe said brusquely. 'Are you certain John Knox doesn't live here?'

The girl didn't reply, just gave a slight nod of her pretty head, ignoring the merchants and washerwomen who stood arguing with the soldiers outside the tenement. Suddenly the firing recommenced. Joe hurriedly followed Nan up the flight of stairs leading from the front of the house above the luckenbooths and through a door towards the newel staircase, failing to help her carry the child up the numerous flights of steep, stone stairs. Round and round they climbed, Joe was getting tired, the child now crying in his mother's arms. He'd only gone in hoping for sex and to pry as to why these rooms were held to be so '*private*'.

'Whew!' Joe exhaled, when they reached an open door into the attic.

'How do you do this...' but he failed to complete the sentence, collapsing onto a bed. Nan sat on a stool rocking the grizzling child, whilst trying to tempt him with a wooden toy.

'Wonder why I thought it was John Knox's house? Well, he's got a good reputation where I come from.'

'Some people think what Master Knox is doing is good.'

'Where's the child's father?'

'They say Master Knox wants to use the treasure of the Catholic Church to rebuild God's kingdom,' Nan continued, as if she hadn't heard the question. 'And I'd be the first to admit that Edinburgh will have more schools and hospitals since our land was taken by the Reformers, well at least that's their intention. I must give that credit.'

'So what about the kid's fath...'

'I'll sing you a song if you like, it's what the minstrels sing for me. Rabbie likes the tune, it goes...the flowers in the garden stopped growing, flowing, the day the gardener used his hoe and plucked the bud, stopped the flow, ripped the stalk and wouldn't let go, and planted his unwanted seed into her garden. And the roses and thistles, are there for the plucking, due to the gardener's raking.'

She had a sweet voice Joe conceded, and the tune of the song was quite catchy.

The young boy started howling when explosions resounded through the Canongate. Joe waited for a while until everything had quieted apart from the child, then decided it was time to leave.

The guns had stopped firing. Some of the burgh's inhabitants now milled about the luckenbooths outside. All were disclosing their fears of the prospect of further attack, or worse, civil war erupting from inside the Flodden Wall.

Joe headed towards the Netherbow, which was more like a market than a security post. A gaggle of geese waddled behind a group of women dressed in rich fabrics and laces, accompanied by equally immaculate footmen. Merchants were at their stalls around the Netherbow Port, nearby soldiers were overseeing those who entered through the arched gate. A couple of horse and carts were being unloaded; the horses reacted whenever they were barked at by the stray dogs. Joe wondered if they were stunted wolves due to their ferocity and matted coats. Standing near the carts were two women wearing metal about their heads, perhaps it was some sort of surgical procedure he contemplated.

It was only when he heard a bird cry that he looked up and saw the three heads stuck on spikes above him. Blood was dripping from the severed edges, veins and sinews dribbling out, eyes popping from their sockets. Who would be judge at the end of the day as to which one was the good guy and who the bad? For, as Joe knew, history books were only written from the perspective of the victor, the survivor.

His eyes now focused on a bell in a small belfry, then moved slowly towards a plaque just above the entrance which read *'beyond here lieth Leith, Wolves and England'*.

'Oh, take no heed of the tétes, monsieur; they usually put them up at the Castle.' The voice belonged to the fool Nicola Ambruzzi.

'They call this place *'World's End'*, as the poor in the town can't afford to leave because of the toll. For them it's here that their world ends.' Joe couldn't stand her, stupid girl. But there was little he could do to rid himself from her whilst she played the fool.

'What's the matter with those women over there, why are they wearing that metal on their faces?' He referred to the women who had their heads incarcerated inside iron cages. There were spikes covering their mouths, and a chain that seemed to be attached to a bridle.

'Scold's bridle,' was her only response. Joe presumed that they must have scalded themselves badly. It wasn't hard to imagine, accidents must have occurred daily.

'Monsieur James Stewart will have to retreat, he's losing the battle,' the girl informed him; whilst she performed a few dance steps over broken boxes lying on the ground.

'Rosslyn chapel is the apple of your eye. Sir William St. Clair, Lord Justice General. A friend to the gypsies and Christ, but the price...'

'Just talk in English, well Scots or French but not this stupid gibberish, yar?'

'If I might say, monsieur, you don't speak like others yourself. All this la de da yar!'

'It's called Received Pronunciation if you must know, Nicola.'

'Well, monsieur, perhaps you can tell me then who received it, or where you received it from. You are a philosopher so I'm told. Did your philosophy show you a spiritual depth of what you received, or did your spiritual depth help you to receive your philosophy?'

'I once studied philosophy, I didn't ever say that I was...'

'Whatever, monsieur, but even you must know that there is a first cause, and all religions believe that first cause to be God. So are you saying you received your special tongue from God? Because if you are and Master Knox hears about it, he'll just have your tongue cut out from your head, just as we do to lampreys.'

Joe ignored her, desperately searching for a cigarette stub amongst the debris on the ground. The pigs that lay in front of the houses and lands began to snort.

'Monsieur, I am upset, tres upset today, a gypsy has been badly beaten. A man, a stranger broke her jaw and slashed her face.' Joe had no interest in gypsies, and shut his ears to her foreign gibberish. Then the girl started to sing, as if thinking that might penetrate his cold heart. Even Joe had to admit he quite liked the tune.

'James Tinkler was a tinker and owned land in the reign of William the Lion, hundreds of years ago. So...Faa, la, la, le, la, le, Faa.

Land was owned by tinkers at Annandale called Tynkler's land only a hundred years ago so...Faa, la, la, le, la, le, Faa.

King James the Fifth made a treaty in the winter of 1540, in favour of a new gypsy Rajah. Hurrah...Faa, de, la, de, la, de, Faa.

Son of the Lord and Earl of Little Egypt...King and Captain Johnne Faa.'

Beyond the Netherbow Port Joe suddenly became aware of the men and women with fancy collars and feathers. Their clothes intricately embroidered, even jewels were sewn into the cloth. Farthingale skirts and neat bodices with puffed out sleeves seemed to be all the rage at this end of town. Even the women's hair was entwined with jewels or ribbons for those who weren't wearing coifs, or hats which appeared to be taller than he'd seen elsewhere. The men too had varying fashions, their beards and facial hair in obvious contrast to those further up the hill. Here no one seemed too fazed by the recent gunfire, although news had arrived that Moray was defeated.

Coaches were pulling up carrying those of high rank, coachmen and servants danced in attendance. The houses here were more like mansions with their beautifully designed gardens. Some of the windows were covered by wooden facings pierced with round holes instead of glass, which were now being opened by servants.

'You can see their grand gardens from here, even their trees and flowers are better than anywhere else in Edinburgh. Oui, nearly as good as the Queen's gardens.'

'What were you saying before about gypsies? And in ordinary speech if you wouldn't mind, yar.'

'So, you want to know about Rosslyn, monsieur? I'm a gypsy you know. There are laws against gypsies here. Sir William St. Clair, although some now call him 'Sinclair' even though he sins less than Clair, less than most,' she rambled.

'Mais oui, he has done his best to protect us and even saved my uncle's life. He would have gone to the scaffold. And do you know, every May and June my lord invites us to his fields by Rosslyn Castle to perform our plays? And he even loaned my relations, distant relations of course, he loaned them two of his towers to live in during the festival. Robin Hood and Little John.'

'Oh, yar, so they're the plays you perform? I believe they were popular amongst the medieval and renaissance heathen.'

'No, monsieur, Robin Hood and Little John are the names of the towers at Rosslyn. Mais oui, you are correct when you say plays about them are popular.' Nicola suddenly performed the splits causing Joe to wonder if she were quite mad.

'Although they have been made illegal. The Scottish Parliament and Master Knox think all theatre immoral. Ah,' she gave a sigh. 'If only our Queen's mother hadn't been murdered, this wicked land would still be Catholic.'

'Why doesn't this St. Clair mind you performing at his castle then?'

'Parce que, monsieur, he also worships the green man. See over there,' Nicola pointed across the street. 'That's Plainstanes Close, the Queen's French tailor Jacques de Soulis lives there.'

'What do you mean the green man, like the jolly green giant, something to do with sweet corn? Corn dollies? Or do you mean he's seen some extra terrestrial?' But Nicola wasn't listening.

'Her Majesty has her silk directly imported from Italy, and wool from the Netherlands. She even sent to Paris for gloves. She prefers dog skin to deerskin, and detests the Scottish cloth, Scottish food, Scottish culture. In fact, monsieur she detests Scotland!' Nicola made a funny clown's face feigning tears. 'She has another French tailor Jean Decumpanze, but she prefers Jacques de Soulis. Her Majesty also brought her master of the wardrobe with her from France, Servais de Conde.'

'So, if you're a gypsy why aren't you Indian looking, I mean I thought gypsies originated from North India?' Joe sized her up and down, dark hair, swarthy complexion but not Asian. Pretty girl, good tits Joe conceded, although not very feminine in her jester outfit.

'Don't know why you didn't stay in France if you like it so much!' Joe snapped, exasperated by her non compliance. 'They probably threw you out due to your stupid ramblings.'

'At least I can ramble in many different languages, monsieur!'

'Yar, I've heard that gypsies speak Hindustani, well so my history teacher taught us. Before the Romany thing it was Hindustani, or maybe that wasn't the gypsies, I can't remember.' He coughed up some phlegm from his throat. 'Probably too stoned at the time to have listened. Perhaps you speak some bastard language like Romany. Did that originate somewhere like Romania? To be honest I didn't even know there were gypsies in Scotland in the 16th century.'

'In 1541 the council ordered gypsies to leave here with their families or else they'd be executed. But King James died the following year so the gypsies were reprieved,' she laughed. 'Scotland is now the only land where gypsies are safe. They say every gypsy is a voleur, but it's not true. And authentique gypsies aren't tinkers.'

Joe listened, not really interested, but persuaded to extend the conversation when the fool performed a handstand, giving him a more intimate view of her breasts.

'Some say we have royal blood, that we came from the great Pharaohs of Egypt. Others say we originated from one of the Clans of the Holy Land…but many priests of the new church call us the Devil's spawn. King James, he'd loved us once…traitor, coward! Oui, he betrayed us, just as he did his own enfant our Queen of Hearts.' Nicola gave a sigh, 'mais oui, monsieur, that's men for you.'

I thought you sang a song just now about King James liking a gypsy called Johnny Fart?'

'Faa, Johnne Faa. Although some call him *Faw*. Oui, the King loved our lord of petite Egypt, perhaps loved him too much.'

'What do you mean by that, too much? I mean are you saying that…'

But Nicola had moved away, now performing her conjuring tricks and riddles for the lords and ladies as they walked towards the Palace gates.

He felt safer once he got back into the Palace courtyard, depressed from that day's experiences. There was too much to take in and to cope with. He had his own problems, he didn't need other peoples. Anyway, this was supposed to be a holiday, what had he taken to give him such a bad trip?

Bell, book and candle Cockburn had said, but Joe hadn't a clue what she meant.

In the distance he heard the blast of a gun, then more guns and dogs barking. He hoped it wasn't a hunt, he liked deer with their big, Bambi like eyes, so innocent and trusting.

It was drizzling slightly as he roamed through the waterlogged pathways and shrubberies. The flowers were overwhelmed by raindrops, some had been destroyed, trampled on by the numerous dogs roaming around. Butterflies and bees were still winging around the colourful petals. There were no other humans in sight, not even the dog handlers. If there was anyone there they were hidden by the mist. Even Arthur's Seat was obscured by mist.

Again he heard the guns go off. Perhaps he should pray, Lawrence prayed, every Friday night he went to the synagogue. Lawrence didn't believe in Jesus of course, but he caused Joe even more uncertainty by constantly reminding him that Jesus said that he came, *'only for the lost sheep of the house of Israel'*, and that He'd referred to the gentiles as *'dogs'*.

Odd that the word *dog* spelt *god* backwards, he thought. Perhaps God lived in Barking and on the annual Saving of Souls day ate Winalot. Lawrence had thought it exceedingly funny that Joe's mother spent so much time in the Catholic Church praising a guy who didn't even come for her soul.

'Oh, where are you Lawrie, I need you!' he cried into the damp Scottish air, nothing like an August day.

Suddenly, Joe caught sight of an unusual tree planted inside a small greenhouse.

'Pomegranate,' a voice made him jump, it was Mingo, the valet de chambre.

'Can you see me, I mean, is this a dream?'

'More like a nightmare I should say,' Mingo laughed, 'like this garden, never find Morrison the gardener when you need him…just like God.'

'Just thinking about God funnily enough. They say He loved me enough to die for me. But did He die for the evil ones to live too?' How often he'd debated this issue during moral philosophy tutorials. He'd even provoked one of his tutor's, an ordained Anglican minister, by suggesting that if Jesus hadn't self sacrificed then Hitler wouldn't have had the chance of eternal life. What if Hitler had repented at the very last minute, would it mean that he'd spend eternity in the same paradise as the Jewish children he'd contrived to have murdered?

Joe barely looked at the valet de chambre, another swarthy skinned foreigner.

'I was speaking to Nicola before, do you know the Germans killed gypsies too?'

'Oh the Germans! Well, they kill everyone, don't take it so personally,' Mingo replied nonchalantly.

'Even so, it's odd don't you think, that the Germans have a thing about both gypsies and Jews? Do you think there's a connection?'

'God's invisible, sometimes you think He's not there when He is. He just hides, when he wants you to go to find Him. That's what it is with God, He needs to know you haven't forgotten Him, so it's all a game of hide and seek.'

Antony Flew, one of the philosopher's Joe had studied, came to mind. Flew had published a paper; '*Theology and Falsification*':

> '*Once upon a time two explorers came upon a clearing in the jungle. In the clearing were growing many flowers and many weeds. One explorer says, 'Some gardener must tend this plot.' The other disagrees, 'There is no gardener.' So they pitch their tents and set a watch. No gardener is ever seen. 'But perhaps he is an invisible gardener.' So they set up a barbed-wire fence. They electrify it. They patrol with bloodhounds. (For they remember how H. G. Well's The Invisible Man could be both smelt and touched though he could not be seen). But no shrieks ever suggest that some intruder has received a shock. No movements of the wire ever betray an invisible climber. The bloodhounds never give cry. Yet still the Believer is not convinced. 'But there is a gardener, invisible, intangible, insensible, to electric shocks, a gardener who has no scent and makes no sound, a gardener who comes secretly to look after the garden which he loves.' At last the Sceptic despairs, 'But what remains of your original assertion? Just how does what you call an invisible, intangible, eternally elusive gardener differ from an imaginary gardener or even from no gardener at all?'*

Perhaps the only real existence the individual had was their own mind. Performing on a stage of space and time that was merely an illusion; so that every day on waking, the only evidence of existence was the ability to think. Every morning jumping into a new dream, life being merely a sequence of consecutive hallucinations.

'That is a pomegranate tree, one of the King's favourite fruits,' Mingo explained, with slight arrogance in his foreign intonation. His eyes were staring at the tiny, bushy tree dressed with bright, glossy leaves and red flowers.

Joe suddenly recalled the riddle old Ma Ragg had handed to him, as Mingo opened the secured door of the greenhouse and allowed Joe to enter.

'The Exodus and the pomegranate, don't go to hell, so find the bell.'

Cautiously he glanced at the other shrubs on the ledges, his eyes unable to keep away from the tree. Tentatively he inspected the trunk, branches, and leaves, now staring at the small purple fruit.

About to walk away, one of the pomegranates suddenly caught his eye; it looked slightly different from the rest. Waiting until Mingo had left, Joe reached toward the fruit, only then noticing that it was damaged. Prodding it slightly, about to throw it away he suddenly noticed that the flesh had been hollowed out. Poking his fingers inside Joe immediately felt an obstacle, and then carefully removed the object from the fruit. In his wet, purple stained hands lay a small piece of parchment. Another Scriptural reference: Zechariah 14: 20.

Joe fumbled for the small Bible, wiping the juice from his red hands onto his clothes, and then flipped over the pages. Habakkuk, Zephaniah, Haggai, Zechariah…

There, in the Old Testament it read:

'When that day comes, the very bells on the horses will be inscribed with the words, Sacred to YHVH'

Chapter Four

'Their tricks an' craft have put me daft;
They've ta'en me in, and a' that;
But clear your decks, an' Here's the sex!
I like the jads for a' that!' **Burns**

He wasn't certain how long he'd been sober, if at all during that past week. Joe recalled the spasmodic gunfire during the nights. Apparently the Queen's half brother, James Stewart the Earl of Moray, had retreated toward Dumfries. John Knox the Minister of the Reformed Church had hurriedly left the burgh.

Most of his time he'd spent in the servants' quarters. Other times he'd wandered through Holyrood Park and up to Arthur's Seat with a flask of whatever he could lay his hands on. Constantly trying to forget those occasional roars and strange animal noises coming from the Palace grounds. He was fearful this whole experience was nothing more than full blown schizophrenia. Katie had often said that he belonged in a mental asylum. Better to be within a cocoon of insanity than crave a fag or sanity Joe decided philosophically, as he staggered along the Canongate pouring the content of his flask down his young, greedy throat.

Whether it was morning or afternoon Joe had no idea, passing by the lords, servants, holy men and shop keepers who stood outside Mossman's building. It looked as if a bank had been set up on a table outside, filled with numerous scales and coinage. An assortment of

81

bonnets were hanging above the open shutters, and several men were hurrying about with cloth and scissors as if they were tailors.

Perhaps Katie was inside the tenement cleaning, Joe thought to himself.

'No, her name is Nan,' he burped into the mane of a horse standing by the stables, wondering if he was imagining the pigs running wild alongside the hens.

Could do with a shag, he thought to himself, his eyes fixed on St. Giles steeple rising up above the town. Perhaps he should see if Nan was up in that attic room where she'd taken him once before. Well, perhaps, if he got desperate.

Passing the guard house Joe tottered up towards St. Giles Kirk. The Mercat Cross was almost opposite Towris Close. Perhaps Nan was at home he considered when he reached the Kirk.

Suddenly, he heard the sound of men booing, shouting and yelling, but the crowd was too dense for him to see.

The Kirk was the community centre of Edinburgh according to Cockburn. This was the centre of the universe for most of the burgh's inhabitants, where the main burgh market was held. The gothic Kirk stretched 206 feet from east to west, dominating every other building, and every person who lived or worked inside the Flodden wall. The lantern spire encrusted with delicate arches and fretted pinnacles soared above the finely fluted balustrade. Yet there was no statue of St. Giles outside. Beside the Kirk, running its full length were the luckenbooths and tollbooth positioned virtually in the centre of the street. This reduced a broad thoroughfare into a narrow lane that was inundated with traders and consumers bartering their way into hell.

His hazy, inebriated eyes focused on the buttresses of the Kirk, crammed with stallholders who couldn't afford the lock ups. They gave the impression that they themselves were embedded in the church walls like animated gargoyles. The gothic prison stood on the south side; he could hear men, women and children screaming for mercy from inside its walls. '*Mercy*', how often he'd heard that word. Did it bear any meaning in itself, or was it only used to incite an emotion? Perhaps the philosopher Wittgenstein wasn't so difficult to understand after all when he'd said that language only had meaning in the way it was used.

Ignoring the wails, he followed the path which now led him towards a narrow, crooked lane that wound between the high walls of the tollbooth and houses on the one side and the Cathedral buttresses on the other.

Behind the Kirk was the graveyard, and below that were the elaborate gardens belonging to the houses.

His head was still exploding from the cries that resonated from inside the prison walls as he staggered back towards the mob that had trebled in size around the Mercat Cross. He was too drunk to notice the woman in the pillory, least of all note the temporary absence of the '*Maiden*'. The screams had now transferred from inside the prison to the mob outside, louder and louder, until they became shrieks.

A child was being lifted up above the crowd that had gathered around the Mercat Cross. The child, who looked barely older than Chloe, was lifted up towards a makeshift scaffold. No, it wasn't real, Joe told himself. No, they couldn't do this to a child. Not to a real child, a living one, not outside a church.

Too drunk to even stand straight. Joe's ears hurt with the infant's screams, his ears and his head. Its wails echoed through the summer air, a child too young to even comprehend what was about to happen. The child was too small to reach the scaffold, the noose too big for its tiny neck. The hangman's face was covered in a black mask, his long ginger hair dangled over the child's naked body. Dressed in black clerical attire he resembled a demonic raven waiting to tear the flesh from his prey. As Joe drew close he could see that the executioner was none other than Wolfart Bruce.

'In the name of our Blessed Lord Jesus!' he heard the minister shout.

Falling over his feet Joe staggered back across the rough, cobbled road, sliding through the horse manure which was thick on the ground. Away, he had to get away from the screaming, the wailing. Get away from the inhumanity of man.

Suddenly he heard someone whistling his tune, *'Joe Hill'*. It was coming from one of the four closes where Nan lived, opposite the Mercat Cross. But, when he turned to look there was no one in sight.

'Where are you? Come on, show yourself!'

The tune, he could still hear it, louder now. There was a smell like flowers; it grew stronger as he strained to see who was whistling.

Then, a mist rose up before his eyes. The smell was sweet, like a meadow.

Joe stared into the mist. Slowly, out of thin air, the form of a woman materialised. Not as a solid mass, only a vague, hazy outline.

'Do ye ken Alexander Cant wa' murdered here? Craig's Close, finest hoose in the burgh they said. Called me a murderer, and ma daughter. Alison Rough's ma name,' she gave a curtsy.

'Ma husband wa' killed at Flodden, left wi' four young bairns. I became the greatest merchant in the burgh. Of course all the men were jealous of me. Dinnae like a woman doing sae well. Aye, I made a fortune. One son joined the priesthood, t'other son John married a wealthy widow and became one of Edinburgh's first Protestants. Although he shamed me by saying that his sister Isobel wa' a bastard, just tae disinherit her.'

Joe's feet seemed to be stuck to the ground, his legs caving in, like his brain, just like it had in Paris. Last job they'd said, but it hadn't helped. Although the task hadn't been executed by Joe, he'd been well away by then. Nevertheless, it was still too much to deal with.

'My other daughter Katherine married a wealthy merchant, Alexander Cant, in 1531,' the ghostly voice continued. He could still hear the tune whistling in the background, blocking out the noise of the screams at the execution.

'Aye, he complained that her dowry ha' nae been paid and he sued me, me his mother in law. Beat up ma bairn often, e'en beat me. Anyhow, one day ma daughter and I just killed him.' The apparition appeared to sob. 'He'd attacked me over ma heid, and whipped Katherine's belly, she wa' pregnant. Wanted tae kill his ain unborn bairn. I mean, wha' would any mother do?' Joe just stood transfixed, like the victim of a stroke.

'Aye, we were arrested, condemned tae death. I ken why, they dinnae want a woman tae be sae rich withoot a husband. It wa' a set up. It wa' planned. Accused of being either a murderer or witch, it dinnae matter. They'd kill me whatever crime they'd invent just tae get ma treasures.' She lifted her shawl to dry her eyes.

'But wi' Katherine being pregnant her execution wa' postponed. Efter the bairn wa' born she ran awa' tae England…married a Scots Protestant, Alexander Allan, then went tae Germany. It wa' only recently she left her property tae her wee lassie she left at hame.'

Too traumatised to speak, Joe wanted to run, head was spinning and whirling, but his legs wouldn't move. He could still hear the shrieks from the Mercat Cross, screams in the distance like he'd fallen into the bowels of hell, or opened Pandora's Box.

'Aye, I ken wha' ye want tae ask, did I bring up the wee one by mysel'? Nae, lad, I tried tae run, but was caught and they drowned me in the Nor Loch along wi' the eels and trout and lumps of neeps and shit.' She began to laugh hysterically.

Joe looked around him, but no one was nearby. No-one appeared to hear or see her; all absorbed at the goings on by the Mercat Cross.

'It wa' efter ma death King James V ordered that all ma wealth should be given tae the crown, but the council wanted it for themsel's, ha ha ha!'

The whistling was louder now, the tune '*Joe Hill*' droning on and on.

Another woman suddenly appeared beside Alison Rough. He could feel the blood slowly drain from him. If only he could get away, but where could he run?

'I am nae born yet…nae until 1616. But a widow like Alison, a wealthy merchant tae. Like Alison I will also be widowed wi' bairns. Name is Mary King.'

Mary King, that was the name of the close the tour guide had mentioned.

'We moved into Towris Close where Nan lives, called Alexander King's close by then.'

The women began to laugh, louder, louder until they were shrieking. Their mouths wide, tongues overpowering the broken teeth inside their screeching heads. Their shrieks keeping in time with the bloodcurdling screams coming from the Mercat Cross. An orchestra of horror, all dancing to a tune from hell.

Bang! Bang! Bang! He battered the door so loudly that voices shouted at him from various open shutters of Towris Close, until someone threw a bucket of sewage just missing his head.

'Gardez l'eau, ye English bastard!' a voice shouted.

'It isnae yet 10, ye hae nae call tae throw oot yer shit now!' An arm suddenly grabbed him and dragged him in through a door. It was then when he fainted.

His mother suddenly appeared, sitting by him whilst he slept, stroking his hair, singing to him.

I dreamed I saw Joe Hill last night, alive as you and me...in the sweet by and by...but Joe, you're ten years dead. I never died says he. We shall meet on that beautiful shore.' She was crying as she sang, he was about to ask her why, when suddenly Katie came into the room. She looked different.

'This is Chloe,' she introduced another young woman who stood beside her. But this was a grown woman, not a child. Her sapphire eyes, the same as Joe's eyes filled with tears.

'Why did you leave me, daddy? Didn't you love me, daddy?' she pointed to a scaffold where she was hanging by her neck, a man with ginger hair clapped and danced as she screamed for mercy. Her mother now lying on the ground beneath the scaffold. Her neck broken, eyes popping, tongue hanging out of her dry, cracked, bloody mouth. His head hurt. Thump, thump, a hammer against his brain, consciousness hammering into the unconscious.

'I dreamed I saw Joe Hill last night, alive as you and me,' his mother sang in the background.

'I'm sorry. I'm so sorry!'

'You had a bad dream.' The voice belonged to Nan, she was sponging his forehead, it felt so nice, so cool. Was this reality, or was this also a dream? How many dreams could fit in to a timeless zone, like a Russian Matryoshka doll? One fitting inside the other, never ending, one dream inside another inside another ad infinitum. Was this all there was to eternity, was there no end? No awakening?

He'd sobered up by now, although his head was still erupting as the August sunshine pierced through the wooden shutter.

Accepting the bread and jug of ale Nan offered, Joe was unable to converse, the dream, the alcohol had all been too much.

'Cockburn was looking for you.'

Joe gave a brief nod.

'Hello, Nan lass, want some mair bread, the Palace baker sent it up...sorry, didn't ken ye ha' guests.'

Joe glanced up to see one of the Palace servants standing before him. She was carrying a basket laden with loaves under one arm, the child Rabbie under the other.

'They just had a hanging, wee laddie, did ye see?'

'No. Suppose the hangman was Wolfart Bruce.'

'Who else tak's such joy in murdering bairns and lassies? Looks like the Devil, wi' his lang red hair and black clothes.'

'He'd best not lay hands on my wee Rabbie,' she kissed her child and took him from the baker's arms.

'Aye, the Devil himsel'. Ha' tae be if he's such a guid fiere of Master Knox.'

Joe took the opportunity to leave whilst they were talking. Perhaps he should find Cockburn, ask her what she wanted.

The stench from the nearby loch made him nauseous. He could see Nor Loch from where he stood outside Nan's door. The local women hanging their washing on their improvised lines, sheep huddled beside a rickety old shed watched over by a mangy dog. Pebbly, grassy banks framing a world unknown to those down at the Palace. A world of its own, hidden from view.

The banks on the other side of the marshy loch harboured random cottages and barns that were scattered arbitrarily across the fields and moor land leading to the sea of Leith. How clearly he could see the tall ships with their sails, even the larger fishing boats. They seemed just a step or two away, and he would be free to swim across to the Kingdom of Fife looming up just across the water. Leith had carried Queen Mary to Edinburgh. Leith or Lethe, the river that flowed through Hades. River of Oblivion. Waters for the dead to drink, to forget. A baptism of new life, with the obliteration of memory.

'I hae nae interest in the nuns, Master Robertoun, even though ye are the master of oor hie school,' a man in richly embroidered clothes and feathered hat retorted to his companion dressed in a plain black gown.

'Sae ye are mair interested in the Skinners and all their plots?'

'I dinnae ken wha' ye mean.'

'Och aye ye dae. I've seen ye whispering tae those such as George and Thomas Redpath...even Thomas Levyngstone.' The said Master Robertoun gave a knowing wink.

Perhaps Joe should find the chief bottle washer of the town to ask how to get out. He wouldn't need to find a key then, he could just walk. Maybe there was a president or a mayor or someone like that.

'Excuse me!' the men looked up at Joe, then seeing that he was well attired relaxed with a smile. 'I wonder if you could tell me if you have some sort of mayor.'

At first the men look bemused, and then suddenly the headmaster understood, 'oh, ye mean a provost! Aye, our provost is...oh Tam, do ye hae last year's lists wi' ye?'

'I'm only looking for the way...' Joe tried to interrupt, but the said Master Robertoun was having none of it.

'Aye, here it is, I wa' on ma way tae lodge it at the council chest afore we get the new one.' Tam handed over two important looking parchments neatly scribed in ink.

'Town councils and deacons of crafts and members 1565
Provost: Archibald Douglas of Kilspindie
Baillies: Alan Dickson, David Forester, William Paterson,
*   John Sim*
Dean of guild: Alexander Park
Treasurer: Robert Glen
Council: John Spens, David Somer, Robert Kerr, Alexander Guthrie,
Archibald Graham, Alexander Clark, William Fowler, James Lowrie,
James Nicol, Alexander Uddart Alexander Sauchie (tailor) Mungo
Hunter (smith)

Craft deacons: (tailors) John Purves, (skinners) Alan Purves, (goldsmiths) James Cockie, (hammermen) Mungo Hunter, (barbers) James Lindsay, (masons) John Paterson, (wrights) John Cunningham, (cordiners) William Hutcheson, (baxters) William Newton, (fleshers) John Blythman, (walkers) James Hunter, (websters) Robert Meid, (bonnetmakers) James Lawson.'

'Of course not everyone's on this list. We ken that the next provost is tae be Sir Symon Prestoun of Craigmillar,' Master Robertoun informed him. 'And Alex Guthrie is the clerk, if ye need a flesher tae recommend tae yer servants, I'd say Williame Thomsoun's yer man. Would ye agree, Tam?' he turned to his companion in the feathered hat.

'If he needs a lawyer which he will do if things carry on like this,' the said Tam replied, 'then gae and see Richard Strang, he's got me oot of a few scrapes in the past.'

'Perhaps the Queen would do well tae replace her secretary Davey Rizzio wi' Richard Strang as her advisor, could do a lot worse.'

'As if she'd listen tae anyone other than a priest.'

'Aye, ye are right, Tam, he's right, Master...?'

'Joe Hill.'

'Well, Joe Hill, ma friend Tam is right in wha' he says. It wa' only a few months back...April, or maybe it wa' March. Or wa' it May? Anyway, the priest Sir James Tarbot had eggs thrown at him in the Kow Gait, and her Majesty was said tae be very angry,' the headmaster, Master Robertoun expounded.

'I believe it took place at the one remaining Catholic institution, the old people's hame.'

'Ha, she got even mair angry when her brother James had her lover the poet executed, ha ha.'

'Tak' nae notice of Tam, Master Hill, he disnae ken wha' he rants on aboot, just ha' tae much barley and rye. Ah, and here's Cockburn!'

True enough Cockburn had appeared at last.

'Nae bletherin' in yer Latin taeday, Master Robertoun? I ken why, ye are feart of being accused of attending a Latin Mass!' She laughed good humouredly, before leading Joe away.

'Sae, Master Joseph, ye hae been introducing yersel' tae the local sights eh? Well, I'd best give ye ma ain guided tour afore ye get any nonsense told tae ye by others.' Cockburn then proceeded to lecture him on his surroundings as they headed down Hog's Back Ridge.

Cockburn stopped by some huge scales that dripped with blood and old bits of flesh and bone. The stench was unbearable.

'The Tron, the toon's weigh hoose. Trade's done here ken…ye must hae seen the tradesmen going doon the wynds. The private closes in the Canongate are where ye'll find the mansions.'

'It stinks! Everything stinks! Blood and guts everywhere, what's the point in having nice paving if it's bloodstained?' Even the smell of fish filled his nostrils. His eyes suddenly caught sight of a piece of flesh that appeared to move, the animal was still alive even though it had been partially dissected.

Joe hurriedly moved on.

'What I have noticed is that so many of the houses have wooden frontages,' he digressed. 'The houses are stone…well most of them, so I don't understand why the balconies project out over the street.'

'It isnae over the street, Joseph, it's over booths or stables. Ye'll see that there's nae glass windows, nae e'en doon by the Canongate, nae since James IV.'

'Of course there are…I've seen…'

'Bit of advice for ye, dinnae e'er wash in the Nor Loch, it's fu' of shit. E'en the pigs gae there tae wash.'

'Thanks, Cockburn, thanks a lot!' he swallowed hard, wondering what Cockburn meant about the glass windows. He'd seen numerous glass windows during the brief time he'd been there.

'See the notice above the Netherbow Port? *Beyond here lieth Leith, Wolves and England.*' Cockburn then proceeded to tell him all about the whys and wherefores of the Canongate. That it was a separate burgh to Edinburgh, and it had something to do with Augustinian canons, but Joe had little interest.

As they stood below the Netherbow Port, Cockburn explained how those who entered the walled city at the top of Hog's Back Ridge near the Castle would have to come via the West Port into the West Bow and Lawnmarket.

'The butter tron is at the top of the West Bow. There used tae be a meal market further doon Hog's Back Ridge, but it was shifted in 1541 because it was in sight of all persons. And that a multitude *'of vile, dishonest and miserable creatures convene tae the said market daily.'*

As they headed back up past Mossman's house, Joe was disgruntled to learn that the tour hadn't yet finished.

'Then there's the cloth market…14 markets in all. Then ye have between there and the poultry market, the luckenbooths. Ye ken the luckenbooths by St. Giles, get ye servant tae tak' ye there.'

'I don't have a servant, Cockburn,' Joe muttered, trying to forget what he'd witnessed when he'd approached the market at St. Giles earlier. The child would be dead by now. He should have saved him, but would they have hung him instead? What if the child had been Chloe, would he have swapped places?

Had the executed child ever known any happiness in its short life? Joe wondered, did happiness have any meaning?

'Aye ye are right, laddie. Dinnae fret, I'll get ye a servant tae care for ye as soon as I can,' Cockburn offered enthusiastically, interrupting his melancholy. 'Now as I wa' saying. Between the luckenbooths and St. Giles are the *Krames,* if ye need…'

'Krames?'

'Aye, stalls for the traders who cannae afford shops.'

'Oh, yar, you mean those awful stalls lodged so tight into the structure of the Cathedral wall.' Joe pondered as to whether that was where the word crammed originated from *Krames.* Unfortunately he'd never been a great scholar of linguistics at Oxford.

'One can't even squeeze in there to purchase anything, least of all see what one is purchasing…not that anyone would want to purchase anything from such an outlet naturally.'

'And then ye hae the poultry market by the top of St Monan's Wynd, and the fleshmarket that runs doon both sides of the King's Hie Gait from Niddry's Wynd tae Blackfriars Wynd.'

'Hog's Back Ridge, make your mind up what this street's called. Hie Gait, Low Gate, Watergate…Hog's arse!' Joe grumbled sarcastically.

'The Ironmarket is below St Mary's Wynd. And the Grassmarket runs below the Castle and joins on tae the end of the Kow Gait. One end of the Kow Gait heids in the direction of the Palace, the other the Grassmarket,' she expounded. 'Ye can see a guid hangin' in the Grassmarket. E'en a beheading if the Maiden's up and running, tae cater for the execution of one of oor elite,' she smiled.

Joe wasn't certain if she were joking, but somehow thought not.

'Ye can get tae the Kow Gait that way, if ye can avoid the cows… the fishmarket is doon there tae,' she pointed across the way. 'I suppose ye could look at it like, well, like the Kow Gait running parallel to the road we're on…but below it. I ken it's confusing, even I admit that.'

'You can say that again! All I need to know, Cockburn, is how the fuck I get out of here. I really don't need to have an in depth map of the area as I don't intend to stay.' Joe was now resorting to pleading. It made little impact, as the tall, beautiful Cockburn continued her dialogue.

'If ye dinnae ken already, the Mercat Cross is the trade centre of the toon, ye'll hear the royal proclamations from there. Prison's there tae, sometimes public executions. But as I said, ye'd need tae gae tae Grassmarket for most hangin's and choppin's.'

Joe felt sick, the memory of the child filled his whole being, how could it have happened?

'Ye ken the Mercat Cross is opposite the close where Nan li…'

'Can I get a get a can, you know coke? Even Irn Bru would do, I'm really thirsty, Cockburn.'

'Ye want ale, lad, then just say ale! Dinnae blether, ye have a mooth.' Cockburn led him to a nearby inn, inhabited by a better class of men who had left their horses outside the stables. She sat Joe on a bench near the horses whilst she ordered the refreshments. Sixteenth century Edinburgh seemed to be one vast world of smells he reflected, one stench overpowering another. Horse shit like icing on the cesspit called '*Edinburgh*'.

It was half an hour and two jugs of beer later when Cockburn was in full swing.

'Sae ye ken, Joseph, the Privy Council thinks themsel's above the Queen hersel', the council meets twice a week at the tollbooth. Ye ken they e'en put her name tae things she says nae tae.' She sighed disheartened. 'Controls trade, law, made up...well, it used tae be made up of clergy and barons.' Cockburn took another swig of beer, leaving Joe to wonder how a female could get away with being a hermaphrodite in 16th century Scotland. Katie had once said that she wondered if the perfect humans were hermaphrodites. Her reasoning was based on the theological assumption that if God were both male and female and Adam was made in His image, that meant that pre-fall, Adam was also a hermaphrodite which was why men had nipples.

'Aye, privy council thinks it's above the Queen now. E'en given itsel' the power to mark the Queen's name tae charters and papers she opposes. Wha's the point in a Queen if nae one tak's any notice of wha' she says? Dae ye fancy some pig, Joseph, the innkeeper ha' some roasting?'

Joe gave a nod, pig in shit was better than nothing, and he was hungry.

'When Arran was regent, Scotland was still a Catholic country and the clergy were a part of the council,' she continued, clicking her fingers for the landlord to come and serve them. 'But now that Marie is Queen, and the Protestants are in power, there are nae clergy in her Privy Council, just Protestant bastard aristocrats. Did I tell ye, Joseph, most of ma family, the Cockburns, they are Protestant and I'm asha...'

'Yes, Cockburn you've already told me.'

Joe had barely put his fifth jug of beer to his lips when Cockburn offered to carve the roasted pig that had been carried to their table by a large breasted female. This left Joe bemused why most women he'd seen had their heads covered, and yet had no hesitation in allowing their bosom to flop out for the eyes of the world.

'I see ye like yer titties, Joseph,' Cockburn teased, 'the Scots have guid titties... and the magistrates wear blindfolds.'

'I'm sorry, I don't understand what you're talking about.'

'Lassies aren't supposed to work in taverns…but the lairds prefer it this way, and sae nae one cares. Would ye care for a wee dram?' she offered to pour whilst he chewed into the burnt chunk of pig's head, with eye still intact.

'Scotch?' Joe looked at the colourless liquid, reminding him of vodka, wondering if it were blended or single malt.

Eagerly Joe put the pewter goblet to his lips and swigged back the contents.

'Fucking Jesus! Fucking Jesus… fucking Christ!'

His mouth on fire, blistering, exploding spluttering out the fluid.

'Nae used tae a dram, Joseph?' Cockburn laughed, as Joe coughed copiously. 'Aqua Vitae, fire water of the Scots.'

After the pain had subsided, Joe began to laugh.

'This is good…if one can survive the first swallow. God, it burns doesn't it? Think my whole throat's ripped bare.' Joe slowly took another sip, followed by another, his smile broadening with each mouthful. 'I was just wondering why that woman who brought the pig to our table is allowed to show…you know…what you call *titties*.'

'Oh, ye are sounding like Master Knox. He's forbidden lassies from taverns…but naebody tak's notice,' she smiled. 'If ye glance aboot, ye might e'en see women wearing chin cloots, although oor Queen ha' banned them. Ma Queen Marie loves dancing, gambling, and although she allows others tae worship as they will, she will ne'er be one in a chin cloot nor cease her dancing.'

For a short time there was silence. Their attention was focussed on the aristocrats who, assisted by their numerous servants, emerged from the inn and were mounting horses that resembled large donkeys.

It was early evening when Joe made his way back up towards Towris Close. Cockburn had departed having given him a further reminder about the bell, book and candle. The blacksmith, whose forge was in the close, was in the throes of hammering shoes onto two horses at the top of the narrow alley when Joe arrived. The smith had no intention of moving the animals, so Joe found himself trying to squeeze through the narrow gap between their tails and the wall, in order to access the tenement.

'Hello, Joe,' old Ma Ragg greeted him.

The pig lay on the floor sprawled out in the centre of the room by the unlit fire.

'The lassie should be on her way back now frae Master Mossman's. Ye can wait in her room, I'm going tae ma ain bed now.'

He'd fallen asleep by the time Nan returned. The child wasn't with her, but Joe had no interest as to where he was. The sky was still light. No need for the candle that flickered dimly, stinking of fish oil intermixed with the smell of urine that hung in the air. Neither smell was combated by the numerous posies and pomanders that were dispersed around the squalid, draughty room. Joe was baffled as to why her bed wasn't raised.

'I'm getting under the blanket,' Joe informed her, too frozen to care about manners.

'You have to leave, Master Hill, the curfew will soon be here.' The girl was about to move away from the bed when he grabbed her wrist.

'No, you get into the bed beside me!'

Nan pulled away.

'I was sent to court you, you know...the royal court instigated this. Look, I'm sorry, I didn't mean to scare you. It's just you're so beautiful. Here, have a drink.' Joe pushed a flask of wine into her hand. His penis was growing hard. Just needed a stroke or two, nothing more. Just a few strokes up and down.

'Orders you see, direct from the Palace. You know the sort of thing. They think you and I should...well, should marry. Ha ha.' Joe pushed the flask towards her lips. 'Seeing that I'm a titled man.'

'What's your title?'

'The Queen has strictly forbidden me to disclose it, you see, I'm undercover, my name's a secret. That's why you see me eating in the servants' kitchen.'

'But marriage, it has never been mentioned to...'

He pressed the flask against her lips.

'There's a good girl,' he smiled, lifting her hand to kiss it, looking directly into her eyes.

'Drink it all up, it will do you good. Have another, go on, it won't hurt. It's a special mixture to give you health.' The girl tried to refuse, but there was to be no arguing with Joe that day.

'There's a good girl,' he kissed both hands. 'So pretty, Nan, yar, so pretty. Perhaps I'll marry you. Cockburn told me that the Queen herself wishes for our union. That one day I should marry you. What do you have to say about that?'

'I hardly know you, sir. I am not in the habit...'

'Well, you will be in the habit if you don't find a husband,' he laughed. 'Now just relax, you're too tense, that's your trouble. Just lie down beside me, Nan, just for a moment. There, I can see you're sleepy. Just relax for a moment,' he smiled, forcing the flask to her mouth. 'No, don't pull away, I promise on my honour I won't touch you. I only want someone to talk to. You see, I have nightmares.'

His eyes began to water, and the fear in her own eyes had now turned to compassion.

'I get so frightened on my own, I just need someone to lie beside me until I fall asleep. I suppose you think I'm weak, but you'd be right, Nan. I'm not tough like other men, too sensitive my friends say.'

Like an obedient servant, Nan climbed nervously into the bed, almost as if she were scared to disobey. Is this what he wanted, sex under pressure? If he were honest he didn't care. His loins throbbed, he needed to relieve himself of the pent up semen, needed to penetrate her warm, moist haven of relief.

'Yar, Nan, I want to marry you, but we must find out if we're compatible, you know, down there.' His eyes motioned towards their lower parts.

'We need to know if we're to stay together forever. It's what her Majesty would wish for...I spoke to the priest already, he's in agreement.'

Nan looked at him surprised. He could see the confusion in her eyes, so many questions that she would be unable to ask, he was the man after all. He'd got over the first hurdle, now he had to work out how to make the high jump.

'I know this sounds odd, but the priest told me that I must test you, that's the latest fashion on the continent yar? A husband must test his bride before the wedding.' Joe looked about the room feigning he was speaking in confidence.

'Apparently instructions were instituted by the Holy Father himself.'

'What…what tests, sir?'

'I have no choice…I realise this is very upsetting for you. But Rome has said that if a good Catholic man wants a bride he must test her breasts before the wedding to see if she can feed his babies.'

'Ha, don't be silly, a wet nurse would do that,' she gave a suspicious smile.

'Yar…yar, you're right of course, dearest Nan. But I too need to see them before the wedding. Please, Nan, you will marry me won't you?'

Nan relaxed slightly.

'There, good girl. You are just so beautiful.'

Joe didn't bother to kiss her lips, merely battled to release the ties of her bodice; his face sank into the soft flesh of her small, firm breasts. His eager, hungry mouth sucking at the hard nipples.

He preferred bigger breasts, ones he could suffocate between. Nan's were too small, like Katie's. He'd shagged a fat girl once, he still recalled her belly flopping onto his stomach when she sat astride about to gobble him off. That wasn't too much fun, but it was those enormous breasts of hers that he'd never forget. The size of giant pumpkins, great, huge, overflowing breasts that he'd sucked on throughout that tempestuous night.

Removing his gloves, Joe placed his fingers high up between Nan's thighs. His greatest turn on now would be to shag two bisexual nymph-ettes side by side. But then, that was every male's fantasy. Yes, perhaps he could get Nan to bring a friend and have a session. Well, so long as the friend wasn't Katie. He'd never do that to Katie; after all, she was the mother of his child.

Attempting to replace his fingers with his penis, Nan suddenly tried to stop him. Joe grabbed her arm forcefully, refusing to let her move.

'Please, you must let me…please,' he implored, looking into her young, blue eyes.

'And will you stay with me after I have your bairn?' she whispered, he could see her tears.

'I won't get you pregnant, I've seen doctors about it. You see, Nan, I swear on my mother's life I can't have children,' he said soulfully. 'Do you really think that I'd have such a good standing at the Palace if I were a charlatan? Anyhow, Nan, my sweetest Nan, who God wishes to join to me as my other half. With or without children I'd marry you.'

Again Joe tried to insert his enlarged penis into her taut body, but this time she fought harder digging her nails into his neck.

'Ahh! Stop it! Look! I command you, do you understand? I am the man, your master, and you will obey!' His breath raced with his heart, his penis throbbing between his own thighs, hard, full grown, and needing to be placated. He pressed her head down. 'Go on, go on, I love you, Nan. Go on put it in your mouth, push, yeah just like that. It's good. Now a bit of tooth, harder, Nan, harder!'

Hadn't come yet, saving that, building up to it. Not too fast, pulling her head from out of his hairy thighs.

'You've got the best tits I've ever seen, just how I like them,' he lied, rolling over and pulling her down on top of him.

'Yar, I promise, Nan, I'll marry you. I've even had a vision of the Blessed Virgin, she told me that we would be together until…Well, until my second coming.'

He blew into her ear. His eager hands removed her cap from her head, releasing her long, red hair, like a golden waterfall cascading down upon her shoulders. It was dark, too dark to see her face. The candle was extinguished as Joe battled with her petticoat, bodice, stockings, and then….her nakedness.

'Let me feel you, Nan, let me get inside you, make you happy. You want to be happy don't you? I can make you happy, give you what you want. Here, can you feel it? No, don't stop me! I won't hurt you. There you go, just let it slip inside, just a bit.' He pushed his penis against her pubic hair, a fraudulent, uninvited guest, pushing against the door intending to steal what didn't belong to him.

'No, you won't get pregnant, trust me. There, let me in, just relax, good…mmm… good girl, relax.' Now he was slipping and sliding, slipping and sliding.

'Feels good doesn't it? Ooh, yes, feels so good inside. Oh, so good oooh! Bite me, go on, fucking bite me. Yar, yar, you're really doing well, good girl…mmm.'

His breathing was erratic, his mind unable to keep pace with his body. Joe loved a struggle, didn't like them too easy.

'You're a sexy fucking bitch. Touch my balls, Nan. Go on, touch them! Good girl, good girl, squeeze a bit harder, harder!' Joe was panting now, the sweat dripping from his face and chest.

'Yes, good, right there. A bit to the left, there, that's good, you're doing really well, Katie…sorry, Nan. Yar, yar, mmm, so good… harder! Faster! Squeeze, faster, faster, faster…I'm coming!'

He sneaked out of the room just before dawn that following morning, and hurried into the narrow close and back onto the road he'd come to know as *'Hog's Back Ridge'*.

Passing Mossman's home, he pushed his way through the horses and carts outside. Merchants and trades people were already opening the booths under the black sky. Astute looking goldsmiths sat in front of them balancing coins and scales on long tables.

Joe made his way towards the Netherbow Port as the town's cleaners swilled out the sewage from the closes and wynds. He thought he should have been happier; he'd got what he wanted. He'd released the tension in his loins, unwound, sewed all his oats both wild and those not so wild, and yet, somehow he still didn't feel content.

He should have spent his time more wisely, trying to sort out the riddles and clues in order to get home, rather than fuck a stranger. He'd wasted a day. But then, he'd spent half his life wasting days, at least nothing had changed in that respect he ruminated. What was a day in any event? If he'd really travelled back in time, then there could be no days forward, not in the whole scheme of things, only days past. Naturally, as a philosopher he had a get-out clause anyway. If Joe had transcended time, then he was outside time and in a timeless zone. Therefore, no time could be seen as wasted if it didn't exist.

The 17th century empiricist John Locke had argued that to understand time and eternity one needed to consider, *'what idea we have of duration...a man has no perception of the length of duration which passed whilst he slept.'* Was he asleep; was this all just a prolonged nightmare?

The traders hurriedly displayed their produce around the Netherbow. Woven cloth, wool and dead animals were draped about the walls and nearby stalls and luckenbooths

Just as he was about to show his ring to the guards, he suddenly heard the tinkling of bells nearby. It reminded him of the riddles, the clues about a bell.

These bells were attached to the hooves of a shire horse standing outside the stables beside a tavern where he'd sat that previous day with Cockburn. The horse was harnessed to a cart filled with fruit and cabbages. In the centre of the cart he noticed a large crate of pomegranates. Desperate to escape the town before he bumped into Nan again, Joe pulled out the riddles from his purse and held them up to a street lantern. Still unable to read them he took a lantern that hung above the stables and strained his eyes trying to focus on the words.

'Exodus 28: 34 – so find Elijah, but the clue might not be in order.'

'A golden bell and then a pomegranate.'

'The Exodus, and the pomegranate, don't go to hell, so find the bell.'

'When that day comes, the very bells on the horses will be inscribed with the words, Sacred to YHVH'

Also in his gloved hand he held the diamond studded letter **'R'**

Cautiously, Joe crept forward to take a closer look at the bells tied to the hooves of the shire horse. There was one bell, larger than the others; it had an emblem on the front. Joe held the lantern closer; letters were etched on it, Hebrew letters. It spelt YHVH.

Heart racing, Joe grabbed the silver bell. But, no matter how hard he struggled, he was still unable to detach it from the horse. Suddenly the bell split open. Inside was etched another emblem, a man's head. The man was bearded, but the face was green. Beneath the green man, engraved on the silver inlay, was the sign of a fish.

In the centre of the fish was a tiny object made of rubies. The object was the letter '*O*'.

Chapter Five

'O Cannigate, poor elritch hole,
What loss, what crosses does thou thole!'

Allan Ramsay

How noisy it was on that sweltering September morning. It seemed the whole of Edinburgh, not just the Palace was in a rumpus welcoming the Queen home. Musicians were in abundance, lutes, violas and trumpets blasting. Flags were frantically waving from every turret and pinnacle of the Palace.

Every morning since Joe's arrival, he'd awoken to the thunderous beating of the town drum calling the people to work. The worst mornings were those at the weekend. It wasn't so much the drum as the fact that there was no sewage cleansing, so excrement and garbage piled in stinking mounds on the road.

Still slightly hung over from the previous night, although uncertain where he'd spent it, Joe rubbed his bloodshot eyes, struggled out of his room and headed towards the drawbridge. Cockburn had told him that the drawbridge had been removed once, along with the moat, during Marie de Guise regency there. But, with all the trouble, her daughter Marie Stuart had the drawbridge reinstalled, along with wooden shutters and iron grills for the lower windows.

Joe made his way past the guards and proceeded into the gardens, intending to help himself to a further stick of what Cockburn had called *'Adam's snake'* from the greenhouse. It seemed to satisfy his craving for nicotine in place of a cigarette. Although Joe had always believed that tobacco hadn't reached Scotland so early on in history, he'd been certain that he'd seen a couple of women smoking pipes.

Just like his Bible really. English translations were available in England so he'd heard, but Cockburn had insisted on giving Joe a Latin one, '*the only true version*'. Unfortunately biblical studies were not high on Joe's list of priorities. Whilst the maids were sewing their mistresses' gowns, and the farmers were sowing new seeds, Joe was busy sowing his own free range oats. He'd never had such fun before, not even with the twins. Virgins and whores, maids and their mistresses, and as much free booze as he could swallow. Hypnosis or not, Joe had no desire to wake up, least of all find any clues to any riddles. After all, why would he wish to escape from paradise? Yes, 16th century Edinburgh was Joe's idea of heaven.

Resting on the side of the fish pond overlooking the drawbridge, Joe gazed at the ornate fountain spouting water from the dragon's mouth. He concentrated on the white and golden flowers surrounding the rockery. Somehow the golden flowers didn't blend with the other flora and greenery. They resembled narcissi, but they only thrived in dry beds. Narcissus was the mythological figure who supposedly fell in love with his own reflection.

Like Narcissus, Joe could also see his reflection in the pond water that was constantly disturbed by the fish. Of course the fish were as exotic as the pond, gold and silver with fanlike spines on their heads and backs.

This should have been a tranquil day for Joe, given over to relaxation and pleasures of the flesh. But that morning, the 19th September, was like no other, everyone was manic.

Although there was a measurable distance from where he sat on the edge of the pond to the kitchens, Joe could hear Nicolas Boindreid the master cook in turmoil. His voice reached the highest register as he screamed out into the courtyard for more children to come and turn the spits. With every shout Joe thought he heard growls coming from behind the high wooden enclosure to the left of the drawbridge running adjacent to the Palace wall.

Lord Seton, whom Joe recognised as being the man who had shown such care towards Nan the first time he'd seen her carrying the logs, had spent the last few minutes pacing up and down near the drawbridge constantly mumbling the name *'Maitland of Lethington.'*

Nearby, Mistress Carwood was frantically shouting at the butlers, fruiterers, porters, bakers and brewers; and was now in search of the ushers to come and stand in position to admit guests. Even the valets and page boys were all in a flutter. Some in canary yellow and crimson uniform, others wearing the black of the French servants. Coachmen and stable boys, blacksmiths and ladies' maids were hurrying towards the stables that had suddenly filled with horses, coaches, lackeys and footmen.

Heading towards the abbey, Joe vaguely recalled Cockburn mentioning something about it having once been an Augustinian monastery. He was uncertain if she'd meant the abbey or the whole Palace. Between the English army and the Reformers much of the original structure had been destroyed and the abbey rebuilt. He'd only ever seen it from outside, not being someone over enthused by worship.

The abbey that Joe now saw was about 250 feet long, the main oak doorway exquisitely carved. He entered tentatively as the workmen were still in the process of repairing the roof. Uncertain what to do if a priest nabbed him and forced him onto his knees in repentance mode, but upon opening the door he discovered the aisles were empty. The church was brightly coloured with flags and regalia, tapestries and stained glass windows. Even the paved floor was patterned in yellow, green and brown glazed tiles. Above the rood screen hung the holy rood with Jesus on the cross. There were four doorways into the nave, two in the south wall connected to the church and cloister, one in the north wall leading to the cemetery, and an exquisitely embossed main door.

On the east side of the abbey stood the choir stalls guarded by numerous statues, the sunlight danced eerily across them into the shadows.

Yet no matter where he looked amongst the icons, carvings, tapestries, he just couldn't find God.

The trees had been picked almost bare as he entered the southern gardens. Autumn leaves were now falling thickly, carpeting the ground, swept up by the elderly head gardener John Morrison. Even the ornamental fountains and ponds had the odd leaf floating in their waters.

Joe found himself another bench beside a dovecote. Doves had been roasted outside St. Giles Kirk on the first of that month. All the cripples of the universe seemed to have congregated there due to it being the Catholic Feast of St. Giles. That was until soldiers and the Protestant clergy had forced them to leave on penalty of death. Many of the cripples received a beating as they tried to drink from the fountain. Even a local blacksmith had been whipped for trying to protect them. Joe had heard later that several cripples had died as they'd crawled away from the church. Perhaps they should have realized sooner that a God of cripples could not exist by definition, a contradiction in terms.

'Where is she?' A tall, exceptionally handsome youth aged about twenty, stormed past the bench where Joe sat chewing his twig. He was followed by an entourage of men wearing doublets and white ruffs about their necks. The youth wore hose on his exceptionally long skinny legs, with a watch about his neck. He carried gloves in one hand and a sword in the other.

'My bloody wife! Where is she?'

'Now calm yourself, my lord, I'm sure that she's not far away. You know how she loves surprising you with her sewing, that's no doubt what she's doing now just to please you, my lord.' The small, swarthy skinned Rizzio appealed to the youth who was thrusting his sword at the floor on each side of him.

'I am not your damned Lord, I am King! And why are you Scots not fighting with more zeal?' he turned on a man in military dress.

'Your Majesty, we are fighting with the greatest army I assure ye. We'll nae forget Battle of Pinkie.'

Joe was surprised to hear the man speak in Scots, for most of the aristocracy he'd heard so far had spoken in French. Although he had no idea to what he referred to as 'the battle of Pinkie'. Joe had been tempted to ask if had something to do with a tournament where they could only use their little fingers.

Upon hearing a coach enter the courtyard and trumpets sounding, the young man dismissed his entourage. The Italian, Davey Rizzio, followed the other servants towards the stables, leaving the young king and his Scots companion to walk alone towards the rose covered trellis.

Joe strained to hear their conversation, but the wind was softly whipping through the branches of the trees drowning out his voice. Although the strong breeze was refreshing, Joe wanted to hear what was said, and so wove his way through the giant oaks to eavesdrop.

It was there Joe noticed the man in military attire slyly hand over a tiny package. Glancing nervously about him, the arrogant youth then held the package to his nose and sniffed.

Joe had little doubt as to what he was sniffing.

'It's that damnable Italian, arranging my marriage, even introduced the priest who performed the ceremony of betrothal. She wore black you know, white to a funeral, black to a bloody wedding!'

'Aye, but ye ken she had nae choice aboot that, sire, what would they hae said if she ha' nae worn her widows weeds? And she did change her clothes efter the ceremony. I saw ye both in the coach as ye threw the money tae the crowds, she looked sae bonny,' his companion tried to pacify him.

'Red hair, black hair, bloody wigs!' the young man was now sounding deranged from the substance he'd inhaled. 'Goes out at night dressed as a man! A man no less. Fucking whore!' He gave a loud fart, and then continued to whine.

'I don't see what she sees in Rizzio, and that's apart from his low birth!'

'Aye, but he is a guid musician,' the other man offered in his defence, 'and he's a guid fiere tae ye, a very guid fiere.'

'He's a blasted Papal agent nothing more! You know that, my wife knows that, even John damned Knox knows that!'

Another man suddenly approached them, it was Mingo. The young man appeared to calm down and the three of them made their way out from the trees.

'Ye ken that the servant who ha' just joined them is one of Lord Darnley's valets de chambre?' Cockburn whispered in Joe's ear causing him to jump.

'Yar, I know,' Joe snapped.

'Aye, and ye ken the prat shooting his mooth off is Henry Stewart, Lord Henry Darnley, the husband tae her Majesty. Fancies himsel' as king. Rome hasnae accepted the marriage because the dispensation needed still hasnae arrived.'

'Why do they need a dispensation?'

'Because they are cousins.'

Marriage, Joe reflected, why did women want marriage? Even Katie had been too possessive. Joe was young, a red blooded male, *'Jack the Lad'*, Lawrence's mother had called him, too young to settle down. Anyway, what did he know about raising kids? Women were better at these things than men. Women knew about feeding, winding and teething, it was all so natural to them.

'He wa' a Catholic priest, ye ken.'

'Who was?'

'Knox, he wa' a Catholic priest. Could'na even stay loyal tae that vow, and married a young lass. She deid, and now he has another, Lord Ochiltree's wee lassie Margaret Stewart. Just 17 she wa', Palm Sunday 1564 the wedding. He'd been tried for high treason only a few months before. Anyhow, everyone kens he only married her because she's a distant relation tae her Majesty. Ye can imagine how that went doon in the Palace. But then she cannae trust e'en her ain kin.'

'What do you mean?' Joe asked, scratching at his codpiece, wondering if he'd caught the pox.

'The Earl of Moray, her brother, Lord James Stewart pretends tae care, went wi' her tae France, ken her since she wa' wee. Yet would happily see her deid and tak' the crown for himsel'. Anyhow, Joseph, I dinnae have time for bletherin.' I promised ye I'd find ye a servant, I'll come back for ye soon.'

'Down came a blackbird and all that,' Joe muttered, his attention now taken by a maid as she carried a basket of laundry. She reminded him of the blonde on the tour bus.

'So are you getting your nose pecked off...or waiting to peck my nose off?'

'Pardon, monsieur?'

'Want some help?' Joe motioned towards the basket. 'There seems to be more of you frogs here than there are Scots. Why didn't the Queen stay in France if she only likes the French. Bit foolish if you ask me, to come all the way here if she doesn't associate with her Scottish subjects.' Joe took the basket from her.

'What's that noise?' he jumped at the loud roar. Often, whilst on top of Arthur's Seat, he'd seen foxes, deer, hares, even heard the occasional howl from a wolf, but these noises in the gardens were different. Of course, he'd put it down to his being drunk. He'd even considered that this virtual reality fantasy had played 20th century animal recordings from speakers hidden in the sculptured bushes.

'Is it a wild boar? No, don't tell me let me guess. Is it a wolf guarding the Palace?' Joe teased. The young maid shook her head. 'Well, then it's…a hyena yar? Chimps? No, no, I know! It's the noise of parrots imitating wild animals?'

'It's a lion, my lord.'

'Don't be ridiculous, as if they would have lions in Scotland,' Joe sneered.

'It was King James IV, he built a lion's house and brought a lion here. It landed at Leith, just like our Queen. Lives in the garden, monsieur.'

'You are joking?' Joe scorned, but was unable to hide his uncertainty as he placed the basket down.

'No, my lord, my mistress told me that the keeper of the first lion here was Sir James Sharp, he was a priest. That's why my mistress mentioned it; she said that all Catholics must have the heart of a lion.' The maid stooped over the basket and began folding the items.

'Its keeper now is Master Fentoun, he's the keeper of the Palace garden. Did you know the lion's name is Judah?'

'Oh, you're talking rubbish! Why then have I also heard other animal noises? You're just a damned fool!'

'No, monsieur, you are mistaken. I am not the fool, although it's kind of you to think I am, my name is Florymonde.'

'Flory what?' he laughed cruelly.

'Florymonde, monsieur, although my mother named me Madallaine, my mistress says that it isn't suitable for me. Oui, monsieur, there are many animals here, we have what is it you say in your English, a menagerie?'

'Well...take me to see this menagerie!' Joe demanded ungraciously.

'Pardon, monsieur, Master Fentoun is very protective of it. I am truly sorry, monsieur,' she smiled nervously. 'It can be very dangerous, monsieur, its teeth are so big it could kill a man. I've seen it tear a young lamb apart with its teeth. See this tooth?' Florymonde digressed, opening her mouth to reveal the large gap in her front teeth that immediately blemished her looks.

'My previous mistress lost her tooth, she made me have mine pulled out to put into her gap.'

'Why did you let her?'

'It's her right, monsieur. Anyhow, she'd have sent me to live with the lepers if I'd refused.'

'I thought there was a leper hospital at Carlton Hill, or a monastery. My friend Lawrence said there was. Perhaps it's not been built yet.'

'Liper Toun – that's where the lepers go. Not that I'm saying you're a leper, monsieur, no, not that I'm saying that,' the girl sighed, trying to sort through the washing.

'Should bring euthanasia here, that would end the problem,' Joe mumbled, as he chewed the twig *'Adam's snake'*, slyly wondering if his own Adam's snake would be up to rattling its poison out again.

'There was a Catholic hospital in the Kow Gait. You still might see an Augustinian canon or two around those parts. I'm told Master Knox will force them to leave on penalty of death, just like they did to the gypsies.'

'So, why should you think it would be of any interest to me? What, do you think that I'd pay for you to be looked after there if you get sick or something? I only asked about your gummy mouth, nothing more.' Momentarily the girl was taken aback; her pretty eyes began to fill with tears. Then suddenly, with a sniff she threw back her head.

'I only thought that you might be interested where James Calvert the priest was caught reading Mass.'

'So what?'

'He was dragged up Hog's Back Ridge and locked in the stocks and pelted with rotten eggs. I can also tell you about the Earl of Bothwell, monsieur, I've just seen him riding into the Palace.'

Joe decided he needed to sit down, the pretty French maid sat beside him, her face shining beneath the sunlight.

'They say that the Queen first saw him at a tournament at Greenside. They've probably torched it by now.'

'Who?'

'Who, monsieur? Who do you think? The Reformers of course, the traitors to God and our Queen.'

Joe sniggered, unable to take any of this too seriously, pushing the stick of his favourite fungus into his mouth.

'They say that it was Protestants who murdered Betsy, you know, Betsy the Scottish domestique. You may have seen her, monsieur, she served in the Queen's bedchamber.'

'Probably a lion ate her. So, tell me about Rizzio and this king person, Darcy or whoever.'

'Darnley, sir, he's called Darnley. Rizzio was lying with the King before he married the Queen,' Florymonde giggled.

'What do you mean *lying?* Lying like telling untruths?' he retorted, wondering whether he should try and bed the maid, or have a day of rest.

'Non, monsieur, don't be so naïve. They were playing arseholes, what else do you think?' the maid began to fold some of the items in the basket.

'I don't understand, why then have I heard that it was this Davey Rizzler who encouraged the Queen to marry Darnley, surely he'd want him for himself?' Joe retorted, having never understood the mind of homosexuals, least of all bisexuals.

'Speaking of Rizzlers...you don't have a spliff do you by any chance?'

The maid looked bemused.

'You know, a blow?' Joe pursed his lips and made a sucking noise.

'A blow. Oh, monsieur, I don't do that type of thing!' she retorted, feigning shock.

'As for my lord Darnley, he never belongs to anyone. He likes the young boys and valets though…and the whores. Oh, don't worry, the Queen knows. She so loved him you know, but soon learned, as all women do.'

Joe chewed hard on his stick.

'So she's interested in the Earl of Bothwell now, or so I've heard?'

'He also goes with boys,' the girl giggled, accidentally dropping a petticoat.

'Has he also slept with Rizzler?' Joe asked, picking up the item from the dusty earth. 'He could form a boy band, the Renaissance Rogers.'

'Je ne sais pas. Davey Rizzio may have slept with the Earl, but they've never been caught if they have.'

'So, don't these men also have mistresses, any juicy gossip about mistresses?'

'I can tell you the secret, monsieur that the dead Queen Marie of Guise wrote to Lord St. Clair of Rosslyn. She swore to be a true mistress to him for all her life as thanks to him for showing her, *a great secret within Rosslyn.*'

'Who is Rosslyn, was this Marie the geese goosing her as well?'

'Your mistress needs you!' a voice like thunder called to the girl, it was Mistress Carwood. The girl jumped up, grabbed the basket and giving a quick curtsy hurriedly disappeared.

It was after she'd gone when he noticed that the maid had dropped something from her washing basket. Joe stooped down to retrieve the piece of white linen. It appeared to be embossed with what looked like an illustration of Moses in the bulrushes. What was of even greater interest to Joe was the fact that this wasn't any ordinary biblical picture. This infant was lying in a crib decorated with the insignia of a square and compasses, and bore the motto, '*Moses Man*'.

The September sunshine blazed down as Joe sat back down on the bench. He could smell the grass, shrubs and flowers that carpeted the gardens in all their glorious colours. The borders and rockeries flowed down the garden walls, dripping colours that dazzled the eye like a floral waterfall.

Bored and hungry, Joe wondered if he'd get the munchies after coming around from whatever illicit drug he'd taken to give him such a long trip. Joe rummaged through his purse to search for a sweet or piece of gum. Even a sugar coated comfit would suffice. The only item that pressed against his greedy fingers was the tiny book bound in crimson and gold with the royal crest in each corner signed by Nostradamus.

'Nostradamus prophesised and the true lineage isn't David's seed. Tamar was Queen of the hive and Deborah was the bee'.

Joe was still none the wiser. Flicking over the pages he noticed that some of the text was highlighted: *'Le tant d'argent de Diane & Mercure Les simulacres au lac seront trouvez.'* (*Diane's large amount of money and mercury, the imitation will be found in the lake*).

Tired, Joe closed his eyes. He could hear the occasional noises; horses trotting, dogs barking and men shouting. But, for the most part it was peaceful, as the smells of autumn filled the air. The warm soft wind played across his face, lulling him to sleep. Everything was tranquil, serene, until a voice called loudly in French to her companions just as they passed Joe's bench where he was snoozing.

The woman wore a green silk dress with slashed sleeves, intricately embroidered with tiny jet pearls and silver and gold thread. Her auburn hair was braided away from her pale face, partially covered by a heart shaped head dress. A white ruff and crucifix embraced her throat, one hung from the rosary attached about her waist.

Joe marvelled at her golden hair glowing beneath the September sunshine, a fire waiting to blaze.

The bodice of her dress revealed the most exquisite embroidery that Joe had ever seen, harbouring small emeralds and black pearls. How hot she must be Joe thought, observing the weight of her gown. She was quite beautiful. Tall, slim and elegant, just the type he could go for, nothing plebby, this was class. Something about her reminded him of Diana the Princess of Wales, but he wasn't quite sure what. Behind her was an entourage of jesters, musicians and a throng of dwarves, some whom he recognised from the servants kitchen.

A page lifted the hem of her gown to keep it from trailing in the dirt as a tiny dog ran out from beneath it. Another page raced about the gardens wiping all the benches, anticipating that she might wish to sit down. Joe noticed the small Italian, Davey Rizzio scurrying alongside her. His dark head was covered in a jewelled cap with a green feather sprouting from its centre. Green velvet clothes were perfectly tailored to his small frame. The clothes were richly embossed with gems that sparkled beneath the sunshine, as he jumped about with a golf club that he carried in his gloved hands.

'Davey my dear, the trouble with you is that you have a generous spirit and faithful heart. Those like my brother James are just jealous of you,' the woman laughed, her teeth white, unlike most of the other women he'd seen.

'I think it's more than a little jealousy, Marie, you are too naïve. Your brother Moray is working with your cousin Elizabeth against you, and he hates me only because I am loyal to you.'

'And there's still the gossip about you and the Earl of Bothwell, James Hepburn, Marie. He's here today you know?'

'James would never hurt me, Davey, you must know that. He's just a little too ambitious. But for a Protestant he doesn't strive towards the making of Catholic martyrs as do so many others here.'

'You seem to have forgotten that Bothwell planned to abduct you not so long ago, and if it wasn't for that madman Arran, God only knows where you would be now,' he sighed, shaking his small, capped head.

'Ah, I know who has upset you, Davey, it's Master Knox isn't it?' the young woman teased, dancing away from him behind an oak.

'I know he started all the rumours. John Knox, the priest who would be king ha ha!'

'Well if you won't be warned, Marie what is the point of my trying?' he rebuked. 'Look how he sneaked back from Geneva practising his blasphemies on Hog's Back Ridge, and distributing the Lord's Supper with a common cup and bread. Your own brother Moray is known to be his friend. Even officiated at your other brother's wedding. Yes, you're correct when you said he is the priest who would be king! Soon he'll have statues erected of himself all over your kingdom. Why else has he married your kin?' The small Italian began to walk away.

'Oh, Davey come back! I was only playing, please don't be angry. Haven't I given you everything? Even Maitland fears you have his job as Secretary of State. What more can I do to prove how much I value you?' she implored.

'Hog's Back Ridge is not a nice way to describe his love making to his young bride,' a dwarf suddenly chuckled in a high pitch. Suddenly everyone began to laugh, the atmosphere no longer strained.

'Perhaps we shouldn't call it by that name,' Marie Stuart smiled, drying the tears of laughter from her pretty eyes. 'Hog's Back Ridge I mean, that's just the local term, I suppose we should use its correct name, *The King's Hie Gait*.'

'But you are Queen, and until it's called the Queen's Hie Gait all your loyal servants shall refer to it as Hogs Back Ridge!' Rizzio declared, theatrically falling onto bended knee to kiss her hand.

'He's a witch. Knox I meant, not Rizzio.' Another dwarf intervened with a chuckle, his voice also high pitched, bearing an Italian lilt.

'Fifty he was when last year he married your cousin of 17.'

'You are too charitable, my Queen,' a jester, brightly attired like a harlequin intervened. 'You constantly pardon that Devil, whom the dwarf rightly names as a witch. A follower of the German Luther, creator of Protestantism in his own image. Luther who wanted to slaughter everyone who refused to do his bidding, blaspheming the name of Christ. Look how many holy people he put to the slaughter.'

'Ev'n murdered God's ain…the Jews. Aye, ye beware, yer Majesty. Ye'll pardon Knox once tae often, and then he'll call for yer ain heid withoot an ounce of Christian charity, for all his lang winded sermons aboot the love of Christ!' another dwarf ran up beside them. His Scots voice was comical, his little legs unable to keep up with the rest of the group.

'Knox spends more time preaching hate than love, so I can't for the life of me understand why he has so many devotees,' the jester added, whilst walking upside down on his hands.

'Money, greed, that's all. The barons lead and the people just do what they tell them.' Another jester now joined him upside down, their hands moving forward in unison.

'But you are the Queen, they should be doing what you tell them,' the dwarf with an Italian accent squeaked. To Joe's ears all the dwarves sounded as if they'd inhaled helium.gas.

'Perhaps if I were a male they would,' Marie Stuart responded with a sigh. 'But if I achieve anything as a female they'll brand me as a witch.'

'A witch only follows the Devil, and we all know of Knox's dabbling with the occult,' the dwarf replied.

'Conjures up demons, my Queen. Master John Knox has been seen flying at night over his own Kirk,' a jester puffed. His mouth was only a few inches from the ground whilst his feet juggled silver balls mid air.

'Aye, but I would bet that nae-one's seen him dance!' the Scot's dwarf gave a short, comical dance movement.

Once again they all burst into fits of laughter.

Suddenly, the Queen's beautiful eyes hit on Joe, who blushed at being caught prying.

'And who might you be?'

'I...I am a guest at the Palace,' Joe bowed, uncertain what to say, least of all how he was suddenly so proficient in French.

'Are you indeed, a very nosy one at that. And do you know who I am?' she demanded haughtily.

'Perhaps you are the Queen?'

'Ah, so then who do you spy for? My husband or my brother?' With that, she stormed off with Rizzio and her army of personal servants at her heels, resembling a circus ringmaster more than a monarch.

Joe had heard the name Knox when he'd been on the tour bus with Lawrence. The guide book had shown a bust of him in St. Giles Cathedral. He'd thought it odd at the time that there'd been no statue of Mary Queen of Scots, well, not one that he'd seen.

'Joseph!' the voice belonged to Cockburn. 'Ye hae tae come tae her Majesty's apartments efter she's dined, ye need tae meet yer servant.'

'Cool.'

'Nae, I would'na say sae so.   Ye'll burn yersel' sitting sae lang in the sun.'

'Yar, burn is correct, Cockburn, probably in hell,' Joe laughed.

'So are you rich, Cockburn? I mean are you some high ranking duchess or something yar?'

'I believe I may hae told ye afore, I am related tae the Cockburns of Ormiston.   I've put some clean clothes on yer bed, ye cannae possibly wear the tunic ye've got on. Hand it tae one of the maid's they'll get it washed for ye.' Before Joe had a chance to remonstrate, Cockburn was gone.

The courtyard was crowded with packs of hounds brought in from the nearby kennels, accompanied by hunters on horseback ready for the hunt.   Above them sat Arthur's Seat, the heather and gorse burning a purple and gold fire across the skyline.

Joe remembered sitting in similar surroundings, focusing on a blazing skyline once before.   It was whilst at Oxford, just before graduation during the milk round, when he'd been persuaded to meet with a Mr. Peacock, a civil servant.   They'd met in a National Trust park due to all the private offices on campus having been booked by other prospective employers searching for the cream of the acne crop. But Joe had no ambitions other than to play in a band.   He'd said as much to Mr. Peacock as they'd watched the sun go down behind the distant Oxford spires.

It was less than twenty minutes later when Cockburn came back to collect him, issuing long winded instructions on how to conduct himself in the presence of the Queen.

'Look, Cockburn, I appreciate all your efforts, but when am I getting out of here? Not that I'm unappreciative of this hands on 16th century experience, it's been quite mind blowing.   But now I think it's time to own up to whatever TV game it is. And if it's Lawrence who's put you all up to this, then I'll pay you doub...'

'Master Joseph, I really dinnae ken wha' ye are bletherin' aboot.'

'Oh what a lot of bollocks, I mean, you didn't even know me. If this was real, how would you have allowed me to stay at a royal

116

Palace without even checking out my credit cards or having a security check by MI5?'

'Who?'

'Yar, you're probably right, MI6. You can't fool me!'

'Ah, sharper than I thought. Sae ye've guessed who's going tae be ye servant? Aye, ye cannae be sae stupid as I thought.'

Guards seemed to be en masse that day. They were standing at the foot of the turnpike stairs, and had what seemed like a whole regiment of them at the top, no doubt due to the Queen's presence.

Upon reaching the top of the stairwell, Joe followed Cockburn into the Queen's banqueting hall where attendants, pages and maids were scuttling around.

The floor was thickly covered in rushes, the walls overwhelmed by tapestries and black velvet reminding Joe of a painting. His eyes focused on the men and women exquisitely attired in jewel encrusted gowns and doublets as they reclined in their chairs. The long wooden table was filled with bowls of fruit, nuts and an assortment of titbits surrounded by jugs of wine. Cockburn placed her finger on her lips to ensure silence, and then crept into the Queen's bedroom. Angell Marie the perfumer was fiddling about with a pomander by the four poster bed. Roars of laughter could be heard coming from the supper room, hidden behind large tapestries and a curtain. Cockburn motioned Joe to follow her to a small gap between the curtain and door of the supper room where they could glimpse the Queen at the head of the table.

Lord Seton was there, causing Joe a sudden pang of guilt knowing how he'd kept clear of Nan once he'd bedded her. Perhaps he'd approach the said Lord at some point and ask him directly what he'd meant about her relations. If any of Nan's claims were true, it wouldn't hurt to go and visit her again. It wouldn't be such a bad move if she were even vaguely related to the Queen. Might even help him get into the royal knickers.

Occasionally he'd seen Nan in the distance, once entering James Mossman's house, and when she came to work at the Palace. But he'd hidden from sight, and thankfully she'd never come to find him. 'Mademoiselle de Puiguillon is in there…And of course Margaret

Carwood, that's her Majesty's favourite woman of the bedchamber,' Cockburn whispered. 'Look at that fool Nicola, wha' is she wearing? She kens nae tae wear green if her Majesty's in green. Would ye just look, Joseph, a green dress trimmed with crimson and yellow braid. Of course that's her favourite.'

'Do you ever wear dresses, Cockburn?' Joe teased, but the said Cockburn failed to respond.

Through the small gap Joe spied on the young Marie Stuart, surrounded by an assortment of aristocratic guests, servants and jesters. Radiant, her golden red hair braided beneath a diamond studded tiara, her dog now perched on her lap. As he stared into the tiny room lavishly decorated in crimson and green, Joe couldn't understand how they all fitted in.

Rizzio was playing a guitar made from tortoiseshell and mother of pearl, accompanied by two other musicians. The Queen appeared to be in fits of laughter from the whisperings of one of her female jesters.

Nicolas Boindreid, the master cook, and Mingo hurried across the bedchamber towards the supper room, where they were greeted by Mistress Carwood. Joe vaguely heard parts of their discussion with the men sitting nearest the door, one of them being Lord Seton. It had something to do with the logistics for a forthcoming melee, a tournament the Queen had planned where the participants fought on foot. Then Mistress Carwood left the supper room immediately followed by the cook and valet.

'…And, so I told him, the last Mass in Edinburgh was said in St. Giles on March 31st 1560. Well, you were there weren't you? You remember it?' Joe heard the man sitting nearest the door inform Lord Seton.

'Oh, yes, I remember it well. Ha, but her Majesty didn't exactly endear herself to her Protestant subjects when she replaced the Reformer, Provost Kilspindie, with the Catholic laird of Craigmillar… ha ha ha!' Both men broke out into roars of laughter.

'Cannae keep everyone happy all the time. E'en the French court was nae happy that she wore white tae her wedding tae her first husband,' Cockburn whispered.

'Why?'

'Because it's considered the colour of mourning in France. Aye she loves tae wear white. Ye ken there wa' an eclipse of the sun on the day she arrived here. Some say that she's an angel fallen frae the skies. Aye, an angel, Queen of Hearts.'

'Are you going to encourage her Majesty to go out dressed as a man again tonight, Nicola?' a young man called over to the fool dressed in her green harlequin gown.

'Her Majesty likes to do it of her own volition, Monsieur Standen, you cannot blame me, I am but a fool.' Nicola began to strum one of the musical instruments.

'So you think her Majesty prefers a fool to a dwarf?'

'You are merely her page, wee or lang the Scots would say. And a page can only do as a page will, whereas a fool can do everything,' she jeered. 'The world envies the fool. Even the blessed St. Paul said in the holy book that any one of you who thinks he is wise by worldly standards must learn to be a fool in order to be really wise.'

'Fool, are you saying I wish I were a man?' the Queen interjected. 'For a man would never have my superior brain. Ah, but then as we know all too well, my subjects only seem to respect brawn.'

'But is Nicola correct my dearest sister, Marie?' one of the men laughed. 'We all know how you love to dress up as a man and go into the city at night. And I'm certain Master Knox would be the first to quote you the biblical text which forbids women wearing male attire.'

'Well, dearest brother, Robert, why should only men be allowed to live happy lives? Take my husband for instance. I don't even know where he is!'

'But, my most beautiful Queen, you love your horses and your dancing. You dance as well as any gypsy. Why should you care where my Lord Darnley is? As your brother Lord Robert reminds us, you love to dress up as a stable boy and escape at night,' the Italian Rizzio teased.

'Ah, but her Majesty thinks that Master Knox won't like her dancing. But who cares what a Catholic traitor has to say? You should have him beheaded and have done with him,' one of the pages interjected.

'Aye, Sebastian's right, my dear. I've told you before, you are too kind, too honourable. For if the tables were turned Knox would have no hesitation in parading your head on a spike around this Philistine jail,' Lord Seton warned, then banged his jug down hard onto the wooden table.

'He's just a penis poxing paedophile,' the said Sebastian exclaimed with a bow.

'I must say, dear Marie, I do like that expression of Sebastian's, I must remember it for future use,' Lord Seton laughed.

'So this fool Nicola…thinks she's a gypsy?' Joe whispered to Cockburn

'She is a gypsy, Joseph, oor beloved Queen loves the gypsies. E'en issued a writ frae France in favour of John Faa the Earl of wee Egypt. Nae, I lie, it said, *'upper Egypt'*.

'So does he get invited to these suppers with him being an *'Earl'*?' Joe asked cynically.

'Nae, he deid in 1553…but her Majesty is still guid tae all of his clan. E'en the year efter the Earl deid she pardoned a gypsy Captain Andro Faa for his murderin' Niniane Smaill.' Cockburn suddenly gave a sigh. 'Do ye ken that in England it's against the law tae be seen in the company of gypsies for a month or more? There are over 10,000 gypsies in England.'

She looked melancholy. Joe thought her extraordinary, as if not quite of this world.

'Blether in a language called *'Cant'*, sae I've been told. But Nicola tells me that some blether in Egyptian…or did she say it wa' Latin? I cannae be certain.'

'Can't speak Cant,' Joe mumbled sarcastically, his attention fixed on the characters in the small supper room. He was intrigued by the theatre, yet irritated that he'd not been invited to join them.

'Thieves, many of the gypsies,' Cockburn whispered. 'But guid dancers, danced for the old royal family in Holyrood, lang before oor ain Queen wa' born. The auld Queen e'en had gypsies as handmaids, ken.'

As the royal party headed out of the private chambers into the banqueting hall to partake of dessert, Lord Robert, the Queen's brother approached her.

'You seem out of humour, Marie, we must soon have another masque to cheer you. Come, Fool, entertain!' Nicola immediately stopped juggling grapes into her mouth and began to sing a comical song, but no one seemed to be listening.

'Lord Robert is the Queen's half brother, he wa' made an abbot when he wa' but a bairn,' Cockburn whispered to Joe.

'So it was obviously a prayerful decision, having noted his life long commitment to the faith and innate and mature spirituality,' Joe jibed.

'Yes, Marie, your moods are swinging again, is it your digestion playing you up?' a woman wearing a damask and velvet gown asked, as she followed the Queen towards a cluster of chairs.

'I'm well humoured, sister Jean, just so long as I have my loyal family and friends here with me. Loyalty is what really matters, perhaps even more than love.' The Queen gave an artificial laugh, and then turned to a young woman of similar age who had sat down beside her.

'Marie Seton, you have always been the loyal one.'

'The mistress of your wigs, methinks,' the page Standen laughed.

'Do you know, Master Standen,' the Queen turned to him as he fell to his knees and bowed. 'My dearest lady in waiting here refuses to marry in order to stay with her mistress. Yes, that is loyalty don't you think? And what man can ever appreciate her as much as her Queen does?'

The said Marie Seton responded with a blush, 'we will always be your four Maries.'

'Well, not if Lord Maitland has his way with your Marie Fleming,' Lord Robert lifted his goblet and gave a wink.

'In fact, we were the five Maries!' the Queen retorted.

'Yes, with you included five. The flower with her four loyal petals travelling all the way to France when you were what?...barely six years old,' Lady Jean, the Queen's half sister joined in.

'My four Maries. Been with me all these years. But Marie Seton, well, you are the rarest petal of them all.'

'Oh, your Majesty, I shall blush,' the young woman waved a fan across her face, and then started to fiddle with the Queen's hair.

'But loyalty is in your blood of course. Even your mother, maid of honour to my own mother. Yes, Marie, loyalty is in your blood.'

Marie, a devoted lap dog continued to rearrange her mistress's hair entrapped in the diamond tiara. She was plain, almost genderless if it weren't for her gown.

'Ah, but Marie Fleming is your chief maid by virtue of her royal blood. And what a wonderful wedding you gave to Marie Livingston only a few months back on Shrove Tuesday,' Lord Robert interjected. 'Which of course was only right with her father being your guardian.'

The fool, Nicola Ambruzzi suddenly whispered into the Queen's ear, causing her to burst into laughter.

'And you were the first female to play golf in Scotland,' the fool continued in a louder voice for all to hear.

'Shame my husband Lord Henry wasn't the golf ball, it may have proved even greater fun.'

'Perhaps your Majesty would like me to send my Lord Darnley two of your golf balls to sew into his codpiece. They can replace those that are missing by nature,' the Italian dwarf offered.

'My Lord Darnley was invited to supper tonight but declined; his loss Marie,' Rizzio piped up.

'No one can blame you, and remember you did nurse him from measles and that was before you were even married. April last, if my memory serves me well,' Lady Jean added.

'Yes, you are right, it was around that time my brother James signed an agreement with Ruthven, Morton, Glencairn and Chatelherault to stop my marriage.'

'Speaking of the Devil's own,' Lord Robert interrupted, 'I must remind you, dear sister, that our brother Moray was at Stirling four days ago. So you can't stay here for much longer as our most devoted brother and his cronies are intending to continue to war with you.'

'Her Majesty has returned for just a short interlude, Lord Robert. But he is right, Marie, you mustn't leave this unfinished business too long, your army awaits you in Stirling,' Lord Seton confirmed.

'And my Queen led her army without her husband; and I hear she wore a helmet on her head and carried a pistol!' the voice came from the top of the turnpike stairs.

'Ah, James, so you're here…but too late for food, we've just eaten. Why didn't you join us?' the Queen cried with delight at the stocky man sporting a short moustache and cropped hair.

'That's James Hepburn, the Earl of Bothwell,' Cockburn whispered into Joe's ear.

'George Buchanan describes him as looking like, *'an ape in purple'. Y*et, he appears tae get all the lasses.'

'And the men from what I've heard,' Joe mumbled cynically.

'Just returned frae exile. It won't please ma Lord Darnley,' Cockburn grumbled, pulling Joe behind a nearby screen in order to re-fill his goblet.

When Joe next looked at the Queen she was playing backgammon.

'I thought you were going to introduce me to her,' Joe complained, wondering how he'd get the said Marie Stuart into her four poster bed.

'Hae ye worked oot yer clues yet, Joseph, for ye only hae a limited time here. Soon the glass of sand will run oot, and then where will ye be?'

'I've solved a few clues if you must know, Cockburn, I do have an honours degree. In fact I found a bell, book and the letter '*O*', and I also found a letter '*R*' before that, see Ro. Is that the answer, '*Ro*' or '*Rho*'…like in the Greek alphabet?' But Cockburn failed to answer.

'Okay, so is it '*Or*' is that the word '*Or*'?'

'I'm off tae collect ye servant tae introduce ye.'

With that Cockburn left him to play his word games alone.

Joe anxiously watched, hoping that he was about to be introduced to the Queen, he'd never fucked royal fanny before. The problem was, once back home there'd be no one to boast to. He could just imagine saying to his fellow drinkers at the Sloane Square wine bar, *'guess who I shagged last night? Marie Queen of Scots'*. A good shag was like a pint and whiskey chaser, it didn't have quite the same bite without the morning after boast.

It was after the guests had vacated the room for a stroll in the gardens that Joe heard the animal noises louder than ever. He moved towards the window and looked down into the courtyard. To his horror, just below the Queen's apartments lay a narrow enclosure with high walls giving refuge to a fully grown lion.

So the French maid was right, the roars he'd heard for the past month belonged to a lion. Why anyone, least of all a Queen would want a lion in her Scottish Palace Joe had no idea; let alone how it survived the winters.

The large den extended beyond the north west tower, bordering the western gardens where the enclosure became wider. It was divided into three separate sections, the lion being in the largest compartment that contained a small, stone house. The exterior stone and timber wall of the den extended from the drawbridge and overlooked the main courtyard. In the western gardens that were private to the Queen, the lion was visible through the high, black, iron railings.

After a while Joe turned his gaze from the lion's enclosure to the western gardens that were private to the Queen. An aviary stood near the centre of the western gardens, but the only birds he could see were partridges and peacocks that roamed freely across the flower beds.

It was beyond the aviary that Joe noticed a fountain shaped in what appeared to be a man's head. It was too great a distance to see the emblems on the fountain, but he had little doubt it would contain at least one lion and a thistle.

Beyond the fountain was an open air theatre. Men were on the stage, but they were too far away for Joe to see exactly what they were doing. One carried a box towards the Palace. As he approached the north-west tower Joe noticed that the box was filled with puppets. Ravens were swooping down at the box, omens of death, so Lawrence had said. He'd never seen them there before, least of all associated them with Holyrood, only the Tower of London.

'So, I'm to be your servant? ha ha!' the mocking voice belonged to Nicola who had walked across to where Joe was hidden in the shadows behind a tapestry of a deer hunt.

'What do...no! Cockburn, there's no way I'm having...'

'Master Joseph, I would'na argue, be grateful.'

'I see you have your Bible,' Nicola said, glancing down at the miniature book in his gloved hand. 'I'll sing you a song, Englishman. Normally I choose to have no dealings with the English, but as you are a Catholic then I'll make an exception.'

Joe glared at Cockburn.

Nicola Ambruzzi began to strum a lute. The tune was quite catchy, reminding him of 'Greensleeves'. But then most tunes he'd heard since his arrival reminded him of 'Greensleeves'.

'Not house of David, it was Saul, whom God chose as their king.
Was God's judgement so wrong? Then David was ordained as King.
Deborah was a judge, a warrior too and a Nazarene.
Deborah fought and won a war, with courage like Esther who was a Queen.
Ruth was a Moabite cast out, from the chosen of God it said.
A sin to marry one so low, Naomi's sons their God let go.
Deborah was a judge, a warrior too and a Nazarene.
Deborah fought a war, with courage like Esther who was a Queen.
The book of Ruth was an after thought, put in to cover for David's crown.
Grandson, a half breed couldn't lead the race whom God embraced.
Deborah was a judge, a warrior too and a Nazarene.
Deborah fought a war, with courage like Esther who was a Queen.

'Am I supposed to clap?' Joe grunted cynically, noticing that Cockburn had gone. Then suddenly he thought that perhaps she'd be good for a shag. Not as good as the Queen herself, but there was still time for fanny royal.

'How's Nan?' The unexpected mention of the girl's name caused Joe to jump. He hadn't expected that, didn't think he'd have to face the woman again. Of course he'd forgotten that Nicola knew her, perhaps far better than he'd imagined.

'How should I know?' he retorted, annoyed, ashamed. 'Surely you've got better…or worse things to occupy you than bother me. I mean, if you're the Queen's jester then shouldn't you be annoying her?'

'A fool, not a jester. And anyway, monsieur, her Majesty does not have just one *'jester.'* There is Jacqueline. She is very good…but not as good as me!' She gave a little jig and clap, producing a bunch of roses out of nowhere, and then resumed her song.

'Jesus a Nazarene, house of Benjamin and Levi
Father's line not of worth, if He were the son of a virgin birth.
Deborah was a judge, a warrior too, the Queen of bees
Deborah led her army bold, and sat beneath her own palm tree.
Tamar and Jeremiah went to sail, across the seas with fishing nets
Came with treasure and the stone, and with all of heaven's secrets.
Deborah was a judge, a warrior too and a Nazarene.
Deborah fought a war, with courage like Esther who was a Queen
Tamar the line of Benjamin, and the line of Levi redeemed
David not the blood royal, the crown of Judah was meant for a Queen.
Deborah was a judge, ruled all the land without a man
The bee of all hives, honey filled well, the mighty mother of Israel.'

'Of course, monsieur, many mistake Jacqueline for me, or is it me for her? They incorrectly refer to both of us as *'La Jardinière'*. But I don't mind, that is the riddle for you, monsieur, as to which one of us has the right to be remembered as the true gardener?' she raised her painted eyebrows teasingly.

'For scripture speaks of a gardener in the gospel of St. John 20:15 if you recall…and many speak of Gethsemane as a garden. Sweet Lord Jesus took Simon to his garden, called him His *'rock'*. Don't you think it strange, monsieur, to use that appellation when rock is not the name of a person?' But Joe made no response, he had no interest in gardens, least of all in Jesus.

But the fool would not be silenced, she was still chattering whilst flipping her body upside down and dancing on her hands with legs in the air juggling lemons.

'I like gardening. And anyway, Jacqueline is very good, as a fool I mean. Ha, but not as good as me eh, Cockburn?' she gave a saucy laugh to Cockburn who had reappeared with a jug of whiskey.

'And of course there's Jane Colquhoun. I'd prefer that one of them should have to do this job training you. I definitely objected when Cockburn came to fetch me to serve an Englishman.'

'Ye'll behave yersel'. Joseph, have a guid drink.'

'Oh, here goes, fire water. I can still feel the blisters from when you last gave me this, Cockburn,' Joe laughed, eagerly drinking from the goblet embossed with the Queen's official crest.

'Ah! Ah! Ooh fu…mmm. Tastes good, mmm.'

'Monks used tae distil it in their monasteries. But now it's hard tae come by since the Protestants burned doon their brew hooses. Some say that St. Patrick wa' the first tae drink it here.' So it was the Christians who were the manufacturers of whiskey Joe laughed to himself, what a surprise. Methodists, Salvationists and so many others who refused alcohol as if it was the fuel of the Devil, yet they were branches of the same tree which had introduced the alcoholic to his addiction. Just like the white man taking whiskey to the Native Americans and causing their degeneration. Fire water, was that the cause of why they'd lost their land and civil liberties?

Joe refilled his goblet, this was indeed good stuff.

'Single malt?'

Cockburn made no reply as she filled Nicola's cup.

'Yar, it was a stupid question, this isn't malt at all. Hiawatha. Wasn't his wife called Fire Water?' but again Joe got no response.

Then he suddenly started to laugh, 'no, not Fire Water, Laughing Water. And no wonder, if she drank any of this, ha ha ha!' His two companions, upon seeing him doubled up in fits of laughter also joined in, the three of them heady from the drink and the heat of the day.

It was still only mid afternoon when they entered the gardens. The autumn sun shone brightly as Nicola Ambruzzi led Joe to the greenhouse where he could take more sticks to chew.

'Her Majesty was so pleased to see James Hepburn my Earl of Bothwell. Such a fine soldier. Did you see how she beamed when she set eyes on him?' Nicola offered Joe a stick which he grabbed and immediately pushed into his mouth.

'Why did the Earl of Bothwell turn up so late in the battle when it has apparently been going on for quite a while?' Joe spat out a piece of the twig onto the ground.

'Her Majesty led her army from l'Islebourg on the 26th of last month, you know?'

'L what?'

'L'Islebourg…it's what the French call Edinburgh because it's surrounded by lochs. Half the burgh's French. Well, it is since her Majesty came home. Brought half of the French court with her.'

'Yar, fine, but what about James Hepburn, the one you call Bothwell? Why did he come to her aid so late in the day?'

'Well Marie headed for Linlithgow, but her message to Bothwell asking for urgent aid didn't reach Paris until the 27th.'

Nicola handed him several more twigs then sauntered away from the greenhouse.

'Of course the Earl of Bothwell had to avoid the English who were trying to stop his crossing the channel. Well at least this battle has frightened off her brother Moray. Even John Knox has run from l'Islebourg. Pardon, monsieur, I mean Edinburgh. They say she lodged with Lord Ruthven at his castle before she came home. I don't trust him,' the young woman confided.

'Doesn't she feel odd in male company? You know, one female with so many men?'

'I admit Bothwell's brought with him hundreds of men and munitions. But my Queen holds a special place in her heart for him.'

'I thought she had him exiled,' Joe retorted sarcastically.

'Well, we mustn't speak of that anymore. My Queen is content now, and that is all that matters. And of course she has her four Maries to keep her company and her chief lady in waiting Mademoiselle de Pinguillon. That's not forgetting her half brother Robert and half sister Jean, the Countess of Argyll, whom you saw in her apartment.' Nicola Ambruzzi then proceeded to turn a cartwheel over one of the larger plants in the greenhouse.

'How many brothers and sisters does she have?' Joe asked, wondering if the whole city was related to the Queen in some way.

'No one knows, monsieur, her father, King James V, was a very sociable man.'

Just as the fool was about to turn another cartwheel she was interrupted by a group of men who waved to her as they headed towards the Palace.

'Those are her chaplains and physicians, the one wearing the big black hat is her surgeon,' she whispered, slightly breathless from her acrobatics, 'but he is not a barber.'

'Who's the man sitting by the fountain with the satchel?'

'Oh, that's Mr. Archibald Crawford, he distributes her charity to the poor.'

'Does he…does he give Nan any?' Joe tried to say it with nonchalance, but didn't quite manage it.

'Nan, why, sir, she would never accept charity. Although she has no real need to take any, she could claim her natural inheritance, but she won't. Stubborn like her father.'

'Where is her father?' Joe again tried to be nonchalant, but, for some reason, the mention of her name caused him severe discomfort.

'Took his own life. Although we are not supposed to know.' The girl pointed at two men nearby. 'See those men who've just gone up to Monsieur Crawford, that's Pierre Oudry and Pierre Martin, they repair the tapestries and bed hangings.'

'I've seen them before.'

'I doubt you've seen Jacques de Soulis before, Cockburn has instructed me to take you to see him to have some outfits made for you. He is her Majesty's own tailor.'

'A female having a tailor, so what I've heard is true, your Queen wishes to be a man? If she's finding it so hard as a woman then why doesn't she just let her brother Moray rule if that's what he wants? I mean, it's not right for women to rule. To be totally frank with you I think it's even weird for women to be fools or jesters or whatever you're supposed to be. When did you decide to take over such a male province?'

'Male province, monsieur? Male province! Imbecile!' she shrieked. 'Being a professional fool is the highest artistic talent in the world, and women have always been the masters of this art!'

'Oh yeah, such as?'

'Such as, monsieur, those like…well…'

'See, you have no names to offer. Women are never masters at anything. They are only good for being mistresses, and not very good at that!'

'Those like Artaude du Puy in 1373, she was the fool of the Queen of Charles I of France. And, monsieur, there was a very famous female dwarf of Philip the Good at Burgundy, Madame d'Or. And also at the wedding of Charles the Bold in 1468 there was another female dwarf Madame de Beaugrant.'

'So, doesn't mean they had talent just because they were freaks.'

'Well, what about Anne Boleyn, the concubine of King Henry V111?' she challenged smugly.

'Oh, Anne Boleyn, spare me! A freak if ever there was with her 6 fingers! Anyhow, she was Queen wasn't she, why do you call her a concubine?'

'The concubine!' Nicola repeated. 'She had a female fool, Lucretia the Tumbler. All great female fools of even greater female Queens receive rich rewards. We do other duties in the chambre, and our clothes are better than any of the burgesses in the Kow Gait. And I can fart as well as any man,' she bent over slightly to demonstrate, much to Joe's disgust.

130

'There, see...no smell! I've even been given Dutch gowns, striped purple satin, even my bodice is lined. I'm allowed crimson satin striped with gold, and I've another blue and damask chequered dress, and kirtles of silk and satin under my gowns,' she bragged, lifting her skirt. 'Even my petticoats are red and I have more than one cloak of yellow and green. Her Majesty has even given me a gown of fur from the white hare for formal occasions.'

A sudden wind blew in their direction, even in early autumn Scotland was rarely without an icy nip.

'Oh to think, monsieur, I could be in lovely hot Spain now, if only Catherine de Medici wasn't such a jealous mother in law.'

'What are you talking about, you idiot?' Joe snapped. The girl irritated him, too independent, unrestrained.

'Catherine de Medici was Queen Marie's first mother in law. Mother of Francis, the boy who died. Marie then set her sights on marrying the heir to the Spanish throne, Don Carlos. Catherine soon put a stop to that...jealousy!' Nicola spat on the ground.

'Jealousy is a very dangerous game. Oh, how I miss France! Even Brantome hates this country and its depressive culture.'

'Brantome, is he another fool?'

'Non, monsieur, he is a poet who came with her Majesty from France. He hates the music, hates it. But I don't discriminate against the music, I hate everything Scottish, not just the music.'

Joe was now feeling better since he'd chewed the stick, and followed the young fool from the gardens and headed towards the main gates of the Palace.

The aristocracy swarmed around the forecourt awaiting their litters and servants. Packs of dogs were also waiting with their handlers to join the hunt. Several dwarves were hanging onto the backs of the carriages doing acrobatics to amuse their audience.

The Canongate was also filled with litters, gentry and of course beautifully laid out gardens, many displaying the design of the fleur de lys. The gentry who inhabited the area were as decorous as their gardens. Joe knew all too well that the fashions and cloth worn by the populace deteriorated the further up Hog's Back Ridge one went. Cockburn had told him that there had been a law passed in 1457 forbidding the ordinary citizens to wear silk, scarlet cloth or furs.

Joe was now beginning to understand Lawrence's grievance against a church whose manual stated that it was a sin to own two coats, yet its hierarchy did as it pleased.

As for his own silk, scarlet and fur, Nicola grabbed his arm and headed up the Canongate and into the sewing rooms of Jacques de Soulis.

The Netherbow port was busy as usual. Merchants blocked the entrance with their produce. Soldiers standing with guns and swords were demanding the toll fee from non residents who wanted to trade. Joe rarely needed to show his ring to the guards, most recognised him by now. As always there was so much noise, Joe could barely think. There seemed to be more animals than people, but by now he was growing accustomed to the stench. His arms were laden with new clothes, shoes, hose, purse, hats, and daggers that he'd received from the obliging Jacques de Soulis.

'Did you know, monsieur, that the first Protestant minister of St. Cuthbert's was a tailor?'

'Well, Jesus did tell us to sew our seeds.'

'He was a tailor in the Canongate, Harlow.'

'Came from Essex then? Nicola, tell me, why have some of the closes got gates fixed to the ends?' He asked, puffing his way towards the port.

'It's only because they're locked at night, it's where the rich people live,' she gave a hop, skip and jump.

'Walk properly, Fool! But why are they locked, have you no knowledge of the area in which you live?'

'Well, if you must know, monsieur, I can quote the law verbatim. I have been told that it was the winter of 1554 when the burgh council issued a regulation for, '*eschewing of evil doings of various vagabonds and others which required traders and inhabitants of closes to ensure there be nightly from this day forth until the 23rd day of February next lanterns and street lamps set forth at 5 o'clock in the evening and remain until 9 o'clock.*" She momentarily paused for breath, then continued. 'The statute specified that each barber, candle maker, apothecary, taverner, baker and common cook should burn a lantern each evening in front of their booths or else a two shilling fine!'

'So. Even a monkey can learn to peel a banana.'

'I am not a monkey, sir, but I can get you one if you require. There, monsieur, you can see the statute for yourself', the fool pointed her finger towards a notice:

'that thair be nychtlie fra this day furth quhill the xxiiij day of Februar nixttocum, lanternis and bowettis sett furth at v houris at evin and remane quhill ix houris'.

It was just as they'd passed through the port when he noticed an old woman locked in the stocks.

To his dismay he saw that it was old Ma Ragg. Uncertain what to do Joe looked to Nicola. But she was already busy telling her riddles to the traders. How they roared, but Joe never found her jokes funny. Obviously 16th century humour was different to the comedians he'd grown used to on TV.

Poor Ma Ragg, her dirty, torn shawl and ragged skirt soaked in the gunge that had been thrown at her. Of course, there were no moral souls around to save her. As he stared at the pathetic figure on the ground, head and arms locked into the apparatus, he recalled Lawrence lecturing him that over 300 women were strangled and burned between 1479 and 1722. To Joe's mind there were no eternal truths, morals dictated only by the trends of the day, like fashionable clothes.

Joe suddenly felt slightly ashamed of how he'd argued with Lawrence that women deserved their lot. Lawrence had constantly tried to point out that women were treated as the blacks were in 20th century South Africa. Forbidden by law from progressing, to ensure that the white master class kept their wealth and pride. But, as Joe pointed out to his friend, for all Lawrence's altruistic objections, he still wouldn't have married a black girl. Also that he happily attended a synagogue where Rachel, his fiancée, was forced to sit separate from him, and forbidden to even touch the holy scrolls due to her gender.

A passing baron suddenly thrust his boot into the side of Ma Ragg. Joe had managed to avoid looking directly at her, avoiding her bloodshot, vacant eyes until now. Joe put the boxes of new clothes on the ground, preparing to hit her assailant when the old woman shook her head at him.

'Joseph,' Ma Ragg mouthed. Joe, unable to turn away gave her a reassuring nod, but she wanted him to draw near. Again he looked for Nicola, but she was now flirting with the young soldiers at the gate. Nervously, Joe moved closer to the stocks, struggling beneath his bundles of clothes. He noticed that her wrists were bleeding. Even from where he stood he could smell her foul breath, and the urine from where she'd wet herself.

'What was your crime?' Joe mumbled, embarrassed for both himself and the woman.

'I went to Mass…I ken it's a crime. But if I fear man mair than God, then why go tae any Kirk if God is less powerfu' than the sinners who beat me?'

Demented, Joe thought to himself, at least in the 20th century they'd have locked her up for her own good. Yes, he reflected, not too many martyrs and visionaries in Knightsbridge.

'Joseph,' she wheezed, 'ye must go tae see Nan, ye must. She needs ye, lad.'

Joe smiled and gave a nod, relieved that Nicola had suddenly grabbed his arm to lead him off from the Netherbow up the steep hill of Hog's Back Ridge. Of course Joe had no intention of seeing Nan again, nothing to see her for. He'd had his fill, she had nothing more to offer.

The streets were crawling with beggars, but Joe barely noticed them. Not even those who'd had parts of their bodies forcibly mutilated. How they stank, almost black with filth, eyes red. Children old before they'd even been weaned, hands stretching out, fingers raw, pleading to a world that didn't care, and never would.

'Church ordered most of these tortures,' the fool mumbled, noticing Joe turn to look at a child with only part of a foot and badly deformed, scarred legs.

'The Scots invented the bootkins, it ensures maximum agony, monsieur. They place a wooden frame around the legs and drive wood or iron through and crush the legs and feet. Sometimes the Reformers use iron frames and heat the boot.'

Joe searched his purse, removed a few coins and threw them in the child's direction avoiding any eye contact.

'Don't worry, monsieur, they don't kill too many these days due to there being no space to bury them. St. Giles Kirk is full so they're being buried in Greyfriars…but that's also getting full. They burn as many of the poor as they can, think no one knows what's going on. The barbers buy some of the dead to practice on, but we know, we're not stupid.'

'No, you're not stupid, you're just a fool!'

As they passed James Mossman's home Joe caught sight of the effigy of Moses pointing up towards the sun as if he were trying to say something. But for the life of him, Joe couldn't fathom out what.

'I'll send Nan some bread and cakes…where's the bakers? Does she need medicine for the kid?'

'Non, monsieur, she needs your help.'

'So let Nan get a husband. Suppose that's what she wants, someone to put a ring on her finger,' he tapped the ring finger of his left hand.

'Non, monsieur, you touch the wrong finger. You know full well that the wedding finger is on the right hand, that's where the vein flows directly to the heart.'

'Why does she need my help?' He snarled, he'd only shagged her that once, not given a life long commitment.

'Does she need a doctor? Maybe you don't understand what I'm saying…you know, a doctor,' he spoke more slowly, louder. 'Maybe here doctors are referred to as bailies or maybe they're the barbers? I'm never certain, Nicola,' he tried to change the subject. 'It's surgeons who are barbers aren't they?'

Nicola gave him a glare, 'you must go to see her!'

'Perhaps she wants food. Is it a bailie from whom one buys bread or is it a baker?' he snapped, infuriated by the hassle he was getting from Nan's numerous supporters. To think that if he got this much grief over Nan, what would have happened had he shagged the Queen herself, Joe wondered.

'Will it be very costly if she needs a doctor, or baillie? Oh, won't you come home Bill Bailey, won't you come home?' he began to sing flippantly.

'No, monsieur, she is not ill. Anyway you use the wrong word, it is baxter you mean. Baxter is the baker and bailie is the magistrate. You do talk strangely, monsieur. Although there are gypsies called *Bailie*.' Nicola poked out her tongue at him; a fly perched on the tip, then flew up and landed on her nose.

'There are the surgeons and barbers. According to Cockburn prices have soared in the last ten years,' she gave a fart.

'Why?' Joe gave a louder one in response.

'Why? Well, because...' and she gave a louder emission.

'Oh, you are disgusting!' he yelled, 'bloody disgusting. You fart arsed fool! You bag of hot air!' and they both fell into fits of laughter. This was good, Joe thought to himself, just like being back at school.

Swine were being herded from the Kow Gait, squealing from the beatings being administered.

'Easier for the cobblers to make shoes if the skin is soft,' Nicola explained. 'Getting them ready for the slaughter. They'll take them to the fleshmarket. There's not enough feed for the winter, the autumn is the last chance you'll get to have fresh meat. I expect it's the same where you come from.'

Joe suddenly noticed several important looking men running up behind the pigs.

'Who are they?'

'That's Monsieur Symon Prestoun the Provost. The Queen replaced the Protestant Provost Kilspindie with this man; he was the Catholic laird of Craigmillar'

Nicola was now walking on her hands much to Joe's embarrassment. Yet, being upside down didn't stop her tongue.

'The men with him are his bailies John Prestoun...he's the Dean of Guild. I'm not certain who the other man is, the one with red hair and the sword, think he might be John Western his treasurer. And the man carrying the satchel is Alex Guthrie.'

'Who's the man covered in blood?'

'The man herding the pigs is Monsieur Gilchrist, and the other man helping him is Williame Thomsoun, they're both fleshers, they butcher the beasts. Some say that Monsieur Thomsoun's grandmother was a witch.'

'Why?'

'Because one day when she was looking after the beasts in the highlands, they fell off a cliff into the sea, just like when our blessed Lord Jesus put the demons into the pigs.'

'So are you saying that my friend Lawrence is right for not eating pork?' he laughed. 'Lemmings do that don't they? You know, jump off cliffs. Are you a witch, Nicola?'

'I'm not a witch, monsieur so please don't suggest that. Ah, bonjour mon ami,' she called over to a man heading in the opposite direction. His face was bleeding slightly, his clothes torn.

'This is Gordon Thomsoun, Joseph. His brother in law is the man running with the donkey, he's a poet. Forgive me, I forget his name.'

'Martin,' the man panted. 'We've been fighting wi' the mingin' Reformers by the Tron, they're efter us...hae tae run!' The said Gordon Thomsoun then took off, racing down towards the Kow Gait.

'So, even he can't wait to get away from you...I know the feeling,' Joe tormented, wondering if he should shag Nicola to get him in practise for the big night in the four poster. Perhaps the Queen's ladies, the four Maries', watched over the bed. He had heard that servants slept in the same room as their master or mistress. Now that would be something to brag about. Joe smiled to himself, imagining telling Lawrence he'd bedded 5 gorgeous women all named Marie in the same bed.

'If you don't know, monsieur, over there, that's our Tron,' she pointed to the weigh-beam.

'I know. I can smell!' he purposely avoided looking across at the weigh-beam dripping with dead flesh.

'And our tollbooth, the jail...and where our council meet...'

'Yar, I know. And a toll is a turnpike and a port is a gate and a port is also where ships dock,' Joe mumbled disinterestedly. 'And why you call both the toll and your strange twisting stairs *turnpike* is beyond me.'

A troupe of soldiers on horses galloped by, indifferent to whether they knocked anyone over or not. Joe jumped out of the way, the disturbed debris on the ground hitting him in the face.

'Bloody fools!'

'Did you know that in 1086 the female fool Adelina owned 20 acres in Hampshire, it was the cousin of William the conqueror who gave it to her?'

'This gets more like a blasted history lesson…an eternal bloody lecture than much else.'

Nicola laughed, wiping Joe's face with a cloth she'd conjured from nowhere.

'One of the greatest acrobats ever was Matilda Makejoy,' she continued, unperturbed by Joe's protestations. 'And I, monsieur, I am a gypsy, so I dance…I read the stars…and I know the future. And although my Queen leaves the Palace soon, she will return safely by the Feast of St. Luke.'

By now they'd reached the Mercat Cross. A black man, semi naked was locked into the pillory, positioned between the cross and the Kirk. The victim made no protest as his head bled from the constant assaults from passers-by.

'How is it that there's a nigger? Thought Africans or West Indians only came over in the 60's to drive the buses,' Joe laughed disparagingly. 'Oops, sorry, I didn't mean to say nigger, I meant black brother, ha ha.'

'I don't understand, monsieur, buses? But we are still now in the 60's. Even King Henry of England had a black trumpeter in his court in the year of our Lord 1507. Some say that even the Blessed Virgin was black.'

'I wasn't referring to the 1560's you idiot! Oh, what's the point?' Joe snapped irritably.

'I take it as a compliment you calling me an idiot, it is the ultimate accolade you can give to one of my profession,' she grinned. 'It was only about ten years ago, or so I'm told, that many black slaves were brought over to these islands.'

'Throw out Jews, bring in blacks, what's the point?' he grumbled, searching for another chew stick whilst trying to balance the boxes of clothes that weighed heavy in his arms.

'Ah, monsieur, but the Jew was free to get rich. The black, they keep him in chains like an animal.' She threw out her hands in continental fashion, suddenly producing a dozen eggs which she juggled in the air. 'Perhaps we all get a chance to be black, all return as a Jew, as a female, as a...'

'So what are you saying, that we are reincarnated or something? How crass!' he scorned, as she dropped one of the eggs onto his foot.

'You stupid...' he suddenly stopped, accidentally making eye contact with the black prisoner locked in his chains. Joe hurriedly moved on.

On the far side of the pillory he found himself being confronted by numerous traders trying to entice him to buy their wares. Stalls bulging with cloth of various colours, ribbons, laces and coifs. Nearby was a poultry market. It appeared that the whole of Edinburgh congregated here by the Kirk.

He looked up at the Gothic entrance of the new prison. Being so close to the church it gave the impression that it was an annex. In the middle of the street beside the Kirk were the luckenbooths. The ground floor shops of the nearby tenements that were busy selling meat and bread, as if in competition with the stallholders standing by their own portable booths, 'krames' crammed and jammed between the luckenbooths and Kirk.

Joe now reflected on what he'd said. Lawrence would have condemned him for using the word 'nigger'. Even Katie had occasionally sobbed aloud due to some of his sentiments. But, he'd only said them to shock, to provoke a reaction. Even Lawrence knew how much time he'd put into the anti apartheid society at university, and the free Nelson Mandela campaign.

'The chapel of Holy Rood used to stand in the lower part of St. Giles churchyard, it was destroyed by the Reformers. They used what was left to build the Tolbooth in 1562.'

'I just love the spiritual morality of your leaders...well, nothing changes over generations, the nature of man.'

'Most of the minor crimes are dealt with at the Tron. Ears cut off for infringing the game laws…or maybe their right hand for a second offence. Perhaps it is the same where you come from, monsieur. Where is it exactly you…'

'Look at the state of my boot, you dropped egg on it!' he glared at her.

'Please don't worry about the egg, I can easily get another. The main poultry market is near St. Monan's Wynd and the fleshmarket reaches all the way down to Blackfriars Wynd, parallel to Hog's Back Ridge. Pardon, monsieur, you probably know this as '*the King's Hie Gait*'.'

'Yar, or even uncle Tom Cobbley and all!'

'Ah, so you know uncle Tam the cobbler too. I need to contact him about money the Palace owes him for leather. He left L'Islebourg for the highlands before Lent last year…how is his gout?'

Joe ignored her apparent stupidity.

'So if I head towards the Castle at the top of the hill I'll come to Lawnmarket where I can purchase milk?'

'Oui, monsieur, and the fish market is…but you've been here long enough, monsieur, you must know all this well. So why do you want to buy milk?'

'I don't.'

'But you just said that you wanted to *purchase milk*. They were your precise words, monsieur.'

Joe's eyes sought sanctuary by gazing at the local peasantry running around wearing flat blue caps even though it was summer. The women wore shawls, many had bare feet.

Most days he'd spent climbing to the top of Arthur's Seat, sampling the spice and herbal mixtures he'd managed to purloin from one of the boys who turned the spits in the Palace kitchens. If he didn't know better, Joe would have sworn it was cannabis.

'Odd how the Pope didn't help,' she muttered, whilst making funny faces to the stallholders. 'Did you know that Pope Clement VII gave King James V a fortune to keep the Kirk Catholic…and the Holy Father rewarded him by giving his illegitimate sons bishoprics.'

A couple of minstrels passed by, Nicola waved to them whilst Joe sipped from a fountain trying to get rid of the bad taste of the stick.

'Ah, when we first arrived from France how my Queen was welcomed by pomp and splendour, even the fountain here at the Mercat Cross flowed with wine...even Lord Huntly seemed less dangerous then.'

'Who?'

'The Earl of Huntly, Catholic, but a lunatic. Wanted to kidnap the Queen to marry her. Didn't bother him that he was already married.'

'So, where is he now?' Joe belched into the autumn air.

'Dead. Moray, her brother, and Maitland rode with the Queen, and Huntly was captured and dropped dead and his son was executed'

'So the Queen married Darnley...why?' His eyes focused on the fountain, wishing that it still flowed with wine.

'His father Lennox is descended from a Stewart princess and his mother was the niece of Henry VIII. After Marie, she's Elizabeth's next heir. Even Monsieur James Melville told Elizabeth the bastard, that no woman of spirit would choose Darnley for a husband, as he was more like a woman than a man,' Nicola declared, whilst performing a handstand on the handle of a wheelbarrow. 'Monsieur James described him as very lusty, beardless and, ha ha...he called him *lady faced*, ha ha ha!'

Suddenly he noticed a man having his ear nailed down by the Mercat Cross. The women nearby were obviously peasants, wrapped in filthy, dull shawls vaguely resembling tartan, but nothing like the tartan he'd seen in 20th century shops.

'So, you think we are barbaric, do you not do such things where you come from, monsieur?'

'Well, the difference is, where I come from one has to pay to have one's ear pierced. Oh, God, hide!'

Just beyond the krames Joe caught sight of Nan with her son Rabbie. She was the last person he wanted to see.

Grabbing Nicola's arm he pulled her towards one of the nearby gardens behind the Kirk beyond the cemetery. Bloody women, Joe groaned, they could never let go, claws in, nothing else in their little heads but to trap a man.

Was someone playing his song?

'Can you hear that?'

'What, monsieur?'

The tune of *'Joe Hill'* suddenly whistled through his ears. Haunting the Edinburgh wynds, blowing across the luckenbooths, the krames, the Kirk…*'I dreamed I saw Joe Hill last night alive as you and me, says I, but Joe, you're ten years dead, I never died, says he, I never died says he.'*

A sudden gust of wind blew, as if someone had walked over his grave. A voice? Or was it the breeze that cried:

'The Countess of Ross, female warrior, a Scot! I led my troops in 1297 against the English, but no one remembered me after I went to heaven.

And Scots Protestants cried, "we have truth, our fruits of which Christ is the core!"

As they burnt to death Janet Allen in 1661, and in 1594 Alison Balfour.'

'Hello, Nicola,' a tall, dark haired man with an intricately designed beard emerged from one of the gardens carrying a small silver casket. His accent was a mix of Scot and French.

'Ah, bonjour, Monsieur Mossman…please allow me to introduce my companion. Monsieur Joseph Hill…he is not from around here you understand?'

'Ah yes, Cockburn told me about you. Good to meet you, Master Hill, I was just going home to see to some business, would you care to walk with me and perhaps come in and partake of some food and ale?'

Joe looked at Nicola, uncertain how to respond to the well dressed man in brown doublet and hose. Joe noticed that Mossman also wore a ring like the one he wore, engraved with the lion, square and compasses.

'We'll walk with you, monsieur,' Nicola volunteered. Joe didn't care where he went so long as he avoided Nan; his eyes scanned the area to ensure they wouldn't meet.

Nicola and Mossman went on ahead, Mossman having relieved Joe of his boxes of clothes, leaving Joe to skulk behind. His mind was elsewhere, thinking about Nan and Rabbie, Katie and Chloe, and wondering whatever had happened to Lawrence. A bit much to believe that he'd somehow regressed in time. If so, Lawrence could have regressed with him.

'*Mossman*', the same as Lawrence's surname. He missed him; Lawrence was his anchor to sanity. Even his own philosophical studies didn't help.

The philosopher David Hume, a Scotsman, was born in Edinburgh. Joe recalled seeing his statue in the High Street near George IV Bridge. But now there was no George IV Bridge, no statue, and Edinburgh High Street had become Hog's Back Ridge. Hume had argued that the idea of existence was no different from the idea of any object. Joe never really paid much attention to Hume during his studies. He'd never paid much attention to anything at university, well, apart from women and booze. Hume had written about cause and effect, but Joe couldn't recall anything he'd said, other than one of the quotes he'd memorized verbatim in order to write down during his final exams.

'All the colours of poetry however splendid, can never paint natural objects in such a manner as to make the description to be taken for a real landskip. The most lively thought is still inferior to the dullest sensation'.

Joe had concentrated on the rationalists rather than empiricists like Hume, who, Joe had badly argued, had failed to appreciate those under the effects of hallucinogenic drugs. At what stage did word become flesh?

It was just as they reached the luckenbooths at Mossman's house when the priest, Wolfart Bruce, in long black gown and greasy ginger hair made his way towards the tenement. Bruce was accompanied by an older man who sported an exceptionally long grey beard that almost reached his waist. Balancing a flat cap on his head and holding a Bible in his hands the older man shouted, 'mermaid's spawn!'

James Mossman ran up the steps above the booths into his home, immediately re-appearing with a gun.

'You may be able to bully our beautiful Queen, but you can't terrorise me!'

The man with the long beard laughed and walked away. He was followed by the priest, and a bunch of simpering devotees dressed almost identically in drab, dark clothes.

Relieved that there was not about to be another battle, least of all with him in the range of fire accidentally getting shot, Joe looked up at the building resting on the Doric style pilasters that adorned the first floor windows. Such a beautiful piece of architecture, even Joe's Philistine mind could appreciate its continental influence. The luckenbooths were like a 16th century shopping arcade, choc a block with scales, coins, trinkets and caskets made from precious metals. They were the focus of the hubbub of the populace who pushed and shoved their way towards the booths. Many had their own goods to barter, be they swine, donkey or servant.

From below ground, men and women emerged from Mossman's cellars carrying huge sacks over their shoulders, and heavy kegs of what Joe presumed to be ale.

Nicola Ambruzzi had now run up the side steps above the booths to whisper something to Mossman. The man gave her a nod in response and then disappeared into his home with gun intact, leaving Nicola to return to Joe.

'What did that chap with the long beard mean, *mermaid's spawn*?'

'John Knox, haven't you seen him before?'

'So, that's the famous Knox is it? I thought he'd done a runner from Edinburgh.'

'The Devil's son is a like a dog, monsieur, returning to his vomit. Monsieur Mossman is one of the Queen's most loyal subjects. Knox calls our blessed Marie a '*mermaid*'.' Joe looked bemused.

'Mermaid means '*whore*'.'

'So, is Mossman a Reformer or a Catholic?'

'Ha ha, monsieur, James Mossman is a Jew of course! Grandfather had to marry a Christian wife and convert to Catholicism, but even so, everyone knows they are Jews.'

'Yar, thinking about it, Nicola…Nicola! Please come down from that pole!' he shouted across the road to the fool who had now climbed up a pole outside a barber's shop. Obediently the girl ran back across the road.

'Mossman could be a Jewish name, same name as my friend Lawrence. But, surely if he's a Scot he'd have Scots name.'

'He does, monsieur, James.'

'No, Fool! I can see you're well named. Even I know that in Edinburgh the majority of men here seem to be called James. I was referring to the name Mossman, that's not a Scots name.'

'Don't you let the Queen hear you speak ill of him. Oh, and if you ask anyone, even the Mossmans if they are Jews they will deny it.' The girl picked up a couple of small silver weights from the nearby scales to juggle but they were too heavy. Instead she made them disappear inside her clothes. But, Joe wasn't impressed; he'd seen too many conjurors doing the same tricks. Noticing his lack of response Nicola returned the weights to the booth, and threw her head up with contempt.

'Why would he deny his being a Jew?' Joe persisted with his questions, desperate for another piece of stick to chew now that he'd chewed his last piece up by St. Giles.

'Because in England he would be put to death for being a Jew, and his ancestors were only allowed to remain in Scotland so long as they converted to Catholicism. In Scotland it is far worse to admit to being Catholic than to being a Jew.'

'So, it's not illegal to be a Jew here...not like in England and Europe? I didn't know that. So when did the Mossmans arrive here, did they come from France with the Queen?'

'They were here long before the Queen. I think they've been here for at least a hundred years. Pawnbrokers and bankers. As you know, monsieur, only Jews are allowed to be money lenders. Master Mossman told my Queen that one of his distant ancestors was Aaron of Lincoln, the wealthiest man in England.'

'What bollocks!' Joe retorted, fervently searching for another chew stick. 'Even if Mossman's grandfather, or great grandfather, or whoever it was happened to be a Jew it doesn't mean that they still consider themselves as such. I mean, as you say, they converted to Catholicism a long time ago and obviously married Christian wives.'

'Oui, his wife is Mariota Arres.'

'Well, a Jew is only a Jew if his mother is a Jew!'

'See, look up there.' Nicola pointed up at a stone carving set into the corner of the house above the luckenbooths. 'Look, that figure's Moses, he's receiving the commandments. And see the sundial? Look at what's above him. Moses is looking up at the sun; you understand? Like a philosopher.'

Joe gazed up to where she pointed. Plato's '*Republic*' suddenly came to mind:

> '*The sun is not sight, but isn't it the cause of sight itself and seen by it?...when we turn our eyes to things whose colour are no longer in the light of day but in the gloom of night, the eyes are dimmed and seem nearly blind, as if clear vision were no longer in them....yet whenever one turns them on things illuminated by the sun, they see clearly, and vision appears in those very same eyes...*'

'What does that motto say?'

'Why, monsieur, can you not read? It says, 'love God above all, and your neighbour as yourself.'

'Even so, this doesn't make Mossman a Jew!' Joe snapped.

'But, monsieur, why else would he have a figure of Moses on his house and not one of the Blessed Virgin or one of the saints? And where do you think the name Mossman originates? It means '*Moses man*'.'

Suddenly Nan appeared as if from nowhere, the girl he'd tried so hard to avoid was now standing facing him. Joe was used to these situations, and although inwardly he heaved, from outward appearance he remained unfazed.

'Oh, hi, Nan, what a coincidence. I was only just thinking about you. I've really missed you... and those beautiful green eyes. In fact, I was coming to visit you today. Well, to be honest I came up several times, but there was always a chap hanging around outside. I thought it might be your kid's father.' He gave her a quick peck on the cheek, catching sight of the priest Wolfart Bruce watching them. Joe gave her another kiss on her other cheek just for effect. The priest turned and walked away.

'I wasn't concerned for myself,' Joe continued to excuse his caddish behaviour, 'I just didn't want to cause you any problems, and then I saw that old girl in the stocks today.'

'Ma Ragg,' her voice was trembling, she looked pale, upset.

'Yar, Ma Ragg. Well, when I saw her like that I knew that I must find you in case you were in trouble. You know, in case you had no one to look after the kid.'

'Rabbie.'

'Yar, Rabbie. So I've just been up to your place and guess what? No one was in.'

'What about our wedding day…you haven't forgotten?'

'Monsieur, Sir James is wanting to speak with us,' Nicola interrupted.

Joe glanced up and noticed that James Mossman had come out of his door and was beckoning to him.

'Well, nice to see you again, Nan, we must get together sometime.' Joe gave her another peck and headed off towards Mossman's house.

'No, monsieur, Sir James wants Nan to come too, Nicola insisted, much to Joe's dismay.

Joe and Nan followed Nicola up the flight of side steps above the luckenbooths leading into the man's private home.

'We can't get married without the Queen's permission. Cockburn advised me to wait,' he whispered to the young woman beside him. 'She said that because of the battles the Queen is fighting, you know, with her having to lead her troops, it wasn't an appropriate time to hold such a celebration.'

Of course Joe had been into the Mossman home once before, but he didn't think it proper to mention it to Sir James. The Mossman coat of arms was attached to the wall, the initials *J.M* (written in the Latin form *I.M*) and *M.A* after Sir James and his wife Mariota Arres. This was complimented by the same renaissance sundial and motto as that outside the building: *'Luve God abuve al and yi nychtbour as yi self.'* The figure of Moses was also there, but this one was carved from wood not stone, and in place of the sun was a lion.

He was invited to take a seat by the window.

147

The gun was lying on the table beside him, along with his boxes of clothes.

Noticing Joe's gaze Sir James expounded, 'made of ivory and horn, German. Germans make the best guns.' Joe gave a nod, he wouldn't mind one himself. All he had was a dagger, not a great defence if someone was about to shoot him. Until this authentic encounter he'd never realised they had guns in the 16th century, only swords and swash buckling men prancing about in tights.

Joe noticed James Mossman whisper into Nan's ear. In order not to eavesdrop, he turned away to gaze out of the window at the customers bartering at the luckenbooths below.

'I believe that Nicola Ambruzzi is ordered to teach you royal protocol,' Sir James Mossman interrupted Joe's ruminations.

'Even so, I would have thought that someone of your breeding would have already been trained. Ah, but times are changing, nothing's the same anymore. When my father was young...'

'You cannot trust anyone these days, Monsieur Mossman...well, apart from the few.'

The fool gave Mossman a strange look, and then practised some sly conjuring tricks with 3 gold coins, only to make them reappear as six.

'Master Hill, I'll get to the point,' Mossman suddenly interrupted the performance. 'We need you to look after Nan, we believe her to be with child. Raped again I shouldn't wonder. If I discover who the father is I shall shoot him myself.'

'But...but why me? I mean I hardly know...'

'Because we have no other men of your stock available. Most of our lords are with her Majesty in battle, well, those of your age.'

About to remonstrate, James Mossman immediately interrupted him.

'Of course, you shall be well looked after for your trouble.'

'But, why would you care so much about...well, I don't mean to be rude about Nan, but she's just a servant.'

'A servant, ha, but you know nothing, Master Hill! He doesn't know, does he, Nicola?' The fool shook her head; a smile crossed her pretty lips.

'Master Hill, Joseph, if I may call you that. I'm told that you already have a special task for which Cockburn has sent Nicola to assist you, so I will offer you my personal protection if you would oblige me in this. As to why we laughed when you refer to our beloved Nan as a worthless servant, I think you must sit down, and Nicola and I will tell you a story.'

Joe found himself being cajoled into a carriage beside Nan, young Rabbie, Nicola and of course Sir James Mossman. The horse-drawn carriage headed in a north-easterly direction, past the Palace and through Holyrood, passing numerous soldiers, carriages and a small loch graced by several black swans.

Joe glanced up at Arthur's Seat. As the carriage left Holyrood, entering the fields and copses of unknown terrain, he noticed several cottages scattered around. His eyes focussed on the peasants working the land, many were harvesting, some were sitting on high branches of apple trees.   Others were on horseback or leading oxen yoked to ploughs trudging through the thick autumn leaves.

Suddenly the horses descended down a steep hill passing a couple of pretty servant girls lifting their skirts from the ground exposing their ankles. Perhaps this wasn't going to be so bad after all.

'And remember, Joe, if you need anything you only have to ask. I'm sure that you'll be very happy here,' Sir James said, when they arrived at the small cottage in the middle of nowhere. There were donkeys in a nearby paddock, along with chickens and a couple of goats. The cottage was pleasant enough, thatched roof, quaint, situated near a brook of clear running water. Autumn leaves floated down stream alongside the ducks that adeptly manoeuvred around the wooden pails belonging to the other cottagers. Even the local peasantry looked cleaner and plumper than those he'd seen in the town. How different the smells were, fresh grass and flowers, even the cow dung didn't have the same stench out here in the slightly salty Scottish air.

Inside, the cottage was sparsely furnished. A few stools, bench, table and cooking range, but clean nonetheless. The chimney was just a hole in the roof and fire in the centre of the room. A cot and bed were tucked into a corner, nightwear hung above a large chamber pot.

'We couldn't put you anywhere too grand…it wouldn't be safe. You'll fit in easier living here,' Mossman explained, as if reading Joe's mind.

'Where do I sleep?'

'There's a loft up those stairs.' Sir James pointed to a ladder by the side of the entrance, 'your bed is up there, but it's clean and warm. Your food will be supplied by my own workers, and your clothes of course.' The man smiled, heading away from the cottage leaving Joe running after him.

'And remember, Joe,' he whispered out of Nan's hearing, 'if you ever have an inkling as to who the father of her unborn child is, you must tell me immediately, you understand?' Joe gave a nervous nod, and then the well dressed man pushed a bag of coins into his hand. 'Of course, I objected to her not having a female companion here, as it will do her reputation no good living alone with a man. But, she assured me that you were honourable, and that the Queen herself had plans for you and Nan.

As Joe's blue eyes watched James Mossman drive away, he knew that there was nothing he could do to avoid the situation he was in.

Why Joe had been chosen to be her minder he had no idea. He couldn't even look after himself let alone anyone else.

Suddenly, Rabbie ran towards him, Joe picked him up, swung him around by his arms. He felt guilty for having to care for her child when he had done so little for his own. Was this child any more special than Chloe? According to Sir James it was Nan who was the special one, but Joe still couldn't understand why she had been working as a servant and living in squalor when her life could have been so different. Of course Mossman and Nicola had tried to explain that Nan and her supporters had thought it safer for her to live in obscurity. But, what had once been a carefully guarded secret was now out. It had only been since the Protestants had taken over that no Catholic was safe, and of course now there was not merely Rabbie to think of, but Nan's unborn child.

Joe looked at the pale girl who was busy carrying a bucket of water towards the cooking range. Who'd ever think that she was the daughter of a king, half sister to Marie Queen of Scots?

Chapter Six

'For when the web is at an end,
'tis then too late a fault to mend.
Let thought of this awaken dread –
repentance dwells not with the dead'
– Michael Bruce (1746-67)

The following two months went quickly. Much of the time Joe found himself back in the Palace, with Nicola teaching him royal protocol and Cockburn inviting him to various suppers now and again. He'd spun so many lies that everyone believed him to be an honourable man, and one who needed to be prepared for court life. Nan was excused from accompanying him. Cockburn had put it down to her pregnancy, and wanting to keep a low profile away from the Palace. The truth was, Joe had never invited her along. Mossman had even financed a new wardrobe for him, velvet mainly. Fitted doublets, spanking new breeches, perfumed gloves, hose, stockings, shoes and ruffed shirts. Joe loved those evenings at Holyrood, except for the fact that he had not dined with the Queen.

After such suppers, more often than not, Joe would fail to return home to Restalrig. Instead, he headed into the Canongate and through the Netherbow Port in order to instruct his assortment of renaissance lovers in the art of pelvic thrusts.

In fact, Joe wasn't doing too badly at all, many of the women he now even considered as regulars. None gave him the grief that they would have done had they'd lived in 20th century London.

Yes, Joe was settling into this fantasy very nicely thank you.

Missing his daily tabloids, he'd occasionally take a peek into his Bible. He'd even opened his crimson and gold bound book containing the prophesies of Nostradamus, but the prediction that made the most impact due to its being marked in red ink was far too obscure: *'d'Arthemide: Allant murdri par incognu du Marne'.*

The best translation he could glean was: *'Diana going to be murdered by the unknown man from Marne.'*

As Joe had no idea where Liper Toun or even Stirling Castle were, let alone a Scottish village called Marne, there was little he could do. Least of all prepared to search the whole of Scotland to find a girl called Diana.

One of the French maids, Ellie, with whom Joe had fornicated amongst the flower beds of the Palace in late October, had mentioned a major row between Marie Stuart and her husband Henry Darnley on the 2nd of that same month. From what Joe had been told, it was something to do with her reappointing James Hepburn, the Earl of Bothwell, as lieutenant-general instead of Darnley's father Lennox. Joe didn't know what all the trouble was about, uninterested in the silly French maid's gossip whilst she sat astride his naked body, his own eager mouth busily sucking at her breasts. She'd mentioned that Bothwell hated Moray the Queen's half brother, although the earl wasn't a Catholic, and that there was a rumour that Moray knew some secret of the Queen's. Ellie whispered that there were bets going on in the servants quarters as to whether this secret was due to the possibility of her having slept with Rizzio or Bothwell. But, the whisperings into his sensitive ear merely caused his penis to enlarge, Joe was now more engrossed in satisfying his infantile need to breast feed than court gossip. Although, he was none too impressed when Ellie noticed the Kirk minister Wolfart Bruce spying on them through a hedge.

When Joe had complained to Cockburn, she'd merely rebuked him for not getting on with his task, that being to complete his mission in solving the riddles and finding the key. In fact, Cockburn had become so enraged by his lackadaisical attitude, that eventually she'd ruled that he would cease getting a free ride and work for his keep. Joe didn't care, he was having a great time, so he'd borrowed a lute from Nicola and went into the streets to busk, mainly in the taverns; and the public loved him. Of course his main song was a favourite of both his mother and Lawrence that he'd vaguely adapted to suit the style of the day. He'd managed to retain the lyrics re-written by his namesake Joe Hill, to the tune of '*The sweet by and by*', that had been originally composed by Samuel F. Bennett and Joseph P. Webster.

'Long-haired preachers come out every night,
Try to tell you what's wrong and what's right;
But when asked how 'bout something to eat
They will answer with voices so sweet:
You will eat, bye and bye,
In that glorious land above the sky;
Work and pray live on hay,
You'll get pie in the sky when you die.'

If his audience grew tired of his singing, he'd then offer to paint their portraits, trying to imitate the style of the day. The gentry paid well, they'd invite him into their private mansions and wine and dine him. They'd even offered their servants for him to sleep with. To the poorer folk he gave sketches for free, some even offered their daughters.

He'd painted a portrait of Nan, merely to impress Lord Erskine and James Mossman. He thought it one of his best, although Nan didn't seem too thrilled. It was at least a week after completion when he had sobered up enough to look at it more critically that he noticed the portrait bore little resemblance to Nan, but was the spitting image of Katie.

Of course, during this time Nan was suffering morning sickness. He knew without a doubt that the child was his. Occasionally they slept together on the nights he stayed home, Nan believing that he intended to marry her, loved her.

'Nan, you are my world, everything I've ever wanted. Blasted Reformers! If it wasn't for them and the English we would be married by now.' Then he'd sing her one of Burn's poems. He'd recalled the poet's works from when his younger brother Kieran had hassled him to test him on Burns for his A level.

'Please sing *Ae fond Kiss* again, Joe, you know how I love it,' Nan had begged, and then joined him in the song as he strummed the tune on his lute.

'Ae fond kiss and then we sever, ae farweel and then forever. Deep in heart-wrung tears I'll pledge thee. Warring sighs and groans I'll wage thee.'

Sometimes, if Joe felt excessively randy and required extra tricks performed on his genitals he'd sing, '*My Nannie O*'.

'Now, each time I sing, '*O*', Nan; you copy with your mouth the word, '*O*'; Got it?' he'd instruct like a schoolmaster. 'See, push it in like that...wider, Nan. Form an O with your mouth. Push it right in, good girl.' Penis happily swollen, throbbing inside her wet, taut mouth as he'd sing:

> '*Come weel, come woe, I care na by, I'll tak what Heav'n will send me O; Nae ither care in life have I. But live, an' love my Nannie O.*'

It was always on the final rendition of '*Nannie*', when he enthusiastically ejaculated an '*Oh!*'

But Joe never planned for a future, well, there was little point, he didn't intend to stay around that long. Anyhow, if this was more than a hypnotic dream state and he did return to his normal time zone, it would mean that he'd bred his own ancestor.

Characteristically, Nan never complained about his lack of emotion or commitment, but he did help her in the cottage making the fires now that the winter had drawn in. Nan seemed to like it when he spent time with her, content when he was there, he even played with the kid. But most nights he frequented the taverns in Edinburgh, the cottage being within easy walking distance of Holyrood and Arthur's Seat. His main problem when he entered the town was the stench.

Every night it reeked of excrement, like an open sewer.

'Gardez Lieu!' the all too familiar cry, and Joe would jump to one side of the road as the filth poured down, narrowly missing his head. Excrement and urine was all he ever smelt, day and night it hung in the Edinburgh air.

But, life was fun, even now he laughed when he recalled his initial visit to one of the taverns, when asked by the innkeeper if he wanted a chopin. He'd replied with all seriousness, '*a chopin' board or Nocturne in F sharp minor?*' But Joe learnt soon enough that the innkeeper had referred to the liquid measure, equivalent to 1 ½ pints.

More often than not he'd see Henry, Lord Darnley, sprawled out drunkenly across a bench, sometimes even on the floor.

All too often, local whores would brazenly sit on the King's lap, placing their hands on his codpiece, without any shame for humiliating their Queen. But, now Joe had other things on his mind than bedding Marie Stuart.

For, like Nan, she too was pregnant, so sex with either of them would soon prove more of a hassle than pleasure. Joe would wait until the Queen gave birth before he made his move. Obviously, he'd heard what had happened to the poet Chastelard for being found under the Queen's bed. Apparently everyone in the Palace knew that he'd been her lover, but Moray had discovered him there and forced his sister to allow his execution. Perhaps Joe had got it wrong after all, sixteenth century married women indulged in adultery as eagerly as the men. It was merely that there were different penalties for men and women, perhaps even a different Bible.

Of course, he had doubts about Nan. On more than one occasion he'd returned home to Restalrig only to find the priest Wolfart Bruce standing by the cottage door, once even speaking to Rabbie. Joe had challenged Nan, concerned that the Protestant minister intended to hang the child on the scaffold, having never forgotten the time when he'd done it to another infant. Nan's explanation was that the priest lived nearby and that he'd just come to offer spiritual guidance. To Joe's mind, the only spiritual guidance the man could offer was the directions to the local scaffold.

'You have the sexiest dimples in your cheeks, Joe,' Nan would say, trying to calm him, to bond with the man she loved, share a moment of affection, of sentiment.

'Not as sexy as the one in my dick,' he'd reply, pushing her pretty head down towards his groin. After 20 minutes of oral sex, Joe was placated.

It was during a few days of what he termed as, *'raving'*, when he'd bumped into Cockburn, escorting a tall woman with exquisitely braided black hair, outside James Mossman's house.

'Hello, Joseph, allow me to introduce ye.'

Joe gave a bow.

The woman was not beautiful in the conventional sense, although her skin radiated a glow reminding him of a wax candle. Her skin was darker than most of the locals, perhaps she was from the Middle East, he thought. Her almond shaped brown eyes sparkled as she smiled.

'I don't believe I know your name, my lady.'

'Lady of the Fishes, that's what I'm known as.'

'Oh, you work in the Kow Gait?' he referred to the fish market down in the Kow Gait.

Cockburn raised her eyebrows in protest.

'I'm often to be found in the Kow Gait, that I admit. But my main occupation is to save people from drowning.'

Joe looked puzzled, now wondering if she was a lifeguard, or maybe helped with a lifeboat somewhere.

'That's very honourable of you, my lady, but I don't suppose you have many fish that drown.'

He'd only said it to make her laugh, but once again Cockburn glared at him, now visibly shaking her head. Joe didn't know why they both seemed bereft of a sense of humour.

Suddenly, the woman spoke.

'I save fish from drowning, Joseph. Fate is mapped out for all the fish of the sea, but they still have the power to change their course.'

He'd so longed to respond with, 'what, do they pray to Cod?', but thought better of it.

'You see, Proverbs 3:16 tells us, *'Length of days in her right hand, and in her left hand riches and honour'.'*

'How does that link in with fish? Are you something to do with deep sea diving?' he asked, seriously wondering if there was some treasure in a loch somewhere, or a shipwrecked vessel out in the ocean.

'The choice the fish have to make is between the left hand of Boaz or the right hand of Jachin. Of course the meaning of the name Benjamin is *the son of the right hand*, just as the length of your own days is mapped out in your right hand.'

'Fish can't think, of course they can't. Or do you mean dolphins?'

The woman began to walk away, ignoring him. Cockburn followed as they headed down towards the Kow Gait.

Bored and intrigued, Joe decided to follow from a distance. Just before they reached the Grassmarket they stopped outside at a church. The Kow Gait had numerous wells, and Joe was thirsty. It was just as he approached a well when he caught sight of what looked to be a playing card flapping in the breeze. Joe bent down to retrieve it, it was a tarot card. The illustration on the card was of a broken tower. Perhaps they belonged to a court jester or gypsy, he thought, glancing back to the church where Cockburn and his companion had stopped. But, when Joe looked, they'd vanished.

Nan, not yet showing signs of her pregnancy, had a visit from Sir Arthur Erskine. He'd arrived on horseback on a windy November day with Nicola riding beside him. Sir Arthur, as Joe well knew, was devoted to the Queen as her equerry and Master of the Horse.

The Queen, whom he'd barely set eyes on, had left Holyrood on 8th October for Stirling Castle to lead yet another battle with 18,000 of her troops. She was trying to put down the rebel lords, and didn't return until the 18th October. Even then she only remained until the 30th of the month, proceeding on to Dalkeith House for the day.

Only home for a few days, by the 12th November Marie Stuart was off again, this time to Linlithgow Palace. It was now the 14th of November, and she wasn't due back until around the 20th of that same month. Her absence would amount to about 6 weeks. Joe wondered how the Queen managed to ride so far and for so long in her pregnant state.

'Nice legs,' he observed to Nicola as he watched her attempt to dismount.

'Why, thank you, monsieur,' she smiled, re-positioning her cap.

'Not you, the horse.' Joe stroked the dapple grey mare. Sir Arthur beckoned two men working by the nearby stream to attend their horses, leaving little Rabbie to toddle after him.

'We didn't think we'd find you home, thought you'd be in the burgh practising your favourite sport…penis poxing!' Nicola sneered, giving a fart as she jumped down from the saddle, Joe laughed as he followed Sir Arthur into the cottage.

Nan poured a jug of wine into their goblets as they sat around the table. Rabbie played contentedly on Nicola's lap. Joe didn't speak, he felt guilty. He was fearful they'd called in order to rebuke him for his licentiousness, or worse, execute him for his treatment of one of royal blood. Was this classed as treason he wondered? His palms sweating, pulse racing.

'At least I know you're safe, Nan, with Master Hill here to protect you.' Arthur Erskine smiled; Joe heaved a sigh of relief.

'Although, as I've told you before, I still think you should have a maid living with you…even Nicola would be better than no one.'

'Thank you!'

'No, no, I didn't mean that as offensive, Nicola. But I think Nan should have a lady's maid due to etiquette. It's not at all good for her reputation, even though you're soon to be married.' Joe turned his eyes to the window.

'If I were known to have a maid, it would merely confirm to my accusers their suspicions,' Nan replied.

'Yar, might blow her cover,' Joe added, fearful that any maid who presented herself he would have already bedded.

'Ah well, you young people have your own style of doing things. In fact, I could use your modern brain to help solve these murders that are becoming too frequent of late.'

'Yar…yar of course, I'd love to help. In fact, I'm quite good at solving clues. I just love murder weekends…I mean I love challenges.'

'Well, thank you, Joseph, it's very re-assuring that you're going to be such an asset to the court. I'll discuss the details of the task with you later.'

'Come, Joseph, let us leave them to talk in peace,' the fool said, practising a card trick that went wrong.

Joe, relieved not to have to remain in Sir Arthur's company, hurriedly followed Nicola away from the cottage. The haunting sound of wedding bells was peeling from inside his own head.

In the near distance Joe noticed a loch half hidden behind some tall horse chestnuts, where a large group of people were gathered. They sat on the muddy grass and boulders, many in prayer. High above them stood a small castle, beehives and a dovecote. Their donkeys and horses grazed nearby, beaten mercilessly by the fierce November winds. Even from here Joe could see the ocean in the distance, in the opposite direction Arthur's Seat soared upwards into the grey winter sky.

Joe was surprised to see aristocrats and peasants mingling together, many were blind or had some visual impairment. The wealthy wore long gowns covered by thick, fur lined cloaks. The poorer females wore coarse, grey shawls and ragged cloaks or plaids. The majority of the men with them wore flat blue caps and saffron shirts, covered by filthy cloaks, just the same as some who lived inside the towering Flodden wall. As he studied the faces of those who were obviously blind, Joe once again recalled the words of the Edinburgh philosopher David Hume. Did he mean that the world of the blind was inferior in every way to the world of the sighted? Joe looked into the blank eyes sitting before him. Would life for them be only 100% authentic if they could see?

Suddenly, Nicola decided to liven things up, and began to entertain the pilgrims singing her favourite song accompanied by her lute. Joe stood by, embarrassed and totally bored.

'Not house of David, it was Saul, whom God chose as their king...'

'Thank God you've stopped that awful racket,' Joe sneered, as they headed towards the trunk of a fallen horse chestnut lying near the loch. 'Did someone lie to you, Nicola, and tell you that you could sing? God, you have the most awful bloody voice I've ever heard.'

They both sat down on the cold, damp tree trunk. Joe's attention momentarily distracted as he glanced at her audience.

'Has all of Edinburgh moved to Restalrig?' Joe mumbled sarcastically, eagerly accepting the piece of chew stick Nicola had offered.

'Pilgrims, Joseph, they come from all over the world to worship at St. Triduana's well.' She wrapped her shawl tightly about her shoulders as the winds whipped up.

'Where's the well?'

'In the Kirk here in Restalrig, the blind come here. Well, they used to, and they leave with their sight.'

'Yar, if you say so,' Joe muttered cynically.

'Mais oui, why don't you know this? You live here, surely you know this!'

Joe belched loudly.

'Restalrig is very important to Catholics. Why, it was the Dean of Restalrig who performed the marriage ceremony of the Queen to Lord Darnley. Sir William Maitland was against the marriage you know? I don't trust him, monsieur, and he's having a love affair with one of the Queen's ladies, Marie Fleming. She sleeps in the Queen's bedroom with her, privy to all her confidences.'

'And I suppose you trust your Sir Arthur Erskine do you?'

'Perhaps your question would have been better served if you had asked me if I trusted Marie Fleming, monsieur. As for Sir Arthur, well he hates Davey you know, they all do.'

Joe looked bemused.

'Davey, you know the Italian Rizzio. Oui, he is truly hated. Because he's closer than anyone to the Queen's heart, she adores him, monsieur.'

'You see, monsieur, my Queen and all her loyal entourage didn't arrive in Scotland until 1561, and Restalrig Kirk was destroyed by the Protestants in 1560. It grieves her that she will never see it as it was.'

Joe was bored. Although Catholic himself, he'd shown no interest in his religion. Not even when his aunt had returned from Lourdes ranting and raving about miracles, holy baths and the grotto of St. Bernadette. Then his father had a blazing argument with his maternal uncle about Bernadette's vision at the grotto. According to Joe's father, Bernadette claimed to have seen a girl of her own age and not *'a pagan goddess'* as he'd put it. Joe's uncle Paddy had insisted that the statue in the Lourdes grotto accurately depicted the saint's vision. 'When the Duke of Chatelherault opened the Scottish Parliament and made Scotland Protestant in 1560…'

'My friend Lawrence said that Constantine did the same in Rome,' Joe interrupted her. 'One man has a thought, and the whole world's perception of God changes.'

'Pardon, monsieur? Of course all this wouldn't have happened if he hadn't been Regent after the death of Marie de Guise, or should I say after her murder.'

'Why should anyone murder the Queen's mother?'

'Only you can answer that for yourself, monsieur. But remember that the duke believed himself to be next in line to the throne after my Queen Marie.' Then Nicola digressed, 'pilgrims aren't supposed to visit the ruins here anymore. But they still do, in secret. Anyhow, monsieur, the pilgrims need to be entertained, and if you don't like my voice, then you must sing to them yourself.'

Joe just gave a laugh, took her lute from her and walked back towards the mass of people in the field by the loch where he began to strum. The winds were howling through the thick, wet grass. Mists were rising in the distance, with the smoke from the chimneys.

'Obviously they haven't got the miracles they came for…suppose I'm the next best thing,' he mumbled to Nicola. But she wasn't listening, busy guiding the numerous blind pilgrims to sit closer to the performance. Joe, feeling niggled by his own insensitivity, strummed with greater vigour than usual.

> *'Give your money to Jesus, they say,*
> *He will cure all diseases today.*
> *If you fight hard for children and wife,*
> *Try to get something good in this life;*
> *You're a sinner and bad man, they tell,*
> *When you die you will sure go to hell.*
> *You will eat, bye and bye…'*

And the pilgrims cheered and clapped, blind and sighted, rich and poor firmly convinced that it was a spiritual ballad; that Jesus would indeed cure all their diseases that day. By the end of the hour on that miserable, cold November afternoon, Joe had his 16th century audience eagerly joining in with the chorus, *'you'll get pie in the sky when you die!'*

It was beyond the loch when Joe suddenly noticed two boars being chased. Not wishing to see the boars slaughtered in front of him, least of all hear them squealing and screaming when they encountered their bloodthirsty death, Joe handed the lute back to Nicola.

'Argyll, Knox said, you did us harm, too tolerant of Catholics.

Most powerful magnate in the highlands, too tolerant of God and the Blessed Virgin.

Argyll, Knox said, you did us harm, too tolerant of her you amour so well.'

The fool's falsetto notes rose up into the grey, misty air as he headed off towards what looked to be the ruins of the Restalrig Kirk.

Even away from the meadow he could still hear her singing, although he didn't have a clue as to what the lyrics meant. If Joe was honest, he didn't really care.

'Epileptic cursed, by a sorcerer from hell, Patrick Ruthven conjured his dark spell,

The Queen his evil cannot tell, for gold their souls would sell.

I am but a gypsy, Ruthven, I can see your curd. You are her enemy, and not Chastelard!'

Suddenly, he found himself face to face with the priest Wolfart Bruce. He was riding an ass, heading away from the ruins of St. Triduana's Kirk. Joe wanted to thump him, instead, he spat at the ground as the hooves trotted by.

'What are you thinking, my lord?' the voice greeted him the moment he stepped into the ruined grounds of the Kirk. It belonged to the maid whose breasts he'd once sucked, Ellie. At first he panicked, what if Nan found out? Then he remembered, this was the 16th century, he was allowed to have lovers, it was only females who weren't…

163

officially. Although the majority of the church was destroyed, the graves and tombstones hadn't been demolished. He noticed several pilgrims inspecting them, some appeared to be praying.

'Hello, Ellie, I was just thinking why anyone bothers to come to Restalrig, I mean it's just a tiny hamlet of no significance.'

'Why, my lord, great men from all over Scotland used to come here for pleasure and to rest.'

'Ha, Restalrig, Scotland's greatest tourist resort.'

'Mais oui, that is correct, monsieur. Restalrig reaches all the way from the far side of the Nor Loch and all the way to Leith shore and then goes eastward. It's a shame you weren't here on St. Triduana's Feast Day, the eighth day of October. But, then the Reformers appeared and caused havoc. No, it was best that you weren't here.'

'So, who's this St. Tridant?' Joe asked, as he bent down to pick up his chew stick that he'd dropped.

'Triduana, monsieur, she was a virgin. They say when the blessed saint was put in her tomb, a well of pure water sprang up from the ground.'

Joe looked around, unimpressed by the remains of the demolished church, although there were sections of wall and a few windows still intact. Nearby, he noticed a small well, beyond which was a large graveyard. Some of the tombs and stones were highly ornate with carvings and emblems, most appeared to have been left unscathed. Only one building had not been demolished. It was hexagonal in shape, not in keeping with 16th century architecture, like him it was somehow lost in time.

'Oh, monsieur, if only you had seen it as it was, so beautiful. Why, even the Pope himself praised it. Oui, even the Holy Father had sent a part of his own heart here to Restalrig.' A tear dropped from her pretty eyes, but Joe had no time for neurotics.

'So, what's the St. Triad's story then?'

'St. Triduana, my lord. She had an altar dedicated to her. Many miracles were performed at her altar, monsieur. Ah, but that was also destroyed. If only you'd visited before this desecration, you'd have seen it for yourself.'

'Unless I was blind,' Joe scoffed insensitively.

'True, monsieur, so you do know about St. Triduana without my telling you!' Ellie brightened with enthusiasm.

'What?'

'The blind came here to get cured. Bathed in the blessed saint's well. You see, St. Triduana was so beautiful, her eyes, they say, were the most lovely in all Scotland and a certain great king adored her.' Ellie spoke like a child in a world of fairytales.

'They say that he wouldn't leave her alone to worship as she wished to worship, in peace. Refused to allow her to retain her virginity because he adored the sparkle of her magnificent eyes. So to curb his desires she plucked out her eyes and handed them to him on a thorn.'

The maid smiled, as if this was the most wonderful accomplishment she'd ever heard.

'Mad, the woman was mad. Was she certified?' Joe scorned, spitting out a piece of the stick.

'Oh, yes, my lord. Rome issued certification of her saintliness almost immediately!'

To Joe's mind, Ellie made Nicola seem almost intelligent. As he climbed up onto one of the broken boulders that lay in the ruins of the demolished Kirk, he wondered if the fool had grown bored with her singing. The loch was too far away to see anything other than several donkeys and horses tied up awaiting their owner's return from their pilgrimage.

'So, the sinners are needed to authenticate the saint? Interesting,' Joe scoffed.

Some of the pilgrims were praying nearby at the well, constantly signing the cross over their faces and breasts, some mumbled in Latin as the seagulls screeched overhead in the dreary, grey sky.

Resting on one of the tombstones he invited the maid to kneel beside him. The winds were louder now, almost screaming through the Kirk yard. Nearby, he noticed an assortment of amber beads scattered around about the muddy earth.

'Cures blindness some believe…the beads I mean, not the mud. But then, our blessed Lord Jesus did cure a blind man with mud. Perhaps they got it wrong,' she mumbled, her eyes squinting almost in pain, as if her sanctuary of ignorance was no longer secure.

'Until this Kirk was destroyed, my lord, this was one of the most renowned shrines for pilgrimages in the whole of Scotland. Oui, it was the Chapel Royal of King James V.' Joe merely responded with a sigh to show that he was bored.

'I can get you some wine, my lord, good wine. I know where to find it…in the lower chamber.' She suddenly jumped up and hurried off without waiting for his response.

Joe didn't have to wait long for her to reappear with two large flasks.

'The lower chamber here is still used by the lairds of Restalrig as a burial vault.'

She handed Joe the flasks. 'And you can see the remains of the eastern window and chancel walls, monsieur, but it's not good for much else. Except the well of course, and even that Master Knox has plans to destroy.'

The seagulls had now landed in the graveyard en masse. Seagulls were timeless, Joe contemplated, their dress code never changed, once a seagull always a seagull.

'John Knox hated our last dean, Dr. John Sinclair. He's the son of Sir Oliver Sinclair of Rosslyn. Have you ever been to Rosslyn Kirk, my lord?' Joe ignored her, hoping that his lack of response might stop her tongue.

'Oui, John Knox hated Monsieur Sinclair, and that's why he caused this disaster to both heaven and earth. Poor Monsieur Sinclair only recently died. They say he died of a broken heart.' She moved closer, her breasts accidentally rubbed against his arm, large, heavy, full blown breasts.

'So you're like St. Tridu whatsit, with your gorgeous eyes… waiting for your prince to come. And this one's about to. Come on, let's take these flasks to the vault, I want to see this lower chamber of yours.' He smiled, exposing the dimples in his cheeks, the dimples no girl had ever been able to resist. The winds whipped through the heather crying like a banshee, thrashing against his legs. His hand reached out to cup one of her breasts as she walked ahead of him. His other hand was holding an opened wine flask to his greedy lips as he headed towards the hexagonal temple; the only building still left standing amongst the debris.

'My codpiece is too tight, ooh, I'll have to remove my breeches. Here, put your hand down there…God, your tits are the best…you're beautiful…what's your name again?' Joe slobbered, as his penis grew like Pinocchio's nose.

They descended down into the partially demolished, damp crypt, barely able to see where they were going. Inside, the floor was submerged beneath a huge pool of water, surrounded by a bank of rocks and broken crucifixes.

'Here, lay on this.' He pulled a wooden chest towards her, throwing his cloak on top.

Ellie obligingly lay on the cloak as Joe climbed on top, her breasts were already hanging out, ripe. His lips opened and pressed her hard nipples into his mouth. His fingers descended between her skirt, lifting her smock, slyly climbing like a preying mantis up the sweaty tower of Babel towards heaven.

'Here, take this,' he exposed his penis. 'This is what parliament means by a Private Member's Bill.'

Suddenly, there was a noise coming from above them.

'What if it's the soldiers, they will kill us!' she cried.

'Why?'

'Because it's forbidden to worship here, it's Catholic, they forbid us to remember the Blessed Virgin.'

The footsteps came nearer, Joe's heart started to beat faster. Was the nature of God about to be revealed by a gun or sword? He wondered. The evolution of religion, enforced by murder. The footsteps crunched over the fallen leaves and foliage, crunch, crunch, louder, nearer, until the huge black shadow appeared at the entrance of the crypt. As it loomed closer he recognised it as being Wolfart Bruce. The minister hadn't appeared to have noticed them. Waiting until he'd disappeared from view, Joe resumed where he'd left off.

Brushing the cobwebs off his hose, Joe headed back up into the sunlight. He took the flasks of wine with him, leaving young Ellie to her own devises down in the lower chamber. Now the winds were even stronger, forcing him to lose his balance as he fought his way across an open field towards an empty barn. Leaning back against a pile of straw, Joe opened a flask. Outside, the winds howled, he could hear shots being fired, animals screaming like babies. Of course, if he'd been a gentleman he would have invited the young maid to partake of the alcohol. In hindsight, Joe thought he should have done, now that he'd found the barn with its straw covered floor. It was more comfortable than the cold stone crypt.

After he'd consumed all the contents of the first flask, Joe started on the second. He didn't remember much after that, except falling asleep and hearing his song '*Joe Hill*' being sung somewhere in the distance, and then having a strange dream of a female reciting a poem.

'Remember me? Elsie Inglis. I saved their lives. Place your hand down the well to claim your surprise.'

Joe didn't know who the woman was. Elsie Tanner he'd thought the voice had said at first, his grandmother had told him about Elsie Tanner when he was a boy. She told Joe he'd end up with someone like Elsie Tanner if he didn't mend his ways. He didn't know to whom she referred, other than his mother explaining she'd once been a character in Coronation Street.

Although the wine had seemed to have knocked him out, once awake he was completely sober, not even a headache.

The winds appeared to have died down as Joe headed back towards the Kirk.

The pilgrims had gone, so had Ellie, stupid females. He spat at the ground, churches always had more female than male worshippers, women were just more easily conned.

What was that? A breeze, had someone walked over his grave? A voice, but no one in sight, was it the wind? Joe listened, following the direction of the voice. Was it a woman wailing?

Louder, louder until it was just like any other voice. Then a figure slowly began to materialise, as real and solid as his own body.

'Who are you...what do you want?'

The figure smiled, then began to dance, singing whilst her small feet tapped out the rhythm.

'Isobel MacDuff, Countess of Buchan. Took my war horses and never said, '*truce*'.

Risked my life, opposed Lord Buchan. Led the war horses to fight for the Bruce.

In Scotland women will be called witches, burnt at the stake or else drown.

But Scotland won't ever remember, Janet Bowman and Janet Brown.'

It was then that he noticed the well where the pilgrims had gone to pray.

From where he stood he couldn't even see the water, most probably it had been drained. Joe stared down into the deep pit.

'Reach out your hand, place it down the well' the voice had said.

Tentatively Joe bent down and knelt by the side of the small, stone well.

Out of the corner of his eye he noticed a handle attached to a rope. He began to turn the handle, faster and faster, so fast that at one stage he almost fell in. As he turned, a wooden bucket that was attached to the bottom of the rope slowly began to ascend. When it reached the top he saw that the wood was splintered and worn. Joe rubbed his tired eyes. It was when he took a step back that he noticed the strange markings on the bucket, it vaguely resembled the face of a man with a beard. In fact, Joe thought it looked remarkably like the paintings he'd seen of Jesus, even a little like the impression on the Turin shroud. But, as he knew all too well, most bearded faces found in unconventional settings gave rise to the myths of them being Jesus. Yet, this face had a tint distinct from the rest of the bucket...the face was green. Mould most probably, Joe decided. He looked inside the bucket expecting to find it filled with dirty water, maybe a spider or even a dead rat. But, to his disappointment it appeared to be empty.

He rubbed his sore, tired eyes again. Then suddenly, he noticed a tiny package lying in the bottom of the bucket.

Dipping in his fingers Joe eagerly retrieved the object and tore open the protective wrapper.

Inside, lay a small object made from topaz, it was formed in the shape of the letter 'S'.

Now he had three letters, 'S', 'O', and 'R'.

It was dusk by the time Joe went back to the loch. He'd expected to hear Nicola singing but, as he neared the field surrounding the loch, all he could hear were shrieks of pain. A flock of seagulls suddenly rose up from the field as the screams grew louder, it was then when he saw the cause of the commotion. Wolfart Bruce, the priest, had tied a man and his wife to a tree, stripped them naked and was in the process of beating them with a bundle of thorn studded brambles until they bled. Their five small children were standing nearby, too frightened to cry. Their shocked eyes witnessing the blood drip down onto the grass, their tiny ears unable to shut out the sound of their parents' screams.

Joe stood still for a moment, then walked forward and removed the instrument of torture from the startled priest. Then he calmly punched him in the face so that he fell to the ground. The other pilgrims looked horrified; the majority suddenly grabbed their belongings and children and hurried away from the scene, helping their blind and crippled comrades to leave with them.

Joe untied the victims from the tree and allowed them to run off into a nearby copse, struggling to dress in their torn clothes along the way.

Wolfart Bruce picked himself up from the ground, swept his long, ginger hair from his eyes and dusted down his black cloak. He reached inside his mouth to remove a tooth that had been punched out, his lip was bleeding. The priest then walked right up to face his assailant full on, so close that his nose almost touched Joe's nose. His bloodshot, dark eyes glared, an animal ready for the kill.

'I hae a guid memory, Master Hill, a very guid memory. Ye hae nae heard the last of this. Dinnae e'er turn ye back, dinnae e'er walk alone on a dark night. Dinnae e'er sleep, as I'll be there waiting. And I can wait a lang time. Aye a very lang time tae get wha' I want!'

'Monsieur, where did you go? I have been very worried about you.' It was Nicola. Her voice was agitated, her face flushed. Joe made no reply, his eyes fixed on the priest as he skulked off into the copse leaving Joe to follow Nicola back towards the cottage.

'The soldiers came here, led by Wolfart Bruce and cleared the area. They won't allow us to worship here anymore,' she wiped away the tears. 'I've been looking for you everywhere, monsieur, we must go back now, Sir Arthur will be furious at our prolonged absence.'

The fool had been correct of course, Sir Arthur Erskine was not happy, and had just mounted his horse about to return to Holyrood alone. On seeing the two latecomers he immediately dismounted and followed them into the cottage.

'I have some sad news,' Sir Arthur Erskine began. 'But you understand, what I am about to tell you is not to be breathed to another human being...ever!'

The two of them nodded, whilst Nan went to put Rabbie in his cot.

'Her Majesty lost her unborn bairn today, she's now confined to her bed.'

'Oh mon Dieu!' Nicola cried, 'and I wasn't with her. Where's the King?'

'Calm yourself, Nicola, your gypsy blood is too passionate, calm yourself.' Sir Arthur rested his gloved hand gently on her shoulder. 'I'm afraid my Lord Henry Darnley can't be found. His friends say that they think he's gone hunting in Fife.'

Nicola was sobbing now, but Joe didn't understand the fuss. Surely she could have more kids.

'But no one must know she is back in Edinburgh, least of all that she has miscarried. We hope to have her in Linlithgow by the 1st December next.'

'But, my lord,' Nan protested, 'how will my sister be able to ride on horseback having just lost her bairn?'

'She'll have to travel in her coach...she has little choice, Nan. If your cousin Elizabeth should find out...or anyone. Least of all her husband or even your brother Moray, then it would be the worse for her, and for Scotland.'

'Yar, but what has it got to do with us?' Joe interrupted, only now wondering why this Sir Arthur had ridden out to the cottage in order to share such an important secret of national security.

'Joseph, I've already discussed this all with Nan, and she's in agreement, and of course so is her Majesty. What I'm about to tell you must remain in these walls, and if we can pull this off we'll be able to keep the crown for Scotland and the Stewarts.'

It was around midnight when Joe found himself being accompanied into Edinburgh Castle by Sir Arthur Erskine. The moon was full, their route easy to follow, causing Joe to wish the moon was full every night to save him from falling into the excrement, which happened all too often when he was drunk.

Sir Arthur Erskine removed his gloves as they reached the Castle gates, motioning Joe to do likewise. It was only then that he noticed that his companion wore the same ring as himself, embossed with the lion, square and compasses.

The soldiers on duty at the Castle gates stepped aside, allowing them to enter beneath the raised portcullis. Joe found it a hard climb from the gates up the rough, steep pathway to the Castle as the winds raged. He was exhausted by the time they eventually arrived at their destination. Sir Arthur led him into a small, empty room with just a few stools and a table. A servant had followed them inside, carrying goblets and a jug. No sooner had they drunk their wine and taken a short rest when Sir Arthur rose and urged Joe to follow.

'We've put the child here.' Sir Arthur Erskine moved towards an open gap in the wall where a large block of stone had been removed.

'Put your hand inside, just to verify there is a body for your own peace of mind.' Joe knew that he'd have had more peace if he'd not been involved in this conspiracy at all. In fact, if he'd just stuck it out with Lawrence instead of lusting after those girls he wouldn't be in this mess.

Against his better judgement, Joe nervously placed his trembling hand into the hole. Of course he had no idea what he was feeling for; the foetus would be too premature to have resembled a formed baby, all of two or three months at the most. Joe's fingers felt around the sides of the tiny coffin, it was still open.

'We have given him a Moses basket.'

Joe presumed he meant those odd looking carrycots Katie had once pointed out in Mothercare.

'Sir Arthur, would you mind leaving me alone, just for a moment… In order to say my prayers?'

His companion nodded sensitively, and hurried out of the cold, draughty room.

The infant's remains were covered in a flimsy material. Carefully, Joe retrieved the shroud from the coffin as the moonlight poured in through the windows, casting shadows around the cold morgue.

In his fingers lay a small sheet of white linen embossed with an image of a red lion and Moses in the bulrushes playing with a fish. It was similar to the piece of material that had fallen from the maid's washing basket all those months before in the gardens of Holyrood Palace, this was also decorated with the insignia of a square and compasses, and also bore the motto '*Moses Man*'.

For a moment Joe genuinely wanted to pray, it seemed the only moral thing to do. But, other than remembering a few lines of, '*Holy Mary, mother of God pray for us sinners now, and at the hour of our death. Amen*', Joe just didn't know how to pray.

Heart thumping, thump, thump, thump; his fingers trembled as he tentatively placed his hand back inside the gap in the wall, intending to replace the shroud over the coffin. As he did so, Joe suddenly felt a small, hard object attached to the inside of the opening in the wall.

He glanced around apprehensively; there was no one else in sight. Hurriedly, he removed the item. It was made of crystal, formed with exact precision. It was another letter '*S*'.

It was the early hours of the morning when Joe was woken by a commotion outside his old room at the Palace where he'd spent the night.

'Another wench murdered!' a voice cried. Perhaps he should have told Sir Arthur that previous night of his own suspicions of who he thought the murderer was, but he still wasn't certain. He had thought that it might be Sir James Mossman.

Mossman, Moses man, it was from where the name originated if the title bearer were a Jew. After all, didn't he have the emblem outside his home advertising his link to the biblical Moses? Too many references to Moses, none of them made any sense to Joe, unless of course Sir James Mossman was the killer.

From what Lawrence had told him of the psychological profile of serial killers, they liked to leave their mark, some macabre signature. Joe opened the shutter and stuck his head out into the windswept courtyard. Ravens were swooping down amongst the debris, fought off by two maids, one who was sobbing. Yet, from what he was able to overhear there hadn't been a murder after all, a girl's body had been discovered in the lion's den. The lion Judah had apparently mauled his victim to death.

Joe gave a sigh of relief; probably a wild animal had also savaged the maid Betsy. He recalled the animals he'd occasionally encountered on his way home on those nights he'd returned to Restalrig, wolves, boar, even bears. No doubt all the deaths were due to natural causes after all.

Well, at least the night hadn't been entirely without results, he'd got another letter, '*S*'; although, of course it was sad about the baby. But, there was another matter causing Joe concern. If the Queen's baby had died, then who exactly was the man who one day would be named heir to both Marie Stuart's throne of Scotland and Elizabeth's throne of England? The King known as James VI.

The winds howled with the wolves down from Arthur's Seat as Joe headed towards the Netherbow Port later that morning. All seemed normal, the market traders battling against the winds to set up their stalls. The beggars took up their usual places on the ground, narrowly avoiding the donkey and horse excrement. A few women defiantly wore chin clouts, others forced to wear a scold's bridle. Their heads suffocating inside the iron cages, unable to eat due to the spikes covering their mouths. Washerwomen struggled beneath their baskets, bakers and hawkers selling their wares, oblivious to the fact that the future heir to the Scottish throne had died.

Cockburn had accompanied him with Nicola. As far as Joe understood they didn't know what had happened, Joe had been sworn to secrecy.

'Sae, how's Nan?' Cockburn broke the silence, munching into a hot pie, her breath visible in the dawn air.

Joe didn't answer, just evaded the issue with a grunt.

'I hope ye are looking efter the lassie, Joseph, I ken wha' ye dae tae women, but ye'll learn the hard way if ye dinnae listen now.'

'She's alright I said!' he snapped. Disgruntled by lack of sleep, the cold and the stress of too many secrets. 'Anyhow, I've got to paint the portrait of some Burgher's kid today, wants him to wear black. Odd colour for a kid.'

'Reformists, Joseph, Protestant demons, led by the king of the witches. Aye, Protestants dressed like the Devil himsel' in their black clothes. Ev'n the Queen's brother Earl of Moray is always seen tae be wearing black.   Compare him tae Lord Seton in his bright scarlet outfits encrusted with golden thistles.   Would ye care for a pie, Joseph?'

Joe shook his head as they passed through the Netherbow Port.

'Nae matter, ye can have a dish of roasted doves when ye return tae the Palace, they're slaughtering most of the doves in the dovecote taeday.'

Sir James Mossman suddenly waved down to them from an open shutter above his luckenbooths. Nicola waved back, but seemed too fatigued to perform any tomfoolery that morning.

'So much for artistic talent, Nicola, you couldn't even manage a cartwheel. You've become boring as a fool,' Joe sneered cruelly.

'Nae sae lang ago Hog's Back Ridge would have been inundated with Abbots of Unreason and Queens of the May...but now, with these Reformers all the fun ha' gone frae this burgh,' Cockburn spluttered out the contents of her mouth.

'It is November, Cockburn, the Abbot of Unreason comes in May!'

'Used tae come in May, used tae.   Nae any mair, nae any mair.'

It was just as they reached the top of Towris Close when they heard the commotion.

'Bairn droonin'!' the numerous voices cried. The three of them hurried down the close towards the Nor Loch. Joe began to run through the excrement and rubbish that filled the stench ridden narrow path. Ma Ragg put her head out of one of the doors.

'Wha's all the...?' But no one answered, as Cockburn had now taken the lead.

Down by the bottom of the close overlooking Nor Loch a crowd had gathered. It resembled a poor man's seaside. Women mending fishing nets, upturned boats, buckets of eels and mangy looking fish filled the muddy bank. Fish, there was so much fish in the city, salmon, cod even porpoise if they could catch it. His father had taken him fishing as a boy; he'd vowed to do the same with his own children. In Paris he'd seen an infant who looked the spit of Chloe. The car belonging to the parents of the toddler was packed with fishing gear. They'd sold the car to one of Joe's contacts, a white Fiat Uno. His associate hadn't been overly impressed with the purchase, particularly as it smelt of fish, but he wouldn't need to keep it for long.

Joe now focused on the far side of the loch, marshland leading out towards fields sparsely scattered with buildings and cottages leading towards Leith, the harbour where Marie, the Queen of the Scots had docked when she first arrived in Scotland. Why she ever came here Joe could not imagine. Having to sacrifice her beloved France and its vastly superior culture and climate for this uncivilised pollution. A distant speck caught his eye, a ship sailing into the horizon. Obviously Nan's cottage wasn't so far from the sea, seeing that Leith was also a part of Restalrig, Joe deliberated. Suddenly, his attention was caught by a small boy bobbing up and down in the filthy water of Nor Loch. Not far from the child was the priest Wolfart Bruce, he was standing above a woman tied to a ducking stool, his wild, ginger hair whipping around his bearded face. Onlookers were shouting down at him to help the child.

'It's Rabbie, it's wee Rabbie!' Old Ma Ragg called from behind.

Rabbie, but how could it be? He'd left him back at Restalrig. Where was Nan?

'Chloe!' Joe cried, before jumping into the ice cold water. But Joe couldn't swim through the thick muck and gunge. It was like swimming in a sewer. Excrement, urine and discarded rags full of blood, bits of wood, dead animals and even bits of human flesh floated around him. Not a good swimmer at the best of times, the water filled his mouth.

Women collecting pails of water stood motionless watching Joe swim towards the child whose head was now below the surface. Battling through the numerous objects that blocked his way Joe continued to swim, breathless, trying to lift his head. He was swallowing too much water, too much excrement. He could hear the voices in the distance calling, encouraging him, cheering him on. Not far to go now, almost there, he couldn't give up, not now. He could still see the child's head bobbing up and down beneath the surface, could almost touch him, so close now. Joe stretched his arm forward trying to reach Rabbie's hair, one more kick of his legs and he'd be there. But just as he stretched his arms to grab the child, a large object resembling a kettle drum banged onto his own head. Crash! Smash! Crash! Joe lost consciousness.

He woke up in Nan's old bed at Ma Ragg's. Voices were coming from the adjoining room. From what he overheard from Cockburn's conversation with Ma Ragg the priest Wolfart Bruce saved Rabbie.

'But he didnae save oor Joseph...nae, he would'na save oor Joseph.'

'Now dinnae go upsetting yersel', Ma Ragg, Joseph is fine. Lucky for him that Jacques de Soulis was there, he's a guid swimmer.'

'If he'd been a woman they'd have said that he was a witch.' Joe recognised the voice as belonging to Nan. Yet, he still couldn't understand why either she or Rabbie were in the city.

Joe fell asleep, but was roused again when someone rapped against the wooden shutters of the window above his bed.

'It's only me, Cockburn...Nicola!'

Joe listened as Cockburn hurried to the door and let the girl into the room. He heard her ask after him and the child, then joined the others around the fire.

Nothing caused Joe to take an interest in their conversation, that was until Nicola suddenly said, 'I don't trust one of the Queen's ladies, Cockburn, I just don't trust her.'

'Be careful who ye confide in aboot that, Nicola, dinnae e'en tell the Queen, she would'na thank ye for that information.'

'I know I can trust the three of you here, I would trust you all with my life,' the fool confessed. 'And I know without you speaking, that you all feel the same as I do, the Queen is in danger from those she trusts most. The very one she shared her bed with.'

Joe didn't know to whom she referred; there had been so many rumours of men who had shared the Queen's bed.

'Tae many Maries here for ma likin',' he suddenly heard old Ma Ragg interject, her voice hoarse. 'I will tell ye this for nought, I ken who ye dinnae trust, Nicola, ye dinnae trust that Marie Fleming.' Cockburn glanced nervously towards Nicola, silently instructing her to make no comment.

'Her ain mother wa' a bastard of King James IV,' old Ma Ragg continued, unaware of the danger of speaking so liberally. 'And ye ken how she wa' made the Queen's governess but ended up shagging King Henry II at the French court? Bad blood, mark ma words, aye bad blood. Open their legs as swift as their mooths that family.'

Their gossip quickly turned to other subjects, mainly the problems in the Queen's kitchen and the future facing the gallopene boys, the children who were used to turn the spits in the Palace kitchens. From what he overheard Cockburn say, it seemed likely the boys would soon be replaced by dachshunds that would be turning the spits in their stead.

As Joe visualised the dogs running in a wheel to turn the spit, possibly wearing aprons and a chef's hat, he began to think about his own wheel he seemed to be running on. He was like a hamster, around and around but getting nowhere. He still hadn't completed his mission, although one problem had appeared to have been solved, that of a serial killer, seeing as the lion was to blame for the most recent death.

Now his mission was to find his way out of there, to solve the riddles. He had four letters now, 'S', 'O, 'R', 'S', what did they mean? 'SOSR' or 'OSRS', or were there going to be more letters to complete a longer word? Perhaps an 'E', 'Sores'. Was that the word? Or perhaps 'Orses', or maybe even 'Roses'. Suddenly Joe sat up, yes, that must be it, there was the war of the roses. This must be a clue to solving the riddle, 'Roses', it had to be the answer, didn't it? Lying back down on the smelly bed, he tried to remember some of the other riddles he'd found, but what did they have to do with roses? If only that song Nicola kept singing didn't constantly run through his head.

'Deborah was a judge...the bee of all hives...the mighty mother of Israel'.

It was some time later when Ma Ragg approached Joe's bed with a bowl of broth.

'I heard you mention Marie Fleming...can you elucidate?' he wheezed.

'I dinnae mess wi' mysel' in nae dirty way like that, laddie. Ye can play wi' yersel' if ye wish, but dinnae expect me tae.'

'What? Oh...no, no! I didn't mean...no. What I meant was could you please explain why you don't trust Marie Fleming?'

'Why, sae ye can hae me put intae the stocks or worse?' 'Oh no, no, certainly not. Surely you don't think I'd do anything to hurt you, Ma Ragg...why, Ma Ragg, you are my friend...aren't you?'

'Aye, suppose that I am, laddie, and frae wha' I hear, ye dinnae hae sae many fieres as most. Well, the mother of ma Queen's lady, Marie Fleming, ha' a bairn tae the king of France. The bastard of Hang Goolie Me.'

'I think you mean Angouleme.'

'Aye, that's wha' I said, Hang Goolie Me. Anyhow, as ye ken Marie Fleming is the grand bairn of King James IV, just the same as oor Queen Marie. And Marie Fleming is jealous. But she is the most bonny of the four...favourite of her Majesty. E'en slept in her room.' The old woman moved closer to his ear, her breath foul. But Joe no longer cared, now used to foul smells, and having been in Nor Loch himself, he didn't doubt that he smelt just as bad, if not worse.

'But Marie Fleming is now bedding that Maitland of Lethington. Her sister's a witch ken, the Countess of Atholl. Aye, mark ma words, she's plotting against oor Queen.'

'What do you mean?'

'Ye must ken wha' I mean, laddie, she's plotting wi' that Marie Beaton. Writes beautiful...just like the Queen.'

'What do you mean? I mean, are you saying that she forges the Queen's signature?'

'D'ye ken it's strange how King James IV deid when his son wa' a bairn, and his faither did the same tae him? Hang Goulie Me's daughter Jeanne d'Albret is a great poet, her son Henry is now aboot 12 years lang.'

But Joe didn't have a clue what she was talking about.

179

'Ma Ragg, what do you know about a bell, book and candle?' he wheezed again, it was still difficult to breathe having swallowed half the Nor Loch.

'And can you tell me where I can find a special key to get out of here?'

'Only Master Mossman kens aboot those things, Joseph…or Nostra Larmas, but I dinnae ken he abides in the Canongate.'

'Well at least we know that there wasn't a murder.'

'Wha' do ye mean?'

'Well, the maid that they thought was murdered…It was discovered that a lion killed her. I confess, I once thought Mossman may have been the killer. Now I feel awful to have blamed him.'

'Aye, laddie, sae ye should. Sir James Mossman is the best fiere anyone could have,' the old woman sprayed her words across his broth. Toothless gums unable to control the saliva.

'So, have they killed the beast?'

'Nae, why should they kill Judah?'

'Don't know, depends if the girl's life had any worth I suppose.'

'Why, the lion didnae murder her,' Ma Ragg retorted, as if horrified by such an idea.

'I thought she was found in the lion's den?'

'Aye, but Ellie was murdered. Her neck was braked, her titties… ye dinnae want tae ken what the beast did tae her titties. Aye, and other bits.'

But Joe wasn't listening his mind stuck at the name, *'Ellie'*.

'Of course some still blether that it were the lion Judah, but I ken better. The evil wa' done on a full moon, God bless her soul.' She made the sign of the cross over her wheezing breast.'

Judah, stupid name for an animal, Joe reflected. Leo or Lenny would be more apt, even Rudyard, after 'Jungle Book', although it hadn't yet been written. It was odd for a parent to name their child *Rudyard*. On thinking about it Joe decided that the name Judah for a lion wasn't so bad after all.

'So tell me…' Joe stretched out his hand towards the old woman in an attempt to keep her by his side. 'Why…why was it that Jacques de Soulis the tailor had to save me?'

'Monsieur de Soulis is a guid man. Quilts the linings of all her Majesty's winter gowns, and creates cloaks for her as elaborate as any of her frocks. Why, only March just gone, he ordered special lace and ribbons for her frae abroad.'

'I meant why did that priest save Rabbie and not me? Why were Nan and Rabbie there? I'd left them safe at Restalrig. Why would Wolfart Bruce jump into that filthy water to save Rabbie?'

'Oh are ye an idjot or wha'? Ye ken why, laddie. Wee Rabbie's his ain son!'

Joe ate the broth after Ma Ragg had left him, muttering aloud to himself, 'Nan didn't tell me about ginger dick being the father of her kid. So much for her love for me!' Yes, he thought they'd shared everything, well, at least he'd presumed that she had.

Too weak to get up, Joe thought it was time he found the key out of there, he'd had enough of all this crap. Tipping open his purse, Joe emptied its contents onto the bed. Letters, Scriptures, pieces of parchment, two tiny books, the Bible and Nostradamus. What clues did he have?

'Nostradamus prophesised, and the true lineage isn't David's seed. Tamar was Queen of the hive and Deborah was the bee' .

Then he looked at the reference to Exodus 28:34, the command to find Elijah and a golden bell and a pomegranate. Well, as far as he knew he'd found that, hadn't he?

The letter '*R*' lay in his palm, sparkling with diamonds. *R*, rosary beads, *R* for Royal something. Then he looked at the letter '*O*' sparkling with rubies. He still had the silver bell inscribed with '*YHVH*' and the head of a green man and sign of the fish. Christ was the sign of the fish, but he wasn't green. Perhaps he was when he was crucified Joe ruminated. Sighing with frustration, he placed everything back down onto the bed and opened the tiny book of Notradamus. He re-read the passage about the images of Diana and Mercury being found in a lake. There was the Lake of Galilee, but he didn't recall his Sunday school teacher mentioning a Diana being there. Perhaps she was one of Christ's followers who was healed and just didn't get a mention. Loch was the Scot's term for lake, perhaps there was a Diana who worked down by the side of the Nor Loch.

He'd often seen women sitting on the shore mending nets, washing clothes, bathing; even digging for worms and fishing for eels. If only the name Ellie didn't spasmodically jump into his memory, if Nicola's song would just stop playing in his head.

'The book of Ruth was an afterthought, put in to cover for David's crown. Grandson, a half breed...David not the blood royal, the crown of Judah was meant for a Queen...'

What did the song mean, *'King David a half breed'*?

Chapter Seven

'But tent me, Davie, ace of hearts!
(To say aught less wad wrang the cartes,
And flatt'ry I detest)
This life has joys for you and I;
And joys that riches ne'er could buy;
And joys the very best.
There's a' the pleasures of the heart,
The lover an' the frien.' — *(Burns)*

It was snowing heavily as Joe opened the wooden shutters and looked through the grill of his window into the noisy Palace courtyard on that Saturday afternoon, the 9th March. He'd spent the night in his old bed that he'd somehow managed to retain on the ground floor of the Palace. Although unable to recall how he'd got into it, least of all what time and with whom. How dark the sky was, the winds whipping up manically around Arthur's Seat, a white mountain shrouded in mist.

The familiar roar of the lion, Judah, was echoing from the western gardens, Joe was still unable to comprehend why it was there, or how it survived in this merciless climate. Of course, that was apart from the ongoing accusations of it having mauled young Ellie to death. Perhaps she'd died not long after they'd had intercourse; it would mean that his semen would have still been inside her. It would mean that she died whilst part of him still lived in her. Of course it begged the most fundamental question, were his own potential children also killed?

The priest had taught him at Sunday school, that when a man and woman came together they were one flesh. But he'd had too many women, did he become one with them all, did Solomon become one with all his concubines?

Ellie, poor Ellie, so willing to please, what had she ever done to deserve such a savage death? *'You really will marry me, monsieur?'* her naïve words now haunted him. Yet, no one had been arrested for her murder, and the lion still lived.

The courtyard was heaving with coaches, litters and horses being tended to by the numerous servants. Packs of dogs eagerly waited by the gates, surrounded by even larger packs of humans carrying guns and swords. The noise colossal, constant blowing of horns, shouting, whistling and the incessant beating of a drum.

The snow had made a mess of the pathways, obstructed by numerous heaps of slush. One of the larger ponds was being used as a skating rink. Mademoiselle de la Zouche, the governess to the younger girls of the court was amongst those who were skating alongside her pretty charges. They were being watched over by the Countess of Atholl and Madame de Cric, Marie Beaton's mother, who applauded the girls whenever they slipped on the ice.

Yes, Joe loved court life, although somewhat disgruntled for having never been invited to one of the Queen's masques or balls for which she was renowned.

The last time Joe had been home to the cottage in Restalrig it was freezing. One small fire by the cooking range, unable to stop the draughts seeping in with the damp.

The hamlet was boring, even the animals had been slaughtered for winter. Only a few odd pilgrims appeared randomly at the shrine of St. Triduana, braving the sharp winds that howled across the snow covered meadows, whipping beyond the fields and into the distant sea.

But, Joe had little cause to complain. Most of the winter he'd spent in the Edinburgh taverns where he'd often seen Lord Henry Darnley, the Queen's husband lying in the arms of others, mainly young men of late. Although it was no secret that he'd been conducting an affair with a female of the Douglas house, and had impregnated yet another lady of his wife's court.

But, how could Joe criticise the young man? He was merely sowing his wild oats just as Joe was doing, nothing wrong with that. It was a man thing, that's what men were created for. After all, Joe told himself, ejaculation was the male's raison d'etre.

Joe threw his long cloak around his naked body and headed out of his room and over the drawbridge, wondering what the day held in store. For a while he watched Rizzio play cachepull with Darnley in the snow covered courtyard near the fountain of Diana. They appeared to be the best of friends. They weren't playing in the courts allocated for the sport; Joe presumed it was due to the weather, as he watched them hit the balls across one of the frozen ponds. Obviously they must be pretty close, if what he'd been told was correct, that Rizzio had helped arrange his marriage to the Queen. Suddenly his attention was distracted by the tall, beautiful figure of the Queen herself, Marie Stuart. She was approaching the pond, gliding towards it as a goddess with her entourage of dwarves. Joe knew by now that many royal courts had at least one resident dwarf, but it appeared that this particular court retained a whole circus of them.

Joe, naked beneath his cloak, quickly hid behind a litter that had parked between two carriages. The Queen momentarily removed her purple velvet cloak lined with ermine, in order to put down one of her small dogs that was hiding inside. Her crimson gown overlaid in gold damask was now exposed to the world, saturated with black pearls, huge as grapes. Even her earrings were drop white pearls, matching those about her neck. A rosary fell from her waist, constantly touched by gloved fingers.

Yet, the exquisite jewel embossed gown did little to hide the bulge in her stomach. Convincing? Perhaps. But Joe knew the truth.

Although he'd spent much of his time hanging around the Palace area he'd rarely seen the Queen. Either she was touring the country with her troops, or else relaxing a few miles away at Craigmillar Castle with her French servants. The place the locals called '*Petite France*', or '*Wee France.*'

'Not riding today?' he heard Darnley shout out to her, as several of the dwarves ran around the perimeter of the pond to retrieve the balls scattered on the icy ground.

'Ha ha…you'd love it if I broke my neck on the snow. Or better still our unborn child's neck. They'd call you King then!' the young Queen gave an artificial laugh, her courtiers uncertain whether it was appropriate to smile back at her.

Darnley seemed unimpressed by his wife's response, and shrugged his shoulders at Rizzio who was in the process of bowing to her. Just as she was about to walk away, Darnley shouted, 'I care about you no matter what you think!'

'In what way do you show your care?' her face serious, as if waiting for a magic word, hoping for some metamorphosis in her immature husband. But there was never to be any similarity between him and the butterflies that had invaded her garden during that previous summer.

'Well, I would suggest that you don one of your Highland mantles in this weather. You have a magnificent tartan plaid…you remember? The one lined in black taffeta.' He was cold, aloof as he shouted. Not even bothering to make the effort of moving towards her in order to speak more intimately.

'You know the plaid to which I refer, the one trimmed with gold. Although knowing you as I do, you'd rather sneak out dressed as a man and go riding, sitting just like a man.'

'Yes, you are right, Henry, I would rather go riding. But I'm forced to sit sideways on a horse wearing a gown, when I'd much rather wear hose and sit astride. But would I rather be a man than a woman? Never! Nothing is more base than to be a male!'

'Don't you let Master Knox hear you say that, your highness,' one of her entourage interjected.

'Why? Because he denies the true religion? Refuses to give the respect due to a woman?'

'You mean yourself your Majesty?'

'No, I meant the Blessed Virgin, the Holy Mother of God.'

The lion suddenly gave a loud roar distracting Joe from the object of his gaze. Turning his head towards the drawbridge, his eyes caught sight of James Mossman. Joe was jealous of Mossman, wishing that he too could infiltrate the Queen's confidences as other men of the court appeared to do.

Cockburn was his major problem. Whenever she saw him she'd demand why he wasn't home with Nan. But he wasn't her nursemaid. Anyhow, as Sir Arthur Erskine didn't know that he was the father of her unborn child, Joe felt he still had rights of passage. That being the right to invade every eligible female passage in Edinburgh and the Canongate.

But, convincing Cockburn proved a hard task, particularly when she was on his back about his supposed mission to solve the riddles. And that Saturday afternoon on the 9th March 1566, just as Mossman entered the Palace through the raised portcullis Cockburn appeared.

'Joseph, I believe ye have received mair clues. Well, at least some tae set ye on the right path,' she said, marching him back through the portcullis and into his small cell.

'Yar, well, at least I have the bell and book...what are you chewing?'

'Tobacco. Sir John Hawkins hawked it aboot England, and wha's guid enough for the English bastard is guid enough for us. But ye dinnae need tae try it, ye hae ye chew sticks.'

'Don't even need those now, and anyhow, I don't need to find the candle, I'm quite happy staying here.'

'Ye cannae stay here. Ye'll die, lad. If ye stay beyond yer time and space ye'll die. We all hae been given oor personal space, this isnae yers.'

'But we're outside time aren't we? I mean forward could be backward, yesterday might be tomorrow.'

'Stop bletherin' wi' this philopory osery. Now, where is ye candle? Bell book and candle, just bell and book is nae guid?' she sighed. 'Huh, well, I dinnae expect mair frae ye, I think I ken ye well enough now...I could give ye a peep if tha' would help.'

'A peep at what?' Joe grew excited

'A peep. Ye ken a peep wi' tabacci!'

A pack of wolves howled manically from nearby.

'Dinnae complain, Joseph, ye hae mair wolves in Restalrig than here.'

'And don't I know it. One came right up to Rabbie, I could even see the cubs hiding in the hedge.'

'Well, ye must be mair of an idjot than ev'n I ken. How did ye nae ken there were sae many wolves sae close tae ye hame?'

'I dunno, never seen a wolf before I came here. Well, only in a zoo,' he shrugged his shoulders.

'But ye were told aboot the dangers. Ye dinnae listen, tha's yer trouble, dinnae listen,' she scolded. Yes, she was right, he knew he'd placed the child in danger, but it wasn't his kid, although he'd never mentioned to Nan that he knew the father's identity. Just wished the Reformist priest was also the father of the other kid she was carrying then Joe could get away from her once and for all. Of course he'd heard the rumours, something about Wolfart Bruce having raped her, drugged her so the serving wench had said. Apparently he'd some minor claim to the Stewart crown and thought he'd help secure it with a child to the sister of the Queen. But he'd probably raped Nan as much as it could be claimed that Joe himself had raped her. Typical female, blame the man whatever.

'How can I know what I should and shouldn't do if I can barely understand what you say, you all talk in different accents, even different languages. French, Latin, English, Scots. No wonder I messed up. How am I supposed to understand when you speak the way you do. It's incomprehensible, Cockburn, you need to learn...'he stopped himself saying, '*the Queen's English*' just in time. 'You need to learn Received Pronunciation?'

'Ye should be grateful ye dinnae live in Strathclyde.'

'Why, do they birch you there for not speaking in Gaelic or German?'

'Nae, Joseph. In Strathclyde they originally spoke Welsh, and some still dae. Ye may be interested tae ken that in Edinburgh we blethered in Inglis...it was just this century we changed tae Scot.'

'So things are changing for the better, I mean how much worse could it get than 'bletherin' in English.' Must have thought it the Devil's own language knowing how you just love us English,' Joe scoffed sarcastically.

'Aye, it is the Devil's ain language, ye are right there, Joseph. But mention the Devil tae much and ye'll find yersel' tied tae the stake below the Castle and burned. Ye'd hae been better coming here afore 1563.'

'Why?'

'Because it wa' only since 1563 witchcraft become punishable by death.'

The wolves howled even louder now. Joe felt the palpitations rise in his chest.

'Aye, only since the Reformers destroyed God's holy Kirk wi' their demonic religion that we hear sae much aboot witches.'

Joe lay back on his bed allowing his cloak to slip away, exposing his naked chest.

'They e'en say that Master Knox is a witch himsel', they say that's why he condemns women tae execution as witches frae his pulpit.'

'Very Christian.'

'Aye, the Reformers are always looking for witches. Even said oor Queen wa' bewitched due tae her devotion tae her waste of space husband.'

'Is she devoted? I thought she was playing around. Well, you know.'

'Joseph! Dinnae ever let me hear ye speak like that again, nae aboot oor Queen. And ye n'er ken who is listening.' Of course she was right. Joe dropped his head feigning penitence. He'd only said it hoping for a positive response to know if he stood any chance of getting into the royal box.

'Ye must have heard that Knox said: *'Let men patiently abide and turn unto their God, and then shall He either destroy **that whore** in her whoredom, or else He shall put in the hearts of the multitudes to take the same vengeance upon her that has been tane of Jesabell and Athalia. For a greater abomination as never in the nature of any woman than is in her'*…Aye, that's wha' he said aboot ma beloved Queen.'

Joe looked at Cockburn's face, sad, yet beautiful.

'Cockburn, you know I love you,' he gave a saucy wink throwing his cloak away from his legs, exposing his pubic hairs. 'You just need to burn that awful cloak you wear and get into some sexy little farthingale number, with a bodice that lifts the tits. Bet you've got great titties, Cockburn.'

Joe gazed at her lips. Pink, wet, well formed, he could envisage them opening to accommodate his pound of flesh.

'Love, Joe, ye dinnae ken wha' the word means. Now get on yer doublet and hose as I dinnae want tae see yer bits and pieces...they are nought to brag aboot. E'en Elizabeth Tudor's bed buggers are better hung.'

'Bugs, you mean bed bugs.'

'I ken wha' I mean, lad, if I said buggers, I meant buggers.'

'How do you know, Cockburn? Eh, how do you know?'

'Ah, and would'na ye like tae ken? Anyhow, ye're mingin'.'

Cockburn left the room as Joe pulled on his hose and codpiece.

When he re-emerged onto the snow covered drawbridge he noticed that Cockburn was assisting John Morrison the elderly gardener, chasing the partridges and peacocks that had escaped the dinner table. The birds were heading into the path of the Countess of Atholl and Madame de Cric, the mother of Marie Beaton. The two women were speaking with the governess, Mademoiselle de la Zouche, about Marie Beaton who was due to marry in May, two months hence. Preparations had to be made. With the sudden onslaught of birds, the governess was also flapping. Cockburn ran frantically after one of the birds heading for the main gates. Perhaps they would eat peacock for their wedding breakfast, Joe thought cynically.

The fires burned brightly in the royal kitchen. Everywhere he looked there were pots, pans and animals, some still alive, waiting to be sacrificed. Unlike the servants' kitchen, this was filled with the best of everything. No bodies lying around the floor drunk, no dead beat knave urinating into the cauldron as they were wont to do in the servants' quarters. Here the servants were busy chopping, skinning and baking. Faces and arms covered in flour. The smell of boiling jam filled the air, summer fruits amidst winter smog.

Hares were being roasted over the flames. Joe hated hare; they stuffed it, stewed it, and then baked it in a pie, placing its head and ears on top of the pastry. He liked venison pasties, once he'd seen a pasty almost three feet in length. But, staying in the Palace was more like living in France than in Scotland. Everything was exotic, food, clothes, furniture. Even the Queen's cutlery was exquisite. Knives and goblets studied with precious jewels, plates of pure gold, goblets embossed with diamonds.

Both Master Boindreid, the master cook, and Mistress Carwood were now engaged in a heated debate with the Queen's chief lady in waiting, Mademoiselle de Pinguillon, who was overly concerned with the Queen's diet. Joe thought it quite comical that when she was sick, she'd send for her head cook, Monsieur Boindreid, rather than her physician.

'She mustn't have pickled goose eggs, she's pregnant, they'll make her vomit!' the woman ranted. 'I've told you this many times, but you, Monsieur Boindreid are too stupid to comprehend a simple instruction. You cause me mal de tête!'

'I'll give you a bad neck in a minute, not just a bad head. I'll bloody well break it for you!' the cook shouted back.

'Well, if Mademoiselle says that pickled eggs aren't suitable, then surely we can give her Majesty something else?' Mistress Carwood suggested diplomatically.

'I also suggest, Mademoiselle de Pinguillon, that you try to curb your temper.'

'Parliament's assembled taeday,' Cockburn suddenly appeared, handing Joe a plate of what looked to be kidneys and eggs.

He grimaced at the food, uncertain whether to try it, or throw it to the dogs beneath the table that sniffed annoyingly around his feet.

'Ye'll be meeting her Majesty taenight, Joseph, so I want ye tae look yer best. Ye can meet her efter she's supped. She'll want tae ken aboot Nan. Sae I hope ye've been looking efter the lassie well, and of course the wee bairn.'

Joe didn't know how to respond. Looking after Nan. He'd hardly seen her throughout the winter, except for the occasional night he'd stayed home. Not so different to Katie really, but then Katie was more demanding, expected more from him. Nan had demanded nothing.

He should be preparing for the birth of his child, or at the very least be the slightest bit excited. But, if Joe were honest, he was having too much fun to worry. He didn't even care about finding the key to release him from this time lock. Yes, he was having a great time if truth be told. If Nan blabbed, then Erskine might shoot him if he found out that he was the father. But Nan wouldn't, he'd met her type before, sacrificial. Although he still found it hard to believe that she was in any way related to the royals, let alone could claim to be a bastard princess.

Naturally, it had crossed Joe's mind on more than one occasion that she might be justified in her claim to the English and Scottish throne as much as Elizabeth I, or anyone else for that matter. The court at Holyrood all referred to Elizabeth as a bastard, but it hadn't stopped her. Queen Nan and King Consort Joseph. He could see himself in that role, dictating to the servants. The first thing he'd do would be to sack Cockburn.

On those rare days when Joe considered the implications and rewards for any husband of a person of rank, he would decide to stay home and play devoted lover and father to be. Yes, during those rare times he'd declared his undying love. After all, he'd stressed, she was his soul mate. Those frequent nights when he'd ventured into the city and stayed away, sometimes for days on end, he'd return to Restalrig remorseful. How he'd cry tearfully into Nan's loving arms about the starving family he'd helped. On another occasion when he'd been absent for nearly a week, missing so long that even Nicola was about to ask two soldiers to start a search, he'd returned truly penitent. Weeping how he'd stopped the hanging of an innocent child down in the Grassmarket.

How Nan had loved him that night for his brave heroics. As a reward she'd performed all the little oral tricks he enjoyed. Yes, it was sexually gratifying to be thought of as a hero.

'There's still the fuss aboot last Thursday,' Cockburn interrupted Joe's reflections, as she removed the untouched plate of kidneys and eggs from the table.

'Thursday, when her Majesty went tae the Tolbooth for the election of the Lords of the Articles…she looked sae bonny.'

Joe didn't know what she was talking about.

'She wore a silver head dress,' Mistress Carwood expounded, entering with some dirty crockery that the maid had overlooked.

'And the Earl of Bothwell carried the sceptre, Huntly the crown and Crawford the sword,' the voice belonged to Mingo.

'Of course her Majesty put Parliament under pressure to draw up a Bill of Attainder against her brother, the Earl of Moray. I'm told that the Bill will be passed next Tuesday the 12th…but I'm worried.'

'Of course ye are worried, Mingo, we are all worried!' Cockburn snapped agitated, as she poured out some wine for the valet de chambre.

'There are sae many rumours…tae many, of wha' will happen. I fear ma Queen will be murdered afore then.'

'Don't be ridiculous, Cockburn, they wouldn't dare. Anyhow we have extra guards on duty, so you worry for nothing,' Mingo tried to reassure her.

'I dinnae ken…wha' wi' the threats tae her Majesty frae all those wealthy barons and Protestant lairds. Dinnae forget, she's makin' them forfeit their lands, I dinnae think they'll tak' it lightly.'

The kitchen was getting overcrowded due to the weather. The children of the lords and ladies popped their little rosy faces into the large room to gaze at the spectacle inside, their bright bonnets and fur trimmed cloaks flecked with snow.

Cockburn disappeared, leaving Joe to make his own way out from the hot, noisy kitchen. It was at the end of the drawbridge where he bumped straight into James Mossman.

'Ah, Joseph, if you have an hour or two to kill, why don't you come back to my home and have a drink. My wife and children are away. There are some friends I'd like you to meet.' Joe nodded, he quite liked James Mossman, jeweller to the Queen, goldsmith of the burgh. He was educated and as sophisticated as those from the French court, although Joe still felt more than a little guilty for having once suspected him of being the killer.

Outside the home of Sir James Mossman the money lenders and goldsmiths sat behind the long tables caked in snow; attempting to weigh piles of coins on their wet scales. Joe headed up the side steps into the building and then ascended the newel staircase. Upon entering the large drawing room he was greeted by at least a dozen

193

men, many of whom he recognised; men such as Archibald Crawford, who regularly distributed charity amongst the poor.

'Sadly Lord Seton can't join us today,' their host said, handing drinks and nibbles around to his guests, many of whom were local tradesmen. 'David Seton is the Grand Prior of Scotland, head of our Order.'

Head of our Order he'd said, what Order? Joe wondered. He was suddenly fearful that they might expect him to take a sword or gun and go and fight the cause.

'I expect you've met Marie Seton, she's one of her Majesty's ladies.'

Joe clearly recalled the occasion when he'd sketched Marie Seton once in the garden. Her face was badly marked, Joe wondered if she'd once had smallpox. Naturally, he'd not been too true to life in his artistic portrayal. Nevertheless, he'd been almost certain the Seton female was a lesbian of the first order, always fussing with the Queen's hair.

'Now, Joseph, allow me to introduce you to everyone. As you've been in this city for a while now, I think it's about time we invited you to join us. I notice that you already wear the ring on your finger.'

Joe glanced down at his hand. His eyes then focussed on the hands of those at the table. Everyone was wearing the same ring as himself, with the lion, square and compasses. After the introductions were over, their host ensured that their goblets were constantly filled with whiskey or hot, spiced mead wine. The men engaged in small talk for a while, mainly politics and the price of gold. Joe was then requested to sit in the adjoining room with parchments to read whilst the initiated would continue their ritual in private. He didn't care, he wasn't into these brotherhood bonding sessions. His father had tried to rope him into his own Lodge without success. He was quite happy with the jug of booze, chicken and nuts; but gave the parchments a miss. He preferred to spend the time gazing out of the window he'd opened, down towards the Netherbow to watch the pretty girls go by.

If there was a real killer out there, which one of those girls would be next? he wondered, watching their young faces grin up at him whenever he waved down.

It wasn't long before he was bored, now fumbling into his leather purse in order to retrieve the tiny book of Nostradamus. One page was slightly torn, probably crushed due to lack of space in his purse. Joe examined the tear, his eyes scanning the text below.

'Oui soubs terre saincte dame voix fainte, humaine flame pour divine voix luire.'
(The faint voice of a woman is heard under the holy ground. Human flame shines for the divine voice).

What woman? What holy ground? Did it refer to the chapel at the Palace or the Queen's private chapel in her chambers? Was there someone buried there? Or was this a prophecy, would they bury the Queen there? No, Joe decided, the Queen wouldn't die in Scotland, the history books had revealed that she would be beheaded in England. Perhaps the passage in the book referred to St. Triduana's lower chamber where he'd been with poor Ellie. Was Ellie the voice of the woman underground? But, there was never anything divine about her...apart from her breasts.

Frustrated, Joe put the Nostradamus book away and pulled out his miniature Bible in its place, flicking through the pages until his finger stuck on one particular page that was slightly creased.

'1 Kings 13: 28' the reference was etched in black ink.
'The lion had neither eaten the corpse nor mauled the donkey'.
Joe only knew one lion.
Perhaps old Ma Ragg was right after all.

Joe gazed through the window. His eyes focussed on the backside of a milkmaid. Her hips swung from side to side beneath the weight of her yoke and pails? Was there any point in striving for anything if life, death, eternity was already pre-ordained? Joe considered. God, mad professor or merely puppet master pulling everyone's strings? Who wrote the Bible? How could its author know what the future would hold if there was free will? Maybe someone had taken these prophesises and turned them into actualities after the event. Jesus had supposedly entered Jerusalem carrying a palm leaf riding on a donkey, because it had been prophesised that was what the Messiah would do. Which meant that any flavour of the month could have grabbed a palm branch and claimed the crown. If only he'd worked harder with his formal logic at Oxford, he'd never understood Truth Tables.

As he grinned down at a burgess, whose portrait he'd painted that previous month, he began to ask himself the question, if the lion hadn't eaten the corpse, then who had?

'Zerubbabel, Haggai, Joshua, omnipotent, omniscient, omnipresent!' he heard the voices chant from the adjoining room. James Mossman seemed to be doing most of the chanting.

'You have arrived at the crown of a vaulted chamber, into which it is necessary that you should descend. You will therefore wrench forth two of the Arch-stones. Let the candidate be lowered into the vault and attend to the writings of our Grand Master King Solomon.'

Was this vault the reference to '*under the holy ground*'? What if he'd been invited there as some sort of sacrifice, was he the candidate about to be lowered somewhere?

'If thou seekest her as silver and searchest for her as for hid treasures then shalt thou understand.'

There was a short pause; he could hear shuffling, banging and chanting, it reminded him of a witches coven.

He'd heard rumours that John Knox was a witch. Perhaps this was the time in history when he moved into the house, if he ever did. Maybe he held a coven there. Was that the reason why posterity thought of it as '*John Knox House*'?

'She is more precious than rubies. She is a tree of life,' the chanting continued. 'You will now endeavour to find the vault. Our Grand Master Moses. Removing the key-stone.'

Grand Master Moses, how Lawrence would have loved hearing that, if only he were here now. Good old Lawrie, sensible, secure, safe old Lawrie.

'What is above is below, the tree of life. She was the companion of the King, wherever the gospel is preached she will be remembered.'

Then one voice rose above the others, Joe recognised it as belonging to Gilchrist the flesher.

'We honour you, Deborah, the judge of the nation, we honour you, Tamar who brought us truth, we honour you, Scotia who brought us home. And wine is strong, a king is stronger, and women are even stronger.'

Suddenly a messenger knocked on the outer door. He heard James Mossman open it, spend several minutes whispering, and then shut it. Soon after the messenger departed Joe was invited back into the room to rejoin the other men.

'Hail Marie full of grace, blessed is the fruit of thy womb, the Beloved.' The prayer ended their ceremony, followed by a discussion about Moses. Yes, Lawrence would have been in his element, Joe thought, almost guilty that his friend hadn't been invited. Lawrence Mossman, Moses man.

Moses, why all this Moses adulation? From what he understood, Moses was a murderer with a speech impediment who had absolutely no sense of direction.

It wasn't long after they'd kissed Joe's ring and he'd been told to kiss theirs, when Joe made his excuses to leave, as Cockburn was expecting him. Passing the numerous beggars, cripples and big bosomed wenches hanging around the nearby snow covered tavern; Joe was tempted to go in rather than keep his rendezvous with Cockburn. They knew him well, he'd bedded most of the serving wenches. The sky was black, like the snow and slush as he began to hurry down Hog's Back Ridge, not wishing for a chamber pot to land on his head; it was almost 10 p.m. and time for *'gardez l'eau'*. Passing through the Netherbow Port he showed his ring to the guard, who was more interested in torturing a bear cub that he had chained to the wall. His route was better lit beyond the Port, as many of the shops and closes were illuminated by lanterns

Bellmen were out early with it being winter, lamp in one hand bell in the other, passing by the coaches and litters carrying the gentry to their evening feasts and festivities.

'Ye must gae and get changed now, ye are tae meet her Majesty!' Cockburn called into Joe's room through the window.

'Sae put on yer best. She wants ye tae paint her portrait. I'll be back for ye in thirty minutes. Oh, by the way, can ye play chess?'

Nodding at Cockburn as she hurried away, Joe peered out at the snow covered courtyard. His eyes glanced towards the royal kitchen as a group of young children ran in from the cold. How endearing the girls looked as they threw off their snow flecked cloaks revealing red and yellow taffeta dresses and scarlet stockings. Chloe would look lovely in yellow taffeta he mused, now desperate for another stick to chew.

Perhaps he should ask Cockburn for some real tobacco if it were available. Yet, somehow smoking a pipe didn't appeal anymore. No, for now he'd stick to Adam's Snake and the jug of fire water.

The crescent moon was bright. It was odd how the moon controlled the tides, he'd never quite understood that. The stars were in abundance tonight, fixed in their allotted positions within time and space, the same stars he'd seen in 20th century Knightsbridge. Everything in the universe seemed to be balanced. Yet, if just a little off balance, the earth would roller coaster out into the cosmos or else burn up. Lawrence said it was predicted that the earth would burn out, or else fall into a black hole. But he'd only said that after Joe had fallen into a black hole in the Trafalgar Square road works, after they'd been out partying and Joe hadn't seen the gap. He broke an arm, but he hadn't felt it. He was too drunk to feel anything that night when Lawrence had taken him to hospital. It seemed such a long time ago now, all such a long time ago.

The sky was black, the snow falling heavily by the time a very agitated Cockburn led him up the turnpike stairs into the Queen's banqueting hall. He thought it unusual that he didn't see any soldiers. Normally the Palace was swamped with security, particularly now that the Queen was in residence. Joe helped himself to the jugs of wine spread out amongst the fruit, nuts and flowers, whilst they waited patiently near the Queen's private chamber. Suddenly, one of the servants ran over to Cockburn, whispering into her ear. Joe noticed her turn pale, as the sounds of crashing and clanging of armour ascending the turnpike stairs.

'There's trouble brewing, I cannae risk ye staying here taenight. I must get ye oot. Come on, hurry, Joseph, hurry!' Cockburn grabbed Joe's arm pulling him behind a tapestry near the window of the north-east tower. He could hear voices belonging to the supper party in the small room leading from the Queen's bedroom. Suddenly, Joe saw Lord Darnley emerge from the top of a secret staircase hidden behind a large tapestry. The young King didn't see them as he immediately headed into the supper room.

'Come on, lad!' Cockburn whispered, opening the glass window.

How the winds roared as Joe put one trembling foot onto a narrow snow covered ledge below the window. Was this how it ended, Joe wondered, obliterated forever from life's rich tapestry? Never to reawaken, not even in Knightsbridge, never see his family again.

Perhaps there was a Platonic form of his foot stuck on an ice covered ridge somewhere in the heavenly realm frozen in time. Due to his own decadence he'd remain a prisoner in this world of shadows. Never to be liberated, his foot trapped below the window of the north tower playing out the same scene ad infinitum.

But, Joe was unable to step out; it took more courage than he had to climb down from the high window. The wind was too strong, the snow too heavy, whipping into his face, unbalancing him. There was no way he could descend; every ledge was covered in ice, no footholds, nor handholds.

'Why can't we go down the stairs, Cockburn?' he yelled to the guide who was already balancing on the outside of the tower.

'Come on, be a man!'

Be a man, what did that mean? He'd heard it said often enough, his own father had said it whenever Joe messed up, '*be a man*'. By definition he was a man, if that equated with having a penis. But society expected a man to be made of sterner stuff, a warrior, a knight, gallant yet brave. A man, the one who ravaged and raped the whore. A man, the one who sacrificed his own life in order to protect the vulnerable virgin.

There was a loud noise, it sounded like the clanging of armour, they'd find him any second if he didn't get out. Perhaps do to him what he'd heard had been done to others; tortured, beheaded, burned, or even disembowelled.

Joe's frozen hands clung onto the edge of the icy shutters as the snow beat down hard on his head blinding him. Carefully placing his other foot into a snow filled hollow, his fingers refused to release their grip from the wooden shutters. Surely if Cockburn could make the climb then so could he...couldn't he? His hands bled, torn from the ice and splintered wood; wet, frozen fingers dripping blood onto the ice.

The March wind whipped up harder, now raging, screeching across Arthur's Seat. Unable to climb back into the Palace, he could hear the screaming from inside. He could hear a man's voice, could hear Rizzio shrieking. But Joe couldn't hang on, fingers slipping as the wet snow lubricated his grip.

'Cockburn! Cockburn! I can't hold…God help…'

As he sat on the dung sodden ground, Joe thought he'd broken his foot. He had been unable to stop the cough that had commenced on his cry for help from an invisible deity. It had always had been the same, mention God and he'd cough, Katie had said it was because he was demon possessed.

'Bloody females, bloody Cockburn, should never have listened to her!' Joe seethed. Suddenly a shiver went down his spine, as if someone had just walked over his grave. Was that his tune, *'Joe Hill'*, resounding through the sky? Perhaps he'd died. Was it singing or was it a scream from the twisted black branches of the trees? How the wind howled, whistled, wailed all around him. Yet, still the song played through his head.

> *'I dreamed I saw Joe Hill last night alive as you and me.*
> *Says I, but Joe, you're ten years dead, I never died says he'.*
> The voice suddenly became louder, clearer, rising above the elements; he could feel its breath behind him, blowing into his neck, whispering into his ear.
> *'Isabelle of England, I took up arms, then ran to the land of the Scot.*
> *Led an army of women, but my name the world forgot.*
> *Scotland tortured Agnes Sampson and Marie Lamont,*
> *As witches too evil to dip in thistle'd font.'*

Lanterns were scattered across the western gardens and on top of the railings that enclosed the lion's den where Joe now found himself. Struggling onto his feet, desperate to get away from the singing, Joe realised that he'd only sprained his ankle. Thankfully there was no sign of Judah the lion. Even so, Joe knew that he'd have to get out of there with urgency. He was barely able to open his eyes, the snow thrashed down on his face. Cockburn was only a woman, she would never have made it down safely.

The maid Ellie had died there, was he about to find out the truth, that the lion had mauled her to death, ripped her breasts from her with its teeth? Would one of her nipples still be lying somewhere in the den?

Creeping past the stone lodge which housed Judah, Joe momentarily paused to see if Cockburn was lying injured nearby. The animal growled. The snow blinding, he couldn't see anything. Broken twigs and bones cracked and crackled beneath his feet, sounds reverberating, as if the darkness enhanced acoustics.

It was just as he limped past the lion's house that he tripped over, falling backwards into the stinking, putrid lion's dung.

'God! No!' he breathed, unable to accept the possible consequences of his actions. Coughing profusely, Joe reached out his hand to regain his balance. All he could feel on the icy ground were old bones, the remains of the lion's dinner. Perhaps he'd accidentally touched part of Ellie, were they her bones?

Just beyond the bones his ice cold fingers brushed against a metal object, a casket of some sort. He grabbed it in his frozen hands.

Judah growled, Joe struggled to his feet. The small box remained tightly in his grip as he limped swiftly towards the wall adjoining the north courtyard. A sudden noise, a movement came from behind. Closer, closer, louder, splish, splosh, splish louder, closer until the predator was almost upon him; the lion about to pounce. Was his death to be quick and instantaneous, or would it be of the direst kind? Would he remain conscious whilst half his body was munched and mangled; sinews torn, ripped, veins dripping blood, was he to be the living dead?

'God, help me!' But, his breath was lost in the gale.

Splish, splosh, grrr…GRRR!

Joe found himself scaling the icy wall of the enclosure. His numbed fingers tried to grip the sporadic projections in the frozen stone and splintering wood, as if attempting to climb the inside of a giant freezer. Screaming was coming from the Palace above; in the distance he could hear the townspeople shouting and guns being fired.

'Grrr,' the throaty growls vibrated in his head. He could sense the lion drawing closer and smell its breath. Joe struggled blindly, trying to get a foothold onto the ice. He couldn't feel his fingers, ripping his hands and wrists as he pressed them onto the insignificant bumps on the wall. It was when he felt a tug on his boot that Joe suddenly found himself at the top of the wall, immediately falling down into the snow covered courtyard on the other side. He was exhausted, traumatised; his eyes were red, smarting from the sharp sting of the elements and his own tears. Crying for himself, but mainly the tears were for Cockburn.

The casket had fallen from his hands, his raw fingers reached out into the frozen abyss to reclaim it. Already half buried, Joe's numbed hands snatched it back to safety, only to discover that the lock had broken.

'I dinnae ken how we'll get through the Netherbow if it's efter 10...unless ye are wearing yer ring?' It was Cockburn, running through the snow in her long cloak and hood that had transformed from black to white beneath the light of the lantern she carried.

'Oh, thank heavens!' Now tears of sorrow had turned to tears of joy. His ankle was throbbing; he was barely able to stand.

'I think I may have broken my ankle, Cockburn.'

'Nae time to blether, Joseph, just follow me!' his guide shouted, trying to make her voice heard above the raging storm. Her foggy breath highlighted by the lantern.

They made their way into the Palace forecourt just as they heard the sound of gunfire and screaming coming from the Queen's rooms. Cockburn led the way past the snow clad statue of the goddess Diana towards the Palace gates. Joe limped behind in pain trying to keep up, sobbing with relief that Cockburn was alive. As they reached the guard post there was no need to show their rings, there were no soldiers in sight. Suddenly, they heard the sound of the town's bell clanging. Cockburn grabbed a stick propped up in the corner of the guard post and handed it to Joe. It was slightly too long, but it was better than nothing, Joe decided, as he leaned on it.

On entering the Canongate, Joe found himself dodging the chamber pots being emptied onto the street from above his head. The alarm bells all over the burgh were ringing. People were coming out en masse. Men on horseback with swords and guns in hand came charging down the road towards the Palace. The gates of the closes were locked, protecting the gentry and clergy. Most of them were unwilling to participate in the battle, only prepared to play the games where they would have guaranteed control of the rules, and of the numerous pawns to sacrifice on their behalf.

Cockburn suddenly decided to change course, leading him away from the Canongate.

They could hear the pandemonium not far behind; gunfire, shouting, screaming, as if the whole of Edinburgh had taken to the streets. Was this it? Was this how it ended? Perhaps every day was a new life, re-birth, memory erasing the experiences of yesterday on a daily basis. Was the continuation of life purely based on memory? The guns and deafening blasts of gunpowder resounded behind him, as they battled their way through the raging winds. Joe suddenly recalled a quotation he'd once read, written by a Prof. Ronald Atkinson: *'Without memory we should be locked in an infinitesimal present, speechless and without thought.'*

Was this an infinitesimal present? Joe reflected, for he was indeed speechless and virtually without thought.

Neither of them spoke as they trudged across the icy fields beyond the torn, uprooted bushes and raging trees. The March wind whipping up about their heads, beating them mercilessly as they fought their way through the blizzard.

Joe had no idea in which direction they headed, barely able to see his companion.

'Cockburn!' I must rest, I must rest!'

'Okay, Joe, lad, there's a barn just over there!' her voice yelled through the wind. How she even knew where she was, let alone knew that there was a barn in the vicinity, Joe had no idea.

For a while they sheltered in the barn. They could hear the guns even from there. Joe lay down on some old straw, his body frozen, unable to feel his feet, hands or face. Sneezing now, ankle throbbing, swelling. He was in shock from his climb out of the window and fall into the lion's den, and from his climb over the wall. He was warm here in the barn, safe. Even the bats in the roof were safe.

Cockburn lit a few candles, and then closed her eyes, allowing Joe to slyly retrieve the casket from inside his cloak. The contents were barely visible beneath the candlelight, Joe poked his numbed fingers inside. The terrors of the black night howled through his aching head, along with the memory of the unforgettable screams that had resonated from the Queen's chamber.

Suddenly Joe's hand rubbed against a tiny object. Lifting it high up towards the flame of the candle, he saw that it was wrapped in gold leaf. Ensuring that Cockburn's eyes remained closed, Joe carefully removed the object from its cover.

Emeralds, magnificent tiny emeralds sparkled directly into his eyes. Green stars, glittering their magic into the cold, dismal barn. As with the previous gems, this too was shaped into a letter. The letter was '*L*'.

Now Joe had 5 letters, *O, S, S, R, L*, a book and a bell, but the only candle he had was the one now dripping hot wax down onto his frozen hands.

'We must try and get ye hame, lad.'

'I'm not going out in that!'

'And wha' aboot Nan, she's alone wi' her bairn. When ye last saw her, Joseph, did she hae enough food?'

Joe gave a guilty nod, for he hadn't seen her for the past 4 days. Nicola Ambruzzi had caught him in the arms of one of her fellow fools only that previous day. If she told Cockburn, let alone Sir Arthur Erskine then it was all over for him. But then, what with the guns, canons and snowstorm, Joe wondered if it was all over anyway.

'She'll be fine, Nan's a survivor, trust me!'

'Nae, lad, we cannae leave Nan oot there by hersel', we must try and get tae her.' Cockburn insisted, forcing open the barn door against the raging wind.

Joe couldn't even see a metre in front of him, the snow whipping against his face as they continued their journey. There were no animals or other humans in sight as they struggled through the snowstorm, tearing their way through a copse, battling through the broken, wild branches of the trees. Untamed winds, screaming insanely like a banshee, lifting his frozen feet from the snow covered heather. The winds like a poltergeist calling out to him. Ghosts from his past, phantoms lying in wait for tomorrow, never letting him go. Their bloodstained talons nailed into his palms. Joe, their living sacrifice, an eternal crucifixion.

By the early hours of the morning they arrived at the Restalrig cottage, exhausted, numb, and slightly frost bitten, only to find that the cottage had been burnt down. All that remained was the shell. Both Nan and Rabbie were gone.

Chapter Eight

'Haud to the Muse, my dainty Davie:
The warl' may play you mony a shavie;
But for the Muse, she'll never leave ye,
Thof e'er sae puir,
Na, even thof limpin' wi' the spavie
Frae door to door.' Burns

It was four days later when they were allowed back into the city. Everywhere was still white. The snow had stopped falling, the winds had quieted, the Queen had fled.

'Joseph, now that they've re-opened the Netherbow Port ye can go and look for Nan up at Towris Close, ask old Ma Ragg.'

'It's my fault, Cockburn, all my fault, I should have been with her.'

'Aye, and sae it is, lad. But we've searched the whole of Restalrig, Leith, the lochs, the sea, naeone ha' seen her, and that's got tae be guid news,' Cockburn said diplomatically. Everything was so quiet, even the winds had hushed. There was barely a soul in sight. Even the horses outside the inns along the snow covered Canongate stood peacefully, as Joe hobbled beside Cockburn toward the Netherbow. The swelling on his ankle had started to deflate, he knew it wasn't broken but it throbbed constantly.

'How can you be sure she didn't burn to death?'

'Well, Joseph, it wa' snowing. Wet. E'en the cottage walls were still standing, sae the fire could'na hae killed them. I'm just feart now that tae many secrets hae got oot, and someone oot there wants her deid.'

'Do you think it's the same nutter who's murdering all these women?'

'Nae, I would tak' a guess and think this wa' done by someone of rank. Some might see Nan as a threat.'

Joe knew only too well what she was talking about. If one of the Protestant lairds, or even the priest Wolfart Bruce knew that she was pregnant with a potential heir to the throne, what then? Bruce had threatened to get Joe. Was the fire his doing?

'Do you think the priest did it, would he kill Rabbie?'

'I would say nae, although I just heard that Fr. Adam Black, the Queen's priest wa' murdered by Henry Yair just efter Davey Rizzio was killed,' Cockburn confided. 'Ye ken the priest wa' a Catholic? A Dominican.'

'Rizzio's dead?'

'Aye, they killed him in the presence of the Queen...I've heard rumour that her enemies intended tae murder the lairds Livingston and Fleming, and Sir James Balfour. James Bothwell and Huntly appeared tae hae followed oor lead and jumped intae the lion's pit and got awa'.

'If they murdered a priest then they could easily murder a child. I know Bruce visited the cottage when he knew I was away. And I've seen that Knox character near to Towris Close, Nan's old place. Why is he always hanging about there?' Joe kicked his foot against the walls of Netherbow Port.

'And this fucking monstrosity of a port, it's an imposition on human rights keeping those inside virtual prisoners when they've done no wrong. Just for being poor! John fucking Knox, I suppose he can afford to come and go as he pleases.'

'Well, one reason ye've seen him aboot Towris Close is that it's his Kirk opposite. And ye ken there are the luckenbooths and the Council Chambers, nae forgetting the prison. Aye, and the gallows and the stocks are by the Kirk. Master Knox is partial tae torture.'

'Oh, I'm sure he is, very partial, like he is to young girls. All these ministers of this Reformed Protestant Church seem highly proficient at paedophilia,' Joe snapped, still irritated that Wolfart Bruce had slept with Nan befor he'd slept with her himself.

'All the bletherin' frae England reaches the Mercat Cross often faster than it gets tae the Palace. Knox lives opposite the Cross, nae far frae Ma Ragg. His manse is just a wee step awa'.'

'All that man seems to do is cause trouble,' Joe grumbled, suddenly noticing a few late stall holders ambling up to the port long after dawn, to set up their wares. The snow was still settled on the ground, the hooves of the donkeys and horses submerged in slush.

'There was that time Knox helped close the rift between Bothwell and Arran,' Cockburn conceded as she purchased some hot chestnuts.

'Ye must hae heard aboot Marie's brother John Stewart, and Bothwell and her uncle the Marquis of Elboeuf. Ye must hae heard that they raped Arran's mistress Alison Craik.'

Cockburn bit into a chestnut, inviting Joe to partake.

'Hold on a minute, I thought that servant in the Palace told you that all the fiasco was to do with Queen Marie and they thought that Rizzio was her lover.'

'Nae, lad, it wa' tae dae wi' greed and…well, let's just say that the accusation of adultery wa' an excuse tae cause ma Queen grief sae they could keep their treasures and land. That's why I must gae tae the Palace now tae find oot wha' happened efter we left.'

'But why wasn't it alright for her to have a lover? I mean she's the Queen…I mean look at all the half brothers and sisters she has. Her father obviously had numerous affairs, and now you've just told me about her brother and his associates raping a woman yet no one apparently cares.'

Of course Joe's interest in women had little to do with his own enlightened attitude, but more to do with the fact that he still hoped to do his duty in the royal bed.

'Joseph, ye ken aboot Eve, ye dinnae need an explanation. Anyhow, as I wa' bletherin' afore aboot John Knox, it wa' 1561 efter they'd raped Alison Craik when Knox intervened.'

'Why?'

'Bothwell had forced his way intae the hoose of Cuthbert Ramsay. It wa' his daughter in law Alison who wa' suspected of being Arran's mistress, sae they raped her.'

'No, I meant why did John Knox intervene?' Joe demanded, frustrated by Cockburn's inability to converse in a reasonable fashion.

'Because his ain family had been feudal dependents of the Earl of Bothwell's father and grandfather.'

'So all this holy man ever does is what's in his own interests? See there is no God!'

Joe spat out the phlegm from his throat. Perhaps he'd caught an infection from the night they'd escaped from the Palace. It was a wonder that he didn't have pneumonia he mused, recalling the nightmare journey through the snowstorm to Restalrig. His ankle was still throbbing like his head.

'Ye must hae caught a fever wi' a cough like that, Joseph, ye better pull yer cloak aboot ye,' Cockburn momentarily digressed. 'Ye ken it wa' four years ago when Bothwell planned tae abduct ma Queen hersel', but was exposed by Arran. Arran betrayed him because of his raping Alison that previous year. But that's men for ye. And that's wha' they think of God.'

Perhaps they'd raped Nan, Joe feared, having now turned his back on Cockburn in order to spit more phlegm onto the white ground.

'Ye, best get yersel' up tae Ma Ragg's tae find Nan and ask her for some broth. Ye dinnae want tae keep a cough like that, laddie.'

With that Cockburn headed back down the Canongate in the direction of Holyrood Palace, leaving Joe to make his own way up Hog's Back Ridge.

Joe's heavy footprints followed other slushy prints up the hill, climbing higher and higher along the snow covered path. His heart was pounding from fear of what he might find, or what he might be told. Was Rabbie alive? Was his mission to protect the child and he'd failed?

Perhaps it was the Earl of Bothwell and the Queen's own brother who were going around killing the women of the burgh, like Jack the Ripper. It was obvious that if they had found rape so easy in the past, then what was to stop them now? Was it John Stewart who'd set fire to the cottage in Restalrig because he knew that Nan had a claim to the throne? Her claim being that she was also one of the numerous illegitimate children of King James V.

The Mercat Cross was almost empty when he reached there. No '*Maiden*' with a head freshly cut from its body, no corpse hanging limp from the scaffold, no poor soul bleeding in the stocks. Perhaps they'd suddenly heard of Jesus, Joe thought cynically, now heading down Towris Close.

'Ma Ragg! Ma Ragg!'

He was crying by the time the door opened, tears streaming down his cheeks.

'Hello, laddie,' old Ma Ragg motioned for him to enter the dreary, stuffy dwelling. She didn't smile, her face drawn. Was Nan dead? Was someone dead?

'Nan's in there,' she pointed to the adjoining room where he'd seen the improvised fireplace on that first occasion he'd visited. The resident pig had long since been slaughtered and consumed.

A limp body lay on a filthy straw mattress in the corner, hidden in the shadows. The fire was out, the room freezing even though the shutters were closed. Joe opened them to let in some light and fresh air.

'Nan, Nan,' he called over tentatively, 'Nan...why isn't she answering?'

'Lost the bairn, Joe, she lost yer bairn.'

Old Ma Ragg sat Joe down beside the dead fire and gave him a dram of whiskey. He was shaking by now, his whole body as if in a fit, refusing the bowl of cold porridge she repeatedly pressured him to take.

'Ye must keep strong, when she recovers she'll need ye.'

'How did she...' Joe was unable to complete his question, the strength of the whiskey forcing him to cough again.

'She ran oot of food for Rabbie and hersel'. Wolfart Bruce the priest lives in Restalrig, sae she went tae ask him for help until ye returned. It wa' the night the storms were sae loud. I wa' feart that the banks of the Nor Loch would break and we'd all droon.'

'Restalrig, but why would Bruce be there? It's just a tiny hamlet, even the Kirk's in ruins.' Joe looked bemused, and then suddenly recalled the occasion when he'd seen the priest snooping around the Kirk when he'd been with Ellie lying on the bank of St. Triduana's well.

'Nae, lad, nae. Restalrig covers right across Leith, he's still the priest there, although he ha' nae Kirk of his ain.'

'So did he help her...is that where she's been, and this is the result?' Joe wondered if Cockburn would get him a gun, he'd happily shoot the Rasputin impersonator and have no care for the consequences.

'Nae, Joseph, if only tha' were how it wa', lad, if only. Ma bonny Nan left the wee laddie at hame and went across the fields tae Leith. I mean, ye ken wha' the storm was like on that night. Nan knocked on his door on the point of collapse,' Ma Ragg paused to blow her nose into her apron. 'Mistress Bruce, his new wife, came tae the door. Seeing her wi' big belly and the weather, but she refused her food or shelter and sent her back intae the storm.'

She wiped a tear from her haggard, weary eyes with her stained apron. Joe wondered where Nan's God had been on the day He'd mapped out her life plan.

'But when she got hame she foond the hoose on fire...she wa' losing yer bairn. But all praise tae the Holy Mother.' the old woman crossed herself superstitiously. 'Master Gilchrist the flesher happened tae be picking up the beef that had'na been slaughtered autumn last, and he heard her cries. He put her and wee Rabbie in his cart and brought her tae me. But the baby ha' deid...and I fear that the Lord wants ma sweet Nan tae.'

For a moment there was silence. It was his fault, all his fault. Joe was unable to even glance towards the young body that lay lifeless on the straw bed. *Reap what you sow*; he'd read the words in the Bible that Cockburn had given him. This was what he had sown, the fruits of his labour which amounted to lust and inhumanity. As a philosopher he'd spent years reading books on what it constituted to be human. He had the right body sure enough, but not the mind, and it would seem he possessed no soul. Maybe that's what he was, the walking dead. Never to rest, dipping in and out of inauthentic lives, never learning, stuck onto reincarnation's wheel, eternally damned.

'My baby, it was my baby, I've killed it!' Joe sobbed. Ma Ragg didn't speak, just pushed the jug of whiskey towards him.

'But I don't understand, Ma Ragg, I just don't understand,' he gasped for breath, more lucid now since the alcohol had hit his brain. 'If there was a storm then how did the fire take such hold...and why would Nan go to a man like Wolfart Bruce for help, why?'

'Why, dae ye nae ken? Dae ye nae ken, Joseph?' the old woman looked at him incredulously.

'Are you saying because he's Rabbie's father? But he raped her!' Joe cried with frustration.

'Nae, Joe, he dinnae rape her,' old Ma Ragg laughed, exposing her gummy mouth.

'Then why did Nan have his child?'

'Why do ye think, lad? Wolfart Bruce wa' Nan's husband!'

Joe's head was spinning, it was all too much to take in; nightmares, dreams, all mixed up. There was no respite, no hope. He was drowning, like the women in Nor Loch, he could feel himself drowning. Why hadn't Nan ever told him? He thought they'd shared everything, well, at least she had. But, he was wrong; they had merely shared a house, and occasionally bodies, nothing more, no trust, no love.

'So why did she get pregnant to me? Why was she having my child? I mean, if you know the kid was mine, then so must Arthur Erskine...I'm a dead man!'

'Sir Arthur dinnae ken ye were the deid bairn's father, sae ye dinnae hae tae fear, Joseph. And if ye ha' listened ye would ha' heard me say that Bruce *used* tae be her husband, nae that he still is,' she croaked cryptically.

'Why? I mean, did he divorce her...I mean, I thought Catholics couldn't divorce?'

'Because he'd conducted the ceremony himsel', it wa'nae a legal wedding,' she mumbled, pouring the contents of a jug into her cup. But nothing came out, it was empty.

'So why did I get the impression she was raped? And her constantly singing that lullaby to Rabbie all the time about the fucking gardener getting into her knickers!' he yelled.

'She wa' raped, Joe; aye, she wa' raped!' Ma Ragg sniffed.

'Was she fucking raped or not! You stup...Look, I'm sorry.' Joe apologised, having stopped yelling.

'She wa' raped aye, but then many of oor lassies are. We dinnae call it rape, it's just men having their rightful way.' She looked across at the straw bed, and gave a nod of her head, as if she understood the ways of the world.

'Of course, wi' him saying that he'd wed her meant that she could'na do much aboot it, and her bairn would hae been a bastard. Wolfart Bruce ha' powerfu' fieres, she ha' nae choice, Joseph.'

'But why did he want to rape her...and then marry her?' Joe continued his interrogation. His head throbbing, brain pulsating, about to explode.

'The only way he could hae got her tae wed him wa' if he raped her. He wanted tae wed her because she wa' the sister of the Queen. Nan ha' a claim tae the crown. E'en though it's only a wee claim wi' hersel' being a bastard, and a lass, ken. But then Bruce has an even wee'er claim.'

There were still too many questions, the main one being, why had he divorced her?

As if reading his mind old Ma Ragg banged the empty jug on the table.

'The Protestant witch John Knox said the marriage was nae real, gull and voice.'

'Null and void...invalid.'

'Aye, that's wha' I said. But he said that if Nan dinnae say a word aboot it, they'd nae make public her crime.'

'What crime?'

'Why, her crime of getting hersel' raped of course!' she retorted, incredulous at Joe's apparent stupidity. 'And in return, if she dinnae mention that there ha' been an illegal wedding performed, then Bruce would help her feed the bairn and keep her secret that she wa' the daughter of the King.'

'Why wouldn't she want anyone to know?' Joe was only half listening, his eyes fixed on the limp, lifeless body in the corner of the room.

'Her life would be in danger, it is now.   Ye ken wi' the fire at Restalrig. Aye, Edinburgh folk hae always ken that she wa' special, ye cannae keep a secret here, lad. Nae secret's safe in Scotland.' The old woman shook her head, her filthy shawl falling to the ground revealing a head partially bald.

'Of course there wa' nae need for her tae work like she did, or suffer sae,' she slowly bent down to the floor to retrieve her shawl.

'Sir Arthur Erskine would hae gi'en her anything she wanted… but that's oor Nan for ye…tae proud.'

'But why didn't she tell me she had no food…why didn't she ask me?'

'Because ye were nae there, lad, ye were wi' ye whores in toon!' Ma Ragg accused.

'Is that who she was with the day Rabbie fell into the loch…with that ginger haired bastard?'

'Aye. Bruce turned up just efter ye left her, demanding she must go wi' him intae the toon tae get Rabbie some new clothes, as some of his Protestant fieres ha' noticed the wee boy's rags.' Rags, Rabbie wasn't in rags or else he'd have noticed. Hadn't he noticed?

'It would'na surprise me if he ha' a hand in the murder of wee Davey Rizzio,' the old woman whispered, spraying her saliva over his cup. 'Tha's why he wanted Rabbie tae look bonny, ken, because if the Queen ha' nae bairn left in her belly then Rabbie ha' a wee chance of succession. But the priest is an idjot, Rabbie's claim is tae wee tae do him any guid.'

Joe ignored her saliva as he swigged back the dregs of whiskey. He'd learnt to share his goblet with half of the burgh's population, which was still the custom. A few extra drops of spittle would make little difference. His mind was too numb to feel anything, even the whiskey had lost its fire.

'But ye dinnae hae tae fear, Joseph, e'en Master Knox declared it nae a marriage,' Ma Ragg continued to console him. 'She is free tae marry ye if ye'll tak' her. If she lives lang enough. And dinnae fret aboot ye wee deid bairn, ye can hae mair.'

Even now in his mind he could hear Nan singing that song of hers.

'The flowers in the garden stopped growing, flowing, the day the gardener used his hoe and plucked the bud, stopped the flow, ripped the stalk and wouldn't let go, and planted his unwanted seed into her garden. And the roses and the thistles are there for the plucking, due to the gardeners raking.'

'Where's Rabbie?' his red eyes drowning in tears, searched around the room for the child who should have been like a son to him, but who he'd seen as no more than a burden.

'Wee laddie's wi' Sir James Mossman. He wanted tae tak' Nan too, but she dinnae want tae move. In tae much pain ye ken. But she ha' great and powerfu' fieres who will protect her. Fieres who are trying tae help our Queen return tae her throne.'

'So what has happened at the Palace?' Joe suddenly thought of Cockburn, and wondered why neither she nor Nicola had come to find him?

'Murdered Master Rizzio, ye ken? Murdered him right in front of the Queen. Wanted her tae drop her bairn then. Wanted her tae drop deid, and Lord Darnley would rule.'

'You mean like a puppet ruler?'

'Aye, he's a puppet, that he is. All just sae that the greedy barons can hae their pickings. Aye, nae done for God, just for mair gold for their ain purses, ken.'

'So where's the Queen, what have they done to her?'
'She's nae in the Palace, Joseph. They tried tae keep her prisoner but she escaped wi' her husband. The Earl of Bothwell led them tae safety tae his castle at Dunbar.' She sniffed back the tears, the same tears she'd spent her whole life crying, they never dried.

'David Rizzio dead? But he seemed such a pleasant little chap.' Joe recalled the small Italian. If only he'd studied history, he'd have known the outcome and could have changed the story. How the Queen would have adored Joe then, but now even sex seemed unimportant. Everything he'd once held of value now had little appeal. All that mattered was Nan and Rabbie; and the death of his child.

'Aye, Joseph, tha' he wa'. Wee Davey Rizzio wa' a guid man. Queen Marie adored him. Aye, she adored him tae mooch.'

Joe looked at the old woman with her unkempt hair and toothless mouth, yet she seemed to know so much about Palace life. But what did she mean about the Queen and Rizzio?

'Are you saying…? Well, what I think you're saying is that Rizzio was the father to the Queen's unborn child? I presume you must know about the arrangement with Nan.'

'Aye, laddie, and now both bairns are deid. But I cannae say ought aboot who the father of the Queen's bairn wa'.'

'So, could it have been the Earl of Bothwell then? Or maybe it was Darnley's after all? They should have called the Palace *Hollywood* not Holyrood.'

Nan began to rouse. The moans began softly then grew louder, she was obviously delirious, Joe hurried over. Her face was ashen; her body so thin and skeletal that he wondered if he'd been blind throughout that winter when he'd left her at home to starve whilst he went gallivanting.

'Nan, Nan…please, please forgive me…please! You must get well. I'll make it up to you…' Joe broke down and wept. His lips pressed against her limp hand.

'Ma Ragg, here's a purse full of coins, go and get some food and firewood, I have to go to the Palace to find Cockburn. Shall I get a doctor?'

'Nae, lad, Lord Erskine arranged for a barber and Nicola tae call when she first ha' her bleed…nae a thing he could dae. Aye, nae a thing he could dae tae save the poor wee mite. Ye can help me bury it though…later. Aye, call back later, we'll give it a Christian burial.'

Joe sat on the side of Nan's bed as she lay still, his mind going over and over his failings. He was unable to change past actions or intentions, unable to reverse time or memories; Joe was unable to sleep.

Suddenly, Nan moved her arms.

'Nan!'

She was burning, a fever had taken her.

'Ma Ragg!'

'I'll get some water.'

'Get the doctor!'

'By the time he gets here she'll be gone,' the old woman replied, hurrying away to get the water.

She was burning; her head was burning, the sweat running down her face.

Everything seemed to be pain and grief. Even before all this, when he was last in Paris, even when he last saw Chloe, it was all such misery.

Nan was crying out now, the hallucinations of the fever causing her to scream into the putrid air. She should have been taken to the Palace and looked after as a princess ought, Joe deliberated. Why wasn't she there lying in silk sheets instead of in Towris Close with its incessant diarrhoea dribbling down the alley?

Screams and mad ramblings issued from her mouth, then came the convulsions.

Was this how her life would end, choking to death on her own vomit; her divine reward for leading such a selfless, honourable life?

'Nan! Nan!' Joe sobbed, sponging her down with water.

'God help her!' Old Ma Ragg prayed on her knees by the bed.

It was then he smelt the flowers. The smell reminded him of roses as they wafted over the body that twitched spasmodically. Whether he'd imagined the three figures that hovered around her bed, he was uncertain. Had he dreamt that he'd heard the names, '*Sophia, James Miranda, Elsie*', being whispered into his ears? All he knew was, when the smell of flowers had gone, Nan had cooled down. The fits had ceased, and she was sleeping peacefully.

It was midday by the time Joe arrived at the Palace gates, his ankle hot and painful, but the guards wouldn't allow anyone through. Everywhere was still white, although the snow was thawing. One of the maids offered to give Cockburn a message for him. Her reply was for Joe to wait in one of the taverns on the Canongate as she would be too busy to see him for at least an hour.

Joe trudged back up the hill and entered the stuffy inn where a fire raged. As usual it was packed with clergy and the gentry. Joe purchased a chopin of ale, gazing about the smoky, wooden room where the whores promoted their wares. The plan had been that as the Queen's child had died, it would be secretly replaced by his own, due to Nan being a Catholic and daughter of King James. A daughter from the Erskine family had also been a contender, but it depended on who produced a son, if either. Now it was too late for Nan. Nothing to keep him now, just find the way out, go. Forget Nan, Rabbie...the baby.

Suddenly, his purse fell open; the tiny Bible dropped onto the reed covered floor. Eyes red from crying, Joe picked it up. It had opened on a page telling the story of Solomon where he'd murdered his brother and married Pharaoh's daughter. Someone had penned handwritten notes into the margin about the temple having the pillar of Boaz facing south, representing Judah, and the pillar of Jachin standing in the right hand corner representing Israel. Then at the very bottom of the page it read:

'Solomon was a bastard, stole his brother's crown, an adulterer of the meanest kind, son of his father. But Simon will have the answer, and wherever the gospel is preached she will be remembered.'

For the next hour Joe went through all the scriptures relating to Simon, but found it so frustrating that his mind wandered as far as the nursery rhyme, '*Simple Simon*'. Joe now considered whether the key was in the possession of one of the burgh's pie salesmen or bakers, or whether he needed to find an imbecile named '*Simon*'. The scriptures relating to Solomon were even more intriguing, as he did indeed commit the crimes listed in the handwritten notes in Joe's Bible. Yet, he was known as '*wise*'; whereas Joe, who'd committed far less crimes, was about to be heralded as a philanderer who'd left a woman and child to die alone. Worse, as the man who'd helped murder his own child by neglect.

Murderer, was he any better than the one who was currently murdering the women of the burgh? Too many philosophers had written about good guys doing nothing, which equated with encouraging the evil guys. Perhaps he was evil' Katie said so. Sometimes she'd called him heartless, other times that he should seek therapy. The nights Chloe was sick, teething or suffering from colic, where had he been? What if Katie were lying dead in her flat, no one would know. Chloe would die. Joe knew then that he had to get out of there, see Katie and sort out the mess he'd left behind. But before then, he had to sort out another mess, the one he was currently in.

'Sae how is she?' the voice belonged to Cockburn.

'Up at Ma Ragg's, really sick…what am I going to do, Cockburn?'

'Are ye asking for her sake, or for yer ain?'

'I'll take Rabbie, I'll make it up to him. I will, Cockburn, this time I'll get it right.'

Cockburn glanced across at a man entering the inn, partially hidden beneath a hooded hair cloak; it was Sir James Mossman.

'I've heard that George Douglas told Darnley that he would throw poor Rizzio off a fishing boat,' Mossman elucidated, purchasing a jug of whiskey. 'Obviously his murder was planned long ago.'

'Aye,' Cockburn replied, accepting the whiskey the serving wench poured into her cup.

'But this was a more complicated murder. Witnesses.' Mossman nodded to the wench to fill Joe's cup. 'They expected Darnley to kill the Queen, but he was too cowardly for that. He's dying of the pox at any rate. Marie is now fearful for her life. The word has got out, they think she might have lost the baby. At least no one knows that she lost it months ago.'

Cockburn and Joe followed James Mossman across the wooden room beyond a cooking range towards an open fire where a boar was being roasted. They sat down on a vacant bench. In the corner, a girl with breasts spilling out of her bodice was sitting on the lap of an opulent magistrate wearing an ermine gown. Cockburn mumbled the man's name to Mossman. Joe couldn't hear what was being said due to the musicians who were playing their instruments on the other side of the cooking range. He decided to move nearer in order to eavesdrop. He was confused that women were allowed into the tavern considering the contradictory information he'd received on laws regarding females. As to how no one questioned Cockburn being there drinking was another matter. But then, as Joe knew well, Cockburn was a law unto herself.

'The Earl of Morton planned all this with the Queen's own brother James, Earl of Moray, you mark my words.'

'Aye, ye are right, Sir James. I heard that Morton's men invaded the supper room the night they killed Rizzio. Ma Queen's ain husband Lord Darnley stopped her getting help when the whole toon were ootside in the courtyard trying tae help her. Aye, her subjects love her.'

'They came with the Lord Provost; she tried to scream to the townsfolk outside for help, or so I've been informed. But Lord Lindsay stopped her, threatened to cut her in collops if she made a move. The Douglas's' held the Palace and refused to allow her attendants to serve her.' Mossman was sweating. Tears in his large, Semitic eyes. 'Lord Semple's son guarded over Davey's chamber. Of course, when her brother Moray went to visit her she had no idea that he was involved with Morton, and was one of the conspirators. So she welcomed him back. Naturally, Maitland was also involved.'

Joe suddenly interrupted.

'Sir James, I'd like to see Rabbie, I wish to be a father to the boy, I wish to marry his mother.'

Cockburn and Mossman stared at him as he kept his own eyes firmly on his whiskey.

'I...I appreciate, Sir James, that I must first approach the Queen herself for permission, but as you appear to be one of Nan's guardians, I felt it only correct that I speak to you about it first.' Too many commitments, moral obligations, each usurping the other, only influenced by the mood of the moment. Were Katie and Chloe his priority, or Nan and Rabbie?

Cockburn picked up her goblet of whiskey and swigged it back in one hit, Mossman fidgeted slightly, then laughed.

'Well, delighted, Joseph, delighted. Here, let me give you this.' He reached inside his purse and retrieved a gold pendant and pinned it to Joe's doublet. 'You are now a son of Jacob.'

'Pardon?'

'An affiliated member of the Tribe of Israel...Jacob became Israel you see.'

Joe didn't see.

'What's that written on it?' he strained to see the markings on the pendant.

'It's Hebrew, it says, *'He came only for the lost sheep of the House of Israel.'*

'Odd, that's what Lawrence used to say.'

'I must go and get Rabbie for you,' Mossman digressed, and stood up, wrapping his cloak about his person.

Both Cockburn and Joe followed him out of the tavern, and walked the short distance to his home. It was at the very top of the house, where Joe had once gone with Nan, that he found Rabbie sitting with Nicola who was singing him a song about Salome, Anna and Judith. He knew that they must be women from the Bible, but he knew nothing about them. The ginger haired child seemed happy enough. A fire roared from the small grate, reflecting a rosy hue on Rabbie's cheeks. Joe, uncertain how to approach the child, tentatively entered the room. He need not have worried. Immediately on seeing him the toddler jumped up from the floor and ran over lifting his arms. Picking up the child Joe held him against his own chest. The tears flowed from his eyes as Rabbie hugged and kissed him.

'I'm going to be your father, Rabbie, and I promise, no one will ever hurt you again, never.'

Cockburn and James Mossman grinned at Nicola as if at least one problem had been resolved. Joe caught Cockburn smiling and wondered why she was happy for this union. After all, she'd been pressuring him to solve the clues, find the key and leave. How could he ever leave if he married Nan?

'What about the mission. I mean I can't take them with me if I leave?' he whispered to Nicola.

'Time, it's all about time, monsieur. Time is only created for you, not you for time. Time has no existence in itself. And now you are outside time...outside from within. For time is relative. And relatives are what you need all of the time.'

As usual Joe had little idea what gibberish she was talking, but now he didn't care, all that mattered was that Rabbie and Nan were safe.

'I'd better go. I promised Ma Ragg that I'd help bury...bury my...the baby. Shall I take Rabbie up to see Nan?'

'No, monsieur,' Nicola intervened, it's too cold for him. I'll give him his broth and put him to bed here, it's warmer.'

'Yes, he's safer here, Joseph. If you can, try and get Nan to come and stay here. I'll send my litter to pick her up if she's well enough to rise from her bed,' Sir James Mossman suggested.

Joe gave a nod, placing the boy down by the fire, and hurriedly left the room.

It was twilight when he emerged into the street. The political tension still wafted through the evening air. Men and women, rich and poor, were talking incessantly about the murder of Rizzio and the assault on their Queen. Soldiers, guards, tradesmen, lords, Protestants and Catholics; all armed with swords, knives and guns. Anger was bubbling in their veins, anticipating an imminent battle as they congregated in the street.

Joe had little interest in their cause; his only concern was to make amends with Nan as he ran up the slushy, snowy Hog's Back Ridge.

He was breathless by the time he got to Towris Close, his ankle was swelling again. Ma Ragg might have bandages or a poultice, he anticipated, hobbling down the garbage ridden alley. Joe was surprised to see the door of the tenement already open.

'Ma Ragg!' he called out, 'Ma Ragg, I'm back!' The room was dark, bitter cold. Joe lifted a lamp from above the lintel and lit it.

'Ma Ragg! Nan!' his heart beat fast, had something happened to Nan?

A noise came from the far side of the room; Joe held the lamp higher and walked over. The groaning came from Nan's bed.

'Nan! Nan!' he could see her lying there, her eyes shut but she was alive.

The dim light from the lamp moved about the small room until it fell upon what looked like a bundle of clothes near the unlit fire. Holding the lamp before him, Joe cautiously gave a kick against the bundle, turning it over onto its side. To his dismay, Joe now saw that what lay before him wasn't a heap of old clothes, but a woman. Her apron and skirt were pulled up over her head revealing her naked

222

lower body. Joe pulled the apron away from her face, only to discover that the poor creature lying before him was Ma Ragg. She was dead.

'What on earth's the matter, Joseph?' Sir James Mossman asked, on seeing Joe run into the room of his tenement, his eyes wild, and face as white as the snow outside.

Joe was unable to speak.

'Sit ye doon, lad?' Cockburn pulled up a stool and handed him a dram of whiskey.

'It's…Ma Ragg…she's dead!'

'What do you mean?' Mossman demanded from his rocking chair by the fire. His wife Mariota ran into the room.

'Don't worry, it's nothing, my dear. Go back to your sewing, please don't concern yourself.' The pregnant woman gave a slight curtsy to those present, closing the door behind her.

'Please, send a litter up to Nan, bring her down here!' Joe pleaded, the moment the woman had left.

Sir James rose and wrapped his cloak about him.

'Tak' yer gun, Sir James!' Cockburn prompted, pulling her hood over her own head.

Nicola pushed Joe into the vacant rocking chair and thrust Rabbie into his arms, then waited patiently while Sir James and Cockburn grabbed swords, daggers and pistols from an unlocked chest.

Wrapped in a blanket Joe sat by the fire with Rabbie fast asleep on his lap. A goblet of whiskey wavered in his hand. The child trusted him, his long, white lashes softly stroking his plump, rosy cheeks. But did he deserve this trust, Joe asked himself, this unconditional love? Did he love his own dead baby, or didn't its life have any meaning if it couldn't be seen? *'Out of sight, out of mind'* so the saying went. Yet, blind people loved their children although they never visually engaged. Love, what did he know about the philosophy of love? They'd never covered that subject at Oxford.

'I'll make it up to you, Rabbie,' he whispered, 'I'll build us a new house, a better house.'

Suddenly, he thought he heard the tune of his song, *Joe Hill'* being hummed.

Perhaps it was a gust of wind, or someone in another part of the house was singing. But the humming continued, louder and louder, closer to his ear.

'Who's there? Is anyone there?'

The noise ceased; no humming, nothing other than his overworked imagination.

Joe sank back into the chair. His eyes now fixed on the orange flames in the fire, roaring, reminding him of the lion, Judah. Why was there a lion down at the Palace? Joe now recalled his treacherous descent into the pit. Curious that they'd bothered to kill Rizzio, why didn't they just throw him out of the window and let Judah finish the job for them? Why didn't they arrange an accident, surely that was the best way to get rid of an unwanted appendage of a royal court? It was easy enough, even during a coach ride out. The carriage could be ambushed, horses drugged or even the driver. Bribe the coach driver to drive along a designated route; perhaps a gun could be fired to startle the horses, a flash of gun powder to blind the driver along a deserted track. Joe wondered if their real intention had been to kill Rizzio, or were all the rumours he'd heard true? That their plan had been to murder the Queen along with her unborn child.

Judah, odd that a Scot's lion was called Judah. *Clan of Judah,* Lawrence had said on their journey up from London. Clan of Judah, Clan of Israel, two kingdoms divided. According to Lawrence, the Assyrians had attacked the ancient Hebrews when they'd been unified, and the Clan of Israel disappeared, some exported as slaves to foreign shores. Only the Clan of Judah remained.

The moonlight filtered into the room through the window, as the burgh's alarms blasted out with the winds, announcing another murder. Even from where he sat he could hear the horses galloping up the hill towards Towris Close; and the locals inside the Netherbow Port crying for old Ma Ragg. Her tears had been unceasing since the day she was born, and now those who'd never lifted a finger to help them dry were crying their own tears in her memory.

Joe's body shivered even though the fire blazed. He was in shock, trembling, sobbing, desperate for Nan to be rescued and brought safe to him. If only he could jump one step further outside time and undo the mistakes, even a few days and his child would have lived.

Time, all was dependent on time, a mere appendage of brain's software.

'*Das Ding an sich*', Kant had attempted to distinguish between things in themselves and things as they appeared to the human brain. Was his baby a thing in itself? Did the unborn child have existence in Kant's philosophy? Or, according to Cartesian principals, did it have a soul if it were not yet capable of thought?

Time. Joe began to toy with the letters…*t, i, m, e, item, emit, mite*, was that his child the '*mite*'?

Rabbie started to move restlessly. Joe began to sing, rocking him up and down on his lap as he rocked his chair.

'It's called *The Preacher and the Slave* by my namesake. It's sung to the tune of the hymn, *Sweet By and By*. Sing along, Rabbie, if you know it yar?…

Long-haired preachers come out every night, try to tell you what's wrong and what's right. But when asked how 'bout something to eat, they will answer with voices so sweet…(Now, here's the chorus, Rabbie)…You will eat, bye and bye, in that glorious land above the sky…'

Joe sobbed as the child slept.

'Do you think my baby's in that glorious land above the sky, Rabbie? What if he gets lost on the way, will someone help him? Do you think Ellie, sweet, poor Ellie will take care of him for me? It was a son wasn't it? What do you think, Rabbie?

Work and pray, live on hay, you'll get pie in the sky when you die,' he finished the chorus, his eyes wet with tears.

Suddenly Joe felt someone behind him, a whispering, like paper rustling. But when he turned to look no one was there. The moon was full, casting its shadows over the room, highlighting Rabbie's soft cheeks. Innocence, was there such a quality? he wondered. Perhaps innocence was an illusion, just like the light of the moon, for that was also known to cause illusions. Words, what were words? The Church referred to Christ as the '*Word*'. What did they mean? What word? '*And the Word became flesh*', his priest had recited when leading the prayers at Sunday school. If Joe were to say the word '*innocent*' over Rabbie, would that then bestow on him a life long quality of innocence, would it keep him safe from sin?

Prayer was just like casting a spell. The only spell he knew was from fairytales, '*abracadabra.*'

Lawrence had told him that it came from Hebrew letters, but Joe didn't recall what it meant. Perhaps it was the Hebrew word for *innocence* he considered cynically, trying to take his mind off the alarm bells outside. The word '*amen*', that seemed to be a word common to many languages. Used like a piece of superstitious sealing wax to end a prayer. So be it. So be what? Let it be. Let what be?

He heard the whispering again, humming, someone was humming his tune. A strong smell of flowers filled the room. The noise grew louder, the humming stronger and clearer until it formed into words.

'I dreamed I saw Joe Hill last night...'

'Who are you? Make yourself known!'

'I'm Lilliard. I led the Scots at the battle of Ancrum,' a voice replied. More like a vibration inside his head, outside his brain. Deaf people heard music through vibration, perhaps he'd gone deaf. He was unable to comprehend why he wasn't frightened. Yet the apparition, if that was what it was, gave him a feeling of calm. It was not like an entity in itself, more like an appendage of himself, uncertain if her words came from his own mind.

'Killed the English commander, gave ma ain life, the bravest soldier on the battlefield they said.' No, this was an independent voice, definitely a female.

'Ancrum Moor, hae ye nae heard of it? There wa' a battle there, 'tween the English and the Scots...the Scots won, wi' me fighting for them. February 1545 it wa'. All tae do wi' King Henry VIII wanting tae unite England and Scotland by marrying his son Edward tae Marie, Queen of Scots. But, we Scots were against the marriage, sae Henry took action. *Rough Wooing* they called it, the battles where the English wasted and destroyed Scottish lands. But at the battle of Ancrum Moor we defeated them. The English army consisted of about 3,000 men, wi' German and Spanish mercenaries and about 700 *Assured Scots.*'

'What does that mean, assured of what?'

'Assured Scots were Borderers, Joseph. They'd temporarily joined the English, and wore the cross of St George on their sleeves. When the English reached the brow of the hill they discovered an army of 1,200 Scots waiting for them. There wa' aviolent battle. The two British commanders were killed, their bodies mutilated. I went tae the battle wi' ma boyfriend…he wa' killed.' The ghost began to cry, tears fell from her eyes. 'Sae I picked up a sword and killed the English…e'en when they cut off ma legs I still fought on ma stumps.'

'So are you known as an Edinburgh Knight?' he asked, thinking that Lawrence may have been right after all, that there had been at least one brave heroine on the planet.

'Why nae, I'm nae frae Edinburgh. And I think yer quest is in vain, as there were hundreds of women on the battlefields. It's just that they've never been remembered, just like the Magdalene. Nae, sir, ye'll nae find yer female Edinbugh knights, naebody remembers them.'

'So why do they remember you then? That's if they do, as I'd never heard of you. And from what the chappie said on the Lothian tour bus, nor had he.'

'The Maid of Lilliard's Grave is a square stone grave that lies off the road at Lilliard's Edge near Ancrum, in the Scottish Borders. I came from the Borders, Teviotdale.'

'Never heard of it,' Joe sneered.

'It's near Hawick, sir.'

'So you led an army? Lilliard, never heard of you. I've heard of Braveheart, William Wallace…but never heard of Lilliard.'

'That disnae surprise me. On my gravestone they wrote:

Fair Maiden Lilliard lies under this stane,
Little was her stature, but great was her fame,
Upon the English loons she laid mony thumps,
And when her legs were cutted off,
She fought upon her stumps.

Men, being cowards want tae keep lassies in chains, it makes them feel stronger. Be honest, how often ye'll see a lassie in branks or scold's bridle. Ha, in fact they were designed for lassies. Nagging wives they call lassies who dare tae use their ain minds. They say they blether tae much.'

Joe thought back to the last time he'd seen Katie, how he'd admonished her for nagging him about not seeing Chloe.

'Ye must hae seen those wi' their heids in iron cages, spikes aroond their mooths, led by chains attached tae a bridle. And where is there tae run?'

He could see her face now, finely chiselled features, small pointed nose, thin lips, high cheek bones. Was she a nymph or banshee? Where did she come from? What was her essence? What was his?

'I'm a philosopher, but I can't work out whether you exist or not. If you do, then do you exist inside or outside my brain? Are you a virtual reality or laser image? Or do you belong to some philosophical category? Rational or empirical, innate, a priori or a posteriori? I think I may have gone mad!' Joe was shaking, perhaps he was having a nervous breakdown.

'A philosopher who never thinks, that's wha' ye are. Do ye ken wha' a true philosopher would hae tae say?'

Who was the true philosopher? Joe wondered. His body was still shaking, trembling as if he had a fever. He wasn't a philosopher, he had never thought about anything much. The empiricist John Locke was known as a philosopher, how would he have summed up the apparition? Was she a primary or a secondary quality? Would Freud have viewed Joe as a schizophrenic, delved into his subconscious or called him 'Oedopus'? If this was madness and the illusion had no existence in itself, then it mattered even less. 'Cogito ergo sum' Descartes had argued. But, there was nothing in Joe's brain that convinced him that he himself had independent existence, least of all the phantoms that constantly haunted him. Was this Kant's 'thing in itself', or thing out of itself? Perhaps he was just out of his mind. But then, who could prove that at one point in time he'd ever been in his mind?

As a philosophy graduate, Joe knew he could no more diminish her existence than he could his own. For, in the black hole of philosophical speculation it was quite possible that she existed and that he did not.

'Adultery is a capital crime, but mainly for lassies.'

'Oh here we go again.'

'Nay, Joseph, nae '*we*', and ye should care aboot lassies just as they would care aboot ye if the situation wa' reversed. I mean, lad, ye've seen enough lassies ducked in the mingin' Nor Loch,' she sighed. 'Well, at least Marie Stuart built the new jail ootside St. Giles, the Devil's Kirk. Before she returned hame there wa' just a porch.'

The Devil's Kirk, was there such a place, a Church where the Devil reigned? Was there an entity raging around with horns, an embodiment of evil? He'd studied the theory of evil in his philosophy classes and got one of his best marks in his finals on a paper about the innate evil in man. He'd even used a Tarot Card of the Devil for his thesis. As for its actual existence, he'd never thought about it much. Christian theology taught that God created the Devil. A big question for philosophers as to how an omnipotent, flawless deity could produce a creature from the bowels of hell. '*Angel of light*', the Bible referred to him. Lucifer, he'd been God's favourite. If God Himself was so badly deceived and made the worst error in the history of the universe by creating His designer monster and then had no control over him, then how did He expect mere mortals to choose between good and bad?

What was God's essence? What was the Devil's? Or were they one and the same?

'Aye, even in this century pregnant lassies are just left on the cold, wct floor tae gie birth...most die.' Her voice, like a sharp gust of wind continued to blow. She held her head high. An air of defiance enveloped her as she raised her sword ready for another battle. Warriors, female warriors!

'Are you an Amazon?' His head throbbed with confusion as he thought back to Oxford and the lectures on John Stuart Mill. Joe had never thought about the name '*Stuart*' before, perhaps there was a connection with the Queen. Mill, as far as Joe could remember, had expounded on Amazonian and Spartan culture where women had advanced levels of equality compared to other cultures of the time. He gazed at the warrior standing before him. Lilliard, sounded like Lillian, but the only Lillian he'd ever known was a Yank at

Oxford. He'd once had a major argument with the fat M.A student who sported a moustache, because she'd constantly ranted on about the plight of the female. Joe had quoted to her what Mill had said, that unlike other tyrannies, the dominance of men over women is accepted voluntarily, being that women are consenting parties.

'It's your own fault, not the fault of men if you willingly play the game!' he'd jeered, before mumbling, *'go and have a shave.'* Even Lawrence had lost his feminist battle when commenting on Muslim women wearing the hijab. Joe had retorted that orthodox Jewish women were the same, covering their heads, the property of their husbands. How he'd enjoyed reminding Lawrence that even in 20th century Orthodox Judaism, a woman couldn't gain a divorce from her husband if he objected, but he could divorce her.

'Ye wanted tae prove that there were nae heroines up here in Edinburgh.' The apparition interrupted his reminiscing. 'Ye e'en made a pact wi' yer fiere tae prove yer theory.'

'Even the Bible tells you that women are inferior to men,' Joe retorted.

'The Bible, that is yer corrupted version of it, conveniently forgets Judith,' she smiled. 'Twice she struck the neck off Holofernes, twice Judith struck and cut off his heid.'

Perhaps he'd gone mad, maybe that trip to Paris just before meeting up with Lawrence had sent him over the edge.

'Am I in Scotland or Paris?'

'Well, I agree wi' ye there. Sae many French here it is difficult tae tell,' she waved the sword above his head.

'Mind where you point that, you'll hurt Rabbie!'

'Judith's maid then put the heid intae a food bag, and the people cried, 'Judith oor saviour ye are the glory of Jerusalem! Ye are the great pride, ye are oor pride! Judith, the beautiful lady of courage ye are the glory of Israel.' Her sword was even higher, flashing and crashing about in the air above her head; its glint reflecting on her face, shining like the sword. 'Ye are the pride, ye are the pride, Judith the lady of perfect grace, Judith the highest honour of God's race.'

'Never heard of a Judith in the Bible. My premise stands. Anyhow, if Judy is in the Bible then she wasn't a Scot, so my proposition stands, my...'

'Yer pendant. Wha' does it say?' she interrupted. 'Ah…it says, *He came only for the lost sheep of the Hoose of Israel.* Ye must find these sheep, Joseph Hill. He said, *look efter ma sheep, feed ma lambs, Peter ha' the keys tae their kingdom.*'

Joe glanced down at the pendent, but he didn't know what she meant. The only sheep he'd seen were on the banks of Nor Loch.

'Isobel Smith, they called her a witch in 1629. Isobel Grierson, burned at the stake by misogynist swine.'

The outline of her body was clearer now, almost authentic if he stared hard enough. She was wearing battledress, sword in hand. Yet, just one slight turn of his eye and the image would cease to exist; as if her very existence depended on his own belief, like Anthony Flew's secret gardener. Like the tree in the field, if no one was there to see it then did it exist? Perhaps she was one of those Gestalt pictures, or three dimensional puzzles? Stare hard enough and it becomes comprehensible, blink and it's gone. Yet he wasn't frightened, nothing could frighten him now after recent events.

'Of course it's nae just yer poor Queen Marie Stuart who suffers, for e'en during her reign the Reformers will strip women naked whenever they can, burn them as witches. It will get worse under Master Knox and the new man made religion. Lassies will be tortured as witches just for having an opinion. Aye, even now in the reign of Marie, Queen of Hearts, wives will hae tae carry the blame for their man's crime. Ye must hae seen them spending their days crying, '*tong, ye leid*', in front of all their fieres and neighbours. All because the wife told the truth aboot her husband.'

'I told the truth,' Joe heard another voice interrupt. It was another female apparition. The room suddenly smelt strongly of roses.

'Please allow me tae introduce ye, Joseph. This is Lady Janet Douglas Lyon, also known as the Lady of Glamis or Lady Janet Campbell.' She had no body as such, it was burnt, only a shell of ashes stood before him.

'So, are you an Edinburgh knight?' he heard himself asking. Both women laughed.

'A trumped-up charge of witchcraft was bought against me,' the woman confessed. 'I was a woman of impeccable character, beautiful they said. Falsely accused of being a witch. You see, I was the widow of John Lyon, the 6th Lord Glamis, and then I married Archibald Campbell of Skipnish.'

'She wa' the grand-daughter of Archibald Douglas, the 5th Earl of Angus ye see,' Lilliard intervened.

'Aye, but that was the cause of my execution. King James V, the father of the Queen of Hearts tried to rid Scotland of the Douglas Clan, so accused me of being a witch. I was arrested with my new husband and imprisoned in Edinburgh Castle. My darling husband escaped, but he was killed.' The apparition began to weep, comforted by Lilliard. 'I was imprisoned for so long, and the dungeon was so dark that I was almost blind. Then they burned me alive at the stake outside Edinburgh Castle. Even my little boy was condemned to death and imprisoned. But thank God they released him after the wicked King James V had died. My ghost is known as *The White Lady* you know. I've haunted Glamis Castle for hundreds of years.'

'Why?' Joe heard himself asking, wondering why he'd asked such a ridiculous question.

'Glamis is the ancestral home of the Lyon. In your time, Joseph, they are the Bowes-Lyon family. The home of the one you know as Lady Elizabeth Bowes Lyon, your own Queen's mother, her younger daughter Margaret was born there. Our Queen of Hearts, Marie, visited the Castle on 22nd August, 1562.'

Lyon, he'd never thought of the Queen Mother's maiden name before.

'But, why have you haunted it?' he persisted.

'Because I can. So that one day someone will know the truth, know how I was unjustly murdered. So that one day the people who were there in Edinburgh watching me slowly burn to death in agony, those who stood there laughing and mocking me, throwing things at me whilst I melted alive and showed no compassion, they will remember me.'

Joe didn't know what she was talking about.

'Well, if they are in the same place you are in now, of course they'd remember, I don't know what you mean.'

'They aren't in the same place, I never said they were. They are all where you are.'

Joe looked bemused.

'What? So you mean that they are people here in Edinburgh now?'

'They return in every age, some live with you in your real time, in your century. They keep returning and returning until the penalty is paid.'

'Am I one of those people who watched you burn?'

But she didn't answer.

'There were lassies ruling amongst the Celts, ye ken,' Lilliard said. 'It wa' sae common that when Celtic prisoners were taken tae Rome they thought the Emperor Claudius's wife wa' the ruler and ignored him. Of course they tried tae stop lassies from fighting in wars, and passed a law in 590 at the synod of Druim Ceat. But it didnae stop us. Aethelflaed wa' the daughter of Alfred the Great, but dinnae suppose ye've heard of her either?'

Joe shook his head. 'But I've heard of her father.'

'Well, proves ma point!'

'So, what did she do, burn more cakes?' he jeered.

'Dinnae ken aboot cakes, but she did conquer Wales and ruled the Mercians and the Danes. She wa' killed in battle in 918 at Tammorth in Staffordshire. But, Wales ha' their ain heroines. Maude de Valerie in 1100 raised an army. But she wa' captured on the battlefield. And, then of course there's Ireland wi' its heroines. Like Maire O'Ciaragain. She led the Irish Clans against the English. I dinnae expect ye've e'en heard of Graine Ni Maille. She's still alive ken.'

'Well, I've never read about her in the Times. Graine…what did you say hcr name was?'

'Graine Ni Maille. she's alive now, in the 16th century. She wa' born in 1550 and will die in 1600. But e'en the bastard English had their ain lass to boast of. Queen of the Iceni. She led a rebellion against the Romans. Boudicca sacked Colchester, St. Albans and London and massacred about 70,000 Roman soldiers and civilians. But she was finally defeated in battle by the Roman governor of Britain, Suetonius Paulinus. She took her ain life by supping poison.'

'But she wasn't an Edinburgh knight, none of the women you mentioned were Edinburgh knights! I've proved my point. Women are…'

But, when he looked up, they had gone.

The child stirred due to the noise outside, if only they'd stop that bell.

'Loud enough to wake the dead,' he grumbled aloud, then began to analyse his own statement. Did it mean that the dead were only dead due to having a hearing problem, that if they could hear they would live again?

'Your mother will be here soon, Rabbie, go back to sleep,' Joe rocked the rocking chair, gently stroking the child's auburn head.

'There's a land that is fairer than day, and by faith we can see it afar...' he began to sing the original words of the song. *'For the Father waits over the way, to prepare us a dwelling place there.* Ready, Rabbie, let's go for it...*In the sweet by and by, we shall meet on that beautiful shore. In the sweet by and by, we shall meet on that beautiful shore.'*

Suddenly, he felt someone behind him.

'Not you again, Lilliard.'

'What else is woman but a foe to friendship, an inescapable punishment, a necessary evil, a natural temptation, a desirable calamity, a domestic danger, a delectable detriment, an evil of nature, painted in fair colours.' The voice ranted, an apparition manifested slowly, shrouded in mist.

'Women are intellectually like children...she is more carnal than a man...an imperfect animal, she always deceives. Women also have weak memories. It is a natural vice in them not to be disciplined, but to follow their own impulses without any sense of what is due. She is a liar by nature!...That, Master Hill, was written in the Malleus Maleficarum.'

As the mist cleared he saw a woman dressed in a doctor's white coat carrying a pistol. But the apparition was not Lilliard, he recognised it as being Elsie Inglis.

'I live just up the road, Joseph, number 219 the King's Hie Street...although I must say I'm disappointed that there's still no statue of me in Princes Street...or anywhere else for that matter. So much for the rights of women!'

'What did you do, breed a couple of kids or bang a tambourine?'

'I studied medicine here in Edinburgh, it's still very close to my heart.'

'An Edinburgh knight?'

'Born in India.'

'Why do you carry a gun, are you going to shoot me?'

The woman smiled, then concealed the gun inside her white coat.

'So why the gun? Did your Swiss finishing school send you on one of those war game weekends?'

'Actually, I attended the very school founded by Sophia Jex Blake.'

'Who? Was she some sort of rock star…were you her groupie or something?' Joe asked sarcastically. The apparition pointed towards another figure standing in the distance.

'There she is, an amazing woman. She founded the Edinburgh School of Medicine for Women. I established a maternity hospital staffed only by women you know. I can see you're surprised. But then you never thought much of women did you, Joseph?

I even took a women's medical unit to Serbia.'

Slowly, she made her way around the back of his rocking chair, causing his spine to shiver. 'I sent fourteen medical units to serve in France. We served in Russia too, ha ha. Do you know what they said of us women out there, they said that it was no wonder England was a great county if all the women were like us.' She gave a laugh, 'of course they meant Scotland too. I was awarded the Order of the White Eagle, the highest honour awarded by the Yugoslav government, and I was the first woman ever to receive it! Decorated by the French and awarded the St. George medal by the Russians. Aye, they said it was no wonder this was a great country if all women were like us.'

'Not all like you, but not so different,' another voice interrupted.

'Oh, allow me,' Elsie smiled, 'Master Hill, it gives me great pleasure to introduce you to Marie…Marie Stopes, born in 1880.'

'An Edinburgh knight?' Joe asked, unfazed by it all.

'Born here in Edinburgh,' the apparition replied, 'No. 3 Abercrombie Place.'

Joe noticed that she was dressed in 19th century attire, but, unlike her companion, was not carrying a weapon.

'Pioneer in birth control,' Elsie Inglis announced. 'Written books you know, of course the Catholic Church hated her.'

'All because I said that birth control is not just for adults, but so that every child may be a loved child. So what's wrong with that?' the said Marie Stopes demanded. Joe tried to ignore her. If he rejected the images, the voices, then they'd cease to exist. Impressions could only be made on an object of passive impressionability. If he were blind and deaf then the apparitions would have no impact, their existence totally dependent on his own software. Just as Kant said, experiences were dependent on two forms of intuition, space and time. If he was, as he'd deduced, outside time and space then how could he be experiencing anything?

'My own child recently died, you know,' he confessed. 'I have to go and bury it…it was a loved child. But then that's a complex term begging so many questions.'

'I opened a clinic for working class women which was free,' the ghost continued to expound on her personal achievements, ignoring his grief.

'But, Marie, Master Hill doesn't believe any of the Edinburgh knights were women. Although, who can blame him, for years they never spoke of us, not at school or in political debate.'

'You are so right, Elsie. Neither you or I were ever deemed worthy of a statue. Are we really so inferior to those like William Pitt and James Craig?'

'Ah, but they are the chest beaters, cave man heroes.'

'Wife beaters more often than not…bullies, Marie. That is the achievement of the majority of males, bullying those they deem to be weaker, only because they know we are stronger. They can only see heroism as being an extension of themselves. In many instances, the male sees bravery equating with physical or mental violence.'

'Comes with their testosterone, Elsie. Perhaps they're the missing link.'

'Aye, maybe you're right. After all, they didn't hesitate erecting a statue of a dog on George IV Bridge.'

Suddenly Joe heard footsteps coming up the turnpike stairs and he turned towards the door. When he looked back, the apparitions had gone.

'Sir James has laid Nan on Mariota's bed downstairs, it was too hard a climb to bring her up here, monsieur,' Nicola explained breathlessly, as she entered the room.

'I must have dozed off.' Joe looked at his watch, he realised he'd slept for at least two hours.

'I see Rabbie's still asleep…the soldiers are out looking for Ma Ragg's killer, the barber said she'd been raped.'

'How many more, Nicola, how many more before it stops?' Joe shook his head futilely. Life, death what meaning did any of it have? There were some lives held as being of such value, that after death a whole country mourned. Others, their lives were considered meaningless, even to those who lived them.

'Will Nan be alright?'

'Oui, she's awake now, monsieur. Mistress Mossman is sponging her down, her own surgeon has taken a look at her and said she'll be fine.' Nicola took the sleeping child from his numbed arms.

'Where's the body of her son?'

'It wasn't a son, Joseph, it was a daughter.' The voice belonged to Sir James Mossman.

'Nan had the priest christen her just now…Islcbourg.'

But, Joe didn't know anyone called Islebourg, James Mossman could see that Joe was bemused.

'It's what the French call Edinburgh, Joseph. Nan wanted her baby to be remembered as a child of this city.'

'Islebourg. Yes, child of Edinburgh, daughter of the 'island borough'.'

But, what he really wanted to say was that it was his baby too. He was the father, he wanted to be free to grieve. Instead, Joe continued rocking in his chair, his tired eyes fixed on Nicola as she left the room with Rabbie in her arms.

'So, the Queen will have to confess that there is no baby. Who will be her heir?

I suppose she can have more children, but would she want Darnley as the father?'

'I have offered my own child, Joseph,' Mossman replied, pouring himself a dram of whiskey. 'Mariota is in agreement, and I'm certain that the Queen will acquiesce in these exceptional circumstances. Of course the Erskines' also have a child on the way, but it depends which of us produces a son.'

'Doesn't the child need to be a blood relative? Well, you know what I mean, Sir James.'

'Depends on what you mean by blood relative. We do have a common ancestor.'

Joe wanted to say, '*yes, Adam and Eve*', but thought better of it. This was definitely not the time to be flippant.

'Wee dram, Cockburn,' Sir James offered Cockburn as she entered the room. Her face was pale, shocked by what she'd seen.

'Aye, Sir James, a wee dram would gae doon well. All John Dee's doing.'

'I can see you don't know to whom Cockburn refers, Joseph, allow me to explain,' Mossman handed both Cockburn and Joe a goblet of whiskey each.

As Joe drank the whiskey, his host expounded on the man known as *John Dee*. Apparently, he was a magician in the English court of Queen Elizabeth. From what Joe was able to understand, Dee was some sort of Kabbalist.

'E'en calls up the deid, ken,' Cockburn interjected. 'Uses mediums…spends his life trying tae make gold. Calls himsel' a '*Christian*', ha ha.'

'There are those in the English Court who claim that he doesn't delve into black magic as such,' Mossman interposed, 'some say that he only wishes to communicate with angels.'

'But he wa' jailed for practising black magic, Sir James.'

'Aye, you are correct, Cockburn, but he was released. Although I agree that he did cast horoscopes for Mary Tudor, and some say that he is now a spy for Elizabeth.'

'A girl I once knew…Katie. She went to this Church, born again I think,' Joe mumbled, after gulping down the remainder of his whiskey. 'Born again, funny, perhaps it didn't mean what they thought it meant…Anyway, they told her she mustn't read her horoscope, it was demonic or something.'

Joe wondered if he shouldn't have mentioned Katie or horoscopes by the expression on the faces of his companions.

'What did I say?'

'Oh, just surprised that ye ken a female who can read. Oor Queen can read. Perhaps your fiere is the daughter of a duke or a baron?'

Before Joe had a chance to reply, James Mossman remarked, 'Dee had a large library of books on witchcraft and magic.'

'Nae as large as ma Queen's library I'll wager. Ma sources tell me, Sir James, that he ha' a fiere named Kelly who sees things in the crystal.'

'What things?'

'Well, ye ken, deid folk. Speaks some secret language tae these deid spirits sae I'm told. Kelly ha' nae ears, ken. Ha' them lopped off for forgery.'

'So, I expect you've already heard, Joseph,' Mossman suddenly digressed, 'her Majesty's expected back here on the 18th March, although this information is top secret you understand?'

Joe nodded; presuming that as he was now a part of the Mossman Lodge and wearing the ring and the locket, he was to be given liberal access to secret information.

'Her Majesty plans to lodge with Lord Herries in the King's Hie Gait on her return. And she'll give the Earl of Bothwell wardship of the Castle and crown demesne of Dunbar.'

'Aye, deprivin' Sir Simon Prestoun the Provost as punishment for his being sae useless during her captivity.'

'So, we must pray, Joseph, as you've never prayed before. You see, the Queen will soon issue a proclamation from Dunbar for her supporters to meet her at Haddington. She's expected to lead her army of 8,000 men back into Edinburgh on the 18th of March or thereabouts.'

'Won't people be suspicious? I mean, they think she's still pregnant.' Joe was shocked that any woman would be expected to lead an army on horseback. How would they believe that a woman who was 6 months pregnant could even get onto a horse, let alone ride into battle?

'She is the Queen, Joseph,' Sir James looked at him suspiciously. 'A Queen, pregnant or not, would be expected to lead her army.' Joe could just visualise his own Queen Elizabeth II galloping off to the Falklands, reins in one hand, handbag in the other.

'The conspirators will hae left the toon by now. Making their secret pacts tae feed their greed. Would sell their soul tae the Devil if it meant mair gold.'

'Aye you are right, Cockburn. Fawdonside, Morton...even Ruthven and Maitland have disappeared. Yet, the Queen will continue to trust that Fleming girl.'

'Ye ken she's now betrothed tae Maitland?' Cockburn turned to Joe, but there was something more important on his mind. He just needed to choose the right time to ask his question.

'I've heard that Tom Scott is tae be the first person ma Queen will execute by the Maiden, wi' him being one of Master Rizzio's murderers.'

Pouring more whiskey into each goblet, Mossman lit himself a pipe. Joe had gone off the chew sticks now, in fact he'd gone off smoking altogether. Perhaps it was lucky he'd not been offered a pipe when he'd first arrived, or he'd surely be addicted to that. He had an addictive personality, due to his Irish genetics so Katie had said.

But, addiction was selective, as he'd never been addicted to Church, faithfulness or responsibilities.

Cockburn was silent as she drank the clear coloured fire water, letting it run down her throat. Even Joe's own mouth didn't sting, it was insensitive to feeling now; he was in too much emotional pain to feel its impact.

'Wha' aboot Rizzio, Sir James?' Cockburn asked.

'I would suspect that the Queen will have poor Davey's body exhumed from its common grave and give him a proper burial in the royal chapel. I believe she has already sent an invitation to his younger brother, Joseph Rizzio, to take his place at Holyrood.'

It was now the time to ask his question, Joe could wait no longer.

'Where's the baby? Where's Islebourg now, can I see her, Sir James?' Joe implored rising from his chair.

'She's lying with her mother I imagine. I'm arranging for her to be interred. But I'm afraid the destination of her interment will be kept secret.'

'But, but can I see her, just for a moment…before you take her away?'

Noticing the tears in Joe's eyes Cockburn glanced at Mossman, who then gave a nod.

'Go down to the floor below, Nicola will take you in.'

Joe hurried out through the door and down the steep flight of steps. He could see some of the French servants from the Palace further down the newel staircase dressed in their familiar black, unlike their Scots counterparts wore crimson and yellow.

'When Jamie and Mark Herbert went to stop Monsieur Ruthvan killing Davey, Monsieur Ruthvan cried, *lay not hands on me for I will not be handled*!' Joe heard one of the French maids whisper to another maid, regarding the night no-one would ever forget.

'Then Monsieur Ruthvan pulled his dagger,' she continued, with more enthusiasm, like a child telling a ghostly tale. 'This was a signal, and his wicked accomplices came into the room from the privy staircase.'

'Oui,' another maid interrupted, 'they knocked the table over, and it was all dark as the candles had been blown out. I'm glad I wasn't there. Did you know that it was the Countess who held the only candle left alight, and they only had the flames from the fire to see by?'

'Who were the other men with Ruthven?'

'Well I think it was Andrew Kerr and Patrick Bellenden…and George Douglas of course.'

'Oui, I have heard the same, and that it was Kerr and Bellenden who pulled out pistols. And they dragged poor Davey from Queen Marie, and dragged him from the supper room right through her bed chamber and presence chamber to the head of the stairs.'

Joe's heart jumped, if he hadn't left when he did, he also could have died. Was God watching him, protecting him that night? If so, why hadn't the same God protected poor David Rizzio?

'But the most amazing thing is, that Damiot's prophecy came true concerning the bastard,' the maid continued in a whisper. 'As it was George Douglas, Morton's bastard brother who stabbed Davey first.'

Joe felt even colder, his spine shivering. He recalled that supper party in more detail, and having overheard mention of someone called *Damiot* and his predictions.

'I do know that when the people of the city heard the commotion and went to the Queen's aid, Monsieur Lindsay threatened to murder her if she went near the window. And all this so that Ruthvan could send the Protestant exiled lords the message to return home.'

'So, did they intend to kill the Queen?' Joe crept up on them. They both jumped, but upon recognition they smiled. If his memory served him correctly, he'd already bedded one of them.

'Oh, hello, monsieur. Oui, they intended to kill Queen Marie, and they were going to murder her unborn baby.'

'Oui, monsieur, I heard with my own ears her Majesty telling Lord Ruthvan that within her belly would one day be avenged. Oui, that was what she said, monsieur.'

'Was Bothwell a party to this murder?' Joe kept his voice low, wanting to prolong the time before he had to confront the real issue burning in his heart. Time, everything was dependent on time. For time past or time forward had to be preferable to time present.

'It wasn't a party, monsieur.'

'My lord doesn't mean that,' her companion intervened, 'No, monsieur, from what I've heard they had planned to murder Monsieur Bothwell, and his friend Monsieur Huntly. But they managed to escape through the back windows of the Palace and past the lion pit.'

Joe almost laughed, the pit was obviously a common escape route in times of life or death.

'I heard they also planned to murder Livingston and Fleming and hang Sir James Balfour…but all they managed was to kill poor Davey.'

'And le pretre.'

'Oui, and the priest Fr. Black.'

Suddenly Joe heard singing coming from a nearby room. As the maids made their way down the stairs Joe crept up to the door.

He recognised the voice as belonging to Nicola, she was singing to Rabbie about William Wallace. The words made no impression until he heard her sing,

'...Old man gave William a jewel, for the Jew was no Godless fool...

A ball of fire caught his eye, and then it fell down from the sky.

When it landed beside him that night, he saw it was a lady oh so bright.

She gave him a wand of Moses...The old man had been St. Andrew, our patron saint the holy Jew. And the lady was Scotia, firebrand, Scotia, the mother of Scotland.'

Joe waited until she'd finished the song and then entered the room. He couldn't see Nan, she was in an adjoining room talking to Nicola who'd gone in to lay Rabbie down, but he could see the dead baby. It was tiny, almost surreal, lying on its back in a basket on the table, partially covered by a shroud. A dog was sniffing it.

'Get off!' Joe kicked the dog in its side until it yelped and skulked away.

'Such tiny fingers,' Joe stared at the miniature form.

'My little girl, wee Islebourg...my wee flower of Scotland.' He could hear Nan weeping in the side room and Nicola comforting her. But he had no words to say, what could he say? It was too late for words.

Slowly, Joe reached out to touch the dead baby's cold, rigid fingers, his own hand brushed against the white shroud. A posy was lying beside the baby's feet, a piece of paper was pinned to the centre. Through his tears he tried to read the smudged ink.

'Zechariah 12: I shall make Jerusalem a stone too heavy for all the peoples to lift; all those who try to lift it will hurt themselves severely...strike all the horses with panic...all the peoples with blindness. But I shall keep watch over Judah.'

He heard Nicola move towards the door. These were his last moments, his last chance to be with his child for the whole of eternity. Time would never unwind; there was no outside time, only inside time, for time was the only prison in any universe. Just as Joe was about to turn away, his eyes caught sight of something glittering around the dead baby's throat. Nicola was turning the handle, about to enter through the door.

Quickly, Joe tore back the shroud from his daughter's body. The necklace sparkled against the infant's pale, blue skin, the only swaddling on offer.

Hanging from the chain was a minuscule amethyst pendent. The pendent was moulded into an initial, the letter '*Y*'.

Chapter Nine

'For gin, frae Castlehill to Netherbow,
Wad honest houses bawdy-houses grow,
The crown wad never spier the price of sin,
Nor hinder younkers to the de'il to rin.'
- Robert Fergusson

It was early evening when Joe returned from work that day, April 30th. He'd been singing outside the nearby tavern, not that it could really be called work. Relieved to leave behind the dire memories of Restalrig, he stood and gazed up at the timber fronted, west facing window of James Mossman's house. Below the window hung the armorial panel, the love lintel carved with two sets of initials: *I.M* and *M.A.*

It had been shortly after the Queen had returned to Edinburgh and reclaimed her Palace when Sir James had invited Nan, Rabbie and Joe to live there permanently.

'No choice,' Sir James had said, echoed by Sir Arthur Erskine and Lord Seton.

'Nan's secret is out, she is no long safe.'

Joe could hear the shrieks rolling down from Arthur's Seat. Like drunken banshees the cries filled the burgh. It was the eve of May Day. The ancient Celts and Saxons had celebrated May 1st as Beltane, the day of fire. Bel was the Celtic god of the sun. Arthur's Seat was ablaze with bonfires and flaming torches. Some of the celebrants intended to enter the Palace courtyard at midnight and bathe in the fountain of the goddess Diana, who was revered as Queen of the May.

Eagerly Joe climbed the newel stairs and entered the large oak room with its wooden panelling where the banquet was to be held that evening. Of course it wasn't a real banquet, not like they had at the Palace, this was just a supper.

As he washed and shaved, Joe recalled how Cockburn and Nicola had reminded him that very morning that he wasn't there to have fun, he was there to solve the riddles and get out after the mission was accomplished. But even they had to concede Joe had definitely changed. Since the death of his unborn child he'd been devoted to Nan. Joe had rarely wanted to leave her side, least of all bed any other women. Even fanny royal had lost its appeal.

'Well, Joe, you look grand!' Sir James Mossman grinned as Joe emerged from his dressing room into the main reception room that was still being decorated for that night's revelry. Joe knew he looked pretty cool in his green velvet doublet trimmed with silver, sleeves slashed front and back as was the fashion, revealing contrasting brocade lining. His breeches were also brocade with silver trim. A velveteen cap perched on his head sprouting a small silver feather. Of course he wore his gloves, as did all the other guests.

He appeared to be early, the musicians were tuning up as the French servants, clad in their black uniform, scurried about offering sweetmeats and drinks to the guests as they slowly filtered in. Joe's eyes eagerly searched for Nan, uncertain if her health was sufficient to sustain her for any prolonged social event.

She'd taken the baby's death well, and appeared to have recovered, although she often cried out in her sleep for old Ma Ragg. Even Joe missed the old lady, recalling the time she'd sat in her own urine whilst in the Netherbow stocks, and the occasion when she'd cared for him after his heroics in Nor Loch. Perhaps this was the night he would find her assailant, his eyes scrutinizing all the guests as they entered.

Joe recognised many as being from the higher ranks of Palace servants: Those such as the tailor Jacques de Soulis, Mistress Carwood, Monsieur Boindreid, Mademoiselle de la Zouche, Archibald Crawford and Sir James's younger brother John Mossman. There were also others, like Master Gilchrist he recalled from the gathering he'd attended on the day of Rizzio's murder.

The musicians were playing now, a poet recited verse beside them as the guests made their way towards the table. They were overseen by their hostess, Mariota, whose obvious pregnant state merely caused Joe even greater depression. Could one of them be the murderer?

It was as they were about to make a toast to the red deer that had been roasted and carried in on a spit when Nan entered. Suddenly, everything went quiet. The musicians stopped playing, even the dogs ceased to bark.

At first he didn't recognise her. He'd never seen her like that before. Her body, although frail, seemed to float in. She was cloaked in a crimson dress, brocade, with silver and braid trimming. Like a lantern, she glided across the overcrowded room. Her brocade underskirt was bedecked with emeralds and pearls, as were the ruffs about her wrists and neck; her sleeves fashionably slashed between emerald and jet beading. A tiara with silver and pearl trim sat upon her fiery golden-red hair, matching the pearls hanging from her ears.

'You look bonny, Nan my dear,' Sir James kissed her on the cheek.

'Oh you do. Just beautiful. A princess...as you rightly are,' his wife Mariota concurred.

'Aye, the most bonny lass to ever grace the court...other than our Queen,' one of the younger men said, falling onto one knee to kiss her hand.

Joe also wanted to kiss her, boast of her to the others as his future bride. But he remained dumb as the other young men danced around her with their compliments. He had no right to even be in the same room as her.

'Well, how do I look?' the impertinent voice belonged to Nicola.

Joe slowly raised his eyes accompanied by a rude yawn. The fool was wearing red and black velvet shoes with matching gloves and a dress of red and yellow taffeta, embroidered with gold rose leaves and jewelled buttons.

'I've seen that dress before.'

'Oui, monsieur, it belongs to the Queen…like these gloves.'

'Poor deer having to cling to your nose picking fingers.'

'Non, monsieur, these are not deerskin, they are dog skin…not as fine as those from France.'

'France! Huh, nothing good ever came from there.'

'Monsieur, you are mistaken,' Nicola laughed into his face. 'Even King Louis XI said that his royal house of France was descended from the blessed Mary Magdalene.'

'That doesn't surprise me, you're all a lot of whores.'

'She wasn't a whore, monsieur, no more than she was a virgin. She was the Holy Mother.'

'Don't be ridiculous, even I know that the Holy Mother was Mary, the Virgin Mary, who was virgin' on the insane when she got the visit from the midwife Gabriel. Anyway, you're well suited to dog skin gloves, so go off and bark elsewhere!'

'You haven't a clue about her, not a clue, monsieur,' Nicola sniggered into his ear as she walked away.

Clue, yes, he was supposed to solve the riddles, find the way out. What did Cockburn expect from him? One minute she'd say his time was limited, the next she was encouraging him to marry Nan. What if his baby had lived, was he expected to leave it behind? Yet, what argument could he have put forward that he couldn't leave his child? He'd left Chloe. He should leave, go and look for Chloe, make sure she was okay. But then, who'd take care of Nan, didn't he owe it to Nan to stay? Perhaps remaining here just wasn't an option, whoever was in control of this strange game had made the rules, not Joe. The game master was writing the riddles, and yet this wasn't a game of Cluedo. There was no Miss Scarlet or a library, in fact there were too many clues, that was the problem. Even the lion was called Judah. What with that and all the Biblical references and the verses from Nostradamus, Joe had virtually given up even trying to find the way back into the 20th century.

Suddenly the musicians broke into song, inciting many of the guests to join in, mouths full of wine, spluttering out the contents with laughter and revelry.

'One of Knox's anti Catholic songs!' someone shouted above the noise, causing Joe to be even more confused as to why they enjoyed singing an anti Catholic song.

'John Anderson my jo...'

It was as Joe reached down to stroke a dog that had hidden beneath the table, pondering on whether the gloves worn by Nicola had once been related to the said animal, that Nan made her way over.

'You...you look...unbelievable. So beaut...' But he was unable to look her in the eye; feeling guilty, too guilty to even finish the compliment. He had no right to even be near her. Had he been blind? Only now able to see the beauty of the woman who had given him her heart so long ago. He'd rather have sex with sluts and slags from the local taverns. Now sex with Nan had been put on hold.

'I have been placed beside Lord Seton,' she smiled, 'I think you are beside Mistress Carwood.' He gave a bow as she made her way towards the far side of the table in front of the musicians and poet. His heart was now beating with longing. Was this love? Was this what the poet's words were all about? Love or desire? No, desire was the passion he'd always indulged, this was different. His eyes took sly glances at Nan as she took her place beside Lord Seton.

Now the song had changed its tune to the cheers of the guests.

'A response to the words you just heard,' Jacques de Soulis whispered, as the voices sang with greater fervour, their gloved hands clapping to the tune.

'John Knox must gae, we will say guid bye, or we'll backen yer ain heid in a pye. John Knox afore ye make oor ain Queen greet, ye will die.'

The musicians began to play softly in the background once the laughter and cheering had died down. The guests were now seated around the table, arranging their napkins over their left shoulder, or arm if their ruff was in the way. A damask tablecloth, barely visible, peeped out from the small spaces between the piping hot dishes that the servants were placing onto the table. Lamb seemed to be the dish of the day, accompanied by smaller platters of swan, salted beef, salmon and dried haddock. All were bathed in spices; some soaked in claret, walnuts and butter. The centrepiece was a giant bustard surrounded by pigeons. A red deer's head perched on a side table, antlers intact, eyes wide open, a silent guest observing all. Around the same gold platter perched small quails seasoned with ginger, and a goose that had been basted and stuffed with hardboiled eggs and sage. Some of the pigeons, along with a couple of sparrows, had been rolled in a paste and boiled as dumplings. Pigeon dumplings were Cockburn's favourite, Joe recalled, wondering why she wasn't there.

Cockburn was such a strange being, she didn't fit the mould of servant. How was it that she knew so much about his supposed mission? Perhaps Cockburn would fit the bill of psychopathic killer. Yes, she'd fit perfectly into the role; unconventional, fingers in every pie. Or maybe it was Jacques de Soulis, he wouldn't be an obvious suspect. Then there was Nicola, she'd suit the part to a tee. Wouldn't that be a surprise? Joe suddenly turned towards the fool, Nicola. She'd been in the vicinity when the murders had been committed, and of course no one would have suspected the Queen's fool, least of all a woman.

The conversation around the table had now turned to the policy of fast days. But Joe was uninterested, although he knew that the Palace never cooked meat on Fridays. On those days he'd been given fish on sops, with warm melted butter oozing over them, garnished with gooseberries or grapes. His favourite food at the Palace on fast days was the fresh lobster and mussels covered in wine. Perhaps being Catholic wasn't quite so bad after all.

'Well, Sir James,' Arthur Erskine smiled at his host, 'did you get this fruit from England? As we all know that figs, apricots and quinces don't grow well here.'

Sir James Mossman laughed heartily, 'the only produce that comes from England is all pickled and preserved like their Queen.'

The guests roared with laughter, banging their goblets and tankards down on the table to show their support of his comment.

'France, the pears are from France,' Jacques de Soulis said, when the hilarity had died down.

'Frittered pears are very popular with the Queen,' Mistress Carwood said with her mouth full, as she shared her piece of beef with Joe. 'Marie of Guise brought pear and plum trees from France.'

'Oui, and our present Queen planted an unusual pear tree in Holyrood,' Monsieur Boindreid joined in, 'you must have seen it, Joseph.'

Joe hadn't heard, his eyes unable to keep away from Nan. His mind tormented over the wasted months he could have spent loving her, now even more beautiful than the Queen herself. Beauty was only skin deep so they said, but Nan's beauty was both outward and inward. Did he only adore her now because her looks were transformed? Perhaps she wasn't even transformed; maybe he'd just been blind.

'As you see the meats are covered in wild berries and dried fruit,' he could hear Monsieur Boindreid continue his exposition of culinary delights. 'Honey, now we have the best honey, Joseph. Our bees are taken to moor land in summer time, for the heather. It's the best in the world because of the clover and heather.'

'Yes, it's full and rich in nectar,' Mistress Carwood reiterated as she sucked the end of a pig's trotter.

'Swine, Mistress Carwood, needs spice, and you will see that, as with all the flesh, I have added pepper, ginger, cloves, saffron...'

'Where's the tomato sauce?' Joe goaded.

'Tomatoes belong to the deadly nightshade, Master Hill,' Mademoiselle de la Zouche retorted, incredulous at his apparent faux pas. 'Ah, but I see you are joking, you are a one for jokes. Where is it you come from?'

'Knightsbridge.'

'Ah, I knew it. Oui, you had to be a knight to have such humour.'

'A knight or a fool,' Nicola muttered within his hearing.

'Quiet, fool! Or you might be sent to Germany!'

Joe turned towards the admonisher, Mademoiselle de la Zouche.

'Why Germany?'

Nicola began to laugh, 'parce que Germans kill gypsies. They think us subhuman and have gypsy hunts.'

'You mean the same as fox hunts?'

'Mais oui, exactly the same, monsieur…shoot mother and enfants together, just like a vixen and cubs. We are considered animals in Germany.'

'This venison is delicious,' Sir Arthur changed the subject, complimenting his host. The juices from the roasted flesh dribbling down his chin.

'Depends on the stars,' Monsieur Boindreid whispered to Joe.

'You look stunning, Nan, just like Arthemide, Diane.' The compliment came from the handsome John Mossman.

His jealousy was put on hold due to the names the young man had mentioned. One of the clues from the book of Nostradamus had also mentioned those names, *'d'Arthemide: Allant murdri par incognu du Marne.'* Was that a clue to the name of the next ghost?

'May song!' John Mossman suddenly shouted.

Now it was time for Nicola to do her party piece, and as before, the guests joined in. Even Nan was singing, his beautiful Nan.

All those months he'd been blind; as blind as those pilgrims at St. Triduana's well, perhaps more so. Katie had often accused him of being blind to what was right in front of him. Yes, Katie had said a lot of things, mostly true.

Joe watched Nan's lips move to the words of the song, perfect, pink moist lips that had once, not so long ago, warmed his penis like a glove.

'The Gowans are gay my jo, the Gowans are gay. They make me wake when I should sleep the first morning of May...'

The singing stopped the moment the sweetmeats were handed around by a black servant and child. The sweet biscuits, comfits and wine were served, followed by pineapples, jellies, tarts, fruits and florentines. Only the wealthy could afford sugar.

'The Queen loves simnel cakes,' Mistress Carwood smiled. It seemed as if any joy to the Queen brought even greater joy to herself.

'See these figures, they're of Sir James Mossman and his wife Mariota.'

Joe looked to where the woman pointed at two gingerbread figurines, moulded with such precision that they looked as if they'd been carved from wood.

'Can you smell the perfume, Joseph? The food's been perfumed just as they do at the Palace,' Mistress Carwood said. 'Mmm, I can even smell the musk and ambergris. You must be able to smell the sweet confections, it's rose water, Joseph.'

But Joe wasn't listening. His attention was now fixed on the three dimensional sugar cast figures of birds and castles. One coloured green and shaped as a bearded head had been brought into the room. Although there was no space on the table or shelf for anything else.

'Sugar paste…and a brick of marmalade. Did you know that the bastard's surveyor gave her a marzipan model of St. Paul's Cathedral and her master cook gave her one in the shape of a chessboard?' Joe knew all too well the bastard to whom she referred was Queen Elizabeth.

'Don't eat the green head.'

'Why, will it speak?'

'Because it's coloured with saffron…it might kill you. It's made with verdigris.'

'What's that?' he sniggered, thinking it was probably a tomato.

'Lead and mercury beaten together with the piss of a child. But you can eat that one.' She pointed to a sculptured sugar paste figure of Diana the huntress. 'No lamb in August nor artichokes in March.'

A tiny Negro child came up and bowed, holding a silver salver in his hands containing strawberries.

'And no strawberries except in June,' Mistress Carwood said, with tongue in cheek. Joe had rarely seen a black person in the town other than a few semi clad servants being whipped up the Canongate. Perhaps Mossman had purchased him in the market. The child was followed by another black servant who carried in a lifelike marzipan model of James Mossman sitting on the back of a lion. In his right hand he held the Torah, in the left, a playing card, the Queen of Hearts.

It was whilst indulging on the strawberries that he noticed a small sugar paste block with lettering iced onto it, hiding behind the largest strawberry of the bunch.

Joe gazed at the tiny words, *'Marie F will betray...Its Gules, a chevron within a royal tressure Argent. Azure, six strawberry flowers.'*

'Strawberry flowers are from the arms of Fraser,' Nan whispered, after he'd repeated the words to her. She claimed that she couldn't see any words, although he didn't believe her, as she leaned over his shoulder peering down at the sugar paste.

'Marie F is Marie Fleming, but the Queen adores her and would never be warned.' As she bent forwards, the exquisite black pearls that hung around her throat fell against his face.

'Scottish pearls finest in Europe,' she smiled. He'd never seen her like that before, so confident. He was unable to compare her with the grubby girl he'd first met carrying the bundle of logs into the Palace.

'Although the pearls of the orient are the best.'

'One day, Nan, I'll get you those oriental pearls, you wait and see,' he smiled, moving towards her cheek. She flinched at his touch.

'Oh look, ice cream! Did you know that it was the mother of our beloved Queen who was responsible for taking ice cream to France from Italy?'

'Surely it would have melted on such a long journey.'

Nan could not help but laugh.

'Idiot, she took the recipe I mean!'

The music played as the servants refilled their goblets with wine, ale and mead which had become a favourite with Joe. The Scots referred to it as *brogat*. It was only at the very end of the meal when they drank Hippocras, a sweet, spiced, red wine. By then most were drunk, but not Joe. He'd barely touched a drink, his mind overloaded with clues and deaths, and a throbbing heart for the woman whom he adored, now untouchable.

'Joseph,' the voice belonged to James Mossman. 'I need a favour,' he whispered.

'My wife Mariota left her rosary in the room where you placed the baby. She'd gone to pray for it, and it must have dropped. It's crucial that no one finds it and asks why she was there. Could you...'

'I'll go now, Sir James.' Joe gave a respectful bow, turned once to look at Nan, then took his cloak and hurried out the door.

The street lamps were extinguished.   It was well after the night curfew as Joe hurried towards the Mercat Cross, keeping in the shadows.

'Gardez L'eau!' echoed through the night air along with the all too familiar stench.

Suddenly he heard footsteps.   Yet whenever he stopped, the footsteps behind also stopped. Joe turned around. There was no one in sight other than the odd soldier pacing up and down Hog's Back Ridge. Above him Arthur's Seat was ablaze with pagan fires, a last stand against the *monstrous regiment* of Protestant clergy. Flames of resistance, fires of unrest that would continue to burn in their hearts and those of their descendents for eternity.

Even from where he now stood, below the rugged path leading up to the Castle's portcullis, he could hear the wolves howl along with the celebrants. They were wailing and shrieking, worshipping on the braes above; the chanting absorbed into the Edinburgh winds.

It was well past midnight when Joe found himself climbing over the craggy precipice which supported Edinburgh Castle.

The guards were playing cards inside the guardhouse; the two soldiers at the gate were flirting with the pretty whores whom James Mossman had sent to distract them. It was as the girls began to kiss and fondle the soldiers that Joe slipped past and made his way into the grounds of the Castle. Higher and higher he climbed up the steep route, lit by lanterns that hung randomly overhead. Footsteps! Joe knew it was the same person who'd been following him since he'd left Mossman's tenement. The screams from Arthur's Seat were still audible, the distant fires burned bright as Joe's heart raced. Plod, plod, plod; the footsteps came closer, crunching along the rough ground behind him. Crunch, plod, crunch, plod, nearer, faster. It was too dark to see anything, was this how it would end?
Closer, they came so close, almost upon him.

Joe raced around a corner, jumping behind a large crag; plod, crunch, plod, plod. Everywhere was so dark and silent, even the wolves had ceased to howl. Not even a glimpse of the flames on Arthur's Seat lit the scene, nothing.

Plod, plod, plod, the footsteps went past and didn't falter, Joe breathed.

As the stalker headed towards one of the lanterns, Joe caught sight of him. It was the Kirk of Scotland minister, Wolfart Bruce.

The priest was disorientated, wondering where his prey had disappeared to. Before he had a chance to redirect his search a soldier approached.

'Wha' ye doing here? This is the Queen's property, ye hae nae right tae be here!'

Joe slyly peered from behind the rock to watch the priest being promptly escorted back down the steep, rugged track towards the portcullis.

Joe knew the room he needed to enter well enough, he would never forget it. Tentatively he opened the oak door into the cold, empty room. A lantern hung above the door, Joe lit it, making straight for the wall where he'd once seen the tiny baby. The rosary was lying on the floor beneath the stone that concealed the small vault, Joe stooped to retrieve it. Unable to leave immediately, he moved closer to the wall. Heart beating fast, Joe found himself removing the stone. Placing one hand inside, he was shocked to find there were now two tiny coffins. The one nearest the opening was covered in a shroud, Joe pulled it out to examine it. As he'd guessed, like its counterpart, it was embossed with an image of a red lion, Moses in the bulrushes playing with a fish. Of course it also harboured the insignia of a square and compasses and the motto '*Moses Man*'. Something fell from the cloth and Joe picked it up from the floor. It was a playing card, the Queen of Hearts.

Joe was crying now, tears streaming down his face, hands shaking as he held the card.

Without needing further examination, Joe knew that this was the coffin belonging to his own dead child, Islebourg. A baby royal, placed beside the other dead child who had also been heir to the throne of Scotland. The coffin lid was fixed down, but just as Joe was about to replace the shroud he caught a strong whiff of strawberries. Feeling about inside the vault his fingers hit upon a small package.

His eyes were blinded by tears and memories of Islebourg, Chloe, of what might have been. He was their father, protector and failure. How often he'd had those same dreams, usually on a full moon, waking in sweats dreaming of a dying baby, was this the baby? Nothing was left to chance, all events planned. Only the games master mattered, he alone held all the aces; Joe being the joker of the pack.

Unwrapping the object, he discovered it was just a candle, an ordinary white candle. The wax was partially serrated, damaged by the stem of a strawberry plant strangulating its base. Bell, book and candle; now he had them all.

Joe held the lantern closer to examine a mark on the wax. It was of a tiny lion. Above the lion, stamped into the white wax was the face of the green man.

The night watchmen were too busy kicking a drunken vagrant to notice Joe heading up the stairs into Mossman's house. The dishes and cloth had been removed from the table. Only a large, golden, seven branched candelabrum sat in the centre alongside a few scrolls of parchment.

'Ah, Joseph, please join us,' Sir James Mossman welcomed Joe back into the room. Joe gave a slight bow of his head, slipping the rosary surreptitiously into Mossman's hand.

'Nan's asleep upstairs…the fool's with her.'

Joe again gave a nod, wondering how she could sleep with the noise Nicola was making, plucking her lute strings, which echoed down through the ceiling.

'Did ye ken, Master Hill, that in the year of oor Lord 1475 the masons and wrights of Edinburgh secured a seal of cause frae the authorities,' Williame Thomsoun said. Joe recognised him as being one of the fleshers he'd met before. 'Later coopers were included, and then other trades. We ha' the first official Lodge. Aye, way back in 1491.'

'We all believe in a supreme being of course,' John lifted his jug of ale. Joe was uncertain whether he was toasting him or an invisible deity.

'We believe in the supremacy of the feminine.'

Joe groaned, then smiled cynically on noticing the total absence of any women there.

Master Gilchrist, the flesher, handed Joe one of the scrolls whilst they continued with their drinking.

'The key is there, Joseph,' Sir James called over, 'the key you're looking for, it's all in there!' His tired eyes, still sore from crying, now fixed upon the parchment laid out before him.

> *'The Lodge is hung in black, strewn with white tears. The seven-branched candlestick is burning in the East, and over the East is a large circle composed of a serpent with its tail in its mouth. In the circle, three triangles are interlaced to form a white nine-pointed star. In the centre of the star is a Hebrew YOD, and in the nine outer triangles are the letters E, A, J, J, Y, A, O, A, H, which are the initials of the nine sacred words.*
>
> *The number of the key is 7 x 7.*

The Lodge is hung with green cloth from eight white columns, and a black altar is in the East, with the coffin of Hiram. The nine-pointed star is now blood-red, and the blood which was spilled in the Temple still is in the northeast. The Lodge is hung in black, strewed with silver tears. Twenty-seven lights (divided equally between East, West, and South) are distributed. The Lodge, styled as a Court, has two apartments. The first, for the reception, is a small dark room with an altar at the centre, upon which is a dim light and three skulls. In front of the altar is a skeleton. The second apartment represents an encampment of the Twelve Tribes of Israel, near Sinai. The Tribes are arranged, with standards (of specified colour and device) clockwise from the East, as the following:

1	Judah	crimson stripes	Lion, couchant
2	Zebulon	light green	Ship
3	Simeon	yellow	Sword
4	Reuben	brilliant crimson	Man
5	Gad	bluish green	Starry field
6	Manasseh	agate	Vine
7	Ephraim	opal	Bull
8	Benjamin	violet	Wolf
9	Asher	blue	Tree
10	Dan	gold-stone	Eagle holding serpent
11	Naphtali	bluish green	Running doe
12	Issachar	greenish yellow	Ass, couchant

YHVH, Holy to the Lord! Worthy Benjaminites. The number of the key is 7x7

The Master is styled 'Mother Scotia' and wears a saffron robe'.

James Mossman gave a nod to the young John Mossman who put down the jug of whisky in his hand and made his way to the table.

'How do we hope to arrive? By the help of a ladder,' the young man began to recite. 'What is it called? Jacob's ladder. Who is the guide onto the ladder? The bee. Who is the guide up the ladder? The Egyptian. What is at the top of the ladder? The pillar... Now can I go back to my fire water, James?'

Joe was too tired to read the other manuscripts Mossman had placed before him, although his eyes caught sight of the odd phrase and the names of Hiram and Moses. There had also been a reference to a key and something about a twisted pillar. He was too tired to care much about anything, although a Latin quotation had intrigued him: 'In arc leonis verbum inveni' (*in the lion's mouth I found the word*). But one thing Joe knew for certain, there was no way that he was ever going near a lion's mouth again, even if it meant him staying in 16th century Edinburgh for eternity.

'Oh, incidentally,' John suddenly interrupted. 'You notice on that bit there,' he pointed to a section of the parchment. 'Well, the bee to which it refers is interesting. This year is the year of the Bee and the Palm Tree.' Joe had little interest in what he said, although he was intrigued by another parchment.

Gautama: *Buddha born of the virgin Maya 600 b.c.*

Dionysus: *Born of a virgin in a stable and turned water into wine.*

Quirrnus: *Born of a virgin.*

Attis: *Born of a virgin Nama 200 b.c.*

Indra: *Born of a virgin around 700 b.c.*

Adonis: *Born of a virgin Ishtar*

Krishna: *Born of a virgin Devaki 1200 b.c.*

Zoroaster   *Born of a virgin 1500 b.c.*

Mithra: *Born of a virgin in a stable on 25th December 600 b.c.*

So virgins weren't a Christian invention after all, he reflected, recalling all those boring Masses he'd been forced to attend as a child. Blessed virgins seemed a popular commodity. Except that he rarely found one in Knightsbridge.

'I presume you already know this by heart...but, just in case,' Sir James handed him another parchment whilst the other guests bid farewell to their host.

The parchment was The Declaration of Arbroath. Joe was surprised, as he didn't realise it had been written by the 16th century. Some of the parchment was torn, obviously well read. Finger marks and food stains were randomly smudged down the side margins, the occasional word erased with time.

To the most Holy Father and Lord in Christ...Given at the monastery of Arbroath in Scotland on the sixth day of the month of April in the year of grace thirteen hundred and twenty and the fifteenth year of the reign of our King aforesaid.'

Attached to the back of the declaration was another document.

Edinburgh Knights

ה   ר   ב   ד

Da-leth = 4, Beth = 2, Resh = 200, He = 5.

ר   מ   ת

Taw = 400, Mem = 40, Resh = 200.

ה   ת   ע   ק   צ

Ca-dhe = 90, Qoph =100, A-yin = 70, Taw = 400, He = 5.

'Deborah means bee,' John explained, 'D has a numerical value of 4. Tamar means Palm tree. You see, Deborah sat under a palm tree which is the connection to Tamar.' But Joe didn't see, he didn't see anything, he was blind.

'Of course Hebrew names are written from right to left, so they don't correspond with the English below, if you understand, as that's written from left to right. The final name there is Scotia, the mother of all Scots.'

But Joe neither understood nor cared.

As he sat there in the silence of the room after the others had gone home or to bed, the lyrics of Nicola's song about Deborah filled his mind.

'Not house of David, it was Saul, whom God chose as their king...

Deborah was a judge, a warrior too, the Queen of bees
Deborah led her army bold, and sat beneath her own palm tree.

...David not the blood royal, the crown of Judah was meant for a Queen.

Deborah was a judge.... The bee of all hives, honey filled well, the mighty mother of Israel.'

God by definition could not make mistakes. Did that mean that David was not God's choice? Joe opened his Bible, now searching for the book of Ruth; such a small book, such a strange story, so strange that he couldn't work out why it was in the Bible at all. What was it saying? Just that Naomi's sons had disobeyed God and married Moabite wives, which meant they were cast out of the House of Israel. When they died Ruth followed her mother in law back to her homeland and entered the tent of a stranger, offering sex in exchange for protection. That seemed to be her only achievement. Why was she mentioned? Why had the Bible revered her? His professor at university had once informed his class that much of the Bible had been radically edited, the truth removed and lies entered. But how was he to know what was truth and what were lies?

But Joe was now fixated on the story of Ruth, it just didn't fit in. Apart from the Book of Esther and the Apocryphal book of Judith, the Book of Ruth was the only other book in the Bible dedicated to a female.

Then it hit him; just suddenly hit him in the face like a thunderbolt. Of course, it was obvious. The book of Ruth had been put in as an afterthought, just like the lyrics of the song said. Deuteronomy 23:3. *'No half breed may be admitted to the assembly of YHVH, not even his descendants to the tenth generation may be admitted to the assembly of YHVH, and this is for all time'*. King David was Ruth's great grandson. Therefore, in Jewish law he had no right to even participate in their religious services, let alone be their king. That was why the book of Ruth had been stuck in. Yes, an afterthought to somehow make David's reign legitimate. If he were a half breed, it meant that not only did he have no right to enter the temple or lead the nation, but his descendents could not claim royal lineage from him. Was it Saul then who was the rightful king? Joe recalled the lyrics; the father's line wasn't of worth. In fact, Lawrence had told him that Jewish children took the religion of their mother, so it wouldn't have mattered who Saul was. No, it wasn't a king Joe needed to find, it was a queen, or at least a woman.

It was just as dawn broke when Joe worked out the number puzzle. The Hebrew words spelt Deborah, Tamar and Scotia, and their numerical value according to the Hebrew alphabet, if he eliminated all the zeros, amounted to the number 49, 7x7. Deborah was from the Clan of Benjamin, but they said that Jesus was from the Clan of Judah. What if the theologians had got it wrong and that the claim that Jesus had to the crown was not via David but Deborah? *Forty Nine*, this was the key; not a metal one, it was a numerological key made up of three female names, all bearing links to both Jesus and to the Scottish crown.

The following day Joe found himself standing in the middle of a field in Rosslyn glen. The trees were full of blossom, the muddy grass covered by a pink and white carpet woven from silk petals. In the near distance he could see a castle, but no soldiers in sight. They'd come for a wedding, but a wedding with a difference. This was to be a gypsy wedding. Joe was tired having spent the night awake with Rabbie who was sick with a slight fever. The riotous pagan celebrations rolling down from the braes hadn't helped the child sleep. Nan had persuaded Joe to go on ahead that morning, and she'd join him later if Rabbie felt better.

In the centre of the field stood a Maypole. A group of gypsy girls were dancing in their flamboyant dresses, with brightly coloured ribbons flowing from head and hands, playing musical instruments. There was a gypsy who played the part of Robin Goodfellow, they referred to him as the *Green Man* and the *Lord of Misrule*.

'Did you know that fools are better than poets?' the voice belonged to Nicola. She was wearing her jester outfit, complete with ridiculous three pointed hat.

'My Queen had her French poet Brantome who came with her from France.'

'You've told me before.'

'So you've never been to Rosslyn before, monsieur…it's 7 miles outside Edinburgh. There's a chapel beyond the wood. Plenty of deer if you should fancy hunting!'

Joe didn't reply.

'It was founded in 1446 by Sir William St. Clair.'

'What the deer?'

'No, stupid, the chapel! He was the Earl of Orkney and Lord of Rosslyn and also held the title of knight of the Cockle and Golden Fleece'

'I wouldn't mind you fleecing my golden cockle, Nicola…I mean, you say you are a clown, yet you've never offered to juggle my balls.'

Nicola ignored him. Joe liked to torment her; she was too strong for him, too independent. This was her one show of weakness and he was milking it for all it was worth.

'He was a member of the Order of the Knights of Santiago and the Order of the Golden Fleece. The St. Clairs' have been very good to the gypsies letting them hold the May celebrations on their land.'

Suddenly Nicola broke into song.

'Gaidelons et Scotia cest piere menerount

Quant de la terre Egypte en Escose passerount.

Ne geres loyns de Scone quant ariveront.

De la noun de Scotia la Escose terr numount.'

The moment she finished her song, the fool began to chatter excitedly.

'Then there was Pierre de Chatelard another poet…oh, oui…but they executed him, his last words were to call my Queen, *cruel*.'

'You're so boring, Nicola, you repeat your stories over and over again.'

'Well, monsieur, if you are so wise, you go and visit Rosslyn Chapel and find the murdered Apprentice. Hiram Abiff was King Solomon's Master of Works when he built the temple in the Holy Land. He was murdered by three jealous masons who wanted to know the secrets.'

'What secrets? Are they Indian?' Joe asked, noticing the band of dark skinned dancers who were jigging around with a huge brown bear attached to a chain.

A girl at university had once told him gypsies were descendents of low caste Indians.

'You know they are gypsies, monsieur, they know all about the quest for the Celtic key and the legends of Rosslyn. Shall I tell you about…'

'Oh shut up, Nicola, I've enough on my plate trying to get out of this weird place!'

'Out? Ah, but I thought you were going to marry Nan?'

'Well, I don't know what I'm supposed to do. Why don't you ask fucking Cockburn, she seems to know everything!'

'See that gypsy there with the turban, her name's Barbara Baptista. And the older woman with her is Helene Andree.'

'So what? Anyhow, I'm going for a drink. Do gypsies make whisky?'

But Nicola had gone to entertain the celebrants with her lute.

Joe headed off towards a stall offering refreshments, a cauldron stood nearby over an open fire. He'd been told that King Henry VIII of England had made it a capital offence to exist as a gypsy. Joe didn't blame him, all they ever did was steal and interbreed. But these gypsies looked different to the vagabonds in London. Their gowns were gathered at the neck and draped over their shoulders. Some carried babies tied in the draped material similar to the baby pouch Katie had used when Chloe was tiny.

'Sent as slaves from Bulgaria you know, Joseph,' the voice belonged to James Mossman. He handed Joe a chopin of ale. 'Did you know that four gypsies accompanied Christopher Columbus on his third voyage to the new world in 1498?'

'My friend Lawrence said that Columbus was a Jew.'

'Martin Luther called them fake friars, wandering Jews and Rogues. In Sweden they aren't allowed to bury their dead.'

'So why did they come here?'

'Scotland gave them sanctuary, Scotland gives many of God's people sanctuary.' Mossman gave a sigh as he lit a pipe.

'The gypsies dance the Flamenco you know? The Queen loves to watch them dance. These gypsies came from Spain. But the Church has banned them from entering Europe, and they can't be buried or christened because they tell fortunes.'

'Well, perhaps the Church is right.'

'Joseph told the Pharaoh's fortune…you should read the book, Joe. Go now, read it for a few minutes, let me know what you think.' Joe bowed and walked towards the crowd that had gathered around Nicola. She was singing about some bard called Blind Harry and William Wallace. He'd heard the song before. The old man in the song was St. Andrew. Her audience appeared to love her. Jerkin clad lords, ladies wearing masks, peasants and gypsies all were enthralled by her singing. The song then changed to, '*James the Tinkler*'. He'd also heard that often enough, her voice shrill and foolish.

'James Tinkler was a tinker and owned land in the reign of William the Lion, hundreds of years ago...'

Joe was bored with Nicola's stupid songs and headed towards a copse in the near distance. The woodland animals scurried away onto the heather as Joe made his way into the thicket and found himself a broken tree trunk on which to sit with his ale. The air was warm; the smells of spring eternal, timeless, the same smells he'd left in Knightsbridge had wafted back in time. Perhaps this was immortality. The smells were fresh, so fresh; flowers and grass, sweet, warm and familiar.

Opening his small Bible Joe gave a yawn, was it really the word of God? It was so confusing, was it a book of myths or fortune telling? Even Joseph, the son of Jacob, was not merely a clairvoyant but also a water diviner, yet that same book decried both activities. Joe couldn't even see the point in the author of the book constantly writing about birthrights of the firstborn son, and then go on to deny the firstborn son his right of inheritance. Esau didn't inherit, nor did Reuben. As to why Judah ended up ruling the whole race was even more baffling.

'I see you are studying the word of God,' a voice made Joe jump. But when he looked up he couldn't see anything except the butterflies gliding from petal to petal.

The sun stabbed through the trees like golden daggers. Perhaps it was Nan, she said she might ride over with John Mossman if Rabbie felt better. Joe had offered to stay with him, but Nan said how much it meant to Sir James for Joe to see Rosslyn, the gypsies and Robin Hood.

'Nan! Is that you?'

'No, Joe, it's me.' The voice wasn't clear, almost like the tinkling of glass. At first he could see nothing, and then the figure slowly emerged like a photograph developing.

'Please let me welcome you to my land. I'd better first introduce myself; I'm Marie de Saint-Clair. Norman family, our name changed to Sinclair after my death.'

Joe remained calm; even he couldn't understand why he wasn't terrified. It was as if he'd just smoked a couple of spliffs, too stoned to care.

'Hereditary Grand Masters of Scottish Masons…although women weren't invited, of course. Nevertheless, Master Hill, I was Grand Master of the Prieuré de Sion!'

Something about the young woman reminded Joe of Diana, the Princess of Wales. But recently that had been a common occurrence. Once even Nan had reminded him of Diana. The face that now smiled down at him was almost transparent like her dress, pink and lilac, similar to the flowers that surrounded him.

The apparition came and went, fading into the flora, only to re-appear each time he blinked his tired eyes.

'I am descended from Henry de Saint-Clair the Baron of Rosslyn. He accompanied Godfroi de Bouillon on the first Crusade. My grandmother married into the French Chaumont family. My mother was a Jewess you know, Isabel Levis, the tribe of Levi. Which is why I was made Grand Master, grandchild of the Fisher King.'

Joe stared at the eyes of his assailant, cornflower blue, just like Diana's.

'Read 1 Chronicles ch.3: 10-16, compare it with Matthew 1:6-11,' the ghost instructed. 'Read about Rahab the harlot, a gentile you know. And Ruth the Moabite, she was eternally cursed due to her race. That is if you believe the book as it's written. Jesus did say *seek and you will find*. Of course, no one does.'

'You mean Deuteronomy 23:3. *No Ammonite or Moabite shall enter the assembly of YHVH even to the tenth generation*…which means that David couldn't inherit the throne.'

'Yes, Joseph, Ruth was a Moabite. David wasn't beyond the tenth generation. And of course although the adoptive father of Jesus was of the tribe of Judah, if He was of a virgin birth then it didn't matter who Joseph was. Mary was a Levite, an ancestor of mine, and of course this meant that Jesus being her son had claim to the priesthood. The Clan of Levi, like her cousin Elizabeth the Baptist's mother. But you already know this.' Joe recalled one of the gypsies Nicola had mentioned, Barbara Baptista. Perhaps he should find her, speak to her.

'Tamar was of the line of Judah, yar?' Joe mumbled, trying to avoid looking at the apparition. 'Perhaps her mother was a Levite or Benjamite.'

But the ghost made no reply.

'From what I've read, Deborah wasn't merely a judge of Israel, more like a Queen if she was also a Benjamite, am I correct?'

'The holy city and capital of Judea had originally been the property of the tribe of Benjamin.'

'So was Jesus married to a Benjamite then, if he wanted the crown? A sort of priest king?'

'Read Deuteronomy 7:2.' A saucy sparkle emitted from her now fading eyes. 'Deuteronomy 28:57…Shiloh, Benjamin's youngest son.'

Joe didn't understand. But, before he was able to question her, she was gone.

The gypsy wedding was well in progress by the time he returned to the field. The groom was dressed as Robin Hood and bride adorned as Maid Marion. During the ceremony the groom referred to his wife as, '*Queen,*' and she called her husband, '*Captain*'.

'Great feast, Joseph!' the young John Mossman called over; he was standing near the maypole. Joe gave a courteous bow, wondering how he was trusted by his Catholic companions; as Nicola had told him that he'd converted to Protestantism.

'Bonjour, monsieur,' another voice interrupted. It belonged to Florymonde, the maid with the gap in her front teeth whom he'd met so many months ago. It seemed like a lifetime to Joe.

'Full moon tonight, lucky for the lovers, monsieur'

'What are you doing here?'

'I have come here to find you today, monsieur, for I learn from Cockburn that you are searching for the murderer. I know who it is…shh, but not here.' she looked around suspiciously. 'If you meet me by the well that sits below the Castle I shall tell you what I know, I have kept the evidence in my locket, monsieur,' and with that, the maid headed in the direction of the Castle.

Joe gave a slight bow and moved towards a group of elderly men. All the history books he'd read insisted that people in the

16th century didn't live beyond middle age, yet he constantly found himself surrounded by the aged. Some of the old men were gypsies; dead animals were tied about their throats; heads of foxes, tails of wolves, a fashion that would be mimicked by the 19th century bourgeoisie.

Then, just when Joe thought the wedding ceremony was all over, a large wooden bowl was handed by the gypsy priest to the bride who suddenly, in front of the whole congregation, urinated into it.

'She just pissed into that bowl!' Joe turned to look at those around him, thinking they'd be as shocked as he was. But it was as if nothing unusual had taken place. The pot was then handed to the groom and he did likewise.

The priest took a handful of earth from the ground and threw it into the bowl with some brandy and stirred it with a ram's horn. Joe looked around for Nicola, he wanted to joke and ask her if that was going to be handed around for toasting the bride and groom, or whether they had to wait for them to shit together in order to dish up for the feast. But Nicola was nowhere to be seen, probably shagging Sebastian or John Mossman. He knew she had a soft spot for both young men.

The priest had placed the bowl of urine samples on the ground and buried it. He said it was done as evidence of their marriage. Joe longed to shout, *are you taking the piss?*' but thought better of it.

The gypsies and their guests headed towards a spit and cauldron where a large boar was being roasted alongside hedgehogs and hares. Still traumatized by the vision of Marie de Saint-Clair, Joe thought he'd take a look about for Nicola. In the distance he could see James Mossman talking to his wealthier guests. Joe recognised many from the Palace dancing alongside the gypsies around a fire. The gypsy children were even playing with the children of the aristocracy, yet Nicola wasn't with them. Joe decided to head back towards the copse where he'd had that strange encounter. The broken tree trunk was still there, even the woodland animals and butterflies, but there was no trace of the vision calling herself Marie de Saint-Clair. St. Paul claimed to have had a vision, yet why the Christian world exalted him, Joe could never comprehend. What differentiated the schizophrenic or the deluded from the religious visionary?

Joe opened his book of Nostradamus, and then he opened his Bible. It was all so complicated and he was tired, too tired to make the effort. Why did he need to leave, he could stay with Nan and Rabbie until he died. Would it make any real difference if he returned to his own time zone if he was going to die anyhow?

There was a sudden whistling. Was it his tune playing, 'Joe Hill'?

One of the butterflies flew past his face, catching his nose with its white wing. There was a whiff of rose petals, the whistling grew louder now. At first he thought the butterfly was hurt, until he looked closer. Before his eyes the butterfly slowly metamorphosed. In its place stood a woman, plump, yet lovely. How her skin glowed, her dark eyes sparkled.

'I am Yolande,' she gave a curtsy. 'Did you know that it was during the 1400's when Rosslyn Chapel was being constructed? The Grand Helmsman of the Priory of Sion was Rene d'Anjou King of Jerusalem. He was succeeded by me, for I'm his daughter. My sister Margaret married King Henry VI of England.' Twirling before him, the full skirt of her elegant dress spun as she began to laugh. Joe looked around for a witness but he was alone, apart from the squirrels, hares and a few birds. But then who should he call as witness, another ghost? A haunting within a haunting?

'My father Rene d'Anjou employed a Jewish astrologer and Kabbalist you know, Jean de Saint-Remy, he was the grandfather of Nostradamus. One of my father's subjects was the Maid of Orleans. You have heard of her, Joseph Hill, Jeanne d'Arc, braver than any man. She was only 17 when she went to the French Court with the Dauphin's brother in law Rene d'Anjou. Ha, and you couldn't even face your own child, at your age. Ha, not even face your own child.'

'What do you mean? I faced my own child last night! My child is dead!'

'Chloe is your child.'

'Chloe, yes. I must go back and find Chloe. I've just been so busy with…'

'The Queen of Hearts she made some tarts all on a summer's day. The Knave of Hearts…do you know who the knave is, Joseph?' But Joe didn't respond.

'I hear you used to entertain the crowds with your singing, but you rarely sing these days.'

'My baby died.'

'You said it, Joe, not me.'

'I'm guilty, I know I'm guilty. No place for free will, eh? Is that why I'm guilty?'

'Jeanne d'Arc, she had free will. She was given the command of more than 7,000 men, which included the Royal Scots Guard. A mere child herself, she led her army and overthrew the English. And you, Master Hill can't even face your own daughter!' she retorted. 'The following year Jeanne was captured, just 18 years of age. Only 18!' The apparition shook her head; Joe thought he noticed a tear fall from her eyes. 'But she used her free will by refusing to submit to rape by her captors. And so she was burned alive at Rouen. They said that she was guilty. What do you think, Joe?'

Joe failed to answer. Yet, what if her story had never been told in the way it had, would she have gone down in history as being mad and nothing more? As for her God, (the one who had failed to intervene in order to save her from being burnt alive), being the same God who'd gone to the trouble to provide Ruth the Moabite with a husband and to supply the gluttonous wedding guests at Cana with more wine, Joe just couldn't see the similarity.

'Do you know why men hate women, Joseph, and keep them imprisoned? Do you really want to know, Master Hill?'

Again Joe didn't reply.

'It's because they fear us. They don't fear each other, they bond with other men. Like uncivilised animals accepting those from the same pack.' She suddenly fell down onto her knees; the squirrels and hares ran towards her like an army of devoted soldiers.

'Ha, animals, I've insulted them,' she smiled, stoking the creatures as they approached her lap. 'Animals would never behave as lowly as men. Men fear women. They have to ensure we remain in chains, or else, should we break loose men would have to face what they are in themselves.'

271

'So what are we in ourselves? You remind me of the philosophers who wrote about things in themselves. I mean we can't be things out of ourselves can we? So it appears that men can't win whatever they do.'

'Men, as you know, Joseph, are inadequate.'

'What was that? Did you hear someone screaming?' Joe turned his eyes away from the apparition, towards the screaming. When he looked back she'd vanished.

Joe made his way towards the commotion. A group of men and women surrounded the body of a young woman lying on the ground. Edging nearer, Joe's heart began to race, was it Nan? Had she arrived with Rabbie and been taken ill?

'She's dead!' someone wailed.

'Murdered!' another voice cried.

Joe peered between the two men in front of him. To his horror he saw that the girl, who lay by the trunk of a cherry tree on a carpet of white blossom, was none other than Florymonde.

The wedding drifted off after that, and Joe still hadn't found Nicola. Poor Florymonde, where was her God? Joe wondered, as he headed back to the main highway, where numerous coaches and horses stood waiting to carry the celebrants back to Edinburgh. What had God ever done for Florymonde? He didn't even let her keep her own teeth.

'Part the Red fucking Sea though!' he ranted into the air.

'Hello, Joseph.'

'Good evening, Sir James,' Joe bowed to the man who'd approached with his younger brother John, hoping they hadn't heard his outburst.

'I wondered if either of you have seen Nan or Nicola?'

Both men shook their heads.

'I know that the fool was thinking of going to Restalrig,' John volunteered. 'Nan said she'd left some timber for the gypsies at the burned out cottage. Nicola said she might go with them...guide I suppose.' The handsome young man sauntered off in the direction of the maypole to watch the girls dance.

'Do you think they're alright? I suppose you've heard about the murder?'

'If you need to find Nicola urgently, Joseph, one of my coachmen will drive you there. Don't worry about Nan, I'll be returning straight home,' James Mossman reassured him.

'What about Rabbie?'

'Sebastian said he's fine. Just a normal fever for a child, nothing to worry about.'

'But Nan said she'd come here if Rabbie was okay.'

'She was tired, Joseph, nothing more. I'll tell her that you'll be home later, she's in good hands.'

"Did I ever tell you, Joseph, about the Mossmans?' he lit his pipe, and Joe knew that this would be a long haul. 'My grandfather was made a burgess in 1492. And my father John, and numerous other Mossmans were goldsmiths…well, obviously some still are.' Joe tried to look inspired, but he was agitated, worried about Nan.

'My father was so well thought of, that the great aunt of our beloved Queen Marie sent miners here from France. Even sent her own Master Mason to work for my father to mine gold on Crawford Muir. My father was made the Keeper of the Royal Mint you know?' Joe listened patiently for another ten minutes and then decided to take up Mossman's offer of the coach to Restalrig.

The journey was wearisome. The horses clip clopping over the rough ground as the moonlight guided them, and Joe thought about poor Florymonde.

It seemed an age before the coach drew up outside the burnt out old cottage which appeared to be in the throes of renovation. Joe felt nostalgic, recalling those times, be they all too rare, when he'd snuggled up beside Nan for the night. How he'd give anything to be able to sleep with her now. He didn't want to find the key out of there, what difference would it make? He'd die just the same on whatever Monopoly board he threw his dice; be it a 20th century or 16th century one. For the games master had made the rules, and the Bible often told how the games master could be pacified. His mind could change, his rules and laws, all could be broken and forgiven depending on whether or not the penitent took His fancy. But Joe didn't want to pass *go*, he didn't want to use his *get out of jail* card. Riddles weren't meant to be solved and keys weren't only meant for escape, but for safety. He was safe and secure; he didn't have to face reality. Philosophical truths were no longer meaningful, only Nan and Rabbie were authentic.

Maybe if he proved he truly loved her then the games master would allow him to stay and forget about the rules of 16th century residency. An asylum seeker, that would be his petition to the Almighty. Others had duel nationality; he would claim entitlement as a registered alien for duel citizenship of two time zones.

Suddenly he noticed something flapping from amongst the rubble outside the cottage. It was a piece of parchment that looked as if it had been torn from a book. Joe bent down to retrieve it, the ink had slightly smudged, but it was legible.

'Lou grand eyssame se levera d'abelhos, que non sauran don te siegen venguddos. De nuech l'embousque – Nostradamus'.

(The great swarm of bees will arise but no one will know whence they have come, the ambush by night).

He placed the parchment into his purse. Was it a gypsy he could see in the distance? Perhaps he'd ask her if she'd seen Nicola.

The old woman was bent over a bundle of twigs as Joe approached, her head covered in a torn, dirty shawl.

'Excuse me...' Suddenly Joe heard the tune, his tune; whistling through the trees, across the muddy ploughed field, through the spring flowers growing around his feet.

'Hello, Joseph,' the gypsy stood up, threw off her shawl and smiled. Before Joe stood a beautiful young woman. Her eyes were the loveliest eyes he'd ever seen, almost too beautiful, he was hypnotised by the woman's eyes.

'Human eyes are blemished with splinters, they erode with time,' she declared. 'If thine eye offends thee pluck it out. Only inner beauty has meaning, that is eternal.' she covered her eyes with her wet hands.

'As you seem so well versed on the higher values, then perhaps you know who's the murderer then...do you know?'

The woman suddenly removed her hands from her face and Joe jumped back in fright. Her eyes had disappeared, only empty, torn hollows remained. Sinews and veins hung shamelessly out of their sockets. Beauty was now transformed into repulsion. With just one piece missing from the jigsaw the rest of the picture collapsed.

The image disappeared, but the whistling continued to play in the breeze. Then Joe caught sight of her, heading towards the Kirk. Cautiously he followed. On entering the ruined site he recalled the time he'd been there with Ellie. Everything was pain now, even memories. Again he'd betrayed Nan, just for a moment of passion.

Joe found the apparition standing in front of a gate, the whistling had stopped.

She turned her head, the empty sockets of her eyes now dripped blood as she walked through the gate of the demolished Kirk.

The apparition led him into the hexagonal temple where he'd been once before. The water in the pilgrims pool remained motionless, framed by the large boulders and rocks covered with numerous reliquaries.

'This is my well,' she declared, placing her foot into the water.

'I'm St. Triduana and this is my domain!' Her chin was raised defiantly; the empty hollows of her eyes were directed towards the roof.

'I don't approve of men being here. Although I do make concessions if they're blind. Blind men are the best sort. Can't sin as much as those who are sighted, although they're all good at leading women down blind alleys.' She made her way towards the centre of the pool and crouched down, immersing her whole body. It was such a strange shaped room, a hexagon. Nothing 16th century about the architecture. Joe was confused as to why most of the Kirk had been destroyed by the Protestant Reformers, yet this structure had been allowed to survive.

The woman suddenly rose up from the waters like an Arthurian Lady of the Lake. She held a figurine of Moses crowned with a sun, high above her own wet head.

'In the book of *Revelation*, there is a woman with the sun, and even though the lion will lie down with the lamb, the wolf will reclaim her crown.'

'What do you mean?' His eyes fixed on the statuette in her glistening fingers. The blood still dripped from the black eye sockets onto her hands.

'Jonathan was from the tribe of the wolf. He loved him as his own soul. Made a covenant with him, stripped himself of the robe. Gave it to him…the robe of colours, the royal coat that Jacob handed down to Joseph.'

'Who did Jonathan love?'

'David of course, David the half breed. Bewitched his lover and stole his crown! Locked Jonathan's sister away for the rest of her life so that she couldn't breed the true heirs to the Benjamite crown.'

'I thought it was Saul who was the evil one. Didn't he visit the witch of Endor? Anyway, Nostradamus seems to be the flavour of the month and has bewitched many royals. Well, at least in France from what I've heard, and the Church doesn't seem to object to him,' Joe replied.

'You must know that Catherine de Medici asked Nostradamus to write horoscopes for her seven children.'

'I've heard that he healed victims of the plague, but then I'm told that to tell the future is evil. Does that mean he's bound for hell?' His eyes looked into the water as if he hoped to find the answer there.

'Repentance, Joseph, we are called to repentance. For even as we speak Nostradamus is dying from the dropsy. Just a month or two left for him to repent.'

'So, what's his crime? He predicts the future, just like Joseph in the Bible.'

'He is guilty of reading moles on the body to predict the future. He uses the tricks of Iamblichus, studies all the secret books, divines by reading water.'

'Jacob's son Joseph, the one with the coat, then he must be guilty. He read from a cup. He interpreted dreams. Who can say who is good and who is evil, or who is a sinner and who a saint? If we all have such impaired vision, can any of us see clearly to ever know right from wrong?'

'You are correct, even Moses committed murder, and Joseph married an alien wife and even read omens. But God alone is the judge, not you or I.'

'So who do you think should have received the royal coat of many colours, Reuben as firstborn son?'

'Reuben! Ha, no of course it wasn't Reuben. It was his sister, Dinah. The blood line is via the mother in Judaism didn't you know?'

And then suddenly she vanished, as if she'd never been. Only the statuette of Moses remained floating in the still water.

Joe threw off his boots and entered the water to retrieve the statuette. He waded towards the centre of the pool and plucked the artefact from the uneven floor.

Rusty, broken rosaries were scattered sporadically amongst the dead rats and flowers that floated beside him. As he made his way back to the edge of the pool Joe tripped over a broken flagstone. The statuette fell from his wet hand and smashed onto the dry rocks. The figurine shattered on the ground before him. One of the broken halves had an inscription carved inside.

'Judges 14.8 - He went out of his way to look at the carcase of the lion, and there was a swarm of bees in the lion's body, and honey.'

It was just after dawn the following morning that Joe awoke in his old bed at the Palace. He hadn't gone home that night, it had been late and he didn't want to wake Nan and Rabbie. He was vexed that Nicola still hadn't returned, and knew that whoever murdered Florymonde was still on the loose. Heading across the drawbridge, unable to forget the scriptural reference, he looked towards the abbey. The workmen were still there, the job still unfinished. Perhaps life was exactly like Keats's *'Grecian Urn'*, he introspected, time captured in a moment. Or maybe the world stopped turning whenever he looked away. His tired eyes continued to glance around for Nicola, why was she so obnoxious, always causing mayhem? Perhaps he ought to report it to the Queen or something, at least tell Cockburn. But Joe had already asked for her that previous night to no avail. It seemed that Cockburn, like the Queen, had also disappeared. He didn't have much time, Nan would be wondering where he was, Rabbie would need him.

A butterfly flew past his head, how quickly spring had arrived. He watched it glide towards the high wall of the lion's den. The fish pond opposite glistened brightly beneath the sky, the rockery enchanting now that it flourished with foliage. The butterfly fluttered towards the flowers. On the day of creation, had God visualised the lava, the caterpillar or the butterfly as being the perfect result? Joe reflected. What part of a butterfly's life was the authentic one? Was Florymonde in a state of flux? Had she undertaken a metamorphosis into a different state, or another dimension? Perhaps everyone was in a continual state of metamorphosis.

The butterfly had flown onto the statue as the water poured from the dragon's mouth. The smaller dragons and lions below spat water into the pond.

A swarm of bees grabbed his attention. Bees were in the clue Joe had found in St. Triduana's well. He ran after them as they buzzed their way towards the Abbey and the small herb garden.

Tiny rosebuds smothered the trellis as the bees landed on them, and then they headed into the eastern gardens where the workmen were packing the donkeys. Joe followed them away from the ruins towards the wells, their fat hairy bodies landing on the arbours and damaged sculptures.

Arthur's Seat looked down scornfully, as if challenging Joe which of them would last the longer. It started with a volcanic eruption, perhaps that was how the story ended. Neither he nor Arthur's Seat could cheat, whatever fate had in store.

The gorse glowed golden flames amidst the purple heather and pine trees. A few horses were near the summit. One day he'd take Rabbie riding...if there was still time.

Eight plots of flowers perfectly designed, patterns of the fleur d' lys were everywhere, not a weed in sight as he entered the southern garden. The trees overhung the ponds and fountains; their pink and white blossoms already starting to fall onto the rock gardens watched over by the figurines and sculpted bushes.

Still no sign of Nicola, not even in the western garden beyond the theatre. Nervously he peeped through the railings into the lion's den, there wasn't a bee in sight.

Disgruntled, Joe headed back in the direction from whence he came, until he arrived at the main courtyard about to head for Mossman's tenement.

Joe glanced across at the litters entering the main courtyard hoping that one would be carrying Nicola.

Again he could hear buzzing. Unable to ignore it, Joe followed the constant drone across the courtyard. His bloodshot eyes were now fixed upon the fountain of Diana holding her arrow in her left hand.

Just like the Benjamites. His mind jumped randomly from one thought to another.

He was almost running now, the buzzing louder and clearer as he approached the fountain.

Diana looked down from her dais into the ivory coloured basin, her breasts still emitting a constant flow of water. Joe wondered why a crescent moon was above her head; the Muslim flag was a crescent moon.

Buzzing, everywhere was buzzing. A huge swarm of bees had now congregated around the statue. Joe suddenly noticed that a nest was between the statues breasts. Then one bee, larger than all the rest flew into the flitch holding the arrows. Something inside glittered. Too far to see from the outside of the fountain, Joe removed his boots and stepped into the shallow water. As he drew close, the queen bee flew off, leaving him free to reach inside and retrieve the shining object. Made from bright blue sapphires, it was the letter 'N'.

Carefully, Joe placed the jewel into his purse. He was about to climb out of the fountain when the bumble bee flew back towards him. He thought it was about to attack, yet, just when it reached his face it flew down between the statue's legs and drowned. Body upside down, its tiny dark legs flapping, applauding its own finale. It was as he stared into the shallow water of the fountain that he noticed a dark shadow. Underneath the drowning bee lay the dead body of Nicola Ambruzzi.

'Lou grand eyssame se levera d'abelhos, que non sauran don te siegen venguddos. De nuech l'embousque'
— *Nostradamus*

279

Chapter Ten

'What else is woman but a foe to friendship, an inescapable punishment, a necessary evil, a natural temptation, a desirable calamity, a domestic danger, a delectable detriment, an evil of nature, painted in fair colours...Women are intellectually like children...She is more carnal than a man...An imperfect animal, she always deceives...Women also have weak memories, and it is a natural vice in them not to be disciplined, but to follow their own impulses without any sense of what is due...She is a liar by nature!' (Malleus Maleficarum)

Throughout May and June, Joe spent most of his time with Nan and Rabbie, although she still hadn't invited him into her bed. No one had mentioned him solving the riddles anymore, no more clues or apparitions, not even a haunting from Nicola. How he missed her incessant gibberish, her pranks, the happy go lucky attitude of an untamed gypsy. Why anyone should want to kill her he couldn't imagine. But he'd never forgotten seeing Wolfart Bruce hanging around St. Triduana's on the day Ellie was murdered.

He'd been down that road once before, then changed his mind when the priest rescued Rabbie from the Nor Loch. But, Joe knew that first impressions counted, and he not only looked like Rasputin, but had executed the small child at the Mercat Cross.

Worse than all this, he'd raped Nan.

Had he raped Nicola also? Had he strangled her on the day they were celebrating the gypsy wedding at Rosslyn Glen?

Even Nan didn't know how often Joe had cried, sneaking out to the shores of the Nor Loch. Tears could flow there unnoticed amongst the inhabitants. They were too busy with their own tears to spare him compassion. It was where he belonged, amongst the refuse of the loch. Surrounded by gulls and eel catchers young and old. Garbage, they were all garbage, born to die, temporary parasites nothing more.

'Nicola! l'jardiniere! Were you the gardener? If you were then tell me…where's Gethsemane, where's your tomb? Please come back. Please give me another chance! Conjure yourself back like Lazarus!' Reduced to tears he'd stood on the edge of the loch, his red, swollen eyes focussing towards the sea of Leith in the distance.

But, she didn't oblige.

During those two months Joe would occasionally say to Nan that if Marie Stuart was the Queen of Hearts, then Nicola had surely been the Clown of Hearts. He was guilty of constantly ridiculing her, ashamed for all his derisive comments when all she'd done was to try and make him laugh. Even the stench rising up from the Nor cesspool didn't affect him. Not even the sight of Wolfart Bruce indulging in his favourite pastime, strapping females to the ducking stool and watching them drown, had little impact. All that Joe knew, was that someday the priest would be made to pay the ultimate price.

But it wasn't all doom and gloom. Some days he'd go down to the Kow Gait and entertain the bourgeoisie with his singing or painting their portraits; lords, ladies, clerics, lawyers dressed in their finery and feathers. Even the hierarchy of the burgh council eagerly posed as Joe painted in varying styles according to the demands of his sponsors.

Occasionally, he'd head along to the far end of the Kow Gait towards the Grassmarket, carrying his paints in a knapsack over his shoulder. He'd stop to sketch the exquisite stained glass windows or the beggars who'd congregated near the alms house and various drinking wells.

The Kow Gait, a deep valley surrounded by countryside, renowned for its water supply and resident aristocracy. It was lined by hedges and impressive carriages with harnessed French horses, and equally harnessed French servants. Timber fronted mansions sprouted between the landscaped gardens. Accurately measured plots enclosed the fashionable geometric knots.

A wholly different world from the Nor Loch and the area beside the Flodden Wall inhabited by the poorest residents of the burgh. He'd even sought out the barber surgeons who worked there, hoping that he might bump into Cockburn on his travels. If only she'd call to see him, or at least send for him. But she was always unavailable whenever he'd gone to seek her out at the Palace. Perhaps his mission had been cancelled, he'd done his penance and maybe he would be allowed to stay. After all he had nothing to go home to.

Perhaps Lawrence had called the police when he'd found him missing. Maybe there'd even been a funeral for him. His family would have grieved. Lawrence would cry, blaming himself. Had they found a body, was he floating in suspended animation?

Many of his customers wanted paintings of the Magdalene. Some even claimed to have seen her standing outside the Magdalen Chapel in the Kow Gait, '*outside her Kirk*'.

Sometimes he'd just take a walk up and down Hogs Back Ridge, or as the lawyers preferred to call it, '*The King's Hie Street*.' If the Reformers hadn't become all powerful, he could have enjoyed the tournaments he'd heard about so often. They were once held at Greenside by Carlton Hill. The hill a leper colony would dominate by the end of the century, or so Lawrence had said.

It was the morning of 28th August. The sun was blazing as Joe headed down along the Canongate towards the Palace carrying his paints in his knapsack and an unfinished portrait of a wealthy Duchess that had only just dried. He was proud of this work, having captured a true likeness of his sitter; perhaps she'd give him a large tip. Of course he hadn't made it too true to life, tactfully avoiding the dark bags beneath her eyes and marks of the pox on her cheeks.

Rabbie wasn't with him that morning, although there had been numerous occasions when he'd taken the boy down to the Palace when he'd had a portrait commissioned. Usually he'd left him with one of the grooms who'd let him ride his favourite white pony around the courtyard. Other times the young maids would eagerly offer to take him for treats in the kitchen, or to play with the puppies bred for the hunts, or with the other children on site. It was during those times, when his sitter had gone for a rest, that Joe had taken the opportunity to go into the Queen's library. He'd browse through the thousands of books which filled the room from corner to corner, floor to ceiling in various languages, mainly Latin.

It was as he arrived at the Palace gates that morning that he noticed it was quieter than usual, apart from the all too familiar roar of the lion Judah. Queen Marie Stuart had left Edinburgh on the 13th of August and returned on the 20th. But Joe had no idea as to whether she was at home or not today. Suddenly changing his mind about where he was headed, Joe altered direction. The weather was too glorious to waste; the Duchess would have to wait a few more hours for her painting. Holyrood Park beckoned the fit young man, as did the climb up to the top of Arthur's Seat. Exhausted by the time he'd reached the summit, Joe sank down onto the grassy earth. Arthur's Seat, had King Arthur really been here, to this very place? His blue eyes squinted away from the glare of the sun, as he looked around at the heather clad hill which overshadowed the Palace. Was Arthur's ghost still roaming somewhere in the park? What was a ghost, was it some build up of ectoplasm or the residue of a deceased person's DNA? Were they in the same physical space as the living, but occupying a different dimension? Leibniz had argued that God had chosen to make the best of all possible worlds. Yet, would all those women who'd been murdered agree with him? David Hume argued that God didn't even exist, perhaps he was right. If God did exist, Joe wondered why he'd never met Him. After all, Bishop Berkeley himself had said, *'esse est percipi'*, to be, is to be perceived. But wasn't it also about sacrificial love for others, that's what Jesus had said. Even the Jewish philosopher Levinas discussed the concept of otherness, the moral obligation we all have to the other.

Perhaps only Socrates got it right after all, Joe speculated, as he spread himself over the hot grass interspersed with prickly gorse. *'The only thing I know'*, Socrates had claimed, *'is, that I know nothing'*, and in regard to himself Joe was in total agreement with this statement. For he also knew that he knew nothing.

As the sun shone down on him he thought about the name Socrates. It was a good name, like Hercules, Aristophanes. At one time all names had meanings, not any more. Arthur, was this where he was buried, on Arthur's Seat?

Chloe, now that was a good name, but he didn't know if it had a meaning. If she didn't like her name she could always change it. Even biblical characters constantly changed their names; Jacob to Israel, Abram to Abraham.

Peter, why did he change his name from Simon? Joe scratched his head, ridding himself of the flies that were crawling about in the earth. If Peter meant *rock* then it was a description of an object, not a personal name; no more than if Lawrence had been given the title *Menorah*, or Joe the label *spliff*. According to his Bible, Jesus was the *Word*. What was the real title of Jesus? He apparently referred to himself as, *'the way, the truth, and the life'*. Joe glanced down at his book of Nostradamus, with it's illustration of the High Priestess. Perhaps the disciples all represented a tarot card or a constellation, a sign of the zodiac, even Mary Magdalene, but there was no card of a prostitute as far as he was aware.

If the experience he was living was more than a prolonged dream, then it was almost a year since he'd last seen Chloe. Could that be measured in time, or merely emotion? He'd sat in a deckchair watching her play in her small sandpit in the back yard of 49 Magdalene Towers on that rare visit. He'd smoked too many spliffs to remember much, just the sand in his shoes when he'd got home. Katie shouldn't have let him have sex with her that day, she knew what he was like. He'd only just got back from a mission. It was hard sometimes to differentiate between the good guys and the bad. But he shouldn't have shagged her, he knew that the moment he'd zipped up his flies.

A mist suddenly rose, chilling the air. Was it whistling he could hear or merely the breeze whipping across the crag? The whistling grew louder, the nape of his neck shivered. Was it his tune that he could hear?

'Who's there? Nicola? Nicola is that you? Please don't go!'

He could smell a fragrance, sweet, fresh like flowers.

As the mist slowly cleared, the figure of a woman appeared; middle aged, average appearance, dressed in red 1940's clothes. Yet, she was bald, as if her head had just been shaved.

'Jane Haining at yer service…I'm a Scot, nae of this toon, came frae Dumfriesshire, but I've been sent tae help ye. Being that this is the capital of ma country.'

He suddenly noticed the basket of poppies. She held one out towards him.

'Heroes, soldiers…who can say who is the hero? The soldier, the martyr…the dead cannae blether. Or can they?'

'Do you know who killed Nicola? I miss her. Please, if you see her, tell her that I miss her.'

'Of course ye will nae hae heard of me, but then, I'm a female. Ye will hae heard of Dr. Schindler. Although it will tak' aboot 50 years for e'en his name tae be known. Aye, aboot 50 years. But nae one ha' heard aboot me.'

'Feel free to divulge.'

'I ken ye hae a Jewish fiere, that pleases me…really. It warms ma heart.' she smiled, kind and genuine, he could see it in her eyes.

'The Jews gave me the greatest honour any Scot could hae. Could be that I am the only Scot tae hae it. Aye, honoured as the *Righteous among nations*'. That's what the Jews and Israel call gentiles they want to honour. I am a righteous gentile. Oh dinnae gae and fret because ye didnae ken who I wa'. Ye are nae sae rare, lad. E'en ma ain at hame, they dinnae ken ma name,' she laughed. There was a twinkle in her eye.

'Lost ma ain mother when I wa' 5, just a wee lassie. But God is gracious and sae when I grew up I joined a Kirk of Scotland Mission tae Hungary.'

The poppies were so red, so bright, in keeping with her attire. Yet not in keeping with her bald head, Joe reflected.

'Matron of a lassies hame in Budapest, in charge of 400 Christian and Jewish bairns. Orphans mainly…poor wee lambs. Although nae all. Some just came for a guid education.' She now moved towards Joe and stood behind him.

'1944, wa' that the year of the Devil? Joseph, lad, it broke ma heart tae sew all those yellow stars ontae the wee lassies' clothes. Of course I could have gone hame tae Scotland like the rest…but how could I leave the wee ones. I mean, wha' would Christ hae me do?'

But Joe didn't reply, what could he say? Although he'd reached borderline as a believer, there was no way he had a clue who Christ was, let alone claim such a personal camaraderie with the guy that he would know His desires.

'Sae I stayed wi' the bairns. I mean, I could'na just leave ma bonny lassies. It wa' going well,' she sighed, 'until we were betrayed tae the Nazis and I wa' arrested and sent tae Auschwitz.'

'So is that why you have no hair? But at least you weren't Jewish, at least you survived. My friend Lawrence…'

'Ma number wa' 79467. That's a number ye'll need ken, it will be a number tae mention when ye cross over. Course, if I'd been Catholic they'd have made me a saint. Ye've thought the same I ken, that it's odd how sae many Catholics are saints and nae one else.'

Joe laughed, he found her vaguely amusing. Nicola was funny in a different way, perhaps she'd met her on her journey down.

'They gassed me ken, along wi' ma wee ones. Aye, and there were sae many Kirks all over the world and none remembered that they worshipped a Jew. Ye must ken aboot the Lutherian Kirk, refused tae help us, said that there were nae innocent Jews, all Jews are guilty they said. Aye, the Jews, the apple of His eye.'

Joe never much cared for that term, *'apple of His eye'*. Lawrence's mother had mentioned it during an argument he'd once had with her about Israeli politics.

'They gassed me on 16th August, 1944, I wa' 47. Ma death certificate said I'd deid frae cachexia on July 17th…but nae one believed that.' She reached over his shoulder and placed a poppy down on the grass. He could smell the fragrance as she neared him, he felt the cool breeze send a tingle over his body.

'Ye ken, Joseph, men are called heroes when they kill, shout the loudest, or if they're the wealthiest or the most selfish. Given medals, statues made in their honour. But ye ken, lad, there are nae sae many heroes in Scotland, nae sae many heroes in the world. But there is a legion of heroines. The unsung heroines like ma sisters who ye've already met.'

He felt a touch on his cheek, as if she'd kissed him, a touch as soft as a butterfly's wing.

Joe picked up the poppy and examined it.

'Aye, ma wee soldiers. They dinnae die on the battle fields. No military honours for them. They were treated like animals, rejected by their peers. Adults who'd ken them since birth, adults who shaved their wee heids, beat them, starved them, experimented on them, then...'

'Enough!' Joe cried out, he'd had enough.

'Bravehearts they were,' she continued, ignoring his protestations.

'True bravehearts. How could I leave them tae die alone? I ha' tae die wi' them, return the Lord's holy ones safely hame. The apples of His eye.'

His head was bent over the poppy, so many tears but for who were they shed? Joe knew full well that tears were only ever shed for oneself.

'Sae ye need tae solve ye clues, Joseph, ye have all the letters now. An anagram, work it oot and ye'll find yer Holy Grail, and then ye can gae hame. Ye dinnae have lang tae find yer key oot of here, ye must gae hame.'

'Home, but this is my home!' he snapped, his fingers tearing the petals of the poppy.

'Nae, Joseph, ye dinnae belong here. But when ye get hame, dinnae forget tae remind them of me. Dinnae forget tae tell ma ain that I wa' a knight.'

'I do belong here, there's Nan and Rabbie and...' But when he looked up, she was gone.

Joe's eyes were sore, too many emotions, too much pain. The girls he'd slept with, how he longed to free them from their pain. All potential princesses locked in their ivory towers, and he would be their brave knight who'd come to liberate them.

His eyes focussed on the nearby gorse. Golden, deceptive in its beauty, sharp to the touch. Suddenly Joe noticed another woman there in battledress. She threw a rolled up parchment into the gorse bush. Joe went to retrieve it. Carefully he unrolled it. It read:

JUDAH

Egypt to Spain, to Ireland - Ulladh (Ulster). The Irish
Leabhar Gadhala/ Book of Conquests - Iberi, earliest
inhabitants of Ireland.

Iberne abbreviated to Erne, then Erin, and Latinized to
Hibernia.

Hibernians/Iberii Ireland about 1700 B.C. - Hebrews.

Ulster's heraldic symbol - a red hand circled by a scarlet cord
- Genesis 38:28.

A rampant red lion on arms of Scots, Irish, Welsh. (Gen.
49:9)

The Chronicles of Ireland - the branch of Judah known as
Zarah colonized all the shores of the Mediterranean Sea
and as far west as the British Isles and Ireland.

Ezekiel 21:25 - royalty change. Take off the crown, exalt him that
is low, and abase him that is high. Judah had been high and Israel
low Hos.3:4. The daughters were planted 'In the mountain of the
height of Israel' Ez. 17:24. The 'tender one' of the 'young twigs'-
crown princess Tamar.

Chronicles of Ireland - Ollam Fodla came from Egypt to
Carrickfergus with princess

Tamar Tephi - Palm Beautiful.

Jacob's pillow - Gen. 28:18. Jacob prophesied in the last days
stone of Israel Joseph 49:24.

1 Cor. 10:4, Ex. 17:6.

Num. 20:8, Ps. 106:33, Num. 20:11, Ps. 118:22, 2 Kin. 11:14; cp.
2 Chr. 23:13, Dan. 2:35, Isa. 27:6, Ez. 21:25-27.

2 Kings 18:13; Isa. 36:1 -. Over 200,000 Jews migrated to Scotland. The Jutes and Danes of Denmark took their names from the Jews and Danites. The heraldic emblems of Denmark - three lions.

Gypsy chiefs - Dukes of Little Egypt

Benjamites and Levites.

Galilee was Benjamite and Levite territory.

Isa.9:21 - Manasseh, Ephraim shall be against Judah

LEVI

Levites - priests.

Protectors of the Ark of the Covenant.

DAN

Dan is omitted in the genealogies of 1 Chronicles 2-10, absent from the 144,000 sealed and protected from the Day of the Lord (Rev. 7:4-8).

Samson was a Danite.

Tuatha de Danaans ruled in Ireland.

JOSEPH

Gen. 12:2-3, I will make of thee a great nation, and I will bless thee, and make thy name great.

1 Chronicles 5:2 - birthright Joseph's and amen to his sons Ephraim and Manasseh.

Moses said his glory is like the firstling of his bullock, and his horns are like the horns of unicorns; with them he shall push the people together to the ends of the earth; and they are the ten thousands of Ephraim, and they are the thousands of Manasseh.

Manasseh and Ephraim the fruitful bough, the archers and unicorns.

Balaam compared Israel to a unicorn Num. 23:22, a lion - Israel's arrows 24:8-9.

The strength of a unicorn; he shall eat up the nations, his enemies, and shall break their bones and pierce them through with his arrows. He crouched, he lay down like a lion, and like a great lion. Who shall stir him up? Blessed is he who blesseth thee, and cursed is he who curseth thee' (24:5-9).' Israel shall do valiantly' (24:18).

British coat of arms - lion, unicorn, young lions, harp of David, scarlet thread of Zarah.

Hebrew word brith - covenant. Ish - man; British.

Ephraim and Manasseh and eight other Clans of Israel, separated from Judah and Benjamin in the time of Rehoboam.

William Tyndale - 'The English agreeth one thousand times more with the Hebrew than the Latin or the Greek.' Welsh like Hebrew same syntax. Saxon over 50% Hebrew.

BENJAMIN

Benjamin shall ravin as a wolf: in the morning he shall devour the prey, and at night he shall divide the spoil. Ehud, Benjamin, Saul, Shimei, Sheba, Esther, Deborah, Paul.

Characteristically left-handed (Judges 20:15-16).

Benjamin's territory included Jericho, Bethel, Mizpeh, Ramah, Gibeon, and Jerusalem.

It was just as he arrived at the Palace gates when a lady's maid ran up to him.

'My mistress is waiting for you to continue to paint her and she complains the sun is burning her, and she wants her skin white!'

Joe followed the maid across the courtyard and found the Duchess sitting by a fountain in the southern gardens harassed by several peacocks. It took him little over ten minutes to persuade the Duchess to leave the painting for that morning, assuring her that he'd be able to finish it at home, and with it being so hot the paint would dry too quickly. The stout woman had left the garden contented, her consolation, being allowed to see the unfinished work which had greatly impressed her.

The moment she was out of sight Joe tipped the contents of his purse onto the grass.

There were two letters 'S', one encrusted in topaz, the other in crystal.

A diamond encrusted letter 'R', an 'L' sparkling with emeralds. There were the rubies, rich red rubies forming an 'O', and the 'N' was covered in sapphires, as blue as the Aegean Sea. The 'Y' opulently covered in golden amethysts.

'*Ossnlry*', he arranged the jewelled letters carefully on the grass; then re-arranged them. It was an anagram after all; '*Yrlsons*', '*Rysnosl*'. But, no matter how many times Joe tried to form an intelligible word he still couldn't make any sense. He was getting burnt by the sun, he'd been there at least an hour and Sir James Mossman was expecting him for lunch. Even the peacocks had deserted him.

Joe heard a noise, a whistling, his tune. Was it Jane Haining, had she returned to give him the answer?

'Where are you, I know you're there?'

The mist rose up, the familiar fragrance of roses, a sense of peace swept over him. A tall figure appeared dressed in a doctor's coat, sporting a stethoscope.

'My name is really Miss Bulkley,' the figure introduced itself.

'You had a sex change? Lesbian then?'

'Bisexual actually. You see, I had to take the name of my uncle. I was dressed as a boy from the age of 10. Lived not far from here you know, 6 Lothian Street, near the medical school.'

'Are you an Edinburgh Knight?' Joe asked eagerly.

The woman, for her gender was now apparent, didn't reply. Instead, she began to pace up and down, hands clasped behind her back.

'Well, have you seen Nicola? Or that Jane Haining woman?'

'I published a novel when I was 18 you know. I studied in the Royal Infirmary disguised as a male. Worked from 7 a.m. to midnight daily before I was 12 years of age. I passed my degree at 12. Yet, I'm not the heroine I'd have wished to be, how I'd longed to emancipate the blacks in Jamaica.'

'But, are you an Edinburgh Knight?'

'James Miranda Barry I was known as, the Inspector General of the army. David Erskine was a good friend to me, and those like Lord Charles Somerset, they both knew my secret.'

'What secret? Do you mean the secret that Marie de Guise wrote about when she offered to be a mistress to… '

'No, Joseph, I meant the secret that I was a female living as a male, in order to receive a proper education and have a career then denied to women. Dire, don't you agree? That I had to live as the opposite gender in order to be seen as fully human.'

Joe just gave a shrug, he had no answer.

'Aye, David Erskine tried hard to change the way things were for women. I can recall his words even now. *'Let us consider for a few minutes the consequences that have arisen from the barbarous education of women in all ages as playthings or housekeepers…the men of Europe have crushed the heads of women in their infancy then laugh at them because their brains are not so well ordered as they desire.'*

Joe wondered if the said David Erskine was a relation to Sir Arthur Erskine of Queen Marie Stuart's court. They both seemed to have the same high moral principles and courageous spirit.

'Have you seen Nicola, if you meet her can you tell her…?'

'If you go to 3 Abercrombie Place you'll meet Marie Stopes,' she interrupted, lifting her stethoscope proudly as if it were a medal.

'We've met.'

'Ah, so have you also met Sophia Jex Blake? She matriculated at Edinburgh University in 1869. Of course the chauvinistic authorities reversed their decision in 1873, and she had to complete her studies and graduate in Berne.'

Joe recognised the name from the time when he'd met Elsie Inglis.

The apparition lowered herself to the ground and sat beside him.

'Sophia, wise by name and nature. Opened a dispensary in Grove Street for the women of the Edinburgh slums. Then she expanded to a hospital and transferred from Grove Street to her own home at Bruntsfield Lodge.'

'So is she an Edinburgh Knight?' He looked across at her, shadowing the warm grass just a few feet away. Shadow on shadow.

'Born in England. She never forgave those who'd abused her at Edinburgh University, their refusal to allow her to matriculate. So she opened the Edinburgh School of Medicine for Women in 1886. Aye, Joseph, she was unable to forgive Edinburgh for only concerning itself with the religious conversion of those abroad rather than the dire nightmares of poverty at home.'

'But the point is, have you seen Nicola, you know, the fool?'

'You are the only fool here, Master Hill.'

'What me? Why am I the fool? It's you and this Sophia woman and this Marie Stopes going on and on, and what have you really achieved?'

'Don't forget Elsie Inglis, Master Hill.'

'Well, answer me! What is it that any of you women ever really achieved? Let alone why it would be of any relevance to me?'

'I thought you'd come in search of female heroes, wasn't that your game plan?' she retorted. 'One of the things the four of us achieved was to save the life of Nan! Who do you think was there in Towris Close on the night of her fever? We are your Edinburgh Knights, if we hadn't arrived she'd now be dead!'

A noise began, like the rustle of a coat, the rustle of a leaf. The smell suddenly vanished, Joe quickly looked up. Too late, she was gone.

Throughout lunch with Sir James, Mariota and Nan, Joe remained mostly silent. His thoughts were not only on the experiences of that morning, whether real or imaginary, but on the jewelled letters. If he completed the anagram then he'd find the key and leave this nightmare. But what about Nan, once he'd left would she mourn? Or would it be as if he'd never existed? How was one to ever really know if one were outside or inside time?

'Sir James, I wonder if I might ask your advice?' Joe interrupted the conversation between Sir James and a servant. James Mossman looked up and smiled, happy about the birth of his son. Joe had rarely seen the child, rumour had it that he was going to substitute for the son of Marie Stuart.

'Well, Joseph, I was looking forward to being asked advice by you. For, being an initiate of our Order, I have felt for a long time now that your profession does you no justice.'

'Sorry, I think we are speaking at cross purposes.'

'I mean, Joseph, that singing to the drunks in the local tavern, or painting pictures for the ladies of the court is not considered a respectable pursuit for a man of your class. Now, if you want to work for your living then by all means do. There's law, finance, local government, even the Kirk at a stretch. But whoever heard of an artist...'

'Yar, you are quite right, and we will definitely discuss it sometime in the future...I agree with you, Sir James, you are a very wise man.' Joe tried his best to humour him, desperate to change the direction of the conversation.

'But, I have a more pressing question...you see these jewelled letters,' Joe tipped them out onto the table. The women present gasped with admiration at the gems sparkling with colour.

'Where did you get them, Joe?' Nan asked, her voice nervous as if she feared he'd stolen them.

'They were given to me. But they are supposed to be an anagram, and I can't work it out.'

For a moment he thought he detected a note of sadness in her voice, as if he'd hurt her by not sharing the information sooner and in private. Yet, there had been no sexual intimacy between them. She was pleasant, attentive, but her eyes betrayed her. Eyes, the windows of the soul, reflecting all the memories of the nights he'd left her alone to bed the whores and harlots of the town.

'Here, let me see them,' Mariota smiled, lifting each exquisite piece carefully across the table towards her. For a moment or two she studied the glittering gems, cautiously examining each letter.

'Well, it could spell...mmm...let me see.   It could spell...' Mossman scratched his head.

'Rosenly,' Nan interrupted.

'Now that is interesting, Nan dear...but I think I may know the answer,' Mariota said, her voice tinged with excitement.

'I think I've solved it, James. Yes, the word is Rosslyn...there you are, Joseph, Rosslyn!'

It was just before curfew that evening when Joe crept out from Mossman's tenement into the balmy August night. He managed to borrow a horse from the stables nearby and bribed the guards to allow him through the city gates, although it was long after curfew. The sun was setting as he followed the unmade road leading away from the city. If he achieved the quest and found the third item on the list of bell, book and candle would there be enough time to save the Queen of Hearts?

He needed more time. Time for Nan and Rabbie, time to mourn Islesbourg. What if he were to awaken in the 20th century and never remember her. Tears streamed down his face as he recalled the tiny face, fingers, feet of his baby daughter. He knew the black holes in the reincarnation theories well enough, made to forget every previous life, never learning. As Joe knew, progress only came with memory.

Barely any time was left to warn the Queen to cease her yearning for France, cease her public liaisons with men of her own choosing. He must complete his mission, and then hurry back to the Palace to advise her to refrain from swimming in dangerous tides where she was over exposed. He must caution her never to ride through dark tunnels of uncertainty. If he didn't have the time to return to the Palace and disclose his fears then how could he save the Queen of Hearts?

Joe rode his badly shod mare along the Lang Dykes towards Bearford's Park and beyond Kirk Loan into the unknown. The sunset had suddenly disappeared, the sky was now black. Luckily it was a full moon. Even the stars were out in abundance. Above the noise of the hooves clip clopping along the muddy, rough paths, he could hear the wolves howl from the braes. Owls screeched from the sinister black branches above; the Devil inside his own head raged on.

Now he was lost, which way was Rosslyn, which path should he choose from the rough, unmade lanes and tracks leading away from the city?

What was that noise, was that Nicola?

'Nicola, is that you singing?'

'Not house of David, it was Saul...' the voice sang.

'Nicola! Nicola! If that's you, I need to speak ...'

But there was no more singing, nothing, just Joe on his mare looking out into the darkness.

Beyond a broken gate that blocked his horse from crossing a small bridge he noticed a stream glittering beneath the light of the moon. A gypsy cart was parked on its banks beside a small fire.

For a moment he thought he heard someone singing, *'James Tinkler was a tinker...'*

Jumping down from his horse, Joe took the reigns, opened the rusty gate and led it over the bridge. A gypsy encampment, Joe anticipated with enthusiasm, but as he neared the fire he saw that it was only an old beggar.

'What do you want?' the man grunted, without turning around to see who the intruder was.

'I wondered if you could direct me to Rosslyn.'

'Why should I?' the old man croaked in a strange accent.

'I apologise, sir, have I done you some harm of which I'm not aware?'

'I'm Elijah, I brought you the message, gave it to Ma Ragg,' he snapped irritably.

'Elijah…he was a prophet wasn't…'

'He raised the dead!'

'Jesus raised the dead' Joe added, lost for words.

'Elijah never died, Jesus did!'

'Do you want some money? Here, I have…'

'Keep your money…just give me your soul!'

Joe began to laugh, 'my soul, why would you want my soul?'

'To save it, before it's too late.'

'Well, if you show me the way to Rosslyn Chapel I'll give you my soul,' Joe humoured him.

The old man struggled up onto his bare feet, his face reddened from the fire.

'Take that road there!' he pointed towards one of the larger crags in the distance, 'you'll find your Grail, your destiny!'

Faster and faster Joe galloped across the unmade roads and fields. The moon was bright, a perfect orb.

Needing to urinate, Joe jumped down from his horse when he reached the edge of a forest, and led it towards a hollow and urinated by a small rock. The moonlight hit the side of the rock like a fairy light. Crickets and small animals caused incessant noise, helped by the occasional growl of a bear somewhere in the vicinity.

'Men are only interested in virginity,' the voice made him jump. Urine splashed against his doublet and hose, yet, when he looked no one was there. Whistling, he could hear whistling, was it his tune, *Joe Hill*'? Flowers, he could smell fresh flowers.

'Who's there? Is it you, Nicola? Nicola!'

'Virgin births…only due to vestal virgins.'

'Who's there, show yourself!'

Slowly, behind the shadows of the rock a figure of a woman emerged, dressed in white, almost transparent, cloaked in mist.

'Who are you?'

'An Edinburgh knight of course!'

Joe put his wet penis back into his hose. Her outline was translucent and hazy, so that she was almost not there at all, coming and going with each breeze. Had this ghost once lived in a time zone, or was she living her life out in two different time zones? Perhaps he was no more real than the banshee before him. Or maybe, just maybe, she was real and it was he who was the ghost.

Then suddenly the mist cleared and he recognised her as Marie de Saint-Clair.

Her face was quite lovely; in her hand she carried a basket of flowers. In the centre of the flowers was a fish.

'I told you didn't I, that my grandmother married into the French Chaumont family and my mother was descended from the line of Levi, Isabel Levis? You know you have to save the Queen of Hearts?'

'Yar, and I know that I'm also supposed to solve all the riddles, find a fucking key and get out of this hell hole!' he roared, so that all the wildlife nearby scuttled away for cover. Joe was sick of games; this game had gone too far.

'I'm also supposed to find the murderer, Grail and leave Rabbie and Nan without a thought…and apart from that, you now tell me I've got to save the Queen of Hearts! And how long have I got, just a few fucking hours?'

'Yes, it's the 28th of August, almost a year since you arrived. You have until the 30th, after that it will be too late to save the Queen of Hearts.'

'Too late, but everyone knows Marie Queen of Scots doesn't die now. It's Elizabeth who has her beheaded in years to come…it won't be too late,' he disputed vehemently.

'I think you understand me, Master Hill. The spell you have woven cannot be undone.' Joe shrugged and turned away, if he didn't acknowledge her then perhaps she'd cease to exist. What if he didn't find the key out of here? The worst that could happen was that he'd remain with Nan and Rabbie, that wasn't so bad, was it? Or did it mean that he'd be pulled out of that time zone and sucked into space; eternally spiralling into a black hole like a tornado, or even Plato's whirl?

'So, if you're a ghost, have you met the Holy Ghost yet…I mean is the holy ghost like you but sort of holier?'

There was no answer.

'Well then, what about your Blessed Virgin, have you met h…'

'Of course as you must know by now the correct word for virgin in Hebrew is not the one used in the Bible describing the physical condition of the mother of Jesus. Hymen intact, the word '*batulah*' would have been correct. But it's the word '*almah*' that is written, and that merely means *maiden*.'

In the distance he thought he heard Nicola singing her song. Joe strained to listen, but there was nothing, only the sounds of the forest.

'Of course in Arabic *almah* means moon goddess, maiden of Diana the lunar virgin.'

'I thought Jesus spoke Aramaic.'

'Are you really as stupid as you appear? Have I not already said that it is a Hebrew word meaning a young woman?'

'So, do you want me to start a mission to the moon and cause a riot in order to find the Hebrew virgins living there?' he sneered.

'Speaking of Hebrews and riots, did you know that 60 years ago in 1506, 3000 converted Jews were slaughtered in a Lisbon riot?' Marie de Saint-Clair said, her lips so lovely, reminding Joe of a rosebud as the smell of roses hung in the air.

'Why should I care, and how is that going to help me find the solution to the riddles, let alone discover the identity of the murderer and get me out of here?'

'Oh, didn't anyone tell you, you don't have to just find the key, you have to find the Holy Grail itself.' As for the identity of the murderer, you already know that, Joseph.'

'Wolfart Bruce do you mean? Or do you mean James Mossman? Oh, how can I find anything…everything here is so primitive!'

'Don't be so negative, Master Hill, there were some good things that happened this century. Theophrastus Von Hohenheim introduced chemotherapy in 1527…then there was the comet in 1531.'

Joe wasn't listening as he climbed back up onto his mare.

'Although there were also negative inventions,' she continued, her transparent arm reaching up to hold the reins.

'In 1533 Francisco Pizzaro ordered the execution by strangulation of the last Inca.'

'So, where was God when they killed this Inca in His name?' the question accompanied by a sudden fit of coughing.

'You have no faith, Joseph.'

'My friend Lawrence, he's a Jew. I think it was him who told me that in 1543 Martin Luther published a pamphlet on the *'Jews and their lies'*. Odd, don't you think, that all these Church Fathers were such evil bastards, and now they are called *'saints'*. But, I ask you, who named them as saints, God or man?'

She made no reply, her ethereal hand now stroking the mare's face.

'Of course Jesus was a Levite as you will have guessed, of Moses line being that he was a priest, you know the Aaron story?'

'I thought he was a Nazarene from Nazareth or something. Oh no, that was Samson wasn't it, you know, a Nazarene?'

'Nazarene is a form of the word *'Nazrani'*. You must know by now that Nazrani could also mean *Christians*. They were also known as *'The Way'*,' she smiled, apparently unfazed by his behaviour. 'And Nazrani also means little fishes in Aramaic. And as you know, that was the Christian symbol, the fish.'

'So Jesus was of the priestly line then, from Moses?'

'Of the royal line of Joseph as well as the line of Aaron...but surely you've worked this out for yourself.'

'So his mother wasn't a virgin?' he sniggered, as if the revelation brought him immense satisfaction.

'You see, I suppose the problem really began with Joseph of the coloured coat, Jacob's son,' she sighed. 'Everyone wanted to be King. The Clans of Levi and Benjamin joined up under the banner of Judah. Although they are now officially known as the Clan of Judah, they were never descendents of that Clan.'

'So they can't claim the lion as their emblem then?'

'Of course they can...think of it this way, Joseph. It's a bit like when Scotland united with England, there is the British flag, but the Scots also have their own flag...St. Andrew.'

'The Jew.'

'Aye, now you are getting somewhere. Think a bit harder down that road, why did the Scots choose St. Andrew, a Jew, to be their patron saint?' Joe shrugged, as he settled his feet into the stirrups. He bent down to release his left foot that had become trapped, due to the hole in his boot hooking onto a piece of metal from the stirrup. When he looked up, she was gone.

It was after he'd travelled about 7 miles away from the city that Joe noticed a strange looking church. As he drew nearer he saw that it had a curved roof, but the building was unfinished.

Climbing down from his horse, Joe slowly walked towards the main entrance. The chapel was protected by flying buttresses and gargoyles. It was hard to detect any detail due to it being night. It was just a building playing backdrop to the light and shadow from the moon. Shadows that danced about its facade like clowns in a circus macabre.

The huge, wooden door creaked loudly as he pushed it open. Inside it appeared to be designed as a church. Candles and lanterns lit the whole nave, as if expecting him. Yet it wasn't a Kirk, there was no altar. His eyes now ascended towards the barrel vaulted roof covered in stars, lilies and roses.

There were about fourteen pillars and twelve pointed arches, yet it was unfinished except for the choir. No altar, he was bemused. Yet there were three pillars where an altar might be. The one at the far end was intricately decorated with floral swathes spiralling down, twisting around the fluted centre from the pillar's summit to its base. Joe looked up again at the ceiling, the walls. Wherever he looked there was a funny looking stone head with profuse foliage growing from its mouth. At least a hundred heads with that same face. Joe recalled also seeing them on the outside of the building.

Biblical scenes played out on the walls before him, lit by the flickering candles like an old black and white movie.

The fall of man; *the birth of Christ*; were amongst hundreds of stone carvings. Swords, compasses, trowels, squares and mauls abounded. Pillars and arches were covered with carved leaves, fruit, animals, figures, cactus, even sweet corn. Serpents were twisting and twirling their way around the pillars, walls, roof and doors alongside dragons and trees. There were also the ubiquitous heads secreting the copious foliage from stone mouths.

'Designed like Solomon's temple.'

The intruder made him jump. His heart raced, ready to explode. He recognised the speaker without the need to turn around. It was the priest, Wolfart Bruce.

So, had he stalked him here? Was this how it ended? A battle between good and evil here at this strange, half built Kirk.

'See that carving,' the priest pointed his finger. Joe turned and saw that his hand was covered in blood. Joe looked into the man's soulless eyes, the eyes of a rapist, how could such a monster have fathered Rabbie? If Joe left Nan now, who'd protect them from the priest?

'Veil of Veronica holding a cloth, see her heid's removed...and there are the seven deadly...'

'Why are you here?'

'I could ask the same question, but I would'na....and how's ma wee son?'

Joe longed to punch him on the nose, but he could smell that the priest was drunk.

'Aye, ma bonny wee Rabbie...can ye see that heid, Master Hill? That's the heid of the green man, or sae they call him. Looks like vegetables being vomited frae his mooth.'

Joe was trembling with rage. How dared he turn up and chat like an old friend.

'Nicola's dead...the fool.'

'Aye, sae I heard. The gardener.'

'What?'

'They called her the gardener...gardener of Gethsemane. D'ye want a bevy?'

Joe shook his head at the flask he was being offered.

'So where are we? Is this some sort of non conformist church?'

'Aye, ye could call it that. This is Rosslyn Chapel. See there, that's a figure of Moses wi' horns.' the priest pointed his bloody finger at one of the carvings. 'And that's the lamb of God, and an angel wi' a scroll... and there's the Devil wi' the folk kneeling beside him. And see that angel, that's the cross of Saint-Clair.'

What did the priest want, had he also come to solve the riddle, or was he going to murder him?

'I will have that drink if you don't mind,' Joe reached for the flask.

'Aye, Master Hill, I see ye enjoy a guid bevy like me.' Wolfart Bruce burped into his face, his breath foul, his teeth stained, some were black or missing.

Joe swigged down the whisky, his body suddenly returning to life.

'See o'er there, a fox dressed as a priest…some say I'm like a fox, wha' d'ye think?' His laugh was sinister, he had to be the guilty one, Joe thought.

'Preaching tae a flock of geese if ye look, but I ken how that feels. Every Sabbath I preach tae ma ain flock of geese,' he complained, pouring the contents of the flask down his throat.

'Aye,' he gave a nod, followed by a loud belch. 'Ye see all these heids, green heids. The Nazarenes worshipped the heid, ken. Aye, and the Templars kiss the heid. They brought the heid here frae France.' Wolfart Bruce suddenly collapsed on the floor beside the fluted pillar with the floral swathes.

'Solomon's temple ha' two great bronze pillars topped wi' lilies and 200 pomegranates.' The priest slurred his words, he could hardly sit upright, his hands waving before him like a handicapped mime artist. Pomegranates, even here there were pomegranates, Joe reflected.

'Some say this is the Apprentice Pillar, and over there is the Mason's Pillar. Ye must hae heard the legend aboot the murdered Apprentice. Some say he created this very pillar I'm leaning on…his master saw the original in Rome. I've nae been tae Rome.' He gave another loud burp.

'The story goes that when his master returned he wa' very jealous of his student's craftsmanship, sae he murdered him. King Solomon's master builder Hiram Abiff was also murdered by jealous Masons.' The priest suddenly let out a fart, and rolled himself onto his side.

'See the dragons on the bottom of this pillar…some say if ye look closer ye'll see that this wa' nae the Apprentice Pillar at all. This face once ha' a beard and moustache, but it's bin removed. Apprentices were nae allowed full beards, ken.'

Joe grabbed the flask from him and took a swig. The priest glanced up drunkenly and smiled.

On a small shelf on the east wall of the chapel he noticed a crucifix. There was no body of Jesus, only his head. Joe longed to ask the priest about the murders, about all the girls who were now dead. He wanted to ask about Nicola, Ma Ragg and mostly, why he'd raped Nan. Instead, he found himself saying, 'so what do you know about the Saint-Clairs?'

'Well, let me see, wa' it Catherine or Marie who married Hugh de Payens? He wa' the founder of the Templars, ken. Funny when ye think, his coat of arms ha' three severed heids. See this pillar, the one I'm leaning on? Well, they call this...'

'Yar, you've said, the Apprentice Pillar,' Joe interrupted, wondering what he should do.

'Nae, they call it Boaz...and the Mason's Pillar they call Jachin. 1 Peter 2:6-8

'The stone which the builders disallowed, the same is made the heid.' But it is none of them. Everyone kens, it's the Princess's Pillar.'

'What did you say, Princess who?' But by now the priest was lying face down on the stone floor.

'Peter, who was Peter?'

'Peter wa' nae one, Peter wa' a rock,' the gruff voice slurred out his words. 'Merovingian kings descended frae Clan of Benjamin.' The priest started to fall asleep.

'Yar, and what? And what!'

'Wha?...Wha' ye bletherin' aboot?'

'What about Peter?'

'Oh, aye, Peter...1296, Edward I of England stole Lia Fail stone. Peter wa' the Stone of Destiny, ken.'

'What does that mean? Hey! Wake up! What do you mean that Peter was...?'

But by now the priest was snoring his drunken head off.

Slowly Joe walked about the chapel. The candles flickered their shadows across the aisle, the walls, the roof and the hundreds of graven images.

Only a little time left, so much to do. He knew he'd discovered the identity of the murderer long ago, so that was one problem solved.

Now he had to find the key in order to return to the 20th century, and on top of all that he was expected to find the Holy Grail.

Again he looked around him, the candles and lanterns blazed as if the Kirk was on fire.

The centre aisle was separated from the sides by the fourteen, 8ft high pillars, so exquisitely designed that they didn't fit in with a building that was incomplete. It was adorned with foliage and figurines, angels playing instruments, bagpipes and Samson slaying the lion. There was even an image of the prodigal son. Joe wanted to laugh; the Bible said no images on earth of anything in heaven.

Carvings of plants were everywhere; the hart's tongue fern, the curly kale, oak leaves and roses.

Gazing up at the vaulted roof, his eyes focused on the sculptured flowers and the intricately carved arches: A fox carrying a goose, Samson destroying the house of the Philistines, the Dance of Death, a king, courtier, cardinal, bishop and a lady looking into a mirror. There was also an abbess, an abbot, farmer, husband, wife, child, sportsman, gardener, carpenter, ploughman and drunkard. Three heads were staring down at him; the apprentice with a bloody wound to his head, his mother and the master mason. But what Joe was most taken with were the images of the careless shepherd and the rich fool. Who was the careless shepherd, who was the rich fool?

Slowly he made his way back towards the priest who was still snoring, his greasy hair pressed up against the ornate base of the Apprentice Pillar. At the top of the pillar, Abraham was offering his son as a sacrifice along with a figure playing the bagpipes. His gaze followed the four spirals of flowers and foliage down the shaft towards the dragons entwined about its base.

He was in the south aisle and could see the image of the 7 sins and virtues. Above his head on an arch over the aisle was the Latin inscription, '*Forte est Vinum Fortior est Rex Fortiores Sunt Muliers Super Omnia vincit veritas*'.

'Edras chapter three verse twelve!'

Thump, thump, pulse racing; the voice had come from nowhere. Sweat dripped from his forehead. Joe glanced around, but no-one was there; had he imagined it, or was it the priest playing tricks on him?

'First Book of Edras if ye want the correct reference. '*Wine is strong, the king is stronger, women are stronger still, but truth conquers all.*'

Suddenly, Joe recognised the bald head, the shocked, pained eyes; it was the ghost who called herself Jane Haining.

'I don't understand what you're talking about, who was Edras?'

'Sae shall I tak' ye doon tae the crypt?' Joe suddenly noticed steps beside the pillar leading down into an underground vault.

Holding a lighted candle before her, she glided down the broken, steep, stone steps. The smell of flowers masked the damp, musty smells rising from the dark crypt.

'There's a legend aboot treasure. A treasure whose hiding place will nae be revealed, until the day when the trumpet blast will awake her frae her lang sleep.'

'Who will it awake?'

'A certain lady of the ancient hoose of Saint-Clair.'

'What can you tell me about the prophecies of Nostradamus... does he mention any of this?'

'All I can tell ye is, that if prophesies are nae frae God, then they are best ignored.'

'How can anyone know if they're from God? What about this man from Marne business? You know, the prophecy '*d'Arthemide: Allant murdri par incognu du Marne.*' I mean, how could anyone have known about that?'

She made no reply as she reached the bottom of the steps and held the candle up higher, casting shadows around the dark chamber. Tombs lined the walls; some had effigies lying on top dressed in full armour.

'So what is the treasure then, is Peter the Holy Grail?'

'Obviously I hae an interest in the Jewish race, which is why I ken a wee bit aboot the stone.'

'So are you saying that the Stone of Destiny, I mean if there is a real one, is actually here?'

Jane Haining just smiled.

'So is the conveyor of this stone one of the saints? You know, like Paul?'

'St. Paul, who said he's a saint? Only the Lord Himself kens who His saints are.'

'Let me get this right, are you then saying that St. Paul wasn't a saint? But I thought he was chosen to preach to gentiles or something like that.'

'St. Paul! Nae, lad, as if a liar would hae anything tae do wi' holiness.'

'What do you mean, St. Paul was a liar?'

Suddenly it had turned cold and Joe began to shiver. But the form before him had no thought for cold or heat. Whether she was ectoplasm or merely a projection from within his own brain, Joe had no idea. He'd read too much philosophy, seen too many weird films, taken too many ecstasy tablets for him to be certain of anything.

'Iraneus the Bishop of Lyon, claimed that the Ebionites accused St. Paul of being *'an apostate of the Law.'* There wa' a document, the *'Kerygmata Petrou'*, it claimed that the spiritual experiences boasted by St. Paul, such as his visions and illusions, were inspired by devils. Some do say that he wa' nae e'en a Jew, but a gentile.'

Joe was so cold, the smell of the damp too much to bear. Why were they here? There was nothing to see.

'Nostradamus wrote in one of his prophesies, *La grand pesche viendra plaindre, plorer. D'avoir esleu, trompés seront en l'aage. Guiere avec eux ne voudra demourer, deçae sera par ceux de son langaige.'*

'What does that mean? Anyhow, I thought you said that Nostradamus shouldn't be studied.'

'The great fish will come to complain and weep for having chosen, deceived concerning his age. He will hardly want to remain with them, he will be deceived by those speaking his own tongue.'

He could see through her body, she was transparent. Joe wondered what the philosopher Kant would have had to say about what comprised her essence. What synthetic, a priori billiard ball could roll her from illusion to reality?

'Ye ken there isnae much time left tae save the Queen of Hearts.'

She was right, there wasn't much time left.

'What has all this to do with the Queen?'

'Joseph, surely ye've worked it oot by now. The Stewarts are one of the lost Clans of Israel.'

Joe thought back to what he'd read over the last year, there were at least 12 Clans. Were the Stewarts from the Clan of Dan? That was an outsider, or were they of the Clan of Judah, or one of the other ten? Samson was of the tribe of Dan, married a Philistine, killed a lion which attracted a swarm of honey bees. Judah was the lion, Deborah was the bee. A bee produces honey. Even Lawrence referred to the Holy Land as the land of milk and honey.

'Is the answer Samson then? That would have been a better name for a lion. I've never read anything in the Bible about the Clan of Stewart. Anyway, how will that help me find the key to get out of here, and if I do solve the riddle and leave, how can I protect Nan? Can I leave the murderer behind to murder again?'

'There is a killer inside each one of us, Joseph, we are all capable of guid and evil, it comes with the flawed genetics.'

'Flawed…ha ha. That's exactly what Katie used to say, that I was flawed.'

'Anyhow, ye are wrong aboot the Bible, Joseph, the Stewarts are named through-oot if ye'd hae looked. Psalm 22:12-21. *Save me frae the lion's mooth for thou hast heard me frae the horns of the unicorns.*'

'I don't understand,' he confessed, as the apparition glided across the dank chamber towards the sepulchres. There were ten knights in all, Joe was fearful that they too would rise up from their tombs en masse.

'The Stewarts are '*the Hoose of the Unicorns*',' she smiled, stroking the helmet of one of the knight's. 'I must leave ye now, Joseph. Ye hae ma number, dinnae forget it.'

'Just tell me, is the key in the Apprentice Pillar?'

'There's nae such pillar Joseph, although it will be a common error in yer generation tae call it that. It is the Princess's Pillar. Even Daniel Defoe wrote in 1723 that it is the Princess's Pillar.'

'You mean Diana, after the goddess?'

'Nae,' she sighed with despair, 'it's the pillar of the woman who brought the Stone of Destiny tae Scotland!'

The figure of Jane Haining was fading before his eyes.

'Please don't go…please!'

'I hae tae go, Joseph, I hae the bairns tae care for…just remember ma number.'

'What number?'

'The number I wa' branded wi' in Auschwitz, 79467.' And then she was gone.

There were only about 12 hours left to find the key, say goodbye to Nan and leave. There was no Nicola to come and save him, even Cockburn had disappeared. Slowly he wandered over to the coffins of the ten dead knights. It was only then that he noticed the large, black, marble sepulchre standing alone in the far corner. A light hung above it suspended from the ceiling, like the eternal light suspended before the ark in Lawrence's synagogue. It was about 10 feet in length and 3 ½ feet high. On the side was written, '*Is.28.16 'I lay in Zion a foundation stone'*.

There was a panel of buttons fixed to the side, as if secured by a sophisticated lock.

Yet he had no idea of the code to tap in to open the casket, and there seemed to be no other way of gaining access inside.

He stood there for a while contemplating what numbers to press. Then suddenly he recalled what the apparition had said. '*The number I wa' branded wi' in Auschwitz, 79467'*. Was that the code?

Joe tentatively began to tap in the numbers, 7, 9, 4, 6, 7. It was when he pushed the final button that he heard a strange noise like the buzzing of a bee. The dark, marble lid of the sarcophagus began to slowly open. Inside was a large, jet, mummiform coffin; the mask on its head made of pure gold, eyes painted, hair black. The coffin was covered in hieroglyphics and symbols.

A sweet smell of flowers wafted past, mist began to rise.

'Deborah can't come,' a voice retorted. 'I really don't like being disturbed, but, as this is my country, named after me, I must take responsibility. So what is it you want?'

'Who's Deborah? Who are you?'

'Who's Deborah? You dare to ask who is Deborah! She is the greatest judge, leader and Queen Zion ever had. The mother of Israel and you dare to ask who she is.'

'So who did you say you were?'

'I didn't. I shouldn't have to introduce myself, seeing as I am the mother of Scotland.'

She was fully formed now; a tall, black woman, eyes like almonds, lips full, cheekbones high. Her headdress and clothes were made of gold and silver, her throat and arms covered in gold bands. Joe was overwhelmed by her beauty.

'Of course the gypsies know me as St. Sara...their black Madonna.'

'But that's not your title is it? You are Scotia aren't you?' Joe suddenly knew.

'You saw all those green heads up in the Kirk? It was I who brought the cult of the head with me from Egypt.'

'And Gaelic comes from your sons the Gaethli, Scot comes from your name and Hibernia comes from your son Hiber...have I got that right?'

Her ebony skin glowed, eyes bright, sparkling with life.

He noticed she wore a necklace of Egyptian blue faïence beads about her long, bronze neck. She was regal in every sense, this was her land.

'Of course there have been numerous legends about me, many call me Scotia, but it's pronounced differently in Egypt. Some claim I married a Greek prince, Gathelus, the son of the king of Athens,' she expounded with slight arrogance, and began to fiddle with her bracelets. 'Legends tell a variety of stories, some that it was at the time of Moses when we ran away, but why should I run from one whom others claim was my brother?'

'I don't understand, I thought Moses' sister was called Miriam.'

'Ha, and perhaps it was...or perhaps it wasn't. Other legends claim I was the daughter of Ramsees II, and there are some who claim that I was the sister of Tutankhamen.' She turned her head, causing her braided, beaded hair to dance across her shoulders.

'Of course the Irish remember me from when I led a battle against them, so they have some true facts about my history. They know for example, that my heirs became the high kings of Ireland and then invaded Scotland.' Joe was confused, was the ghost claiming to be Egyptian, Irish or Scottish?

310

'Are you the sister of Moses then?'

'Some say I'm the daughter of Akhenaten, others say I'm his sister. Some claim Moses was Akhenaten, others say his name was Tutmoses. Some claim Moses had a Hebrew mother and an Egyptian Pharoah as a father.'

He was unable to take much more, his head was throbbing. Moses, that name kept echoing from every crevice. Wherever he looked there was an image of Moses, even on James Mossman's home. There was even a link to Mossman's name.

'I need to find the Grail…unless, unless you are the Grail?' Joe suddenly paused to reflect. 'Are you the Stone of Destiny, or is it Peter?'

'Ah, the Lia Fail, the Saxum Fatale…well, that's easy. Tamar brought it here, she still keeps it safe.' Scotia smiled slightly, as if the location pleased her.

'Is that your coffin then?' he pointed into the sarcophagus, at the ornate mummiform coffin.

'Why would I need a coffin, I'm not dead!'

'So, what is inside?'

'Open it and see!'

'Is it a head? You know, with you bringing your cult from Egypt?' he was scared, what if it was a head? Perhaps it belonged to Jacques de Molay the last Grand Master of the Templar Order who was burned to death in Paris. But then, Joe decided, this was long after Scotia arrived in Ireland.

Suddenly the mummy made a sound like a bee buzzing. Slowly, the jet black figure split in two. Inside was a huge, un-honed stone.

Joe jumped back, fearful of what might emerge.

On its rough exterior he noticed a green head entwined with vines, figs and olives.

'Psalm 118 *'The stone which the builders rejected has become the cornerstone'*,' the ghost declared.

'Are you saying this stone was taken from Solomon's temple? Was this in the Holy of Holies?'

But she made no reply.

'Is this the Ark…you know, the Ark of the Covenant?'

The Egyptian just laughed, the gold rings about her neck rattling with every movement.

'Thomas, doubting Thomas,' the voice beside him whispered.

Beside the image of the head were images of a red lion, a gold lion, a crescent moon, a five pointed star and a six pointed star. There was also a tau cross and the inscription:

'*Genesis 49: Judah is a lion's whelp; you stand over your prey my child. Like a lion you crouch and lie down, a mighty lion: who dare rouse him?*'

'I still don't understand,' he complained, the solution to the puzzle still eluded him.

'Do I take it that you are asking a female for help?'

'Yes,' he said, eyes directed to the ground, 'I don't understand anything. I mean it's not a head is it? I thought it might even be the head of Elijah, he didn't die did he? But Jesus did. And Thomas, I mean what does he have to do with it?'

'Who was named Thomas?'

Then suddenly it hit him full on.

'Thomas isn't the name is it? It's just the meaning, twin. Yar, I see now, it would be a tautology to say that the twin is the twin?'

Scotia's black, generous lips smiled.

'Was the twin Judas, doubting Judas?'

'Of course Leonardo de Vinci, the great innovator, knew all this long before your time, Joseph...he told the true story in his paintings.'

'Didn't he design a helicopter? Wasn't he something to do with the Templars?' Joe gabbled nervously, recalling the books he'd browsed, and a TV programme about Rennes le Chateau.

Again he heard buzzing.

'Does the stone contain the DNA? Is it...Does it?...' he had too many questions, but no satisfactory answers.

'Is it DNA?'

'Hail, Maria, full of grace the Lord is with thee. Blessed art thou among women, and blessed is the fruit of thy womb and the tribe of Benjamin,' was her only response.

Perhaps the stone was radioactive, he'd read in his Bible about a man who'd tripped whilst carrying the Ark of the Covenant and God had struck him down dead. It hadn't made much sense to Joe at the time, as the guy had only tripped. If God could forgive King David, a murderer; and Solomon, a letch, then why would he strike someone down dead for tripping accidentally? But if this were the very same stone as the one in the desert, if it were radioactive; then it would mean that it wasn't God who'd killed him, it was the stone.

The Stone of Destiny, was this the Holy Grail? But if it didn't contain the DNA of Jesus, his blood, then why had he heard about the Grail being the cup containing Jesus' blood?

'The Stewarts are descendants of Judah, which comprised of the Clan of Benjamin. They are also from the Clan of Dan. Although Dan wasn't originally accommodated for as being one of the 144,000 to be sealed in this stone. But, when Tamar married the King of Ireland who was a descendent of the Clan of Dan, the line of Dan was assimilated and validated under the banner of Judah.'

'I only have a few hours to solve all the riddles, find the key and the murderer and get out of here. And as for the Queen of Hearts, how am I to save her?'

'To which Queen of Hearts do you refer?'

'Why, Marie, Queen of Scots naturally,' he scorned.

'But there is another who also wants to be known as the Queen of Hearts, also descended from the Clans of Ephraim, Dan and Benjamin, descended from the Stewart line.'

'Ephraim. That was Joseph's line wasn't it? The royal line. Do you mean Nan?'

'Remember what you read in Nostradamus. *'d'Arthemide: Allant murdri par incognu du Marne'. Diana to be murdered by the unknown man from Marne.*

Is it too late, Joseph? Too late to find your Holy Grail?'

'I don't want to go, I want to stay and look after Nan and Rabbie. They need me,' Joe pleaded.

'You have no choice but to leave. If you don't leave you will be trapped in limbo forever. You will be unable to go either forward or backward in time.'

'But, Nan…I mean how can I just leave?'

313

'You have no option. And once you've gone she will forget you as if you had never been,' she lectured, showing no emotion. 'Past existence is only dependent on memory. Now hurry, you must hurry!'

'Well, can't you give me a clue, please…please help me!' Tears had begun to well up in his eyes, a little boy, lost, afraid.

'You, who had no mercy for the women whom you encountered, are now pleading with a woman to show you mercy. But, as with all men, respect only comes from fear!'

'I'm sorry, I'm so sorry. I can put it right, it's not too late!' he wept openly now, the tears streaming down his unshaven cheeks.

'As a female I'm obviously of a higher spiritual plane than yourself, I have evolved and therefore I take no pleasure in abusing the weak. I will help you.'

'Thank you, thank you!' he fell to the floor and kissed the area about her feet.

'Don't grovel, Joseph, I can't bear men who grovel! Now the Baphomet, the head is here in the Kirk, but you will first need to find the pillar that will be known in your time as the Apprentice Pillar.' She sat down on top of the stone inside the mummiform coffin.

'It has been said that some foolish men thought it once had a beard, but as you are probably aware it doesn't have a beard, because it's a female. If a beard ever was there, it was an afterthought to obscure the truth. The name of the female, like the names of Peter and Thomas is descriptive.'

Joe looked bemused. 'Like Peter the rock and Thomas the twin?'

'Tamar is the place you need to find, although she isn't considered an Edinburgh Knight, but an Irish one.'

'Are you saying that her name is *Tamar* or *Pillar*? I don't know of any places or women named *Pillar*.'

'Tamar, her name is Princess Tamar. She is the Grail Keeper,' the Egyptian matriarch expounded.

'But I thought her name meant *palm*! That's why I thought she was linked to Deborah, you know, with Deborah sitting under her palm tree and all that?'

'You are correct of course, it has two Hebrew meanings. Tamar can mean palm, but it can also mean '*pillar*'.'

'So are you saying that the Holy Grail is inside that pillar up in the Kirk?' Joe asked, as he scrambled to his feet.

'Is that why Jesus carried a palm branch, because it represented a pillar?' But he didn't wait for a reply, now dashing past the ten dead knights and up the broken, stone stairs.

Wolfart Bruce was just beginning to stir when Joe raced towards the pillar on which he still leaned.

'D'ye have any mair derrink?'

'Move!'

'Wha'?'

'Move! Tell me, what do you know about the Madonna?' he shouted at the priest who'd vomited by the base of the column, covering some of the serpents.

'Black Madonna or white Madonna?'

'Don't play fucking clever with me you bastard! You raped my Nan you fucking bastard!' Joe kicked him hard in the back.

'Ah! I'll tell ye wha' ye want, lad, dinnae kick me! Black Madonna, Song of Songs,' he slurred.

'What?'

'Song of Songs…Solomon, it's aboot the black Madonna. Ye should read it, lad.'

The priest struggled up from the cold, stone floor, holding his back.

'How can I open this pillar? Is this Tamar's Pillar? Does it have a code? There aren't any buttons on this!' Joe was panicking, searching up and down to find a way of entry.

Then suddenly, Joe noticed a small emblem of a palm branch just above the head of one of the serpents. In the centre was a button shaped as a bee. He hadn't seen it before, how could he have missed it?

'Ye cannae touch that!' the priest tried to pull him away.

'Nae! You must nae touch it!'

'Get off me!' Joe pushed him off.

Wolfart Bruce once again raised his drunken arm to stop Joe proceeding.

'Ye cannae open it…ye cannae!'

'Get off me!' he pushed the priest hard. But the more Joe tried to release the man's grip from him, the harder his assailant held on. Foul breath that reeked of alcohol emitted from his broken black teeth.

Joe punched him in the stomach. Wolfart Bruce stumbled backwards. Managing to regain his balance, he then went for Joe.

'I'll teach ye tae attack me ye English bastard!' his mighty fists crashed down on Joe's head. His long, ginger hair was flying about his manic, red face.

Joe was bleeding, his mouth, his nose pouring with blood.

'When Cockburn learns that you're trying to stop me…'

'Cockburn is deid!'

'What? What? Don't you lie to me, how can she be dead! Don't you lie, you…' Joe punched him hard in the stomach.

The priest retaliated, pounding at Joe's head, his eye now swelling and closing. The blood ran down the back of his nose into his dry throat.

'She's deid I tell ye, foond in the lion's mooth!'

With every punch on the head came a momentary blackout. Joe's bruised fingers felt about his jerkin, reaching inside, he removed the small dagger that he'd been given when he'd first arrived.

A mighty thrust of his hand, tearing, twisting slicing through the priest's innards.

'Ahhh!' his screams blood curdling. 'Hel…ahhh!'

His long, ginger hair whipped about his head as once again Joe thrust the blade in. Again and again he plunged the dagger; splicing and slicing, ripping open the skin, muscle and sinews.

'Ahhh! Ahhh! God…' The blood was now pouring from the mouth of the priest, dripping down onto Joe's hands.

Suddenly all was silent, the raging had ceased, the battle fought and won.

Joe trembled as he pulled the dead body away from the pillar, and covered it with the flag of a lamb he'd noticed lying beneath a window.

Blood was everywhere; the floor and the column were splashed and splattered as if a decorator had been randomly brushing with red paint.

Joe hit the button shaped as a bee. He had to find the clue and get back to Nan and Rabbie, there was so little time.

Slowly, very slowly the pillar began to open, revealing the secrets that lay inside.

At its base was a small, gold casket, on which sat a transparent box containing a silver goblet.

'This is my blood...drink this in memory of me!'

The voice made him jump. At first he thought it was the priest resurrected. But, upon turning his head he saw that the voice belonged to Marie de Saint-Clair, she was accompanied by an older, dark haired woman.

'Isabel Levis at your service, Master Hill...I'm the mother of Marie. I believe you wanted to meet me seeing as how I'm another Edinburgh Knight.'

'Are you saying that this is the blood of Jesus in this cup? But if Tamar left the Holy Land before the crucifixion then how...'

'Tamar transported the Stone of Scone. It was the Templars who brought Benjamin's cup filled with the blood from the Holy Land. William Saint-Clair arranged it all.' The woman lifted the box containing the silver goblet from the pillar.

Joe noticed that it was empty.

'So is that the Holy Grail then, where's the blood? Did they spill it over the stone when they arrived? Are they going to resurrect him, or clone him or something?'

But, neither of the women replied.

'So are you saying that when Jesus offered them the cup at the Last Supper, it wasn't just any old cup, it was this cup? You know, Benjamin's cup that his brother Joseph hid in his sack. Is that the secret that Marie de Guise knew?'

'The secret is there,' Isobel Levis suddenly pointed towards the golden casket that remained inside the pillar. Joe held a candle over it, the light flickering into the shadows, and suddenly it became a chest of fire, kissed by golden flames.

The casket wasn't locked, it opened easily. Joe reached inside, his hands shaking, heart pumping with adrenaline.

He could feel something, it was small, round. Joe pulled it from its container.

In his hand was the shrunken, severed head of a corpse.

'Don't drop it!' Marie shouted.

'Who?...Who is...'

Clutching the shrunken head tightly by its dry hair, Joe trembled. Its eyes stared, dead, lifeless eyes; skin yellow, lips thin, some teeth still intact.

'How is this?... I mean why...'

What was it that Florymonde had said; Joe tried to recall her words.

> *Marie of Guise wrote to Lord Saint-Clair of Rosslyn, she swore to be a true mistress to him for all her life as thanks for his showing her a great secret within Rosslyn.'*

'It is the Baphomet, the head of the Beloved,' Isobel Levis replied.

Carefully Joe placed the head back into its secure casing.

'How did you know where it was?'

'Because I'm a Levite. The mother of Moses was also a Hebrew Levite. And so were the mothers of Jesus and the Baptist,' she boasted. Her slim fingers toying with her necklace shaped as a fish.

'I also happen to be descended from the mighty Nazarene warrior Deborah, of the same line as Princess Tamar. We are of course all related to Scotia, the Egyptian mother of Scotland, who was, in turn, also a relation of Moses,' she smiled proudly. 'In your foolish world where men think they know everything, they have still failed to discover that I am the direct heir in the line of the twin, the one known as Thomas. It might be of interest to you to learn that I'm also a direct ancestor of your friend Sir James Mossman.'

Joe stared at the apparition. Yes, she looked Jewish, dark hair, large brown, almond shaped eyes, she reminded him of Lawrence's mother.

'Forte est Vinum Fortior est Rex Fortiores Sunt Muliers Super Omnia vincit veritas.'

Yes, she was right, women were stronger, he'd been so wrong.

'You see, the Templars knew, just as Daniel Defoe knew, that it was via the female line that the true monarchy will rule, and not through the male line. Defoe called this the 'Princess's Pillar.' This is Tamar's pillar, and in the Jewish religion, as you know, Joseph, it is from the mother's line that the child inherits.'

'So why isn't Tamar here guarding her pillar, if this is her pillar?'

'Her realm is Ireland, not here. She trusts others, those like myself to guard it in her absence,' the phantom replied.

Joe was still shaking from the shock at discovering the head.

'But, but I don't understand. If Tamar brought the stone here and not the cup then why is it known as her pillar if it has nothing to do with her?'

'Her bloodline is in the pillar,' was all she replied.

'If the pillar is now known as the Apprentice's Pillar, does that mean that Tamar was an apprentice?'

'It was in order to conceal the truth from those uninitiated. You see, another truth was offered as a replacement in order to safeguard the real secret. A tale was told that the pillar was linked to an apprentice. But they even failed to understand that story.'

'What story?'

'The one about the apprentice.'

'Who was the apprentice?' Joe demanded, confused by so many names.

'St. Paul also claimed to be a Benjamite,' she seemed to digress. 'Known as the liar. You must know that...we have to go now.'

'No...no wait! Are your descendents the true heirs to the throne of Scotland?'

'Seven is the clue, magical number, don't forget,' Isabel Levis called back after her, 'and the sceptre will not pass from Judah until...'

'Is one of them alive now, is one of them God on earth? Wait! What was Thomas's real name? Wait! Please don't go! Tell me, did Jesus have any children?'

But she'd disappeared.

Joe's head felt as if it was exploding, imploding, shock upon shock. Yet, he still didn't have the key out of there. The corpse of the priest was still bleeding beneath the flag of the lamb. Fearing another intrusion, Joe hurriedly pulled it across the floor. The priest was heavy, taller than Joe; as he dragged his body towards the top of the steps leading down into the crypt. The corpse seemed to bounce down the steep, stone steps, yet made hardly any noise.

The ten graves of the knights lay undisturbed, visible by the light of the candles and lanterns, yet who had lit them?

His eyes immediately focused on the sepulchre that stood like a monarch in its own right over in the corner. No sign of anyone else; no spectators, no smell of flowers, no music, no mist.

Joe knew what he must do.

Racing against time, he approached the sarcophagus and manically tapped out Jane Haining's concentration camp number, 7, 9, 4, 6, 7. Again he heard the buzzing noise of a bee and the marble lid opened. The buzzing continued as the black figure, lavishly decorated with precious metal, split apart, revealing that the Stone of Destiny was still in place. Joe examined it again; the green head, olives, figs, vines. Joe studied every piece of the stone that he could see, carefully avoiding touching it. He'd been warned that it was radio active. How would the philosophers have turned any of his recent experiences into any logical system? How would Scotia or Jane Haining fit into any of the four propositions of syllogistic logic? The buzzing suddenly stopped.

His eyes glanced down, it was only then he noticed the small, carved, Hebrew letters and numbers:

ה   ר   ב   ד

(D) ד $= 4$ (B) ב $= 2$ *(R)* ר $= 200$ *(H)* ה $= 5$

Deborah was the bee and the clue's in this hive.

ר   מ   ת

(T) ת $= 400$ *(M)* מ $= 40$ *(R)* ר $= 200$

Tamar is the line that will always survive.

ה   ת   ע   ק   צ

(Z) צ = 90 *(Q)* ק = 100 *(Y)* ע = 70 *(T)* ת = 400 *(H)* ה 5
Scotia lifted her mighty hand, her tribe of Scots then conquered Scotland.

Memorising the inscription as quickly as he could, Joe closed up the mummy then heaved Wolfart Bruce's dead body onto its shell. He didn't want to risk getting any of the priest's DNA into the stone, that was certain. Puffing and panting Joe threw the limbs, already showing signs of rigor mortis, between the narrow gaps of the mummy and down the sides of the sarcophagus. Pushing, shoving, breaking, twisted bones as if the priest were now a puppet contortionist. Joe didn't rest until everything fitted inside and the lid of the black, marble tomb was closed tight.

The moon was full as he rode back towards Edinburgh. There were too many thoughts, too much pain, his mind almost crashed; no more bytes in his hard drive. The stars were bright, sparkling alongside the moon, lighting the rough track as his horse cantered along. The moon had to be powerful to control the tides, Joe considered, recalling his own father often saying, 'time and tide wait for no man.'

What if the tides suddenly stopped, or the moon didn't shine, would that be the end of the world? Diana, the huntress, or was she the goddess of the moon?

August 29th, 1566 and dawn was breaking by the time Joe reached the outskirts of the city. He rested there for a while with a flask of ale. He needed a rest, a long, long rest. Even before all this, when he was still in the 20th century, he'd pushed himself to the limit. Paris hadn't been a holiday, far from it. Everything had been so stressful. He'd crossed too many lines. It was too late to go back unless time would be his whore.

His mare was grazing as Joe looked into his purse, he'd left the jewelled letters back on Mossman's table, but he didn't need them anymore. Nan could live in luxury if she sold them, they would provide a good life for her and Rabbie. At least he didn't have the priest to worry about. Wolfart Bruce had got what he deserved.

Was it true what the priest had said, that Cockburn was dead? They had hardly met up during the past few months, he needed to ask her things, wanted at the very least to say goodbye. Poor Cockburn, if only he'd done something to save her. Had she also been murdered? Wolfart Bruce hadn't said. Had Judah eaten her? It didn't bear thinking about. Poor, beautiful Cockburn.

For a moment he thought he heard Nicola the fool singing her gypsy song. Joe listened hard.

Was it her voice singing, *'James Tinkler was a tinker…'* or was it the early dawn chorus? If only he could apologise to her, have an opportunity to say a kind word. But it was too late now, always too late.

Unless he hurried he'd also be too late to save the Queen of Hearts.

It was just as he was about to re-mount when he saw the four figures standing there. He recognised them all, Marie Stopes, Elsie Inglis, James Miranda Barry and Sophia Jex Blake.

'Your knights, Joseph,' Sophia smiled, 'although we are not the bravest knights; nothing like Scotia.'

'We've just come to remind you about some of the other knights. There was the suffragette Agnes McLaren. She was an Edinburgh Knight. The first Secretary of the Edinburgh Society.'

'Although there are also all the knights in other parts of Scotland, those such as Queen Scathach of Skye, she trained the hero CúChulainn.' The voice belonged to James Barry, still wearing her doctor's coat.

'And there's Aife, some call her Aifa,' Marie joined in. 'She fought against Scathach and CúChulainn in the Highlands.'

'There's the Countess of Ross, Joseph, remember she led her own troops during William Wallace and Andrew de Moray's battles with the English,' Sophia said, stooping down to pick a mushroom. 'And then there's Isobel, Countess of Buchan. Isobel MacDuff left her husband, the Earl of Buchan and took the finest warhorses to go and fight for the Bruce and was imprisoned in a small cage for four years.' The other three phantoms now joined Sophia picking the mushrooms from the dew covered earth.

'There was a Lady Bruce who defended Kildrummy Castle,' Elsie remarked, as a bird flew onto her hand. 'And let's not forget Black Agnes, Lady Agnes Randolph held her castle at Dunbar against the Earl of Salisbury for over five months.'

'Even you must remember Lilliard, Joseph,' Marie said, holding a mushroom. 'She led the Scots at the Battle of Ancrum. And did you know that when the Scots army marched on Newcastle in 1644 during the English Civil War, there were dozens of women soldiers.'

'Shall I tell him about Jean Cameron?' Elsie asked her companions, as she handed Joe the bird. They nodded their response. 'Well she raised 300 men and led them to the raising of the Jacobite standard in Scotland on 19th August, 1745...funny there isn't a statue of her on the Royal Mile. Not even one of Lady Lude, she fired the first shot of the Jacobite attack on Blair Castle.'

'I would take a guess that you don't even know that in 1779 a volunteer for the 81st Highland Regiment turned out to be a woman?' James Miranda Barry retorted.

'But, Joseph, these are just the few women who have been remembered. There are many more who fought in all the wars, died bravely for Scotland. Some have been great scientists, inventors, engineers. Many even martyrs. They are the unsung heroines, their memory erased from history forever. All those unsung heroines whose names have been purposely forgotten, deemed worthless due to their gender, they are your true knights.'

Then, just as suddenly as they'd appeared, the four apparitions vanished.

By the time Joe arrived at the West Bow Port the 14 markets were in full flow. He made his way past the butter tron and cloth market.

The pigs rummaged in the garbage, some lay in pens under the outside stairs of the tenements, creating numerous dunghills.

Joe noticed Master Robertoun the schoolmaster speaking with the tailor Jacques de Soulis beside a stall selling velvet and damask. Joe headed down towards St. Giles Kirk, the chickens and geese noisily greeting him like a feathered fanfare.

He could barely get beyond the prison. The August heat was overbearing as he battled past the beggars, carts and donkeys.

Struggling to get through the market stalls, he was hampered by the merchants as they set up the luckenbooths and Krames.

Joe headed towards the door of the Kirk, it was packed to overflowing. He recognised the voice coming from inside, it was John Knox preaching.

'The Earl Huntly in 1562 departed this life withoot any wound, or yet appearance of any stroke whereof death might hae ensured. And sae, because it wa' late, he wa' thrown across a pair of creels and carried tae Aberdeen, and wa' laid in the tollbooth. Sae that the response that his wife's witches had given might be fulfilled. Who all affirmed that the same night should he be in the tolbooth of Aberdeen withoot any wound upon his body. When his lady got knowledge of this, she blamed her principal witch Janet. But she stoutly defended hersel' as the Devil can ever do, and affirmed that she face a true answer although she lied. She, the Devil, the Mass and the witches hae as great credit of her this day as they ha' seven years ago.'

Joe had heard enough. There was no time left for wasting on John Knox. He had to hurry back to Nan, bid his farewells, ensure she had the jewelled letters to sell. He was just about to run past the Mercat Cross when he saw the 'Maiden' erected on a raised platform. It was operated by a lever situated at the back. A rope was attached to a blade, when the lever was pressed the blade fell upon the neck of its victim. Normally the blade was at the top, but this time Joe noticed that the blade was at the bottom of the guillotine, covered in blood.

Suddenly, he heard a whimpering. Turning his head he saw Rabbie standing alone.

Rushing over to the small toddler, Joe lifted him up into his arms.

'Rabbie, what's the matter?' Joe kissed his soft cheek. 'You shouldn't be here alone watching this. Where's mummy?'

The child lifted his chubby hand and pointed a finger.

Joe turned to look.

Lying on the ground before him was a decapitated head.

Beside it lay the body of Nan.

It was over an hour before Joe could be separated from the child. He'd wept more tears that day than he'd ever wept in his life. There was no point in going on, living or dying, it made no difference. If he went, who'd look after Rabbie? Why had she been executed? It wasn't Wolfart Bruce this time. The sweat dripped off him, the heat was so intense, he felt as if he were engulfed in flames. Where were God and His saints when his beloved Nan had been executed? As he wept, the words of St. Augustine came to mind, the man who'd been declared a saint by fellow sinners.

This renowned saint had described women as being, '*vessels of excrement*'.

Nan was so perfect, so lovely, how could an institution claiming to be founded on love exalt such men as Augustine and affirm them as saints? What was the matter with women? Why didn't they retaliate? Joe just couldn't understand. How he longed to scream down at Nan's decapitated head, rebuke her for being a female. If only she'd been a man she would have lived. His eyes swollen, he watched her body being thrown into a cart, whilst her head was carried off to be placed on a spike by the Netherbow Port.

'Take heart, brother, at least they did nae hang her or chop off her heid with that blunt knife they still use. At least they used the *Maiden*.' It was Master Gilchrist, he was also crying alongside the Redpath brothers and Thomas Levyngstone.

It was Mistress Carwood who took Rabbie from him.

Joe didn't stay to ask why or who, there was little point, it was too late now. It was time to go.

As he focussed on the headless corpse in the cart, Joe struggled to sing her dirge, the song belonged to Nan.

'Ae fond kiss, and then we sever, ae fareweel, alas for ever.

Deep in heart wrung tears I'll pledge thee…warring sighs and groans I'll wage thee. Who shall say that fortune grieves him while the star of hope she leaves him? Me, nae cheerfu' twinkle lights me, dark despair around benights me…' he momentarily broke down and wept. After taking a deep breath Joe resumed the Burns song.

'I'll ne'er blame my partial fancy, naething could resist my Nancy.

But to see her was to love her, love but her, and love for ever...'
He was sobbing uncontrollably now. An arm comforted him from
behind, he didn't look to see whose arm, he didn't care.

Hanging onto the side of the cart Joe refused to let go. The
donkey pulled away with the first lash of the driver's whip.

'Nan!' he called after the departing cart, 'Nan...Nan! But to see
you was to love you, Nan! Love only you, love you forever!'

It was down at the Kow Gait the following day, 30th August,
when Joe walked right into the Lady of the Fishes. She was standing
outside the Magdalen Chapel holding a cage containing three doves
and a basket with one fish poking out.

'Hello, Master Hill...isn't the other end of the Kow Gait the most
beautiful part of the town?' How soft her voice was, gentle, almost
like music.

'Suppose so,' he mumbled nonchalantly, wondering why she
wasn't at that end if she liked it so much.

'The gardens there, so perfectly laid. The smells of flowers
everywhere, the people in their finery,' she smiled, her lovely eyes
focussed on the caged birds.

'I was thinking about the Flodden wall, it just came to mind.'

But his own mind was still entrapped within its grief, as if a
demonic spider was weaving a web of steel around his brain.

'I was thinking about the old Grey Friars Monastery. It stood
inside the Flodden Wall when it was ransacked by the Calvinists in
1558...prisons aren't always safe.'

It was so hot; the sun was beating down, shining onto the lady's
face as if her skin were a mirror reflecting the light.

'But I suppose prisons are created in one's own head and heart,'
she spoke more at the birds than to Joe.

'Don't you think that some of the carriages transporting passengers
to and from the Canongate, and to the other end of the Kow Gait are
quite magnificent? Even the flowerbeds at the far end of this lane are
so lovely.'

'Yar, the fucking wonderful Kow Gait...just around the corner
from the Grassmarket where there's a gallows. It's really fucking
glorious!'

'In 1530 Alexander Alesse said of the Kow Gait, '*where nothing is humble or homely, but everything magnificent*',' she replied, ignoring his incivility.

'St. Michael's well is just along the way. Oh, I remember how they used to come in their masses to perform an act of penance there. But not any longer for fear of the soldiers.'

'So why are you hanging around here?' he focussed on the building behind her.

'Oh, the Magdalen Chapel.' She turned to look at the small chapel where she stood.

'I spend much of my time here.'

'Selling fish?'

'No, Joe, buying fish.'

Suddenly he recalled what she'd said when they'd first met, '*I save fish from drowning*'.

'Shame Cockburn wasn't a fish then.'

'The chapel had its altar removed in 1560…a pulpit was put there instead.'

Her voice trembled slightly; Joe thought he noticed a tear in her eye. Perhaps it was from the sunlight, it was so intense as it blazed down on them. Even the dogs were lying in the shadows trying to cool off. He'd never seen her up at the Tron getting her fish weighed. Maybe it was only meat they weighed, Joe had no idea. Even now he could recall the stench, and never could comprehend why they chose to pave an area that dripped blood and guts, and stank of fish and dead flesh.

'Did you know that the First Assembly of the Church of Scotland was held here on 20th December, 1560?'

Joe made no reply, his mind fixed on Nan, recalling all those nights he'd left her and Rabbie alone in the Restalrig cottage whilst he played away with any whore on offer.

'Master John Knox attended the Assembly here. Some say that he has good cause to stand against Rome. But, I ask myself, is murder ever justified?'

How often that issue had been discussed during his philosophy tutorials. Even Lawrence argued that Hitler's murder would have been more than justified, if by the death of one man it would save the lives of the many. But, Joe had replied that if Lawrence based his argument on utilitarian principles then it failed. As Joe pointed out, what if the majority were all Hitlers' and there was only one Jew?

Cattle were being herded further along the road into the Grassmarket, he could hear them moan as the herdsmen beat them with sticks. The doves flapped their white wings agitated by the distant noise.

'What's that place, a hospital?' Joe pointed to the building attached to the chapel, the sweat now pouring from his forehead.

'It's an almshouse, part of the chapel. But it has no altar,' she repeated herself. 'The hammermen still take charge though…gave donations until a few years back. Many still do. It's an almshouse for 7 poor men, Bedesmen, but no women.' She spoke as if that fact saddened her.

'The priest was arrested you know? Taken to Rosslyn Castle, but they released him eventually.'

'What priest?'

'Sir Thomas Williamson, the chaplain of this Kirk, the Magdalen Chapel. He was arrested because he continued to perform the Catholic Mass. He's still chaplain here and receives a full stipend.' They both moved to one side of the lane as a carriage passed by, followed by a man on horseback. The rider glanced at the Lady of the Fishes, gave a nod, made the sign of the cross on his own breast and then rode on.

'So, what do these poor…or sick Bedesmen do?' Joe sighed, wondering if he should get to a fountain for a drink, or head for a tavern. Anything to stop him thinking about Nan.

'The Bedesmen keep the chapel clean, and they pray for the soul of Queen Marie. They also sweep the floor. It's made from earth and rushes, that's apart from where the altar used to be, that was stone. Go inside, take a look.'

'No, it's okay.'

'Well I suppose the floor could be better, all stone would be nice. The west window was destroyed and the statue and candlesticks removed by the Reformers.'

'How did Nan die, did she suffer?' Joe was unable to concentrate on anything the woman said, even finding his way out of there didn't seem to matter any more. Nothing mattered except the death of his Nan.

'There is one stained glass window still there, quite beautiful you know. Perhaps you'll take a look another time, Master Hill, when you aren't quite so distressed.'

'I shall be leaving Edinburgh,' Joe replied, his eyes smarting with tears.

'Well, they'll still be here when you return.'

'Why do you think I'll ever return?'

'One can't escape eternity, Master Hill. Conscience and eternity go hand in hand. You're a philosopher, you know about wheels, they are never ending'

He suddenly noticed a red rose sticking up from beneath the fish in her basket.

'The chapel's benefactor was Michael Maquhen...did I tell you about his wife Janet?' Joe wasn't listening, his eyes now focussed on the rose. Diana, Princess of Wales had been compared to a rose.

'Janet Rhynd is buried near where the altar used to be. They say she was a wonderful woman. We have her to thank for this Kirk you know. After her husband died she saw this chapel through to completion.' She gave a prolonged sigh. 'This site used to be the Church of Maison Dieu...it's now used as a meeting place for the Kirk of Scotland. If you decide to visit in the future, you should come when Alexander Sym is speaking, you'd enjoy his lectures from the pulpit, he talks about logic. My favourite scripture, I must confess, is Matthew 26:13 and Mark 14:9, *wherever the gospel is preached I will be remembered.*'

'I'm going...' He turned to walk away.

'I can see you're hurting.'

'Hurting! Hurting! You don't know the meaning of the word!' The sweat was pouring from him. He wanted to go; leave her standing there with her doves, rose and solitary fish. But, he found himself fixed to the spot.

'What's your real name?' he asked once he'd calmed.

'Magdala was known for breeding doves,' she smiled. 'Why, Joseph, you've been crying. Clocks can't be turned back, deed's that have been done cannot be undone, not when you live inside time.'

Joe had no idea what she meant.

'Magdala had a large fishing industry you know.'

'What's your real name?'

'Mary Magdalene, she came from Magdala…Migdal means tower. They say she lived in a tower.'

'Who cares?' he replied rudely.

'You have a picture of a tarot card I believe. If you look you will see the Magdalene, the High Priestess sitting between two pillars. One is black, the pillar of evil.'

'What's that got to do with my Nan?' he sobbed.

'It was always a choice for you. We are all given freewill to choose between the black pillar or the white.'

'All the clues I found, all the numbers. Yet not the number of the beast who killed Nan. Is his number up?'

'Numbers always come up…eventually.'

'So what's his name then? His address, what's his number?'

'Joseph, you always knew that the number of the beast was 666. Solomon, the child of the half breed David and the gentile adulteress Bathsheba.'

Joe wasn't sure if she was being flippant or serious. He'd seen too many films, the number seemed almost farcical.

'So, is Solomon the devil in the tarot? Did he kill my Nan?'

But the lady failed to answer.

'Answer me! What's Solomon got to do with the number 666?'

'Now the weight of gold that came to Solomon in one year was six hundred, threescore and six talents of gold,' was her only response.

'I still don't understand.'

'It was only Elijah and Moses who were on that mountain with the Lord. Did you ever wonder why David wasn't there with them?'

Joe just shook his head; it was all too deep, too theological.

'Magdalene Church at Rennes-le-Chateau…you've read about it? You must recall the mention of the figures of Joseph and the Blessed Virgin each holding a baby.'

'So Jesus was a twin? Is that what you're saying? Who was the twin…I bet it was fucking Judas?'

'Shiloh was the place where the tabernacle resided, the Ark of the Covenant. It wasn't meant to reside inside Solomon's pagan whorehouse.' She smiled at the small white doves whilst she spoke.

'But you've known that for a while haven't you, Joseph? You're not as shallow as you'd have people believe,' her eyes twinkled. 'You do have a conscience no matter what you think, it grows stronger daily.'

'So was Benjamin the heir then? The Tribe of Benjamin I mean?'

'Joshua 18:28, the birthright of Benjamin encompassed Zelah, Eleph, Jebus, which is of course Jerusalem, and Gibeath and Kirjath.'

'So the House of David was fake?' Joe mused aloud, as the sun belted down. 'So who was the House of Israel?'

'Jacob was the first to be called '*Israel*' and Dinah was Jacob's daughter. She carried the royal bloodline of Israel being the female,' she smiled. 'Her Clan united with the Clan of Benjamin. As you know they all were eventually unified under one banner, that being Judah.'

'But it doesn't say anything about her in the Bible, does it?'

The apparition didn't reply.

'Paul claimed to be of the House of Benjamin didn't he?' Joe persevered, thinking back to what the ghost Jane Haining had said. 'Ghandi called him a liar.'

'There was another Gospel you know,' she said matter of factly, undaunted by the scorching heat.

'I thought the Church burnt everything they found other than the books in the Bible. Anyway, how can you be certain there was another gospel?'

'Because Paul mentions his followers leaving him and following another gospel...he calls his followers '*stupid*', curses them. Is this a man of God?'

'So Ghandi was right then?' Joe wished he could have met him. He'd seen The Clash in concert and Red Hot Chili Peppers, but never Ghandi.

'It's time for you to go now, Joseph, you don't have much time to solve the clues and get out by three. If you don't hurry you'll be trapped here forever,' she warned.

'Whose head was it that I found at Rosslyn?'

'It was the head of the Beloved.'

'The Beloved? Do you mean Jesus?'

'Why, Joseph, I'd thought that you'd have worked it out by now.' The woman raised her fine, dark brows as if surprised. 'The Beloved is the one whom Jesus loved the best...the one you know as Barabbas.'

'Barabbas, wasn't he a criminal?'

'He was an innocent child, not an adult when they were about to crucify him. Son of the rabbi. Jesus sent Judas with the mission to betray him, only because Pilate held his son to ransom.'

Suddenly, it made sense. Judas would never have betrayed Christ if he'd known who He really was. Of course, if God were omnipotent and all good, then He'd never have betrayed Judas and selected him to be the traitor of the world without the chance of redemption. Would there be any redemption for himself, Joe wondered. Was there an unforgivable sin?

'Yes, Joe, it was the son of Jesus who was the Beloved,' her face was glowing.

'Is that the name I need, the Beloved?'

'The son of Jesus was Shiloh.'

'The name I need then is Shiloh?' he demanded confirmation.

Joe remained silent for a moment or two, taking it all in.

'What have you got to do with this kid called Shiloh then?'

'Shiloh is my son too,' and with that she disappeared into an alley with her doves.

Joe ran down Hog's Back Ridge, it was almost 2.15, he had to leave by 3 or it would be too late. In the distance he could see the hazy figure of Mistress Carwood carrying Rabbie through the Netherbow Port heading towards the Palace. Perhaps Joe would have time to hold the child for just one last time. He had few fears for him, he'd be well looked after either by the Queen or Sir James and Mariota.

But, by the time Joe reached the Palace gates they were out of sight. The sweat dripped from him, his clothes were soaked. The sun was glaring down, targeting him.

There was no time now to say goodbye, no time to warn the Queen of the danger she was in. Where was the lock, he'd never even asked where the lock was for the key. Joe stood in the courtyard of the Palace bemused.

He looked across towards the lion's pit. Poor Cockburn, if only he could have said goodbye to her. Too late now.

Opening his purse Joe pulled out the small books. He'd read all he could, studied the riddles and clues from morning until night. He had the bell, book and candle, but where was the lock? 2.28 p.m.

A lantern was hanging by the guardhouse; a small flame flickered from within. Joe ran across to ignite the candle, but nothing happened.

The horses were being stabled; litters were coming and going, yet no sign of help. A sound of tinkling came from nearby. 'Is that you, Nicola? Nicola!'

The tinkling grew louder, 'Cockburn…Cockburn! Are you the one who's going to guide me out of here?' Joe turned towards the sound; it was coming from the fountain of Diana.

'Le tant d'argent de Diane & Mercure Les simulacres au lac seront trouvez'.

(The great amount of silver of Diana and Mercury, the images will be found in the lake).

The goddess Diana stood gracefully above the small fountain. The bow and arrow pressed against her left breast, spraying water jets down into the marble basin decorated with ornate carvings of lions, thistles and hunters.

'Le figulier cherchant argille neufve Lui & les siens d'or seront abrevez.'

(The sculptor looking for new clay, both he and his followers will be soaked in gold).

But the words of Nostradamus made no sense. The tinkling was even louder now. Joe ran towards the noise, his blue eyes looking fearfully down into the shallow water terrified of what he might see.

But there was nothing; no bodies, no faces, no dreams or nightmares, just water.

Joe looked down at the candle in his hand; Cockburn had said he'd need the bell, book and candle. Used in excommunications she'd said.

'After pronooncing sentence the priest closes his book, quenches the candle by throwing it tae ground, and tolls bell, like ye would for someone who ha' deid. The book symbolises the book of life, the candle...the soul, it's removed frae the sight of God, as the candle is frae the sight of man.'

Joe retrieved the book of Nostradamus, and then he took the candle and placed the flame at the edge of the tiny manuscript. It lit immediately, so fast that it almost burnt his gloved fingers. Joe tossed the black ashes into the water. 2.35 p.m.

Joe rang the tiny bell. Nothing happened, and then something flashed overhead. He glanced up; it seemed to be coming from a crystal or diamond reflecting the rays of the sun. As Joe stared, he saw that the bright flashes came from the crown on the goddess's head. Dropping the candle and bell by the edge of the fountain, Joe climbed up onto the statue. Higher and higher, his foot shoved into her bow, his arm around the crescent moon. He wrapped his other arm about the crown, blazing out under the sun. Light from light.

He thought of the code again.

ה   ו   ב   ז

(D) ז = 4   (B) ב = 2   *(R)* ר = 200   *(H)* ה = 5

Deborah was the bee and the clue's in this hive.

ר   מ   ת

(T)   ת = 400   *(M)* מ = 40   *(R)* ר = 200

Tamar is the line that will always survive.

ה   ת   ע   ק   צ

(Z) צ = 90 (Q) ק = 100 (Y) ע = 70 (T) ת = 400 (H) ה = 5

Scotia lifted her mighty hand, her tribe of Scots then conquered Scotland.

If he removed all the zeros from the numbers, in total they came to the number 49.

7 x 7, 7 was the magical number. It made sense when he thought of the reference to Genesis 49. 'The sceptre shall not pass from Judah, nor the ruler's staff from between his feet, until tribute be brought him.' Gen. 49 the same number as the answer 49.

But where was the lock? Then suddenly it dawned on him.

Time, 2.45 p.m.

Slithering down into the water Joe inspected the statue's feet. He grabbed the bell, ringing it like a mad leper. A bee suddenly flew down and rested on one of the feet, as a panel of tiny numbered buttons emerged from inside the statue's left foot. But the digits were secured behind a thin, wax skin. 2.48 p.m.

Joe reached for the lighted candle.

The small flame burnt into the wax film, splitting, melting reality into illusion, and now the way was clear.

He'd almost completed his entire mission; he'd found the murderer, hopefully found the key, but was it too late to save the Queen of Hearts?

His trembling fingers tentatively tapped out the number 49.

Suddenly he heard a whirring. The statue's chest began to slide open, revealing what looked to be some sort of intercom system. A grill covered it, supporting a metal plate displaying the word, **'Name?'**

Name, did it mean he had to shout his own name, or the name of another?

'Joe!'

But nothing happened. He was panicking now, no time left, no time!

'Name?' 2.51 p.m.

And then he knew, as quick as a flash! As if someone had whispered it into his ear.

'Shiloh!' he shouted for all he was worth. 'The name of the Beloved Son, the name's Shiloh!'

Blackness, spinning, sliding along the tunnel, that long, dark tunnel. Noises in his ears, in his head, spinning, spinning. Spinning in and out of consciousness.

Chapter Eleven

'A web I hear thou hast begun,
And know'st not when it may be done:
So death uncertain see ye fear,
For ever distant, ever near' - *Michael Bruce*

'Ten, nine, eight, seven, six, five, four, three two, one...open your eyes, Joe. Well what do you know, you're on time, I thought you'd be long gone'

That voice, he recognised the voice, it was Lawrence. Joe opened his eyes; he was sitting on the bench outside the Abbey.

'Hope you weren't too bored. I've had the most amazing time, been to the Castle, John Knox House, the Museum of Childhood... well, everywhere really. Oh, and I bought...what's the matter, Joe, you look as if you've been crying?'

Joe glanced around, everything was back to normal. His eyes were puffy and sore, he silently rose from the bench and followed Lawrence towards the main courtyard.

The Palace was altered. It had reverted back to how it was when they'd first arrived.

The lion's pit had gone. The north of the Palace was now the east, the entrance was now where the west gardens and theatre had been.

'Well, go on then if that will cheer you up, not worth seeing you in this state, Joe.'

'Go on what?'

'Have a fag that's what, I know that's why you're being so odd,' Lawrence laughed, as he carried his numerous parcels under his arms, gifts for those back home.

'I don't want a fag…I don't smoke,' Joe grunted morosely. 'Look, I don't feel well, do you mind if I go back to the b and b for a kip?'

'No…no, of course not. I must say you do look slightly strange, perhaps you're coming down with something,' Lawrence glanced at his friend. 'And anyhow we've got an early start tomorrow, the coach leaves at 5 a.m. You go back to the b and b and relax. I'll do some more sightseeing, I want to go and see if I can make it up to the top of Arthur's Seat. Can you take these presents back with you, save me carrying them?'

Joe received the numerous parcels from Lawrence, unable to converse, there was too much to think about.

'I hope you bought presents for your family, Joe, and you must get something for Chloe, Katie as well. I mean, it's only right.' He gave one of his wise looks and smiled.

'Guess what I bought Rachel? Yar, you've guessed it, a kilt. I know, I know, but I think she'll like it. I bought my father some Scotch whisky. Did you know that if you go to the very top of the Royal Mile, just before the Castle, there's a sort of whisky museum, really interesting.'

Joe made no response, his eyes scanning the courtyard, the Palace walls, the windows. But he had no idea what he was looking for.

'Well then?'

'Well what?'

'Well…were there any girlie heroes? Did the hypnosis work?' Lawrence looked at his friend with eager anticipation. 'No,' he gave a despondent sigh, 'I can see that it didn't. No female Edinburgh Knights then?' Joe didn't reply.

'See you later then, I won't be late.' Lawrence gave his friend a pat on the back as he walked away, calling back after him, 'remember, we're going clubbing. We can eat out if you like. Or even go and see a show maybe if you're feeling up to it!'

The sun was roasting as Joe watched Lawrence head off towards Holyrood Park.

Making his way sluggishly back up the Canongate, laden with Lawrence's parcels, Joe pulled out his mobile and frantically began to make calls as he glanced around apprehensively. He'd been dreaming, hallucinating, perhaps he was sick. Passing a sign to mark where the Netherbow Port had once been, he arrived at John Knox House. Tempted to go in, he stood there looking up at the projecting timber galleries and Doric columns. The tavern nearby was gone, no stables, even worse, no music or laughter. His eyes were too sore to see clearly as he gazed up at Mossman's coat of arms with three gold crowns, like an old friend, familiar, time served. Beside it, the initials *I.M* and *M.A.* Moses was still there with his sundial, as were the beggars on the pavement outside. It was as if time had never changed for them, like some perverse immortality. But this was the time to make the phone call, to change fact to fiction, death to life.

He'd reached the statue of David Hume. What was it the philosopher had written? Joe tried to recall verbatim the passage he'd quoted in his degree paper:

'It is universally acknowledged that there is a great uniformity among the actions of men, in all nations and ages, and that human nature remains still the same, in its principles and operations. The same motives always produce the same actions. The same events follow from the same causes. Ambition, avarice, self-love, vanity, friendship, generosity, public spirit. These passions, mixed in various degrees, and distributed through society, have been, from the beginning of the world, and still are, the source of all the actions and enterprises which have ever been observed among mankind.'

Had that been the cause of his own actions? Ambition, avarice, self-love? Would it still be possible to reverse an action or remove a cause in order to block an effect?

But, when Joe had got through to the voice at the other end of the phone, they said it was too late. It was impossible, they'd repeated, everything was already in motion. It was too late to save the Queen of Hearts.

It was soon after dawn had broken the following morning that Joe found himself sitting on the coach beside Lawrence, ready for the long journey back to London.

They'd only just set off along Princes Street when he heard the driver shout, 'oh no!'

'Don't tell me there's no petrol,' Lawrence groaned.

'It's Princess Diana!' the driver shouted to his passengers, 'radio just said...said she's dead. Diana's dead!'

Already some of the female passengers were crying, everyone turning to their neighbour; shocked, eyes filled with questions. How could Diana be dead, she was on their TV, in the press virtually daily. Diana had been immortal. Just like her namesake, the goddess Diana, Joe reflected. The Romans had called the Greek goddess, Artemos, *'Diana'*. Then Mary had taken over the position, not the Magdalene, the role had been given to the mother of Christ. Was this why the Princess of Wales was so venerated? Was there something beyond her and those who revered her that no one understood? Artemis, the pagan goddess, also an eternal virgin; Mary had taken over the title only when worshippers were suddenly forbidden to worship her. They missed her, their Queen, the goddess Diana, and so they had replaced her with another Queen. Now, in full circle the title had returned to Diana. For hadn't the tabloids at the time of her engagement to Charles constantly emphasised her virginity?

Diana couldn't die, not Diana.

Lawrence put on his earphones to listen to the news on his own walkman.

'Joe, it says she died in a Paris tunnel...Point d'Alma. Do you know, I'm almost certain that I once read a book about that area, it used to be a pagan site. Oh, you want to listen to this, Joe. They're saying it was a car crash...oh my God, they're saying that she was alive when they pulled her out.'

Joe's head was now in his hands, weeping.

'Her boyfriend's also dead they've just said...Al Fayed's son, the Egyptian. Oh my God, it's awful,' Lawrence continued, unaware of the mental anguish of his companion.

The coach stopped outside Haymarket Station in order to allow more passengers to board.

340

'Point d' Alma they've just said it again. Yar, Joe, that was definitely a pagan centre for sacrifice you know? How odd, like the Hebrew for young woman *'Almah'*, so very odd.'

Joe looked up as the tears ran down his cheeks; the new passengers took their places in the few remaining seats. He recognised one of them as the busker who'd been dressed in a jester's outfit, except now she was just wearing jeans and a T shirt printed with the St. Andrew's cross.

'They've said it was a car crash. Wait a minute...someone's just said that a Frenchman...a Francoise Levi claimed to be driving just ahead of the Merc and saw a Fiat Uno and a motorbike purposely steer into their pathway!'

Some of the passengers continued to weep as the busker took her seat beside a ginger haired priest. Everyone looked numb, as if it had been a personal tragedy; a woman they'd never met had suddenly stolen a huge chunk of their hearts. The whole coach was in mourning.

'Hey, listen to this, Joe,' Lawrence gasped. 'Another witness claims she saw the bike near her house where she lives in Paris, somewhere called Champignay sur Marne, have you ever heard of it?'

'd'Arthemide, allant murdri par incognu du Marne. She wasn't the Queen of Heaven you know?'

'What?'

'Jesus' mother...she wasn't the Queen of Heaven!'

'Look, I appreciate I lost the wager and you didn't find a heroine, a female Edinburgh Knight; but to be honest there's far more important things to worry about today!' Lawrence snapped.

'You didn't lose the bet, Lawrie. I found your Edinburgh Knight.'

Lawrence glanced suspiciously at his companion. A strange look appeared on Joe's face, his blue eyes were unusually dark.

'Marie Queen of Scots, she's your Edinburgh Knight; the one they called The Queen of Hearts.'

Lawrence just shook his head impatiently, and put the earpiece from his walkman back into his ear.

It was as the last passenger boarded when Joe noticed the police. They were speaking with the driver. Then they headed down the centre aisle of the coach towards the back seats where Joe and Lawrence were sitting.

'Excuse me, sir; we would like you to come with us to answer some questions about Katherine Palmer.'

'Katie!' Lawrence interrupted, 'isn't that your Katie, why what's happened?'

'I'm afraid, sir, we have recently discovered two bodies, we believe them to be of Katherine Palmer and this gentleman's young daughter...we're sorry to say that they appear to have been dead for at least a week.' The uniformed officer stood before them, his stature tall, heavy, intimidating.

'Oh my God!' Lawrence cried. 'Oh, Joe, poor Katie...oh, Joe!'

'I believe, sir, that you were in Paris recently. You were staying at Marne La Vallee.'

'I had some business to take care of.'

'What sort of business?'

'I had to set up some contracts.' Joe stared into their eyes, a smile played on his lips.

'Before I show you my warrant for your arrest, sir, I must ask you, are you Joseph Hill?'

'Me?' Joe gave a nervous laugh, 'why, I'm the man from Marne.'

> *'Some books are lies frae end to end,*
> *And some great lies were never penn'd:*
> *Ev'n ministers they have been kenn'd,*
> *In holy rapture,*
> *A rousing whid at times to vend,*
> *And nail't wi' Scripture.'*
> *Robert Burns*

Printed in the United Kingdom
by Lightning Source UK Ltd.
119796UK00001B/130